AMBER ROYER

Fake Chocolate

**GOLDEN TIP
PRESS**

GOLDEN TIP PRESS

A Golden Tip Press paperback original 2020

Cover by Hari Irawan

Distributed in the United States by Ingram, Tennessee

ISBN 978-0-9914083-4-4

Ebook ISBN 978-0-9914083-5-1

Printed in the United States of America

9 8 7 6 5 4 3 2 1

PRAISE FOR THE CHOCOVERSE

"*Free Chocolate* is quirky, fun, and loaded with sci-fi chocolaty goodness! This book is a calorie-free treat."
– **Beth Cato**, author of *Breath of Earth*

"Exhilarating fun in a galaxy muy loca for Earth's most sublime delicacy! Bodacious lives up to her name, and not even certain death can slow her down. *Free Chocolate* proves that romance, intrigue, space opera, mortal peril, and culinary ambition can be served with a sweet side dish of humor."
– **Sue Burke**, author of *Semiosis*

"You had me at laser monkey robots."
– **Arianne "Tex" Thompson**, author of the Children of the Drought trilogy

"Soap opera drama mixed with sci-fi high stakes, *Free Chocolate* is a muy thrilling ride!"
– **Laura Maisano**, author of *Cosplayed* and *Schism*

"Earth has a monopoly on chocolate. The aliens will do anything to get a cacao sample, and the planetary government will do anything to stop them. What a premise!"
– **Daniel M Benson**, author of *Groom of the Tyrannosaur Queen*

"¡Muy deliciosa! Amber Royer's *Free Chocolate* is nonstop fun on every page! From strangely delicious sounding cosmic treats to Spanglish-speaking intergalactic diplomats to the relentlessly breathtaking feartastic adventure, this is a unique read and a total page-turner! Not only does Royer introduce the first university-student Mexican sci-fi heroine, with a host of wildly eclectic friends, but she builds a believable universe around them that is a true delight to visit. Can't wait for the next adventure!"
– **Eden Unger Bowdich**, author of the Young Inventors Guild Series

By The Same Author

Free Chocolate

Pure Chocolate

There Are Herbs in My Chocolate

PROLOGUE

One Month Ago – HGB Headquarters,
Maui, Hawaii

Daschel Janvier opened the door leading to the sidewalk. He was still inside the compound but for the first time in his brief life, he was outside.

The air smelled of salt, and the ocean crashed in the distance and palm trees laden with coconuts danced in the breeze. Daschel may have never *been* outside before, but he remembered all these things. He knew he was a clone, but he had been gifted with the memories of his original. And his original loved the ocean. When Daschel 1.0 had been a child, he'd lived on the coast of France, and had spent many a cold afternoon collecting seashells on the beach.

He'd never dreamed about power then, never imagined that he'd one day become the CEO of HGB, the megacorp that controlled the only Earth product the rest of the galaxy wanted: chocolate. And he'd never foreseen the need to clone himself in case of assassination attempts, or to escape the public eye.

This Daschel had had enough of being used as a target. All he had to do was get off this island, and he could go anywhere in the world. Be anything he wanted to be – as long as it was far, far from the pops and the feeds.

1.0 had once worked as a barista, in a coffee shop in San Jose, California. It had been the happiest time of his life. There had even been a girl … slim, Mexican, with hair that had felt like thick silk in his hands and a laugh that lit up his heart.

He couldn't go looking for her, though. He shouldn't go back to California at all. If 1.0 came looking for him, it'd be the first place the guy would check.

"Going somewhere?" The mirror of his own voice came from behind him.

Daschel turned. He couldn't tell if it was 1.0 or one of the other clones. Didn't really matter when the guy was leveling a gun at his heart.

Daschel waved a hand towards the ocean. "I just wanted to see it once with these eyes, before I go on that press junket."

Which, given the death threats 1.0 had received, was basically a suicide mission.

"But Dash." So it was 1.0, then. Nobody else called him Dash, just his proper designation of 2.9. "We're the same. You are me. You know what the ocean's like."

"We're not the same. You can make choices. Say I decided not to go." Dash gestured with his chin at the gun. "Wouldn't you shoot me? And send one of the others?" He didn't know when he and his original had diverged, but he suspected 1.0 was harder inside than he was.

1.0 said, "You do have a point. I'd have to live with the memory of killing myself. But you'd be dead."

And yet, Dash was not going back inside that building, not going back into the basement where he'd been kept like a lab experiment – despite the luxurious quarters.

He rushed 1.0, going low to avoid the gun, tried to knock his original off balance. They both wound up on the ground, struggling for the gun. It went off, a horrible sound soon swallowed by the serene crashing ocean.

CHAPTER ONE

I blink at the dot on the nav. The ship it represents is closing fast. Mi corazón es racing, and I take a deep breath to force its beat to calm, even though alarm klaxons are going off.

"Por favor, Kaliel," I tell our ship's pilot. "I know they're pirates, pero don't kill them."

Kaliel's hand hovers over a button, his skin luminous in the emergency lights. The tight cuff of his pilot's jacket emphasizes his trembling.

Kaliel once scuttlepunched a ship he had been tricked to believe was a pirate vessel. It turned out to be a tour bus full of old people. He had nearly died for that mistake. And here he is, a breath away from having to make that same decision, to blow up the pirates.

He pulls his hand away from the button, runs his palm across his stiff short hair. "That ship is a Whisperfitz. We can outrun it."

"No, we can't." Frank leans over Kaliel's chair, adjusts a few settings, and pushes the button himself. Our ship's weapon fires, damaging the other ship. Pero, not scuttlepunching it.

"Oi! Viejo!" I scold. Frank's older, Caucasian with ruddy cheeks, brown eyes and a bit of gray in his hair. The golf shirt he's wearing aboardship is more casual than his usual button-up shirt and wool peacoat.

Outraged cackling comes over the com system. It's a language I don't understand, pero the meaning is clear: the pirates are emotirated we damaged their ship, and threatening revenge.

"We could have blown you up," Frank says towards the com. He turns towards me. "But we didn't. Just like the last guys."

Twice now, pirates have attacked the transport. The last time we *had* outrun them.

Kaliel hangs up the com. He's humming something discordant, with an uneven rhythm, under his breath. Kaliel's human, from Sweden, though the song is Nitarri. Had he been a telepath, the song would be calming. Maybe he finds it calming anyway.

I eye Frank. "You left their vital systems working on purpose, viejo? We all know how you feel about pirates."

Years ago, pirates had attacked the humanitarian aid ship Frank's daughter and son-in-law were on, and had spaced everyone on board.

Frank eyes me, frowning. "You of all people should know I don't take lives unnecessarily."

Ironic coming from an assassin. Frank works for the company that controls chocolate in the galaxy – and by extension controls Earth. He has killed to keep their secrets. Numerous times. He spared the one person he'd been assigned to kill that he didn't believe deserved to die: my boyfriend.

Kaliel's not my boyfriend. No y no. Nunca. I'd kissed Kaliel a couple of times, and I still think he's super hot, tall, with cool-toned black skin and beautiful gray-green eyes. Pero, I'm still in love with Brill, mi alien hermoso from the planet Krom. Who isn't here because he's supposed to be muerto. Instead of killing Brill, Frank had helped mi vida fake his death.

Sí, Frank spared Brill. Only – eight years ago, Frank killed my father. And now he is dating mi mamá, which sounds like something that would happen on a telenovela. Pero, no, this is my life. I've forgiven Frank. He'd been doing his job, y Papá had been on the other side of the conflict over chocolate. Pero, I can't make peace with HGB, and Frank still works for them. And he's still not a huge fan of Brill.

When Earth made its first First Contact, it was with Brill's people. The Krom believe that commodities should be shared, to avoid future conflicts. So that Krom landing party took samples of coffee, and of sugar cane – only, they missed chocolate. Now, Earth has a choc-centric economy. Most Earthlings blame the Krom por todo – *everything* – porque they harvested our commodities. Which has made my love for Brill a complicated proposition – and an inconvenience for HGB.

HGB basically is Earth, despite everything I've done to break their choco-monopoly. Their power has not decreased. They still can kill anyone who opposes them.

As if to make my point, Frank's corgi, Botas, walks into the room. Frank rescued the dog from a shelter after its owner got executed by HGB, the first kindness I ever saw him show. Something is sticking out of Botas's mouth – something covered in teal feathers.

"Don't let him swallow that!" Kaliel says.

"Como? What is it?" I'm already leaning down towards the dog, cooing to coax him to me.

"A half-flying rodent the ship picked up somewhere. I've seen a couple of them already. HGB routinely treats for pests, so it may have eaten poison."

"Oi! Botas. Drop it." The dog wags his tail and backs away as I try to take the feathered rodent away. He thinks this is a game. I catch sight of an animal face amid the feathers. The rodent is muerto – *stone dead*. Of course. HGB has always been fond of its poisons. Siempre. When Earth made first contact with aliens, and the planet descended into war to see who would control chocolate, HGB even weaponized an herbicide to tip the scale in their favor.

Botas runs back across the bridge. Frank comes up behind the dog, pero Botas steps away from him, and when Frank tries to grab the corgi, Botas moves back towards me. The dog chomps down on the rodent again, trying to get un mejor grip on it. I gasp. He had better not swallow it. None of us three have veterinary training.

"Bodacious, please." Frank really is upset. He loves this kalltet dog.

"Bo," I correct automatically. I used to hate when people used my full name. Pero, now, he's showing respect. And, no sé – *I don't know* – maybe I don't mind so much. I am bold and audacious, if you consider everything I've done since deciding to break the choco-monopoly.

"Haza," I say. *Fine* in Krom. I've picked up a lot of Brill's language. I sit down on the floor and then flop backwards, sprawled out and not moving.

Immediately concerned, Botas trots over to me, whining, and paws at my arm. I grab the limp body under the feathers. Frank rushes over and presses at the back of Botas's jaw, gently forcing the dog to release the grizzly toy.

Botas barks, then gives me a reproachful look. It feels more – no sé how to say – human than a dog should be capable of. Frank doesn't know it, pero his dog was once infected with an alien mind parasite. I've often wondered if the experience changed Botas. It changed everyone else who has been infected – including Kaliel. Kaliel takes more time to reason things out than he used to. Which is mal for a pilot, no?

"I'll take that," Frank carries the rodent to the trash receptacle built into the wall near the pilot's chair. He presses the button to open it, throws the rodent in. Then he stalks off the bridge.

"Where are you going, viejo?" I call after him.

"To make sure things are safe." He turns back to look at me. "Like I always do."

He mutters something about making sure this ship is safe for Botas, verdad, pero también the comment reflects how he feels about what he does for HGB. He believes the chocolate monopoly secured Earth's place en la galaxia, and now that a disease is running rampant through the cacao trees on Earth, we're vulnerable. That's only part of the story, pero, he's not wrong.

Kaliel asks, "How did you even think to do that?"

I shrug. "It works on my little sisters." Or at least it used to. They're so much bigger now, and between culinary school and everything that has happened since I stole that cacao pod from

HGB, I haven't seen much of them in person. They're on Earth –
where we're headed – but en un country diferente. They're in
Brazil, with my brother and his familia. This time, I'm going to
Hawaii.

I get up off the floor and move to the station at the other side
of the pilot's chair where I can sanitize my hands. HGB cargo
ships are often flown by a single pilot, so the designers planned
for comfort, and minimizing the need to leave the ship on
autopilot.

I am alone with Kaliel, close enough to smell his cologne. And
I can't help remembering what his generous lips felt like against
mine. Pero, the memory is tinged with nostalgia. I've found a way
to be friends with this muchacho, despite our obvious chemistry.
Porque I have something deeper than just chemistry with Brill.

Kaliel hums the calming song again.

"Does that help?" I ask.

"A little." He looks chagrined. "Not the way it does when
Kayla sings it to another telepath. Telepathy doesn't work the
way I thought it would." Telepaths can't read your mind, can't
even communicate with you if you aren't a telepath too, except
through electronic devices. "But even in the human brain, the
notes hit a few of the right places." He grins. "But mostly, it
reminds me of her."

I still consider Kayla mi mejor amiga – my best friend –
though I haven't seen much of her since I've been on Zant,
participating in Earth diplomacy, and in a Zantite cooking show.
And since Kayla found out she's not human, but rather the
missing Nitarri Princess. She'd be in danger if that became
common knowledge, so she's been staying close to home. "Send
Kayla abrazos y besos from me."

"You should call her," Kaliel says. "She misses you. She
thinks you're scared of her now that she can explode people's
brains."

I laugh at the way he says it. Kayla found out she had the
power to stop an entire plague of mind parasite – if she had been
willing to use her telepathic capabilities to kill all the hosts. Pero,

she didn't do it. No y no. I'm not scared of her. I could lie and say I've been busy. I sigh. "It's not that. I'm a little jealous. We were in culinary school together, and after everything that happened, I'm stuck heading for HGB headquarters and she got to go back to the life I dreamed of."

Kaliel shakes his cabeza. "No, she didn't. She found out everything she'd been told growing up was a lie. And that some people want to kill her because of her DNA. And that other people hate Nitarri, because after the destruction of the home world, a number of displaced Nitarri citizens used their gifts to become undetectable assassins. She's been working things out with her mom, but she needs a friend more than ever."

Pain forms in the back of my throat. "I didn't realize it was that bad."

I pull out my phone and text Kayla. *Hey, amiga.*

She texts back, *Hey!*

It's not much, pero it's a start.

Kaliel says, "It must be killing Brill to have you traveling with me."

"He's not exactly fizzbounced about it." My attraction to Kaliel had been obvious to Brill from the start, and his jealousy nearly got him executed as a murderer, that time Kaliel went missing. "Pero he's been trying to be less jealous."

"Good," Kaliel says. "I don't want him getting the wrong idea. Again."

Frank steps into the doorway. He looks at me skeptically. "Can we talk for a second?"

I follow Frank into the crew lounge. It's connected to the one sleeping area on this ship, which was not meant to carry passengers. Botas scratches at the partition between this space and the massive cargo hold, which is firmly closed. Muy bien that there's only a day left before we reach Earth. This ship just got un poquito claustrophobic.

"I heard what you said to Kaliel," Frank says.

I sigh. Tawny, my publicist at HGB, pushed hard for me to get together with Kaliel, even before Brill's supposed death, porque me being connected with an exonerated Earthling hero looks better than me with an alien from a race Earth still distrusts. I hope Frank doesn't start with it too. "I'm not giving my heart to anyone other than Brill."

Frank rolls his eyes. "I don't care about your love life. And I think Tawny's over that, anyway, since you and Kaliel didn't spark after Brill left the picture. There's no drama she can turn into a love triangle for the feeds unless you show interest in someone else."

"Not going to happen." Brill has risked his life for me. He's forgiven a lot of mi estúpido cultural mistakes. The least I can do is be loyal.

Frank says, "I mean what you said about school. There's plenty of time to get that project done before we reach Earth. Graduating would be good for you. Figure out a future for yourself and move forward. You need a purpose other than anger over things that happened in the past. Things that had nothing to do with you."

I shake mi cabeza. "I – I don't think so."

Pero, no sé how to explain that that's not it. The things that have me paralyzed – they aren't the things that HGB did to mi familia y to Earth. No. Not anymore. If I move forward, I have to deal with all the things that have happened to me. Being bitten by a Myska cop – after he shot me. Having a heart attack on an alien ship. Being marched into a room with a drain in the floor to make it easy to clean up after my slated execution. Believing, for a time, that Frank shot Brill left him in an unmarked grave. It's enough trauma for a lifetime.

And my lifetime is bound to be short. I've lasted longer than any other human who's taken the drug I'm addicted to. Pero everybody caves. There are even malcast polls betting on how long it will take me to overdose.

"It's because of the Invincible Heart," Frank grumbles. "You don't dare dream of a future, because you assume you're going to kill yourself."

I swallow hard. "I probably will, *viejo*. Once this is over, and there's nothing to fight against, and nothing to fill the void, I won't be able to stop myself."

The Invincible Heart is a military-grade Zantite rage drug. I'd been forcibly injected with it aboard one of their warships. I'd come close to taking it again, even knowing that syringe likely contains mi muerte – *my death* – porque just a couple of hits causes organ failure in humans.

"There doesn't have to be a void." Frank sounds surprisingly passionate. He loves mi mamá – and tolerates me. I am constantly at odds with him. Still. He knows how much losing me would hurt her, so he's started looking out for me.

"There's no cure for IH withdrawal," I say.

Frank squints at me. "Then how have you been managing while being on Zant?"

As in, near the drug's source. "IH isn't easy to get when everyone is keeping an eye on you. And keeping you busy. I'm only staying on Earth for a few days to film holomercials, then I need to get back to address a delegation of some of Zant's traditional allies. There'll be a limited-enrollment cooking class afterwards, por me to provide one-on-one diplomacy. Garfex may even show."

A coalition of planets, spearheaded by the Zantites, is filing the proper paperwork with the Galactic Court so that they can bust open Earth's closed borders to force trade. The Zantite King, Garfex, is a choco-addict. He also makes all decisions regarding Zant's participation in the invasion coalition.

Kaliel says over the com, "Another ship's on the radar."

Frank looks like he wants to say something else. Pero he huffs out a sigh and heads for the bridge. Frank is tired of my criticism of HGB and of my recriminations of his part in everything they've done. Pero, it isn't fair of him to say I need to focus on my own future when my planet may not have one. I follow him towards Kaliel and the radar holos.

I'm so used to HGB bugging my clothes and my things that I almost expect Tawny to call and offer me someone else to be interested in, so that she can spin some drama around my return to Earth. Which would be horrortastic. If she had a camera hidden aboard this ship, she would have heard our conversations. She would know Brill's alive. And that would put his life in danger.

Pero, she's not with us, and Frank swept the ship for bugs when we got on. Apparently, they respect his privacy, as one of their most trusted agents, enough not to have planted any.

Kaliel mutters, "I guess the pirates know the chocolate supply is limited. I've never attracted this many confrontations before. It's like we're made of catnip."

"Sí, they must know," I say.

"We're going the wrong way," Frank points out. "Ships carrying chocolate are usually going away from Earth."

My chest goes frío. "Mira. Look at this engine signature. That's un gran ship, no?" I've learned a bit about navigation from watching Chestla and Brill. Pero, this time I hope I'm wrong.

Kaliel grimaces. "A lot bigger than the last one. If you do goodbyes, now might be the time."

My heart jolts.

"Don't talk like that," Frank mutters. Though he takes his phone out of his pocket, and I see him send a quick text to mi mamá. He's back together with her, after I'd explained that Frank had spared Brill's life. Mamá was able to deal with finding out that Frank had come into our lives first to kill mi papá, then to keep an eye on us for HGB. Pero, hurting someone close to me had been a dealbreaker for the relationship. Now that their romance is back on, it's getting serious. And I'm not ready for that.

Though, if Kaliel's right, it might be a moot point. Ay! I'd rather not die in transit to Earth, after having survived half a year in some of the mas peligroso – *most dangerous* – places in the galaxy. I've been on Evevron for the past couple of weeks, where the people are alpha predators, and even the food is dangerous.

Before that, I'd spent time on Zant. Zantites are roughly eight or nine feet tall, bald, with rubbery lemon-yellow skin and have giant mouths with double-rows of terrortastic shark teeth. If they unhinge their jaw, they can open their mouths wide enough to swallow a human whole – or rip one in half. They're monsters that aren't monstrous at all, with a complicated code of justice and unexpected moments of kindness. Though if you break their laws, they will eat you.

The ship hails us, and when Kaliel pops up the holo, I recognize the other pilot. I don't know his name. Pero, he was a delegate at the conference voting on whether or not to invade Earth. I'd stumbled into the middle of their speeches on board the Zantite warship I had stowed away on, after stealing viable – growable – cocoa beans from an HGB plantation. This muchacho had called humanity a broken and debased race, due to our proclivity to violence. His long, tangled hair is the same, blocking most of his face, except for a pointed chin.

I'd disrupted that conference, shared chocolate, and yet, Earth is still preparing for an invasion.

"This guy's not a pirate," I tell Kaliel. Which makes me both more and less freaked out. I already have the shakes, so with the amazefusion and the adrenaline, mis manos son trembling visibly now. I ball them into fists. Pirates by definition engage in violence. Otherwise they're gray traders – like Brill – or bounty hunters. And I don't think this guy would agree with mi vida's morality either.

"Don't fire," he tells Kaliel. "It would be a shame to start the war early." Does he even have official authority to be here? He spots me. "Bodacious Babe Benitez. Just the Earthling I wanted to talk to."

A blush heats my face. The first time I saw this guy, in a room full of galactic diplomats, I nearly gotten executed for a cultural faux pas. And now I have to admit I don't know his name. "I am very sorry. We were never formally introduced."

He laughs. "Don't be so nervous, Bodacious."

"Bo," I correct automatically. Then I stiffen. "Bodacious is fine,"

He tosses his hair back from his face for a moment. He has three eyes, arranged in an even row, and instead of a nose, there are slits on either side of face. It's odd, pero not grotesque. His orange eyes look amused before the hair settles back in place. "I may be a diplomat, but I don't stand on diplomacy. My name is Thath."

"What do you want?" I ask.

"You must realize my planet is involved in the Zantite coalition to open Earth's borders for trade. So we have an interest in events on your planet. And there have been rumors." He stops speaking on an expectant note, like he's asked a question.

Mi corazón es beating fast again. "Rumors of what?" He wants me to confirm a plant disease is ravaging HGB's carefully maintained, walled-in plantations. I make him say it, though, because I want a few seconds to think what to say.

"Rumors that something has gone wrong with the chocolate supply."

It's a muy muy bien thing that I used to be an actress. If I confirm that rumor to this guy, the invasion will happen mañana, the borders forced open for "galactic aid" and to make sure we aren't mismanaging the resource to death before they can get their hands on it. The coalition members will be convinced we need their superior intellect and technology to keep from losing chocolate altogether. I paste a slightly confused look on my face. "Are you talking about the redesign?"

"The what?" With this guy's eyes not visible, I can't tell how believable my performance is.

I smile, though inside I'm close to panic. "HGB is doing a package redesign, in alignment with the Mercy is a Gift Campaign. All the bar wrappers will be yellow, and have MIAG printed on them. They've slowed down production while they change gears."

"A redesign." Thath taps at his chin with an equally pointy finger. "This information could be valuable to the coalition. Perhaps even worth selling to the right people."

I feel bad if my lie puts him in danger, pero en serio, he's talked about how much humans love violence, while at the same time making plans to invade my planet. I make a hand gesture like I'm giving him the information. "We just want to get home with our lives."

He knows his ship es más grande and better armed than ours. And that we could tell someone we talked to him. And yet, he breaks off from following us. "I hope you find peace."

I can't help but ask, "You believe this will be resolved peacefully?"

"Sadly, no," Thath says. "But that is humanity's fault. Your unbridled violence cannot be tolerated."

He's acting like we're in the middle of *The Day the Earth Stood Still*, that somehow this invasion will teach Earth tolerance and peace. "Vale, Klaatu." I mumble under my breath. En serio. That's not what's going to happen. There will be bloodshed. And if peace can be had, it will be in the stillness of grief.

I manage not to roll my eyes. "Without chocolate, your coalition has nothing in common. Calling us uncivilizable merely justifies taking what's ours."

Thath says. "Your people have committed murders on numerous worlds, while denying everyone entry to your own, and keep a ring of weapons pointing out at the galaxy."

"Those are matters for the Galactic Police," I counter. "And we are not the only species who have committed murder. Singling us out isn't fair."

"Very little in life is fair, Bodacious." He gives me a sad smile. "Especially for a flawed species."

A chill runs through me. People that self-righteous are capable of exceptional cruelty.

Once he hangs up on Thath, Frank grumbles, "How did that guy even know Bo's on board this ship?"

That worries me, almost as much as what will happen once I get back to Earth. I'm going to HGB headquarters, to talk to the head muchacho himself.

"Should I tell HGB what just happened?" I ask Frank.

He glances at the empty com field. "That would be a bad idea. I have a meeting in a few days to talk to the people who could take the kill order off your Krom. You don't want to make them nervous."

"They've agreed to discuss Brill?" I ask Frank. Es una noticia muy feliz – *happy news*.

He frowns. "I'm giving a report about the situation on Zant, and what I observed when we picked you up on Evevron. I'm still deciding how to broach the real subject."

CHAPTER TWO

The HGB facility on Maui sits like a white jewel near a black-sand stretch of beach, with the island's mountain más grande behind it as a backdrop. The compound contains half a dozen buildings, along with walkways and gardens. Even with misting rain and wind that's set the banana trees framing the entrance bouncing, it's dramatic.

Tawny drives us into the parking lot in front of the main building. She turns off the Humvee. The two of us sit there, the engine ticking ominously as it cools. Rain patters against the windshield.

"I don't want to be here," I tell her.

"I know." She doesn't even pretend I have a choice in all of this. I think she's bracing herself for me being uncooperative.

"I don't plan on fighting you, chica. If it helps save Earth, I will do whatever you ask." And yet, I can't bring myself to open the vehicle's door.

"Really?" Tawny sounds skeptical.

I shrug. "Within reason." I bite at my bottom lip. "You're sure I have to meet with the CEO? I don't see how he needs to brief me for an acting gig."

Daschel Janvier is the "new" CEO. He got promoted when Link Foster, the last CEO, died from a heart attack about four years ago. My theory: it was stress, from keeping all the secrets.

I wonder if Janvier himself knows todo.

"Janvier asked to see you." Tawny squeezes my hand, like we're amigas. The first time she did that, back when we first met me, it felt cheesetastically fake. Pero now, it's comforting. After everything we've been through together, we almost *are* amigas. Almost. "Remember, Bodacious," she tells me, "He's just a guy like anyone else. And you're not in trouble. There's no reason to think this will go poorly."

Ahora bien, that sends my fearfluttered heart rate even higher. Porque *going poorly* is Tawny-spin for *not walking out of Daschel Janvier's office alive.*

I gesture down at the deep green dress I'm wearing. A nice solid color, with no sparkle that could hide a lens. Tawny likes to sneak cameras onto me, to keep track of what I'm saying and doing. And she uses equipment so minúscula, I have a hard time spotting it. "You know, mija, for once I wish I had one of your cameras, to record whatever happens in there. In case my life is worth less than you think."

"Bo!" Tawny looks shocked, her ice-blue eyes wide above her high cheekbones. Tawny is half native Hawaiian, half something I've never been able to place. "Daschel would never spill blood in his office. If HGB wanted you dead, this is the last place they would have brought you."

"Well, that's comforting, no?" It's not.

"It's time to go inside." Tawny rearranges a lock of my hair.

I force myself to open the door and get out, juggling an umbrella, my bag and a cake carrier. The rain suddenly starts blowing sideways, and I get drenched.

As soon as we reach the covered porch, I drop the umbrella and pull out a compact, giving me a glimpse of my own thick eyebrows, high cheekbones and slightly hooked nose. My mascara has smeared and run. "Ay de mi."

"Here." Tawny, pulls a wipe from her purse and tidies up my makeup.

"Gracias." When she's done, it doesn't look too bad.

Somehow Tawny's clear bell-like umbrella has kept her completely dry, and her brown pixie-cut hair looks perfect. She asks, "Where's your pendant?"

"In my bag." My gut feels heavy just from thinking about that mourning necklace. I glance down at the buttery leather purse, splattered with raindrops. I don't move to unzip it.

"You have to wear it." Her ice-blue eyes are intent, as she studies my face. "Honestly, Bodacious. After all the fuss you made over that Krom, I'd have thought you'd mourn him longer than this. I've held off from–" She breaks off abruptly.

Heat flushes in my cheeks. "Held off from what, chica?"

Tawny brushes at the shoulder of her dress, though there's not a speck of anything out of place. "I've refrained from pushing you together with Kaliel, despite the dramatic support in the polls for you to choose him. And I haven't tried to find you a new love interest, out of respect for your loss."

That sounds so much like what Frank said on board the cargo ship. Could Tawny have had a camera there on us after all? Pero, if she knew that Brill was alive, there'd be a new execution order out on him. And possibly one on Frank. And Tawny wouldn't have told us about it. Oi! Could there be someone closing in on mi vida, right now? The thought takes my breath, and I fight not to let it show.

I eye her carefully. "Don't fix me up, por favor. I'm still hurting. I just don't like wearing my grief for people to see."

"Okay," Tawny says.

Que? So simply? No protests? "Gracias."

Does she *not* know Brill's alive? Is she honestly being respectful? I hand Tawny the cake carrier. Mi mamá said not to show up to this meeting empty-handed, pero en serio, will Janvier eat something I give him? You think he'd suspect me of trying to poison him, no?

Chocolate is more expensive than ever, now that the supply is finite, and if he just throws the brownies in the trash, that's dinero – *cash* – I could have spent on un nuevo pair of shoes … or a scarf.

My lips twitch into a momentary smile. Tawny never did figure out what I did with those scarves back in Rio. I'm hoping I won't have to improvise clothing items to climb any walls here. Or have to steal anything.

I don't have to fake the distress on my face as I pull the pendant out of my bag. It's a three-inch disk featuring a sculpted woodland scene, with a crystal representing the sun. Brill had believed he was about to die when he gave it to me. He said it would steady my heart as I grieved. When he survived, he told me that wearing a grief pendant for someone who isn't *muerto* is like asking to be separated from them.

It's true. This necklace makes me feel distant from Brill – mi vida, mi corazón – in a way that seems almost biological. I asked Brill's amigo Gavin about it, and the Krom just gave me a sad smile and said I wasn't likely to see Brill in person anytime soon.

Grimacing, I fasten the pendant around my neck, take back my cake carrier full of brownies, and we go inside, past all the guards, through a series of increasingly thicker doors.

Tawny keeps up a running commentary as we walk. "You'll find this facility quite different from the one you … visited … in Brazil. It caters more towards research and publicity. The no call zones are limited to the restricted workers' areas, so that shouldn't affect you at all. You'll have free run of the grounds, the medical building, the History of HGB Museum, the library, and the spa. Your bags have already been delivered to your room at the resort."

"I'd thought this was where I was going the first time." The first time. Six months ago. When HGB called me home to do holomercials for them – and I took the opportunity to steal a cacao pod in an attempt to restore balance to mi mundo – *my world*.

Instead, HGB sent me to Rio. Which didn't have a spa. Or decent food. Or anything else that they have here – except Tawny, who seems to wind up everywhere with me.

Tawny ignores my comment. "Of course, we still ask you not to leave the gates without a chaperone, for your own protection. The polls show a significant percentage of Earth's population would love to see you shaved. Which is why, if you'd consider pairing off with Kaliel, it would help you gain sympathy." She eyes me. I frown back at her and hold up the pendant. She shrugs. "Oh, look, we're here."

My heart jolts at her reminder of what the vulturazzi want. Mi cabeza en a basket, removed via guillotine. My execution dress going to the highest bidder. Lo he visto – *I've seen it*. The shave is always FeedCasted live, showing the moment of death from half a dozen angles, and letting the social media comments roll in. One execution in particular had gotten to me – a woman also convicted of attempted choco-theft. The same crime as mine. In my nightmares sometimes, I still hear her saying, "No, por favor," over and over before my vision splashes over with red.

Tawny knocks on the door, pero doesn't wait for Janvier to answer before she opens it and ushers me in. The office is ginormous, with high ceilings and a corner view. Floor to ceiling windows show a tropical garden resplendent with macadamia and papaya trees. This place should represent life and plenty. My chest shouldn't have to be filled with ice and fear.

A robot guard stands in the corner, its face melancólica y ominoso.

Daschel Janvier is sitting at a giant mahogany desk. A cacao-pod-shaped bowl of cacao-pod shaped stress balls rests at one end. Each foam pod is stamped with the HGB logo. Behind Janvier, a chocolate fountain dominates the space, with white and dark chocolate cascading like twin waterfalls into separate pools.

Janvier unbuttons the jacket of his suit, loosens his tie and leans back in his chair. His scruff of dark beard gives him a casual "everyguy" look. With his deep dimples, dark brown eyes, and smooth, lightly tanned Caucasian skin, he'd be muy atractivo – if he weren't the head of a corrupt corporation. "Miss Benitez. It's about time we met."

"Why would we have crossed paths? I'm always running away from you muchachos, no?" Heat floods my cheeks again. How can someone so dangerous be so cute?

"You're a spokesperson for this company, Miss Benitez. I should have been more … agreeable." He leans forward and grins. "Perhaps we could have avoided this mess entirely."

I look at the plush carpet. "I doubt that." HGB ordered mi papá's execution. They sent someone to spy on mi familia. They killed innocent people during the First Contact War. How could we not be on opposite sides?

"Hold on." Janvier gets that unfocused look people sometimes get when talking on a sublingual. I just stand there, in front of his desk. I doubt he even heard my question. After about two minutes, he says out loud, "If there's a problem, eliminate it, Akela."

I gasp. His tone just then was ita, ita cold.

Janvier presumably hangs up. He looks at me with a surprising amount of concern. "What's the matter, Bodacious?"

"Did you just …" I can't even manage a complete sentence. I swallow around a dry throat. "Lo siento," *I'm sorry,* "Pero did you just order another execution?"

Daschel smiles. "Is that what you think?"

I'm not playing into any extraño games. "Did you?"

"Maybe." He shrugs, looks even more amused with himself. "Then again, maybe I was rescheduling a golf date. Or finding somewhere to park my private jet."

I roll my eyes. If those things are supposed to impress me, he's chosen his brags poorly.

"Oh, come on Bo, don't take things so seriously." He's teasing me. I have heard he's an incorrigible flirt. En serio, though, flirting with someone you tried to have killed is in poor taste.

"I brought you something, mijo." I offer him the cake carrier, which he takes, arching an eyebrow at me.

"Mijo? I don't think anyone's ever dared call me that before." He sounds stern, his tone chilling. Pero, his eyes are laughing at me. "But I'll overlook it, because I've heard you are a spectacular chef. What was that culinary school you graduated from?"

Out of the corner of my eye, I see Tawny shake her cabeza, and Janvier's eyes go a fraction wider as he realizes his mistake. I *almost* graduated. I left school because I got involved in the whole mess surrounding chocolate. And then I *almost* got to graduate when I did my final, involving edible nanite effects, on the cooking show on the planet Zant that I appeared on – but my project got blown up, along with the show's set.

Like I told Frank yesterday, I can't do the project. Since the bombing, I haven't been able to look at a vial of edible nanites without remembering Verex Kowlk's crumpled, bloody body, his gigante flat yellow face smeared with streaks of blue Zantite blood. The Zantite holostar died shielding mis hermanas from the blast.

Verex had been a rising star. My sisters are nobodies.

Maybe graduation's not that importante.

I take out a datastick. "Eugene, mi amigo y the botanist looking into the disease ravaging the cacao plantations, noticed similarities to a medical case he observed. He asked me to get as much information as I could without arousing suspicion. This is the Evevron's research into a disease that attacks cells in their people in a similar way that the cacao disease affects plants."

Most of that is a lie. Eugene noticed no such thing. The information came from the Evevrons. And the likematches aren't coincidental. The plant disease was synthetically designed.

My sublingual rings. I instinctively answer it. Mi amiga Chestla's voice bubblechatters through my mind. *Are you on Earth yet?*

Sí, amiga. I glance at Janvier. He has a sublingual. In theory he could pick up Chestla talking. *I'm un poco busy right now.* She's picked up enough Spanish to catch *a little.*

Chestla bubblechatters, *Can they use the data? I'm giving you as much as I can without causing problems on my own planet.*

I glance at Janvier, hoping he can't tell I'm taking a call. I hang up before Chestla can say anything even more alarmante.

"Thank you." Janvier takes the datastick, though he's still looking at the cake carrier. What is up with this muchacho? He should be taking the data more seriously. It's almost like he doesn't care if the disease gets cured. Though that is the más importante problem Earth is facing. None of this adds up with anything I've heard about Janvier. He's supposed to be focused, driven, ruthless. Not this guy.

He opens the cake carrier with his free hand, and the deliciosa fragrance of caramel layered with chocolate wafts into the room. Janvier gives me a happy smile as he breaks off a corner of a brownie and pops it into his mouth. So not worried about poison, then.

I shrug. Janvier puts the datastick in his desk drawer.

"Have you gotten to explore the island?" Janvier asks, like he didn't just put a hit out on somebody. Like I'm here for vacation.

I say, "My transport just landed and Tawny picked me up." He should know that. "I waited where I was supposed to."

"I didn't expect you to actually do what you were told," Janvier insists.

"I'm not troublesome on purpose," I say. "Pero, I don't expect you to understand that I have Earth's best interest at heart."

"Believe it or not, I do too. But that requires more hard decisions than I expect *you* to understand." Janvier looks up at me with unexpected warmth in his brown eyes. He moves around the desk and takes my hand.

"Who did you order killed?" I keep mi mano loose in his, despite the comfortable warmth of his soft skin.

He shakes his cabeza. "You remind me of someone I knew when I was about your age."

I'm all of twenty-five. So ten years ago. I smile nervously. Janvier's definitely flirting. I mean, what am I supposed to say to that?

I glance over at Tawny, expecting her to be fizzbounced. What could play better in the media than me shipped together with the head of HGB himself? Maybe she lied about giving me time to grieve, and this has been her plan all along.

I expect her to feed me something scripted, pero her mouth has gone all pinched. Her ice blue eyes gaze at me coldly, and my chest goes just as frío.

Dios mio! Tawny has a crush on Janvier. And since she doesn't know Brill's alive – I'm certain now she doesn't – she can't realize why I won't flirt back with this muchacho.

I pull my hand away. "I need to get down to the set. Tawny has me scheduled for some initial bumpclips this afternoon. And I still have to write my speech for the homecoming reception dinner."

"Stay." He says it with so much intensity, I freeze. "Why go all the way back to Zant after just a couple of days? You're obviously invested in curing the plant disease. Stay and be a liaison between this office and the researchers."

That's loco. I'm not a scientist, and the reason I'm due back on Zant is because HGB – this very office – said I have to fulfil my contract to appear on the Zantite media productions or I'll be back in line for execution. "I need to get back as soon as we're done with the holomercials. I have an event set up where I may get to plead Earth's case to Garfex himself."

I start for the door, before Tawny can stare daggers any deeper through me.

"At least stay for a couple of weeks." Janvier smiles again. Those dimples. "I have a doctor on staff who has developed a treatment for the side effects of The Invincible Heart."

I freeze. "Que?"

IH withdrawal symptoms don't ever go away. Nunca. I live my days with shakes in my limbs and an itch in my blood that I can't scratch. The promise of being free of that is enough to make me ignore Tawny.

"Each treatment's temporary. But it should let you live a more normal life."

Mi manos are shaking right now. If it's temporary, accepting the proposed treatments would tie me even closer to HGB. Pero – even un día, a single day, without the shakes might be worth it. I do have about a week leeway before I need to leave for Zant. "I guess I could stay for a little while."

CHAPTER THREE

An hour later I'm wearing exercise clothes, sitting on a bench in an outside garden, surrounded by plumeria and oleander that are making dancing shadows in the afternoon sunshine, waiting for this mysterious treatment Janvier promised. I'm taking an encrypted holocall from Brill. Brill's on board his ship, which has been repaired. Everything's shiny and new – except for the paint on the bridge's interior. He just couldn't bear to paint over that.

The representation of mi hermoso in the phone's holofield is relatively small. Pero, even in miniature, he's still hot. Krom can pass for human from the outside – except for the color-shifting irises. Their internal biology has significant differences. Their iron-rich blood, more orange than red, contains a natural antifreeze. They can move más rapido than other species, hold their breath indefinitely, and live to an average of 300 years. None of which is fair, no?

Pero, I can't hold those advantages against Brill. Mi strawberry blonde hermoso is tall and built, with a chiseled jaw and a penchant for leather jackets and simple tees. And he loves me, though my life will burn out when his is only beginning.

I miss the way it feels to bury my face in his jacket and inhale the scent of leather and guy, to find comfort when he holds me. It's been a long time since we've been in the same room. Brill and I have been through so much together – good and bad. There are still a lot of relationship bumps to overcome – his familia hates me, and mi planeta hates his entire species – pero I love him in a way I've never loved anyone before. I call him mi vida, because he is the más importante part of my life.

"Will this treatment work, mi vida? I'm not just getting my hopes up over more of HGB's half-truths, right?"

Brill's eyes go a sympathetic deep brown. "I've never heard of a treatment for the Invincible Heart. Most people who take it wind up dead with the first dose, uan it's not a lucrative research field."

The Zantites formulated IH for soldiers going on suicide missions. And sí, for them una dose solitaria es a guaranteed ticket to the grave, as soon as the effects wear off.

"So I'll be an experiment?" Even if I am, I'm not sure if I can resist the possibility of relief from my withdrawal.

"Wal." *Yes.* Brill's eyes shift between gold and purple. "I can't weigh the costs for you, Babe. But I know how horrible your addiction has been. And if you feel like this treatment has a chance of working …"

I nod. "I'm afraid that it may be a placebo to convince me to stay here. Janvier was acting muy extraño."

"Extraño how?" Brill asks.

"No sé – he was playful, almost flirty, while steering the conversation towards asking me to stay. He must need me for something I'd refuse." I hesitate. "Unless his offer's genuine."

"Sthesh. I'll ask Gavin if he's heard anything about Janvier, but I doubt mi amigo would have. HGB plays everything low-key." Brill's face is tight with concern. I love that he's started dropping pequeños bits of Spanish into our conversations. "You could try to find out what he's up to, but you're already in so much danger just by being there."

The lights go out on Brill's ship, though he's still visible in the reflected light from the phone.

"Oye! You okay?"

"Wal. I'm getting a part upgraded, and they warned me they needed to cut power. I'm at a station, so if I start running out of air, I'll open the door."

The wall glows behind Brill's image. Claro está. Brill kept the painting Mertex had done, a design that spans the bridge, flowing up onto the ceiling, made of pink and yellow phosphorescent swirls and flowers, visible only when the lights are out. The painting was part of a prank Mertex pulled -- that inadvertently became a memorial to him. Heat burns at the back of my eyes, and grief weights my chest.

Mertex – the Zantite who had first been my enemy and then become mi amigo – overdosed on the Invincible Heart. Not by choice. At the time, he'd been infected by a telepathic mind parasite. The mind worm forced him to dose himself because it needed the strength and release from fear that comes from an IH high to make Mertex's body capable of carrying out a plan that nearly destroyed everything I care about.

Brill and I stopped the mind worm, pero couldn't save Mertex. The Invincible Heart has no antidote. The Murry worm later regretted causing Mertex's muerte, because while inside Mertex's cabeza, it saw something noble in the Zantite's respect for life, and learned a valuable lesson about what it means to be an individual instead of a hive mind. And it took parts of Mertex's personality -- and Mertex's nickname -- as its own.

"Diay, Babe?" Brill asks. *You okay?* "You look like you're about to cry."

"Wal." Even though tears are misting my eyes. I blink them back, but they're obviously clear in the hologram, because Brill's irises shift toward mahogany in response. "I just haven't thought about that painting en un largo tiempo. There've been so many deaths–"

"I know." His hand moves towards his phone, like he longs to touch this holo-me. He balls his hand into an empty, frustrated fist. "I wish I was there. You shouldn't have to carry this grief alone."

"I wish you were too. Remember the last time you kissed me? Before you got on Gavin's ship?" After Frank helped Brill fake his death, Gavin took Brill away. Heat burns in my eyes and at the back of my nose. "You said that beso would have to last a long time. Maybe forever."

"Don't give up hope. El corazón sin esperanza nunca encontrará la paz." *The heart without hope will never find peace.*

It's a line from one of the cheesecasts I appeared in back when I thought I had a chance at being a holostar – one of my lines. I had only had a few roles before the vulturazzi accused me of horror-heavy things, and I ran away to culinary school – on the other side of the galaxy – to escape the polls and media comments. Brill must have seen the scene where I said the hope line in flashback stardigging interviews. It's the one scene the pops like to show. In it I'm the family's daughter's best friend, and her parents have been ransomsnatched, and I start telling her flash-stories about how they'll escape.

The mist in my eyes gets thicker. Pero, it is tinged with hope. "Frank's somewhere on this island, mi vida. He has a meeting set to try and fix this." I can't do it. Hope is beyond me at the moment. "Pero, what if he can't?"

"What did Mr. Sawyer say about his plan while you were on Kaliel's ship?"

"HGB's ship," I correct. "And that's the last time I'm taking one as transport. Those things are magnets for space pirates. We were attacked. Twice."

"It's not the transport." Brill straightens the cuffs of his leather jacket. "It's you."

"Que?"

Brill hesitates. "Somebody's trying to ransomsnatch you. Gavin found out there's an open contract to pay a half a million Swehns to anyone who can get you off of Earth." Gavin's bound to me as my benefactor, so it makes sense that he would keep an eye on news relating to me.

I squeak out a shocked noise. "Por qué?"

"I don't know why."

Who would want to kidnap me? If someone hopes to use me as leverage against HGB, they're sadly misguided. As much as Janvier had flirted with me, he'd let me die without a second thought rather than jeopardize anything about his company. And I don't have specialized knowledge anyone could use. If it's for the dinero – sí, mi mamá would pay my ransom. Pero, I doubt she

could afford much more than the amount the would-be
ransomsnatcher is offering for someone to take me. Nada makes
sense here. "Maybe HGB has some plan for me that they don't
want anyone to know about. They've used third parties to cover
up their messes before."

"Then why bring you back to Earth, just to have you taken?
Having you disappear off of Evevron would have been easier."
His eyes shift through a couple of different colors. "The money
must be so high because whoever it is expects HGB to try and
stop them from taking you. Revwal?" *Do you agree?*

"As extraño as that is, sí." My relationship with HGB keeps
getting more complicated. "Uan, stay inside the HGB compound
if I want to stay safe? My brain has a hard time accepting that."

Brill's eyes tint violet, the Krom way of laughing without
making a sound. Krom iris chromashift is part of his species'
body language, a gift that lets me know his emotions from
moment to moment – and a drawback that makes it difficult for
him to lie. Pero, it's not impossible. He can hide his true emotions
if he really concentrates in past memories. "It's ita absurd. Last
time you were at an HGB facility, you nearly got killed getting
out."

"I know, right?" Frank had been the one shooting at me. Our
relationship has been … complicated.

"The good news is that the contract specifies the money will
only be paid if you're delivered alive. Uan if one of these morons
does get close to you, at least they'll be careful. I'll be there soon,
to help protect you."

My heart jolts. "You can't come here, mi vida! No y no. Not
into the arms of the company that ordered you muerto. And only a
few aliens have been allowed on this planet, so you might get
arrested before you even land."

"I'll risk it," Brill says. "You passed me off as human before,
remember?"

"For about five minutes," I splutter.

"Gavin has a lead on who might have issued the contract. The
transmission came from some su named Pitch who owns a bar

called The Dead Fish, right on the same island where you are. He's probably just the local contact. I'll dye—"

"Miss Benitez?" A man holding a tablet computer walks towards me.

I hang up on Brill mid-sentence. Holo-Brill disappears, hopefully before the guy got una buena look. "Sí?"

"We're ready for you inside. I do have to warn you, the treatment is somewhat painful, and the results will only last for about two weeks." He leads me down the path and into a building with air conditioning so strong I shiver.

"This is safe, no?" Who have they tested this treatment on? Not many humans are lo suficientemente estúpido to take the Invincible Heart? Being forcibly injected with it aboard a Zantite warship is hardly a common occurrence.

I follow him down a maze of hallways to a small room with a machine that looks like a CAT scanner. "We're going to stabilize the metallic compounds in the drug residue so that it can't interact with your blood. Your sublingual may not work for a few hours after, but don't worry – the treatment won't damage the hardware or your neural patch. Take off your shoes and any metal jewelry."

The guy leads me to an exam table. I hop up on it.

A holofield in front of the far wall is playing medical holomercials while the technician preps me for the treatment. He picks up a remote. "You might like this better."

He puts on a live feed of mi mamá, doing her show with Minda, one of Zant's biggest celebrities. A pang echoes through my chest, nostalgia, homesickness and regret. That was originally *my* show with Minda.

Zantites may be lemon yellow, bald giants with oversized mouths filled with razor-sharp teeth, pero that doesn't mean Minda's not one of the nicest people I know – or that anyone could work harder than she does to bring peace between our two planets. Mamá took my spot in the publicity tour, trying to use the power of media to prove that Earthlings are not savages and that

with the choco-monopoly broken, the planned Invasion of Earth
has no point.

Mamá's sitting on the set's Zantite-sized sofa, Minda on one
side – and Alex Crosskiss on the other. I do a doubletake, and I
must move too much, because the technician grabs my arm and
says, "Careful."

Pero, en serio, Alex Crosskiss, as in the Zantite General who
once tried to use me as murder weapon. I'd stowed away on
Crosskiss's ship when fleeing from both HGB and the Galactic
Police with the cacao pod that had made me guilty of treason
against Earth. I was estúpido y naïve and didn't realize the vessel
I'd boarded belonged to the Zantites. En serio. Nobody would do
that on purpose.

Crosskiss had been agrivengeful towards his stepfather the
King, who, as the highest-ranking officer aboard Crosskiss's
warship, was supposed to execute any stowaways with his teeth.

Pero by the time King Garfex came aboard, Crosskiss knew
that I was a toxic mess of Myska Venom and the Invincible Heart,
poison to anyone who ingested me. Crosskiss planned for Garfex
to execute me, and for the only possible witnesses – Brill and his
friend Jeska – to receive food guaranteed to cause a fatal allergic
reaction in Krom.

We all managed to stay vivo – *alive* – long enough to unravel
Crosskiss's plot. It turned out that King Garfex had no idea that
Crosskiss even existed, because Crosskiss's mother never told the
King she had a son from a previous marriage. Supongo que it all
worked out, since I didn't get executed by anybody, Brill and
Jeska didn't eat any peanut-related products, and Crosskiss got
adopted as the Zantite's Crown Prince.

Crosskiss is a lot less intimidating in a holofield than in
person. And he's blushing green while looking into the camera.
He pulls at the collar of his black uniform shirt. Somebody's
slapped a MIAG bracelet around his wrist. That's a piece of
collectabilia from Tawny's Mercy is a Gift campaign. Minda is
una gran supporter of that concept. She even appeared in Tawny's
initial Show Mercy video.

Crosskiss isn't keen on mercy. Does he even know what the acronym means?

"Tell us about your visit to Earth," Minda prompts in gravelly Zantite. The holo is showing subtitles in Universal.

Crosskiss looks even more uncomfortable. "I had asked to see Paris and my tour guide insisted I visit the Louvre." He makes a face, showing a lot of his feartastic teeth. "I'm not a fan of still art, and looking at a bunch of aliens in various stages of undress didn't appeal to me. But I went, and there was a pod of children out front of the building, launching balloons with notes attached for science class, to see how far they might travel. One of the juveniles gave me her balloon. She said I was going the farthest."

Both Minda and Mamá laugh, and somewhere outside the capture field, the audience echoes that laughter.

"She was right," Minda says. "But you didn't come straight back to Zant. How far have you gone?"

"I haven't tracked the exact distances." Crosskiss looks at the floor. "I love to travel. That's why I chose to captain a warship. I kept the balloon, and I've sent that kid pictures of it at every planet we stopped on for shore leave. The balloon has deflated, but she doesn't seem to mind. And her teacher is ecstatic about the cultural exchange."

It's a charming story, pero It doesn't fit with the Crosskiss I remember. He has to be making it up.

When I showed up as a stowaway on his ship, he forced me to my knees, intending to execute me according to military protocol without even hearing my side of what had happened. Like my life meant nada. He'd unhinged his jaw and would have snapped his teeth shut on my spine if Jeska hadn't warned him I'd been bitten by a Myska. That moment stars frequently in my nightmares.

Pero, if Crosskiss is still on Zant, that means we have un poco de tiempo – *a little time* --left to work on the Mercy campaign. Crosskiss's ship is probable que sea the scout for the Zantite fleet, coming weeks before the Zantite armada, which will lead the coalition forces. Maybe we can still fix the problems with chocolate and save Earth.

I cross the few steps from the exam table to the aterradora machine then sit on the platform that will slide me inside.

The technician says, "Your dependence on the Invincible Heart is more than physical. It's been blunting your reactions to fear and trauma. Once we strip that away, most test subjects have reported feeling raw and at the mercy of emotions they hadn't felt the need to process. It should level out within a day or two. Go ahead and lie down."

I hesitate. What he's describing doesn't sound fun. Pero, neither does killing myself for another high. I lie on the platform. Bands extend from the platform's sides, arcing over me, strapping me down.

"Oi!" Mi corazón thuds in panic.

"Don't worry, Miss Benitez," the tech says. "That's just to prevent you from hurting yourself."

I fight the bands, pero can't move them. Ay-ay-ay! The table trundles me into the machine. I'm still struggling futilely to pry myself off it when a whining noise surrounds me, and then it feels like my blood's on fire. Every nerve ending in my body registers full-scale agony.

I scream, pero they don't stop the treatment. It feels like they're boiling me from the inside out. The fire lasts forever, and I can't think clearly. It's like being in one of my nightmares, sensation and fear overriding todo.

Pero when the technician finally stops and lets me out, the wall clock shows I was only in there for five minutes.

The straps release. I'm too weak to move, let alone stand.

The technician says, "Relax while I go prepare your recovery drink. I'll give you a few minutes. You want to be sure you're not going to throw up first."

"Mhnmhp," I say.

The door snicks closed, y yo estoy complemente sola – *I'm completely alone.*

CHAPTER FOUR

The door snicks open again. I guess the technician forgot something.

"Hello, Bodacious." The muchacho approaching the table doesn't sound like the guy who just left – and doesn't smell like him either. This guy smells of cigarettes and stale sweat. Which makes me queasy with worry and fear. I can't even lift mi cabeza to look at him. He laughs. "This will be easier than I thought."

I thought I'd be safe inside the HGB compound. I was obviously wrong. Kidnappers just stroll into this place.

I try my sublingual. Technician guy was right: it's not working. And my handheld is in a bin on the other side of the room.

My strength is returning, pero not enough yet to sit up, let alone fend off an attacker.

He comes into view, looming over me, his gaunt, pale face aged by substance abuse. "Sucks, don't it? The treatment's worse than the shakes. And I had four hits of IH before they hauled my ass in here."

My chest goes frío como hielo – *cold like ice*. I'm being abducted by someone who took the Invincible Heart by choice. Four or five hits of IH is all the human liver can take before it crashbangs. Which means this guy's well on his way to killing himself. Which makes him that much more unpredictable.

"Por favor–"

He scoops me off the table and deposits me in a lev chair. He opens the door and guides the lev chair into the hall. "You'll be able to speak properly in a few minutes. If you scream, I will kill you. Money's no good to me if I get stuck in a cell before I can get another dose of bliss."

"It. Kill you. Mijo."

He pokes what must be a gun barrel up against my shoulder. "Think of me as a glimpse of your future. You'll get to this point. Or maybe you'll get lucky, and whoever's paying for you will find a more humane way for you to die."

I shake mi cabeza, which still feels wobbly. "I. Made a promise."

I'd promised Mertex that I'd be stronger than this addiction. I'm not likematching this guy, not letting the drug drive me to desperate acts. Nunca.

My abductor knows his way through the building and gets us out through a side door. We're back in the lush garden. I catch a flash of movement on the main path, near the front of the building, pero when I turn my head, no one's there.

I must have imagined it. A lead weight of dread settles into my chest.

Not that I could have called out to anyone without getting myself shot – y them también.

The junkie pushes me deeper through the oleander, to a gate in the garden wall. On the other side, a transport waits on the service road. As we pass through the gate, the guy clicks a fob and the transport's back door swings upward. A metal wall blocks the cargo area from the rest of the vehicle. There's stuff stacked back there, pero not high enough to keep me from seeing there's no windows, no escape routes, just a door into the front of the vehicle – with no handle on this side. My breath catches. Oi! If I go in there, that's it. I'll be offplanet and on my way to the mystery kidnapper.

I've got a little strength back. I push myself out of the chair, hoping the guy won't shoot me. Pero, if he wants his dinero, he needs me alive. I crash to the pavement, shielding my face with my arms. Mostly unhurt, I climb shakily to my feet. I don't make it two steps before he grabs me.

He pokes the gun barrel against my sternum. "Don't try that again."

"Por favor." I take a shuddery breath. "I can get you money. Mi mamá would pay to get me back safe."

He shrugs. "Maybe. But things go wrong with ransom demands. This way, I've got a guaranteed payday and zero chance of the police shooting me."

"Eschucha. I can get you double. And I promise not to run."

He laughs. "Do I look stupid? You're the girl who ran from the Myska cop after he'd bit you. You were dying and still wouldn't turn yourself in to get the antivenin."

Es cierto. I'm not going to change his mind. I sigh and move to get onto the transport.

"Hold it." Frank's voice comes from behind us, near the gate.

The junkie and I both turn. The guy grabs me around the shoulders and pokes the gun barrel painfully into my neck. Mi corazón, already hammering, thuds even faster. I start trembling. It's not the IH shakes, just raw terror at finding myself caught between a cold-blooded assassin and a desperate junkie – both holding firearms.

It's startling. I *don't* have the withdrawal symptoms. And I don't have the buffer against fear the residual IH had given me. Whatever I face this time, I face on my own. And that scares me también.

"Drop it," the junkie says. "Or I drop her."

"That's not going to happen, mijo," I warn him. "Frank's a hired killer."

The guy makes a startled noise. He edges backwards, like he's going to pull me with him into the front of the transport.

"Don't try it," Frank says. "I'm giving you one warning."

"Look old man," the junkie starts. My heart jolts. This guy shouldn't underestimate Frank because there's a little gray in his hair. No. Y no.

"Let her go. Now."

The junkie pulls me backwards, then he stumbles The gun bounces away from my neck. There's a soft kathud and a flash from Frank's gun. A near-deafening bang stabs my ear. The arm holding me goes slack and the junkie collapses to the pavement. I squeeze my eyes shut. I don't want to see his corpse.

Something touches my face. I flinch. It's Frank, wiping my cheek with a handkerchief. The cloth comes away smeared with red. "You okay?"

I nod. A bullet hole from the junkie's convulsive shot marks the pavement nearby. Frank had taken a real chance that I wouldn't be hurt. Pero, he's muy bueno at what he does. And the alternative was letting me be taken.

If he hadn't happened to be here, I would be in atmo right now, headed off Earth. "Why …?"

He gestures at the garden gate. "I was coming to get a physical and psych exam. HGB requires that every six months for guys in my … position. I saw him dragging you out. You what to tell me what this is about?"

"I wish I knew, viejo." I look down at the crumpled figure. Frank just killed a man right in front of me. Again. This time he did it to save me, pero the calm way he pulled that trigger still leaves me frío inside.

A dog barks. Botas, Frank's corgi, comes trotting up to the gate, trailing a leash tied to a broken plumeria branch, complete with flowers. The dog must have grown worried about his owner. Qué dulce. *So sweet.* Frank gestures for Botas to sit. The dog sploots backwards, waiting on the path. Frank smiles at Botas.

Then Frank gestures at the dead man, and the smile slips away. "Who was he?"

I gesture towards the body. "A nobody. I think. Brill said somebody's put a price on me. This muchacho wanted dinero por another dose of IH."

Frank's eyes soften with sympathy. I'm pretty sure it's for me, an IH addict being forced to look at the addiction's tragic result, and not the guy cooling on the pavement.

Frank had watched me the whole way from Zant to Earth, no doubt wondering when I'll self-destruct. Porque I'm a junkie too, fighting the need for that same hit this guy just died over. Maybe Frank's bullet did him a kindness, saving him from an even uglier end.

I look him in the eye. "Would you do the same for me, if I ever got that bad?"

He studies me, considering his words. "If there was no other way to help you, and you asked me to? Without hesitation."

"Good to know, viejo." That thought is disturbingly comforting.

I don't want to tell him about the treatment, no hasta I know it worked. That maybe, just maybe, I have a future after all.

"But I don't think you'll ever crumble like this guy." Frank kneels by the junkie, careful to keep out of the spilled blood, and unzips the guy's jacket. "Let's see what we can learn." He takes out a phone and a wallet.

A slip of paper falls to the ground. It's got a phone number on it and a set of coordinates.

There's not much else interesting. Solamente a stick of lip balm, a pack of cigarettes and some nicotine gum.

"What should we do now?"

Frank shrugs. "Call that number and see who answers. And bury the body, of course."

My heart lurches. "Are you wanting me to help with that?"

He laughs. "This is your problem, but that might push your sensibilities a little far for one day. Go back to your room and get cleaned up. I'll let you know what I find."

CHAPTER FIVE

I'm sitting in an uncomfortable plastic chair in a hunormous studio production room, with no windows and antiseptic-scented air. The production assistants have brought in several racks of clothing from the props department to find me a good look. Craft services has set up in another room, pero, a small table in here holds a coffee carafe. I've had two cups to steady my nerves and try to forget the junkie's muerte. Pero, I keep feeling that slackening arm falling away from me.

I've developed a prodigious caffeine habit, since it helps with the IH shakes. Which I do not have this morning. The treatment worked. Which is freeing. Amazingly so. I should focus on that. I call mi hermano Mario on my sublingual. Gracias a Dios, my internal tech is working again también. Mario was on Zant when I'd held a syringe of the Invincible Heart in my hands and almost caved and taken it. He made me promise to call him any time I felt that weak again. I owe him some reassurance.

Pequeña? Mario's bubblechatter sounds worried. I haven't called him in a while. So, sí, while our relationship is improving, reaching out to him is still not mi primer instinct. Pero, he could call me too, no?

You will never guess what happened, I tell him.

Something chido, for once? You sound excited.

I stifle a laugh. I'm supposed to be studying my lines, not talking on the phone. *HGB came up with a treatment for the side effects of IH. And later, they sent me for a massage.* I skip the kidnapping attempt that happened in between. Why worry him, no? *Me siento como– maybe I have a future.*

Mario chatters, *Maravilloso! Mamá said you were back on Earth. I'm coming out to the compound. Will you still be in Maui when I get there?*

A lump of fear builds in my throat. *They're calling you in?* This has to have something to do with whatever this plan is Janvier has for me.

No. I made an appointment to talk to their archivist about photos dating back to first contact to use for my book on Krom. I want to be fair and interview both sides.

Gracias a Dios. I let out a breath. Y I'm proud of mi hermano. He held on to his assumptions about Krom for a long time, even after befriending Brill. After all, Mario grew up believing that Krom "discover" planets in the name of personal gain. Now he's working on un libro in a quest to understand what Krom actually value.

This may be too soon. Mario sounds hesitant. *But Brill knew one of the Krom who made first contact with Earth. Do you have a way to get ahold of the guy? I'd love to interview him.*

Mario believes Brill is dead. Mamá and Frank agreed – if we told Mario, he would tell his wife and then we'd lose control of the secret. I bite my tongue to keep from telling mi hermano the truth while I pull up my contact list on my handheld. *Vale. I'm sending you Jeska's contact information.* I let Mario go.

Jeska thinks that Brill is dead, también. He sent his condolences, making it clear that I'm welcome to resume contact. Jeska and I had a moment of connection awhile back. He's Brill's somewhat distant cousin. Though Brill's strawberry blond, Jeska's skin is darker brown than mine. They're very different, in ways that go deeper than just looks, pero both are muy atractivo. Pero, even if Brill *was* muerto, getting together with his best friend's brother would be weird, no?

We're about to start holoing preliminary clips. I feel numb wearing this kalltet pendant.

Tawny puts a hand on mine. "You *are* still grieving your Krom."

I manage a wan smile. "What do you think of Frank?"

Tawny blinks. "Look, Sweetie, Frank was only doing his job. It wasn't personal. I think he felt a bit bad about it."

She thinks Frank could have put a bullet in Brill's corazón and not felt it was personal. As much as Tawny's supposed to understand both humans and aliens so that she can manipulate them, sometimes she misjudges people.

I'd hoped to find out what she thinks of Frank, because I'm flusterfused about how to feel now that he killed somebody to save me. Pero, her honest opinion was too much to ask.

"As long as he was doing his job." It comes out with just enough bitter irony. After all, I was a real actress once upon a time. Not una marioneta por HGB's media spinwash. I keep being manipulated into going in front of the cameras. And I don't see an end to it. Nunca. I hold up my script. "Do we have to do the spot with the edible nanites?"

Tawny blinks. "Why not?"

I look down at the tablet and swallow slick nausea. I want to be a chef. And chefs deal with nanites. I need to get over this reluctance.

Tawny puts a hand on mine. "It'll be easy. The nanites are preprogrammed. Just pour the liquid into the melted chocolate, and it will form HGB's Logo and solidify."

"Easy. Bien." I'm still in a feartastic situation, where people keep dying around me. If I let memories of Verex's muerte break me, I become useless to everyone. My gaze moves to Tawny's tablet, where she's doodled a vectorholo. "What's that?"

Tawny smiles. Genuinely smiles. "HGB New. Bodacious, once we get the kinks worked out, people will forget about chocolate."

"Pero, what is it?"

"A rejuvenating health food bar. The prototype tastes like honey." She's got this secretive little smile now. "It's been my project since HGB first hired me. I've been involved with R&D from the beginning. Nobody cared much until we were forced to diversify."

I study my lines, mostly about casa y familia. About how HGB is taking a moment to regroup, suspending the flow of chocolate temporarily, so that they can bring out a line of new, better products.

My sublingual rings.

I don't know what I'm supposed to do here, Bo. It's Murry, like we're already in mid-conversation.

Hola mijo. Not supposed to do where? I always picture just one Murry, though he is a hive mind made of many individuals. Murry is a collection of brain parasites that use the processing power inside brains he has infected to store his memories and power his telepathy. He nearly become a galactaplague, pero Brill and I talked him into limiting infections of himself to one species of non-sentient life -- the flying snake-bug-hippo monsters called spucks, from the planet Evevron. Which happens to be Chestla's home planet.

Evevrons consider spucks pests, because they dig destructively under towns and eat crops. The ones Murry has infected are protected, though only a select number of Evevrons know about the mind worms. In areas outside of Chestla's home city, spucks are still hunted for food, so Murry has to be careful not to cross the river.

Tawny dubbed the spucks dragons, and the media spin stuck. I'd been forced to kill one, and been dubbed Bo the Dragonslayer.

I'm supposed to speak at the Ceremony of Salt for those parts of me that were frozen in the cryostasis pods. What should I say? Murry sounds nervous, one more jangling note in my mind. Pero, at least his problem is something I can understand and deal with.

Evevrons burn their dead and scatter the ashes in special salt caves. This is usually a community-wide event. Only since Murry was engineered illegally, most of the community doesn't know his bloody history. Even so, this low-key ceremony will finally allow Evevron to lay to rest all of the mistakes that led to Murry.

Find Leron, and make peace with him. Then say what's in your hearts. I hesitate. Leron was the lab technician who froze those five individuals in the first place. He didn't have much choice in the matter, pero he still knew it was murder. *And don't eat him. The poor muchacho's been wracking himself with guilt over this for years.*

But that's hard, Murry whines. *We don't want to see him and remember his actions.*

I know. Brill had likematched the mindworm hive mind to un niño. In many ways, that's true. And it's having to grow up fast. *Pero you can do it, mijo. Porque you're brave.*

Okay. Murry sounds a little happier.

And don't eat him. Even if he makes you really mad. Me lo prometes?

I promise. Murry breaks the connection.

I still have trouble wrapping my brain around the complexities of death for a collective being. Even if I don't fully understand, my heart hurts for him.

The brain parasites were originally engineered as a behavior modification tool. These Sympathetic Mindhuggers were never expected to gain sentience – much less form a hive mind.

The first tier of the Mindhuggers' personality came from the criminals it was illegally tested on. The second tier came from the scientists it infected while fighting its way off its origin planet. It learned something from everyone it infected, including mis amigos. Especially Mertex. Y sí, Mertex's personality shines through in every interaction I've had with the Murry worm. It has his love for cheesetastic movies and his unfounded optimism and social awkwardness. Pero it's broken and hurt in ways the Zantite never was and has una lógica fría – *a cold logic* -- all its own.

I hope the part Murry played in Mertex's muerte will help him have sympathy for Leron.

The director calls me into the holocube, which holds a levitating bubble filled with chocolate, a table with a chef's jacket, and a tube of preprogrammed nanites suspended in blue fluid. Nanite gel comes in lots of colors. No sé why they chose this shade of blue. It looks like the tube is filled with Zantite blood.

No, por favor. Why did we have to start with this one? I'm trembling, suddenly lost in memories. Zantite blood all over me, when parts of an executed crewman were tossed on me in a bin where I hid. Zantite blood all over Verex, when the bomb killed him.

The director says, "Put on the chef's jacket. Say your lines, then turn and pick up the nanites. Use the hole in the top of the bubble to pour it in. Okay?"

"Sí." I should be wearing a chef's jacket by now. I should be done with all of this. HGB. The invasion threat. Murry's problems. Todo y todo. I don't think HGB is intentionally mocking me, though. To them it's just a prop. I take the jacket from the table. It bumps the tube, which rolls off the table.

When it hits the floor, the cap pops off. Blue liquid leaks onto the floor. I fall to my knees, just staring at it. La sangre es sangre – *blood is blood* – no matter what the color.

"Don't just sit there. Pick it up," Tawny says.

Tears fill my eyes. I wipe them away. Then without warning, I'm weeping uncontrollably. It's embarrassing, humiliating … and I can't stop.

Tawny bends down, picks up the mostly empty tube, then caps it. "Is it the nanites?"

I move my head somewhere between a shake and a nod. "I've lost so many amigos," I say between sobs. "I always make the failtastic choices." Siempre.

"Not always." Tawny pulls out a pack of tissues and mops up the nanites. "You saved Kaliel – twice. And your mother and Minda. And you uncovered the plan for the invasion and warned Earth."

I stop crying from the shock of Tawny saying cosas positivas about me. I hiccup, fighting to get myself under control. "I guess–" – hic – "this is all in the latest version of my eulogy."

Tawny smiles. "I haven't updated your eulogy. You aren't planning anything that could get you killed, right?"

"Can we continue?" the director asks.

"Give us a minute," Tawny says. For once it's nice to have a starwrangler. She whispers, "Janvier said the treatment for IH would be rough. But most of the world doesn't know you have an addiction. So let me handle this."

I nod and just kneel, hands clasped, while Tawny strides over to the director. After a moment, he calls out, "All right, we're scrapping this one. Take fifteen, and then we'll move on to the Wholesome and Delicious script."

I get up off the floor. I just need to take a few deep breaths and fix my makeup. "I'll be ready in ten."

CHAPTER SIX

I'm back in front of the green screen, doing an initial run-through of Wholesome and Delicious, when Daschel Janvier himself walks in, carrying a hunormous wicker picnic basket. I keep reading my lines.

He sits next to Tawny. She looks shyly at her manos. She is crushing on this muchacho big time.

Sadly, he doesn't seem to notice. He stares at the pendant I'd shoved halfway into my purse when Tawny wasn't looking. With an expression pensativo, he studies my face, especially mi manos, where I've polished my nails a deep red to hide the natural nail, which is puce green – another "gift" from the IH.

The soft smile on Janvier's face is more peligroso than Frank's icy stare. It's the very definition of disgustination – I'm so horrified by Janvier, I find him fascinating – which is turning into una emoción positiva.

I finish the lines. The director glances several times at Janvier, then tells me to take a break. Despite how irritated he was over the break I just took.

When I walk over, Janvier stands, holding out the picnic basket. "This got delivered to me by mistake."

"Que?" Someone sent me a basket? After the abduction attempt yesterday, I'm leery of gifts from strangers. Pero, there is a card. I pluck it from the basket hinge and open the envelope. The front cover is an image of a riverbank, and a few snow-frosted buildings, with the caption "Stockholm." It's a thank-you note from Kaliel Johannsson's mamá. I helped clear Kaliel of criminal charges that could have led to his execution – twice. So of course his mamá was overwhelmed with joy at having her hijo home the second time.

The food inside the basket is as diverse as Kaliel's gene-ties. She's sent a jar of harissa, honey-drizzled semolina cake that looks homemade, Persian pears poached in wine, and a can of Surströmming, along with cookies and flatbreads, preserved meats and cheeses and a giant bottle of Swedish mustard. What would-be kidnapper would have gone to that much trouble?

I pull a sleeve of macarons from the basket and tear it open. I'm not letting this gran feast go to waste.

Janvier takes a macaron. "The weather today is perfect for a seaside picnic. And what could make for better PR than me and you, walking together on the beach?"

I glance at Tawny. Her lips press into a thin line.

Esto es un problema. If I say yes, I'm making an enemy of one of the few people who can help me – right after she showed me such kindness with the nanites. Pero, who can say no to the CEO of HGB?

This is such a telenovela moment, when the powerful businessman singles out the poor girl, subject of pain and scandal, over richer, more worthy, more powerful prospects.

Blech. The same guy who could order assassinations and have people publicly executed via guillotine can't have a secret heart of gold.

"If you don't mind sharing," Janvier prompts.

I flash Tawny a look that means *lo siento mucho, chica.* Ni idea if she gets it. "Do you want to go now?"

"I am a little hungry." Janvier smiles, with the full intensity of those dimples. Raw attraction zings through me. Dios mio! I know how ruthless he is. How can I still be attracted to him?

He's got a car waiting, with a driver and a muchacho in the passenger seat with eyes as fríos as Frank's. At least I'm safe from being abducted off the beach, no?

Janvier pulls up a screen between us and the front seat. This is so oddly intimate. The temperature in my face and chest rises. A few months ago, this guy wanted me muerta. So why would he now, you know, want me?

I have to be misreading his cues.

Janvier taps my purse, which lays on the seat beside me. "I'm glad you've taken that pendant off. It would be … inappropriate for me to be here with you if you were still in mourning."

Ay-ay-ay! I'm not misreading his cues. And he can't know que inapropiado this is.

My sublingual rings. It's Brill. *Babe! I'm here. Set, I'm on the other side of Maui, but I'll be there in a couple of hours.*

Mi corazón freezes. I'm in a car with the man who wants Brill muerto. A man who has a sublingual. Janvier doesn't look like he's talking on it right now, so he probably isn't picking up crosstalk, which can happen when two people are using sublinguals in close proximity. Pero I need to get Brill off the phone pronto, just in case.

I fight to keep my face neutral, while over the sublingual, I'm telling Brill, *I told you to stay away from here, mi vida.*

Brill's laugh bubbles through my brain. *I'm in disguise. Wait until you see my hair.*

I manage not to sigh out loud. *I'll meet you at 7. That Japanese restaurant just outside the complex. I have to go.*

Where are you?

About to have a picnic with Daschel Janvier. I cut the connection before he can react.

"Bodacious?" Janvier asks. "Are you alright?"

"Sí. Sí." I force smile. "Just surprised. We've been on opposite sides, Mr. Janvier."

"Call me Shelly. My friends do."

I snort out a laugh. Muy attractive, no? "Are we friends?"

He shrugs. "Maybe."

I try to examine his face impassively, pero es difícil when he's so present – and so hot.

"Bodacious–"

"Bo."

"Bo, you intrigue me. You should be dead, a dozen times over. But you've proven yourself resourceful, creative and intelligent. And something inside you has let you overcome the destructive need of the Invincible Heart."

I manage a genuine smile. "Gracias por the treatment. For the first time in a long time, I don't feel on edge."

Now that I've had that massive cry, I feel more balanced, more in control.

Janvier puts a hand closer to me on the seat. "The treatments are important, but we could help each other a lot more. Now that the chocolate monopoly has been broken, HGB must take a new direction." He's not accusing me. Even though I broke the monopoly. "If I had you nearby, you could put that resourcefulness to use making sure our direction is a better one."

I can't believe how forward he's being. He must have cooked up some trick, some plan. He wants to manipulate me into agreeing to something even more feartastic than I already face. My heart races, making mi cabeza feel un poco light.

The car pulls to a halt.

"Mira. We're here." I release my seatbelt and open the door. Then I'm out, walking toward the sand, where someone's set up a table with a beach umbrella.

He was that sure I would say sí.

Janvier carries the basket to the table and rummages inside. He holds up the can of Surströmming. "What is this?"

"Don't open that, Mr. Janvier!"

"Shelly."

"Shelly. It's … pungent, no? It's illegal to open Surströmming inside most apartment buildings in Sweden."

"Alrighty then." He drops the can back into the basket and pulls out a hunk of cheese. Then he points to the sand, closer to the agua. "Hey, look at that. A Honey Cowrie shell."

I'm even more sure this is a trick. I collect seashells. Always have, even from beaches where it's illegal. And with Maui's tourist trade, there are never shells on the beach, nunca.

Looking un poco embarrassed, Janvier pockets the shell. "I've never found one of these before, and I refuse to buy things for my collection."

"You collect seashells?" I'm skeptical.

He shrugs and steps close to me. Then, using sleight of hand, he pulls the shell out from behind my ear. "Where do you think I got the nickname Shelly?" He puts the shell back in his pocket. "Let's hope it stays put this time."

The media-spin paints Janvier as a playboy and a flirt. Pero, he's charming. And he's implying I'm positioned to be a force for change, from inside HGB. Even though Janvier's promises are hollow, without mi esperanza – *my hope* -- de seeing Brill again, I could see myself being seduced by them.

Pero, Brill keeps me strong and focused. He is mi vida, my very life.

So why am I smiling at Janvier?

What if this crack of disloyalty in my heart has something to do with the paladzian pendant? A reporter said its purpose was to separate bound corazóns. Could that be more than just a metaphor? It's a horrifying through that makes me feel leaden.

"Let me show you something," Janvier takes out his phone and pops up a holocording of a conversation between himself and a roundish alien with a couple dozen purple tentacles. They're in Janvier's office.

The alien rolls forward, shifting a different set of tentacles towards the floor. Its flat face protrudes a few inches above a bow tie circling its "neck." Of all the aliens I've seen, this one is the strangest looking.

"The bow tie was for my benefit," Janvier says. "He heard it was on-trend on Earth."

In the holo, the alien makes a series of clacking noises, and the security robot steps forward from the corner and translates. "We would be willing to take the mining rights as a lease. Though I don't see why parting with the planet upsets you so. You're not using it."

"Giving away Jupiter would give you too much of a claim in our solar system," Holo-Janvier replies. "We're trying to protect our autonomy, not trade the Zantites for another threat."

The round alien shimmies in a full-bodied nod. "Intelligent, my dear leader human. A lease then. You give us exclusive rights for mining and gas harvesting on the planet you call Jupiter for the next fifty of your years, and we will stand with you against the invasion coalition."

"Why do you believe the Zantites will fear you?"

The alien shimmies again. "Because we know their secret weaknesses. We have observed them for ages of time."

"I will consider your offer," Holo-Janvier says, "and discuss it with my advisors."

During the rest of the conversation, the alien pressures Janvier, who awkwardly keeps saying no.

After the holo ends, Janvier asks, "Could Garfex actually be scared of this guy?"

"I doubt it. Pero, looks can be deceiving. So …" Shrugging, I roll my hand towards his phone. "You said you would ask your advisors. no?"

"I am." Janvier arches an eyebrow at me. "You've met Garfex. Advise me."

I blink. He sounds serious. "Vale." I gesture at the phone again. "I wouldn't trust him. Probably his ships would disappear just in time for the Zantites to destroy Earth – so he can turn around and claim Jupiter."

Janvier's smile gets wider. "Not far from my own conclusion. But why aren't we mining Jupiter ourselves? Why aren't we looking for other ways to make real allies in the galaxy? We've been so caught up in protecting a single commodity, we haven't used that commodity to leverage investment in other galactic industries. We need to save chocolate so that we can build friendships, trade shares in cacao into something more viable long term. We don't even know what's out there to get our hands into."

I gape at Janvier. This doesn't sound like HGB's standard line. In fact, those statements might be heading into the neighborhood of treason. Janvier is ill, or unhinged. Or else he's messing with me.

I swallow to wet my dry throat. "We should focus on saving chocolate first, mijo."

CHAPTER SEVEN

That night, at the Japanese restaurant, even I don't recognize Brill. He calls out to me, and I bust out laughing.

Mi strawberry blonde hermoso with the chromashifting eyes and tough-guy leather jacket has turned into an emo tourist version of himself. Opaque contacts have turned his eyes a muddy brown. When his irises get that way via shift, that means he's upset. These contacts give me the impression that he's perpetually disgusterated.

And his hair. It's solid black. He usually styles it swept back off his forehead, pero his bangs hang down almost in his eyes.

He's wearing a leather necklace with an anchor dangling from it, and leather bracelets adorn both his wrists – making his proximity band, a silver-toned bracelet that tethers him to his ship, less obvious. Por supuesto, that ship is currently on another planet, yet another sign that Brill is out of his element. He lives aboard his ship, relies on it como un escape de tough situations.

He's wearing a long-sleeve black tee layered under a graphic tee. Dios mio! It's one of the memorial tees Tawny commissioned after Brill's "death" – with a coffin and his name written in Krom script. He's hiding in plain sight, with *Rest in Peace, Brill Cray* four inches high across his chest.

A little *too* ironic, no?

Krom lifespans average 300 years, and they age more slowly all along that curve, so Brill who always looks younger than his 29 years, at this point could pass for a human teenager.

I slide into the booth across from him. "Wow, mi vida."

A bottle of sake rests beside a plate of cucumber roll in front of him. Given his apparent age, I'm surprised they served him alcohol. He must have fake ID that matches this appearance.

"Babe!" He sounds un poco embarrassed, pero the contacts hide the shift of his eyes, and Krom can't blush. Which leaves me feeling distant and disconnected from him. The impression that he's angry weighs in my stomach.

I tell him, "You look like you should be in a boy band with that haircut."

He pours me a cup of sake. "It's only temporary."

"Hanstral I'm late." I use the Krom word for *I'm sorry*. "Sneaking out of the HGB facility was un poco difícil, and I had to remove the bug Tawny'd slapped on me. I had to check that I wasn't followed. There was–"

Brill laughs. "You sure about that?"

Heat fills my face. "Que?"

He points at the bar where Frank is ordering a beer. Frank gives Brill's disguise a once-over and frowns.

"Mi vida. Lo siento." Ni idea what Frank's reaction to seeing Brill on Earth will be. The last time Frank saw mi vida, he came a breath from killing him. If it looks like Brill is being careless about hiding the fact that he is vivo from HGB, Frank might change his mind.

Brill doesn't look worried – from what I can tell. "Diay, Babe. Mr. Sawyer told me about the kidnapping attempt. He knew I'd be here."

Brill's culture es muy formal when it comes to names.

"Pero, then why'd he follow me? Wouldn't it have been easier to drive me out of HGB in a jeep?"

"I wanted to see who else might be following you." Frank has come up to our table. Dios mio, that guy moves quietly. He jerks a thumb towards Brill. "Plus, plausible deniability, in case things go wrong with him."

I take a steadying breath, then ask Frank, "Have you met with Janvier yet?"

Frank twirls his beer bottle between his hands. "I'm meeting in two days with the CEO and Board of Directors. I told Janvier this morning that I uncovered some unexpected news on the way back from Zant. When I get to the meeting, I'll tell them you slipped up and let on Cray's alive and hiding in an undisclosed location. And that if they take the order off his head, you promised that Brill won't say anything, but that if we don't, he'll go to the nearest Krom consulate with a hard-to-explain scar and a bullet that matches my gun."

My chest aches just thinking about all the ways that plan could go wrong. Frank put a scar on Brill as a condition for letting him live. If HGB kills or captures mi vida, Brill's flesh will corroborate Frank's story. Pero, HGB could turn Frank over to the courts – where he would be executed for attempting to murder a Krom citizen, something he didn't actually do.

"I don't like it, Mr. Sawyer," Brill says. "Maybe you'll get them to leave me alone – uan there's an equal chance that they'll put a hit on Bo too."

Frank shrugs. "They need Bo alive, at least until this invasion business is sorted."

"But it's still an unacceptable–" Brill starts, pero Frank interrupts him.

"Either I talk to my bosses, or I put a bullet in your head tonight." He gives Brill a friendly grin. "Your choice."

"Viejo!" I can't believe he's almost joking about this.

Frank told me that he's nothing more than a weapon for HGB. Which means that whatever is going on with Janvier, Frank won't like it. Janvier's started talking about change, when Frank's killed numerous people to help HGB maintain the status quo. Which is why it's so extraordinary that Frank went against orders and showed Brill mercy. Something in Frank saw that mi vida had done nothing for which he deserved to die.

Why can't Frank see that he needs to get out of HGB's murky waters before they suck out everything good in him?

"I'd still appreciate you giving me a chance to get Bo out of here before you talk to them," Brill says. "Avell. In case she needs to run."

Frank sips his beer. "If Bo disappears, I'll have a hard time convincing anyone that she's prepared to cooperate."

"She–"

"Oye! Muchachos! I am right here, no?" I take a deep breath. If I flitdash, Frank would be in danger, and I am not explaining to Mamá that I got her hermoso killed. "I am not going to run. Janvier has expressed an interest in me." I can't look at Brill. "Romantically. Pero, I can make it clear that I just want to be amigos. Maybe if I get close to him, I can see how he feels about letting someone close to me live."

"Or give him even more motive to eliminate a potential rival," Frank mumbles.

Brill's contacts hide how he feels. "You'd be tying yourself even closer to HGB."

"Only temporarily." I take Brill's hand. Mine is steady as a stone. Janvier has tied me to him already with the treatments that calm the itch in my blood, and leave me without a craving for power and destruction. I haven't felt this well in a long time. And it would take mucho to make me give up this newfound wellbeing.

"You're sure you can just be friends with this su?" Brill asks.

"Mi vida, por favor." That hurts. I want to marry Brill. Mi corazón physically aches for how badly I want to join my life with his. He's come close to proposing at least twice. Y twice, he stopped himself. The huge levels of prejudice between his planet and mine have given him pause, along with the massive difference in our lifespans. There's nada about myself that I can change, nada that makes me suficientemente buena para him.

"Sorry, Babe. That was uncalled for." He touches his chest over his own heart and looks at me with sympathy. Then he empties his sake cup and refills it. "Who else has a motive to kidnap you? A crazed fan, maybe?"

I pick up a paper wrapper from the table. "Lots of people complain about me in the polls. If you want to sort through my hate mail, check the comments."

"Stop worrying about those polls," Brill says forcefully. "No one would get a good approval rating after everything that's been thrown at you. Revwal?"

I twist the paper. "They want me muerta. They think I'm a horrible person."

"Do you think you're a horrible person?" Brill asks. "That your life doesn't have value just because they say it doesn't?"

"Of course not." I can't explain to him what it was like to be a star and get fan mail instead of death threats. And how it broke me when the paparazzi turned on me, when no one would believe that the people accusing me were the liars.

"I doubt the pops are actively trying to kill you," Brill says.

Frank says, "This may have some connection to Jimena Duarte. I still feel she was part of something bigger."

"Que?" Jimena was my prep-chef, back when I first did the cooking show on Zant. Frank killed her, because he figured out that she planned to kill me. The Murry worm had infected her, and Murry later told me that, before the Mindhuggers took control of her, Jimena was part of a plot to tank relations between Zant and Earth.

"I've been meaning to ask you what this means – 'Pueden encontrar muchos otros para terminar esto.'" The words sound clunky coming off Frank's tongue. Pero, the meaning is chilling.

"Why?" My voice squeaks.

Frank blushes pink across his nose and cheeks. "You didn't want to talk about it at the time. But those were Jimena's last words."

I drain my own sake cup before I answer. "Dios mio, viejo. That means, 'They can find plenty of others to finish this.'"

"Finish what?" Brill asks.

"No sé." I look down at the empty cup. "Pero, Jimena planned to kill me, Minda and Layla to force the invasion." I never explained Jimena's plan to Frank. How could I? Frank still doesn't know the details about Murry. And I only know Jimena's plans because after Murry infected Jimena, he saw her motives. Murry said Jimena only cared about the dinero. Even inside her mind, she never thought about who hired her, or what they hoped to accomplish, and Murry didn't care enough to dig into her memories. "She was scared of what would happen to her if she failed."

"Failed at killing you," Brill says flatly.

"Sí, pero it doesn't make sense for anyone to try now." I shrug. "I assumed one of the Zantites' enemies hired her to start a war that would dilute the Zantite forces. Pero Jimena's last words – they sounds more personal."

"Do the Zantites know what Jimena was planning?" Frank asks.

"Minda does," I tell him.

Brill says, "You should stay away from Zant. At all costs."

"I have to go back. I have a cooking class set up, and Garfex might show. That's a chance I can't pass up."

My handheld rings. It's Kaliel. I'm not expecting a call from him.

"Un momento," I tell Brill and Frank as I answer it as a voice call.

Kaliel says, "My mother asked me to make sure you got her gift basket."

"Sí y gracias. Everything was muy delicioso."

"Good," Kaliel says. It feels like he wants to say something else. Pero, he's silent. I hope he's not in danger, somewhere where he can't talk freely.

"Where are you?" I ask him.

"I'm in a rented ship," he says. "Running an errand for Kayla. Stephen went looking for a DNA database that supposedly survived after the Nitarri home world exploded. He's … well, he's been arrested. I'm carrying a shipload of chocolate to bribe him out of prison."

Nervousness arcs through my chest. "Be careful, amigo. You know how aggressive the pirates are right now."

"I will. Just – did you ever call Kayla? She's alone and worried about her brother."

"Vale. I'll call right now." I let Kaliel go and eye Frank. I don't think he heard what Kaliel said about Kayla back on the cargo ship. No sé if Frank knows Kayla is Nitarri – or if that's a secret I should trust him with. I step away from the table and call her.

Kayla sounds surprised. "Bo! I was about to call you."

"You were?" I wish the call was holo, pero I'm trying to be discreet.

"I've been in telepathic conversation with Murry." She huffs out a breath, like she can't believe she just said that. After all, she'd been quite shocked to find out that not only is she adopted, she's an alien telepath. Y she hasn't had long for that revelation to sink in. "Murry sent a spuck to Earth to help find a cure for Pure Rot."

Researchers are calling the cacao disease Pure Rot, since it mutated from Pure275, the herbicide HGB uses to keep cacao from escaping its plantations. Mutated isn't exactly the right word, though. Before the Mindhuggers made their peace with the galaxy and their home world, Murry intentionally engineered the plant disease, with the intent of ridding the worlds of chocolate. Pero, if the truth of Pure Rot's origin got out, that thread could tug open a whole ball of secrets that would unravel half way across la galaxia.

Kayla sighs. "Murry wanted to make sure I understood that's all he's doing. Because if I decided he's infecting people again, I could still overload all his hosts with feedback."

I swallow saliva from sudden nervousness. Surely she hasn't hurt Murry. And surely, *surely,* he isn't expanding again. "Mi amiga ..."

"Don't worry. It's really just the one spuck. It was trying to fly into the Maui cacao plantation and crashed into Mount Haleakala."

Murry's not supposed to even exist – let alone be on this planet. It's illegal to engineer a mind-controlling brain parasite. And it carries a sentence of muerte with the Galactic Court to *be* a mind controlling brain parasite.

"Is the spuck dead?" Explaining away a spuck being on Earth would be hard. "Do we need to destroy the body."

"The spuck survived the crash," Kayla says. "He just needs a ride."

I turn towards the table where Frank and Brill are still sitting. Frank took that set of keys off the junkie he killed yesterday. He has access to a transport grande enough to hold a spuck. I tell Kayla, "I'll see what I can do."

Kayla says, "I took a catering job for HGB for your reception. It seemed like the only way I'd get to see you."

"I can't wait to see you amiga!" Pero first I have to rescue Murry.

I can't ask Frank to help us outright. It would lead to awkward questions.

I slide into the booth and ask, "Viejo, do you still have the keys to that transport?"

Frank reaches into his pocket and puts the keys on the table. "I moved it somewhere more discreet. Eventually, someone will miss poor Mr. Tanner."

"What did you find on the su's phone?" Brill asks.

"Not much," Frank grumbles. "The phone was a burner. The only number in it was for a bar called the Dead Fish. Nothing to imply a connection between whatever group Jimena worked for and whoever wants to snatch Bo off Earth."

"We need to check out that bar," Brill says.

"Más tarde." I insist. *Later.* I turn towards Frank. "Can we borrow the transport? I told Kayla that Brill and I can pick up some cargo for her tonight."

"For her catering business?" Frank glances at Brill. He knows mi vida's a gray trader who specializes in exotic foodstuffs. Frank looks back at me. "Can you promise this cargo wasn't stolen?"

"Sí, it wasn't." After all, the Evevrons gave Murry access to the spucks.

Frank frowns then hands the keys to Brill. "Take care of this yourself, Cray. If you take Bo farther from the HGB compound, you put her in danger."

"I have no idea what we're doing," Brill says.

"I won't leave Brill's side," I promise Frank. I turn to mi vida, "I'll explain on the way."

Frank looks like he's about to say no. Then he sighs. "You'll have to empty that transport first."

Frank orders another beer, while Brill and I head for the door. It's a beautiful night, and the landscaping is lit to project a romantic atmosphere.

"Gracias, mi vida." I kiss Brill, right there outside the restaurant. It's the first moment we've been alone since Gavin took him away.

Brill may look like a kid, pero his lips are hot and insistent, and his beso tastes of matcha ice cream. Music's playing from the luau farther down the beach. And I still fit perfectly in his arms, which crush me against him.

Pero, the experience feels somehow distant and blunted. Maybe it's the contacts hiding his eyes, or how he looks like a teenager with that ridiculous haircut.

Brill pulls away and puts his hands in his pockets. "You have to stop wearing that kalltet pendant."

"I'm not wearing it now." I lean into him again, pressing my face against his chest, listening to his hummingbird-fast heartbeat. "Lo siento, mi vida. It will just be for the camera. Just for a few more days."

He tilts my face up to his and kisses me more slowly. It takes a minute, pero I melt into the experience. His arms come around my waist and we sway to the music. "I know how much you love to dance."

"I love you, you kek." We'll get back to where we were. Yo lo creo. In two days, Frank will get the death order taken off Brill's cabeza. Either that, or I'll run with him to Krom or into the depths of space, or wherever he wants to go. Because I wasn't kidding Frank. I won't cooperate with HGB if they still want to kill my love.

Either way, the pendant is going deep into my bag. Porque Brill said it's mine as long as I love him. But I don't want to look at it.

CHAPTER EIGHT

After I explain what we're doing, Brill makes a few calls, and we swing by a shady-looking building where he can pick up a signal blocker. I wait, out of sight of any would-be abductors, in the transport.

I get chills, being solo aquí – *alone in this transport*. Where would this vehicle have taken me, if Frank had not happened along?

I call Chestla on my handheld. She appears in the holofield wearing a dark linen-like shirt with flowers at the neckline, over jeans. Chestla, a member of Evevron's alpha-predator species, can be un poco intimidating. Her slit-pupil green eyes have reflective irises, like a cat's. Other than that, and her predator teeth, she looks more or less human, with long honey blonde hair and freckled cheeks. Glittery purple polish coats her claw-like nails, and her smile is infectiously optimistic – if you can get over the instinctive prey response humans feel to Evevron pheromones.

"Hey, chica," I say. "Can you get a message to Eugene?"

Porque, if anyone can, it's her. Eugene is deep inside the walled plantation, in the middle of a no-call zone. Pero, he has to collect data. And Chestla's genius with computers.

"I guess so." She frowns. "Why? Is he in trouble?"

Chestla had a crush on Eugene at one point. I'm not sure if she still does.

"One of the spucks is here. Murry wants to solve the problem he caused." I spoke on the phone with a nervous Murry several times on the way here. He keeps calling, saying something fast, hanging up and calling back minutes later. "He's going to trust

Eugene with the secret of how Pure Rot's designed. I hope that's not a mistake."

"He can trust Eugene to be open-minded," Chestla says. "And not to turn him in to HGB. It will be good for them to work together. If anyone can find a cure to keep Earth's cacao trees alive and producing, it's the parasite that created the disease and the guy who's obsessed with it."

I tell Chestla to have Eugene meet us near the plantation wall. A few minutes later, Chestla calls back and says Eugene has agreed, and that he carries a walkie-talkie. She sends me specifications, which I forward to Brill. Brill sends both of us a thumbs-up, which means he can get a matching walkie.

The front of the transport has six seats and an about teen feet of open area before the door into the cargo space – which has a handle from this side. I hadn't gotten a good look at the cargo with all my panic yesterday, and Frank said we need to do something with whatever it is. Since Brill's still not back, I move through to see what's back there. I'm careful not to let the door close.

The cargo space is full of boxes labeled "HGB New." Extraño, no?

"Eh? Que–" No point in talking to myself. I open a box.

Brill hops back into the transport. He turs around in his seat. "Let's go get Murry." He blinks. "What's wrong?"

"Tawny said they hadn't perfected HGB New. So what's this?" I pull out a bar. The bright pink label is un poco blinding. When I unwrap it, a familiar smell teases my brain. I can't quite place it. I take an experimental bite. "Pauf! It's carob."

"What's carob?" Brill heads back to join me.

"Eso – like fake chocolate. Pero, it's a poor substitute. Carob is the pulp of a tree-grown bean. It's sweet, verdadero, pero not complex. And it's not what Tawny described." I show the ingredients list to Brill. They include crystalized ginger, carrot and coconut. "Carob is fat free and packed with fiber. Tawny will blow a microchip when she finds out HGB stole her product name and stuck it on something that likematches a prune cookie. Think what eating an entire block of this would do to most humanoid digestive systems."

Brill looks at the list and sniffs the bar. Cierto, he doesn't taste it. Krom are prone to food allergies. It's ironic that his species – with their weak cardio systems and allergic tendencies – have chosen to become one of the greatest explorer races in the galaxy.

Brill blinks and one of his brown contacts slips a little. The edge of his iris underneath is green with curiosity. "What does this have to do with Tawny?"

"She's been working on a beauty and vitamin bar since she hired on with HGB. They stole her branding for this … this yech."

Brill shrugs. "It's not like she has room to complain."

"Que?" Tawny is a lot of things, pero she is not a thief.

Brill's jaw goes tense. I can't see the shift anymore, can't tell what he's thinking. "You've seen that ring she wears all the time."

"Sí." It's a trapezoidal jraghite, in an elaborate setting. "I think it's an antique."

"Wal. It's a Krom antique. That's Jeska's ancestral crest on the side." Brill's a bit touchy about jewelry. Pero, I get what's upsetting him. While Krom collect commodities to share con la galaxia, they don't take things they consider irreplaceable, and that often includes art.

Plus, Jeska's brother Darcy was Brill's closest amigo. Darcy was arrested when he and Brill tried to sell illegal mind enhancement drugs, and Darcy got shot while escaping the detention center. Brill believes the muerte was his fault. So every time he sees Tawny's ring, he's been remembering the crest belongs to his deceased amigo's family, también.

"Would Jeska want it back?" Jeska is bit older, so he might not be as touchy about these things.

"If the ring was sold, it isn't his to ask back," Brill says.

"I'm sure Tawny doesn't know."

He nods. "I realize there's nothing wrong with buying antiques. My mom goes to yard sales all the time. You should see her collection of clocks from all over the galaxy."

I blush. Brill's mamá and I aren't friends. Most Krom consider humans an inferior species, so she made it clear that she had no interest in ever meeting me. And now that Brill's faked his muerte, his mother also thinks pequeña inferior me got him killed.

If Frank had gone through with it, she wouldn't have been wrong. And that bothers me. I didn't want to put Brill in danger again. Yet, as soon as he got here, I have him visiting shady buildings to buy illegal gear.

"Oh, hanstral, Babe." His frown does look apologetic – kind of. "I wish everything wasn't so complicated."

Brill takes off and we fly low over the island towards the mountain. It looks like smoke is rising from it, dim against the night sky, ominous like the volcano is ready to erupt. It isn't. The news feeds hadn't reported anything about a potential eruption. That's evidence of Murry's crash.

My sublingual rings. It's Murry. *Bo, is that transport you?*
Sí, mijo. What happened?
I thought I could use the direction ball to control a saucer, like when I was Gideon Tyson. I hit atmo and picked up a weird signal coming from this mountain, and when I tried to set down to investigate, these claws got in the way. The ball slipped, and we crashed. Just because Murry used we doesn't mean more than one dragon waits on the mountain. He has a hard time with timelines and causality, and sometimes refers to himself collectively as *I*, and sometimes even to the spuck and the parasite occupying it separately as *we*.

Tyson's hands are a bit more nimble than yours, mijo, I tell him. Tyson is the reptilian Myska cop who bit me when I fled with that cacao pod. Myska are probably the most venomous species en la galaxia. It was a mostly dry bite, and I still nearly died. Pero we straightened everything out and became friends.

Then Murry infected Tyson and I came very close to getting bitten full-strength.

But I'm almost glad I crashed, Murry continues. It would have taken me a long time for just one spuck to dig through enough of the rock to find the entrance. Come see what's down there before I cave this in to hide the crashed ship.

"Murry wants us to check out what he crashed into," I tell Brill.

"Haza." He presses the transport to move faster. We land at the edge of the dust cloud. We're half way up the mountain, pero foliage still hides Murry's actual crash spot. It's eerie in the dark, walking between the tall, narrow multi-color trunks of rainbow eucalyptus trees. The moon looks huge from up here, full and bright. I imagine I can see the outline of Interface Station.

Brill twines his fingers with mine. "Your planet's beautiful."

Coming from a Krom, that's quite a compliment. I've seen holo of Brill's home world. Almost all of it is lush and green from centuries of terraforming efforts. And flower gardening is a popular hobby in the region Brill is from, which has mountainous crags reminiscent of Scotland.

"Muy Feliz you like it." So happy I can't stop smiling. I'm giddy, just from being here with him, solitario in the moonlight.

He turns towards me. Brill's about to kiss me again, when I hear a crack somewhere in the trees. Oi!

The Murry dragon's there, splooted backwards like the corgi he once infected, his massive cabeza almost level with the ground, grinning at us with long, sharp teeth. His massive front hand-paws sport eighteen-inch blunted claws. Without the IH residue to blunt the reaction, an instinctive prey response roots me to my spot. Pero, it's Murry. And that head-tilt makes him kind of cute. The response fades a bit. Having the IH in my system so long has helped me overcome some of my instincts when dealing with aliens, even if the drug isn't affecting me anymore.

My sublingual rings.

Murry bubblechatters, *Don't mind me. Finish what you're doing. I can wait.*

"We're not going to kiss while you watch," I say out loud. Brill sees Murry, nods to acknowledge I'm talking to him.

The dragon huffs. *Why not?*

Murry still has trouble understanding how individuals form relationships. The only beso the Murry worm ever experienced was when it infected Kaliel and used him to kiss me. Which is already extraño enough, no?

I tell him, *Kissing's private. The individuals involved are making themselves vulnerable to each other.*

The spuck snorts. *Then why do people kiss on those shows Brill likes to watch? The night I became Jimena Duarte, we must have seen a dozen individuals kiss inside that holofield.*

Dios mio, por favor tell me Murry's not addicted to novelas too! *Those are actors. They're pretending, like I used to do when I was in the holos. I kissed people I'd never met before. Pero, it wasn't real. Individuals like to watch shows because they imagine what other individuals' lives are like, uan unlike you, we only get to be one person for always. It's a safe way to practice what it might feel like to be in love or to grieve. We see what actions people take and how they are rewarded or punished, and it helps us decide how we would behave if we were in the same situation.*

Murry taps the claws of one hand against the ground, leaving ruts in the dirt. *That sounds a lot like what we've been trying to do.*

Murry infected hundreds of people, of several different species, with copies of himself. He sampled the life of each host. And he forced some of those hosts, like Tyson and Kaliel, to do things against their nature.

"Sí, mijo, except when it's a novela, nobody gets hurt." Ni idea if Murry understands.

Pero, he smiles bigger, showing more teeth. *Let me give you a ride down. You have to see what's there.*

Brill says, "Next time, su, call my handheld, and I can put you on speakerphone." He sounds miffed to have been left out of the conversation.

"He wants to give us a ride." I make myself walk towards the dragon. I hadn't realized how much I'd relied on the IH residue to give me courage. I've never gone flying with Murry without the taint in my blood to blunt the fear.

Murry complains, *I don't have Brill's number.*

"Mi vida, Murry doesn't have your number." I toss Brill my handheld so he can grab the data. "You have to call him first."

I take a deep breath. Tranquila, yo. I can do this. It won't be like Tawny and the nanites, where having the IH taken away left me weeping. I have to do this. Because if I don't fly on the spuck now, I'm too broken to be of use to anyone. My heartbeat races, and my knees feel like rubber, but I still step up to the spuck and put my hand on his side. The spuck may look like a cross between a snake, a hippopotamus and a giant bug, pero its blood is warm and the scales supple. Its wings are iridescent and strong.

"You okay, Babe?" Brill frowns in concern.

"They said it may take a few days post-treatment to even out my emotions."

"Let me know if I can help. Reshdo." Brill hands me my phone and helps me up onto the dragon before climbing up behind me. I've done this before. Murry's always kept me safe. And Brill is holding onto me too. He hugs me tight, then settles into a more comfortable position.

Murry runs through the forest, trampling plants and nearly knocking us off as he tries to slide his bulk between tress. Every time he shifts, my breath catches, pero somewhere the feeling goes from aterrador to exhilarating.

When we reach the thickest part of the dust cloud, Murry plunges into a hole. My stomach drops. I hold on tighter.

We've entered an oval tunnel formed by Murry's crash. At the back, his saucer sticks partway out from the rock, light from the open door illuminating the space.

Pero, in front of the ship, a shaft heads straight down. This excavation isn't a natural cavern or caldera, and it wasn't caused by Murry's crash. It had to have been drilled with an energy weapon. As the spuck leaps over the edge and plummets down the shaft, taking us into pitch-black darkness, a scream rips from my throat. The bottom falls out of my stomach again, and the force presses me back against Brill.

The falling speed slows, then we level out, and Murry lands lightly.

"Get off." Murry's voice comes from Brill's handheld. "I need to climb under the ship. There's only so much power, so I didn't leave the lights on."

Ni idea what he's talking about, pero we do as he asks.

"We can't see in the dark," Brill tells the Murry worm. "But I take it you can?"

The spuck scrabbles against the rock, and the sound of those claws hits something primal in me. Fear trickles down my spine.

Murry says, "Well enough to be puzzled by what you have done to your hair and eyes. Was this an attempt to look more pleasing to Bodacious Benitez?"

"Not exactly, su."

As lights snap on, ringing the edge of un spaceship grande, I shield my eyes. I look down. Oi! I am standing a foot away from a skeleton dressed in an unfamiliar uniform and holding a smashed terra cotta flowerpot. The skull doesn't look human.

"Dios mio!" I spring backwards. My heart is jumping harder than when I'd climbed onto Murry.

Three other skeletons in the same uniforms lay nearby, all dropped in poses like they were shot or stabbed while trying to get aboard the ship.

Another skeleton sits up against the cavern's far wall. This one wears a dress, in an Earth-style popular in the 2090s. The dress material is embedded with interlocking holograms of hummingbirds, which respond to our movement, even after all this time.

Her skull looks human. She was clutching a backpack when she died. Pobre dama – *poor lady*.

Brill gently moves the bag from her arms. Uck. I'm not sure whether to be horrified that he's disturbing the dead, or curious about what's in the bag. My queasy stomach can't decide either.

"What happened here, Bodacious Benitez?" Murry asks.

"Ni idea." Equipment is piled on the cave floor. The dead guys were probably standing by it when everything went wrong. There's a platform with a divot for holding a three-foot-wide something about four feet off the ground. Pero that something is missing.

"I know who might be able to tell us something." Brill holds up a guidebook for camping in Haleakala National Park. He pulls out an old ident card, dated 2092, that's been acting as a bookmark for thirty years. The name says Frank Sawyer, and the picture's definitely a teenaged version of mi mamá's amor. En serio. With Frank's gobs of shaggy hair and those rosy cheeks, he and Brill could have started a boy band together.

Pero did whatever horror that happened here in 2092 start Frank on the path to what he became for HGB?

"This ship has been down here a long time," I say. "Still, there may still be clues to who its passengers were. Unless someone stripped it."

"Let's find out." Brill flashes over to the steep ramp leading to the ship's front door. He takes a tool out of his pocket and inserts it into a hole that must be the lock.

After a second, there's an odd noise, like a photostrobe charging.

Brill freezes. "That doesn't sound good."

CHAPTER NINE

Brill's stopped breathing, and I realize he's holding his breath, standing there on the abandoned ship's ramp. A voice comes from a speaker system set in the ship's door frame. The words sound like slashing ticks. They are repeated in several other languages.

After the third language, the spuck swings around and stares openmouthed at Brill.

The handheld says, "Don't move. You're standing on a pressure plate. The voice suggests you stay very still until they verify your identity from inside, or until the authorities arrive."

"But nobody's inside," I protest. The shock has my limbs leaden, mi manos gone frío at my sides.

I don't need to see Brill's irises to know they're black behind the brown contacts. He says softly, "There must be a way to deactivate the system. Revwal?"

"You're Krom," Murry says. "Couldn't you just jump for it? Move at your full speed, leap at a high arc, and escape the blast?"

"If you gauge the distance, there's maybe a thirty percent chance of that working." Brill sounds calm. No sé how. "We're fast, but there are limits."

I move towards the ship, looking for a panel or hatch.

"Hest! Babe, what are you doing?" *Now* Brill sounds upset.

"Looking for a way to disarm the bomb." Verex Kowlk pops into my mind, moments before his death, smiling and playing a hand touching game with mi hermanas. The next time I'd seen him … his body had been ruined by the explosion. I cannot lose Brill the same way.

Brill says, "Murry, get Bo out of here."

The spuck turns to me, tilting its cabeza. The handheld says, "Brill Cray wishes for your safety."

"And I wish for his. Don't you dare grab me, Murry."

"Murry–" Brill's voice breaks. "Avell, Babe. If there's disarming to do, the spuck can handle it."

"You crashed the ship," I remind Murry. "And you told me yourself, your eyes don't work well in two dimensions, with symbols."

The spuck stares at me for a long time, considering. Learning something about what love means.

"There are symbols under here," the handheld says, as the spuck ducks its cabeza under the ship, lowering the bulk of its body to the cave floor.

I scramble underneath the ship. Above me there's a square of text about two feet wide, with a divot on either side. I press the divots together, and a panel slides off in my hands, revealing a touch screen.

"Babe?" Brill asks. "Cómo va?" *How's it going?*

Could the screen be another trap? I tap it and wince. It lights up. I don't explode. "Hasta aquí todo bien." *So far, so good.*

I pull up a translation app on my phone. I scan the panel and the touch screen. This language isn't indexed.

I stare at the characters. Sabes que … if you squint a little, this looks a bit like Hegrexian. When I was in school, my dual major was culinary arts and linguistics. Hegrexian is a language many designers use for kitchen tools and starship machinery. I took a semester of it as one of my six language-sampler electives. This could be a colloquial, simplified form. Maybe created by designers who had worked on their own for generations. I pull up a lexicon app on my phone and use what I remember to start a translation.

The symbols explain how to arm the ship's defenses. Pero the only thing it says about disarming said defenses is *Input your personal security code, as provided by your installation technician.*

"Oi!" What am I supposed to do now?

"Everything diay, babe?" Brill asks.

"Wal, mi vida. I just don't happen to have a personal security code."

"I want you out of here." Brill's voice is calm again. "If this ship blows, I have a better chance of surviving than you do."

"Thirty percent isn't good enough." I pull the panel onto my lap and start at the beginning of the instructions. "Mira. This may take a while. I know Krom are good at running. Pero how long do you think you can stand still?"

"As long as it takes." He hesitates. "I wish I wasn't holding this lock pick. If I drop my arm, and the electronic pick moves in the lock, that might set things off."

After a while, that will be muy difícil for Brill to keep up.

"I will translate as fast as I can."

"Translate?" Brill sounds puzzled.

I don't respond. I'm too busy working through how to arm each set of weapons. The pressure plate seems to be attached to a system port called deck B. And if I'm right about the way the toggle system is diagramed, by activating the deck B array, it should deploy outside weapons, but turn off the pressure plate.

I tell Brill, "I think I know what to do. Pero if I'm wrong–" I don't know how to finish that sentence.

"I trust you." His voice gets softer. "With my life."

I need to see Brill's face. I crawl from under the ship and step as close to him as I can. "Te amo. Siempre." *I love you. Always.*

Brill smiles at me. "Don't say goodbye this time."

I try to turn away from him. I can't. "I need to do this before your arm gives out."

I force myself to crawl back under the ship. I work through the activation menus. Claro está, you'd think you'd need a code to turn weapons on instead of to turn them off.

I finally get it to the right screen. If I'm wrong, Brill could die. If the explosion's grande enough, I could die también. My chest overflows with nervous fear.

Ya basta, yo. *Just calm down.*

I take a deep breath and press the button.

There's another whining noise. I throw my arms up over mi cabeza. A repetitive clicking grows progressively louder.

Brill groans. "Hanstral, Babe. This might be goodbye after all."

There's a loud *clack*. I think for a second that everything has exploded. Then I realize a ring of guns has popped out of the ship. Two point down, one barrel just inches from my face. Shtesh! I scramble backwards, out of its path.

I scoot out from under the ship. Brill's not on the pressure plate. He's leapt thirty feet up the rock and is looking sheepishly back at me. He releases the rock and lands lightly. "La!" *Oh!* "The ship's door is open."

"You still want to go inside?" I'm melting with relief that we're vivo. Why push for more danger?

"We risked out lives for whatever's inside. We deserve to see it." Brill sidles to the ramp, tests it with a toe, and then jumps on it. He waves for me to join him. We step inside, where the fermented meat-gone-off smell of decaying plant material permeates the ship.

Brill turns on the lights.

The spuck pokes its cabeza through the hatch. From outside, Brill's handheld says, "Don't forget me."

Brill must have dropped the phone when he'd jumped. He pushes past the Spuck's gran jaw and retrieves it.

I survey the ship's open central area. A ladder leads upstairs, no doubt to crew quarters. This looks like a living/working area, with doors opposite the hatch leading deeper into the ship. Bags of raw cocoa beans are piled high in one corner. One bag has burst open, spilling rotted beans onto the floor. Pauf! I wrinkle my nose. That explains the smell.

If Frank's ID was current when he lost it, this scene hasn't been disturbed since shortly after the First Contact War ended.

A couple of workstations, one piled with papers, are built into the walls. I pick up the map sitting on top. It shows a detailed geographic representation of Maui, with additional information written in a pidgin form of English that I've never seen before.

An envelope contains a contract, alternating paragraphs written in un extraño language of dots and circles and in that pidgin English, spelling out the details so that both parties can understand.

"What's that, Babe?" Brill looks over my shoulder at the document. He doesn't read English fluently, and this is hardly standard usage.

"It's a contract for delivering cacao saplings to a city on a planet called Greftash."

"Never heard of them." Brill looks over at Murry. "You?"

The spuck shakes its massive cabeza.

Brill types on his phone. "I'll ask Gavin. He insisted on staying near Earth while I'm down here. He must be bored out of his skull."

I shudder. I've just seen unos pocos demasiados – *too many* – skulls to want to picture that. "This proves HGB had these people killed just for trying to take a few plants off el planeta." I wish I could release that information. Pero, making HGB – and therefore Earth – look that ruthless would feed straight into Thath's case for our destruction.

The spuck makes an uncertain rumbling noise. It managed to squeeze most of itself through the door. "Whatever happened here, Bodacious Babe Benitez, was not about plants. That platform – that device–" The spuck nods upwards, where something that looks like a giant drill dangles from a harness set into the ship's ceiling. "—these things are for ruining planets."

"How do you know that, su?" Brill asks.

"I once had a hug on someone who had used one." Hugging someone is how Murry refers to infecting that person and becoming partially in control of their thoughts and actions.

I blink. "The contract says nada about destroying Earth, mijo."

"It wouldn't have to," Brill says. "Either the dead su's out there decided that when the planet blew, they'd transfer the monopoly on chocolate to themselves, or the contractors hired them knowing they were planetkillers and hoped they would destroy Earth. Then the cacao trees they requisitioned would be the only ones left."

"Who would do that?" I protest. En serio. That's convoluted and cruel.

"Greftash?" Brill's handheld says.

Brill takes the contract and folds it, then tucks it into his jeans pocket. "The same type of people who would have someone like you killed to start a war."

As we explore the rest of the ship, I call Mamá on my sublingual.

Bee! She bubblechatters. *Mira. Did you just watch the new episode?*

No, Mamá. I hesitate. I need to ask if she knows what happened here, pero Frank is still a touchy subject between us. *Can I ask you something about Frank?*

She hesitates too. *Vale.*

What do you know about his early days with HGB?

I have not pushed him to talk about it, Mamá says. *But he has regrets. He wanted to become a music teacher, and he still plays guitar. El es muy talentoso. Some of the songs he has written allude to much pain. Especially the one he wrote about Xander.*

Who's Xander? I try to picture Frank in a quiet moment, playing guitar. Mamá has seen sides of him that I never will.

I'm still moving through the ship. I open a door to a storage closet, filled floor to ceiling with small boxes.

Xander was his best friend. Mamá's bubblechatter sounds sad. *Xander has been muerto for many years.*

It's easy to forget that Frank has lost as much as the rest of us. His wife, his daughter and son-in-law, his friend – they're all dead.

Lo siento, Mamá. I pick up a box. The label is written in yet another unfamiliar language. *Frank writes music?*

Mamá's laugh bubbles through mi cabeza. *Que? Did you think he grew up training to be a spy?*

No sé what I thought. I have Frank's old ID in my pocket. The guy who wanted to be a music teacher. Who loved hiking and nature. Who, if he is as talented as Mamá says, could have started a band and been a rock star. When he'd told me to move forward with my life, to follow my passions to a brighter future, could part of that have been his regret over not being able to do so himself?

What got you thinking about this, Bee?

I should talk to Frank before I tell her about the cave. Pero, I need to tell her something. *He protected me, Mamá. Someone tried to abduct me, and he killed a man to save me. And I realized – I know hardly anything about him.*

Mamá bubblechatters, *He told me about that. He wanted to know if I have any enemies I hadn't told him about.*

I can only imagine how that conversation went.

Wait, Mamá. Do you have enemies?

Mamá laughs again. *All stars have enemies, mija.*

Minda told me that once. She said I need to develop at thicker skin or get out of the public eye. I've love to fade back into obscurity, pero HGB won't let me.

Well after I hang up, I'm still thinking about who might dislike mi mamá. "Mi vida!" I call. "What is this stuff?"

Suddenly, Brill's at my side. When he looks at the boxes, his hands form white-knuckled fists. "You have to be kidding me."

"Que?"

"These are energy supplements made from Kenski spines. Kenski have been extinct for over thirty years, since their planet had an ecological meltdown." Brill flags down the spuck. "Murry! Help me get these out into the cave. We're going to burn them."

I flash back to when I asked Brill to help me destroy the cacao beans I stole, and Jeska accused him of wevdaglarin, a crime against Krom culture. I've come to terms with Krom discoveries. I've even helped participate in one or two. Brill's attitude now shocks me. After all, in generation's past, Earth went through its own misuse of animals – shark fin soup, rhino horns, elephant tusks. Pero, Brill never demanded I burn mi abuelita's ivory jewelry box.

"What about wevdaglarin?" I ask, confused. "We're looking at an animal-based commodity that has been lost and could be rediscovered, right? You wouldn't help me destroy a handful of cacao beans when it meant mi mamá's life, pero this stuff you will?"

Brill looks at me sharply, his eyes probably the same muddy brown as the contacts. "Each of these boxes represents the life of a sentient being killed for a mineral found in its vertebrae."

"En serio?" I stare at the boxes. "These Kenski were people?"

"They had a weird language and some odd biology. It took a long time for anyone to realize they were intelligent. Their planet was classed for hunting, until a linguist crash-landed there. It doesn't matter that the Galactics had not yet recognized the species. They were people. That big box at the back is an extraction device. If the tech used to do this were rediscovered, it might be used on another species." He grabs a double-armful of boxes and turns for the ship's front door. "Krom won't take another culture's art – and we certainly won't take their lives. It's why we won't trade in things like the Invincible Heart – IH is a drug with no purpose other than death. This supplement – destroying it isn't wevdaglarin, because it's not a commodity. It's a crime."

"Sí. Wal. Of course." I feel awful. All this time together, and I'm still not being fair to Brill. I hadn't meant to upset him.

He dashes away with the boxes, then returns for more.

The spuck stares at Brill. Evaluating. Learning. Seeming to like what he sees in mi vida's passion, and then moving to help by pushing boxes onto the ramp with his nose.

I pick up a half dozen boxes myself and we make a pile far enough away that the fire won't affect the ship. There's hundreds of these repugnante things. Brill opens five boxes, arranging them on top of the pile. He runs the flame from a lighter over the open flaps until they catch.

"It is like a ceremony of salt," Brill's handheld says. "This is a very good thing."

We stand in the firelight as the smoke goes up the shaft in the rock.

Brill's face looks pinched.

I squeeze his hand. "Are you okay?"

"Darcy and I never should have tried to sell those neural enhancers. They're illegal because they're flawed. And we hurt people with them." It's the first time Brill's said that he regrets trying to sell those drugs.

"I know you still miss Darcy." I squeeze Brill's mano again. "You've made a lot of progress dealing with what happened to him, pero, it's okay to still get upset."

"Ga. It's not so much that." He doesn't squeeze back. "I've been thinking a lot about the lines I want to draw for myself, with my work. When I got involved with the Lotvrek, I was young and stupid and taking the Codex way too literally. Most Krom interpret it narrowly, but Jeska is right. Our consciences need to play a bigger part in what commodities Krom are willing to spread through the galaxy." No importa que Brill looks all of seventeen right now – his face seems wise beyond his actual years. "Discoveries are important. Open-sourcing commodities prevents war. Destroying samples of them before they're studied for benefits leads to illegal trade. History keeps proving that. I just wish there was a way to share only good things."

"Things like chocolate," I say, teasing him a little to lighten the mood.

He finally squeezes mi mano. "Chocolate and mercy and hope."

"Now you're just telling me what I want to hear."

CHAPTER TEN

The Murry worm climbs into the holding area in the back of the transport, where my would-be kidnapper tried to put me. Murry doesn't really fit. Using those blunt-knife claws, he slices through the partition. The front of him spills through into the cargo area, toppling boxes of HGB New.

Brill closes the transport door, and we move around to the front. As I get in, I catch Murry snuffling at the boxes.

Brill's handheld says, "What is this amazing smell?"

The spuck's stomach growls. Loudly. Spucks are predominately carnivorous, pero they do enjoy some fruits and vegetables native to Evevron. Which is why they're considered pests.

I never considered what to feed Murry while he's here. I tell him, "That's HGB's first choco-free bar. Carob, fruits, and veggies."

"So no theobromine?" Even una minúscula amount of theobromine, an active chemical in chocolate, can kill a mindworm parasite inside its host.

"Nada, nunca." I turn to Brill. "Though it has a massive amount of fiber. What do you think, mi vida?"

Brill shrugs. "Sounds like Eugene's problem."

I start to unwrap a bar to feed Murry, pero the spuck takes a whole box in its massive jaws and chompcrushes it, wrappers, cardboard and all.

Brill says, "Naramoosh. We'd better hurry and get him to Eugene."

I'd had a hard enough time sneaking myself into an HGB plantation. And now we're sneaking in a giant alien monster?

Impossible, no? Pero, the plan is simple: we'll take Murry to the bionet's edge, and he'll burrow under the barrier, which only extends down to solid bedrock.

Brill gets the transport into the air. I keep glancing at him. He's changed so much. The danger from our adventures have forced him to consider where he wants to go with his life – and who he wants to be when he gets there. Yo también. Claro está, I hope I've changed enough to be worthy of going with him.

Brill's handheld rings, and he pops up a holo of Gavin. Gavin's thinner than Brill, almost awkwardly so, and his lightly hooded eyes are currently deep purple. He's wearing a dark blue denim jacket over a black tee. "I found some information on that planet you su's asked about."

"Doesn't sound like it's anything good." Brill says

"Ga. It's not. The barely habitable world has only one populated continent. But instead of improving their land, Greftash invested heavily in a space program. They keep showing up in this section of the galaxy." Gavin looks over at me. "Did you su's do something to them? They seem to have a grudge against Earth."

"Not that I know of," I tell him.

He looks skeptical. Which doesn't surprise me. Nunca y nope. Before the death-promise that bound Gavin as my benefactor, he'd repeatedly urged Brill to break up with me. "My intel says they're trying to get samples of a disease off the planet."

"They're trying to start an outbreak?" I ask. Earth has some nasty diseases, pero so do otros planetas.

"What if it's the cacao disease?" Brill asks. He's attaching a signal blocker to a collar, so Murry will look like white noise to the drones that patrol inside the bionet. "You just said they have it in for Earth. If they get samples of Pure Rot, they could prove chocolate is endangered."

I tell Gavin, "We found a contract where Greftash tried to get chocolate for themselves decades ago. There could be a connection. Pero, what would make them so horror-happy to see Earth in trouble?"

And what can we do about it?

Gavin doesn't have any answers. Frustrated, I take the collar from Brill move towards the back of the ship. The spuck dips its cabeza, and I'm about to slip the collar around its neck when the spuck arches its spine and goes rigid.

Brill's handheld says, "They're killing us. I thought we could outwit them but they've shot several of Awn. And they're closing in on half a dozen of me."

The spuck roars, loud as a freight train in the transport. I stumble backwards. Whoever *they* are and whatever is happening to Murry, it's not happening here.

Brill looks back. "Jrekt! Don't panic while we're flying."

Individual spucks retain less autonomy than Murry's sentient hosts had. Ahora, this individual is completely subsumed in the experience of the collective. And Murry, as a hive mind, has never been this upset.

"Oye! Oye!" I reassure the spuck, though mi corazón hammers with fear. "It'll be okay."

The spuck thrashes, shouldering the air as though involved in the fight on Evevron. The transport's center of gravity shifts, and the vehicle wobbles in the air. One of the spuck's wings catches on something protruding from the ceiling and the delicate iridescent structure rips. The pain upsets the spuck even more.

"Calm him down, or we'll crash." Brill's doing his best to keep us moving in a straight line.

I've instinctively crouched in a corner. My body doesn't want to move, pero I force myself to stand and face the spuck. "Por favor, Murry. This spuck needs to sleep."

I hold out a hand and hum a bit of Kayla's calming song. In a telepath like Murry, that song can reduce pain. Coming in through my sublingual, it had just sounded like off-key wailing.

The spuck shakes its cabeza, like it's trying to clear away something. Then it snaps at me, inches from my outstretched hand, with teeth that could easily engulf all of me.

"Enrmhpn!" I snatch my hand back, shocked I have all my fingers. My breathing edges towards panic.

I need the Invincible Heart to keep my insides from turning to agua y my legs to Jell-O, and I don't have it. I back up until I hit the pilot's seat. There's nowhere else to go.

I call Kayla on my sublingual. She picks up con rapidez, Gracias a Dios. She sounds slypered.

Can you sing that song to the Murry dragon that's on Earth? It's panicking.

Sure. I–

Hurry, por favor! I hang up on mi amiga.

The spuck thrashes again, banging against a wall, sending us into a spin. My stomach hits the back of my spine, and my chest feels tight as I try to find my balance. Out the front window, the plantation wall flashes by, and then the ocean, and then some trees. Time has gooed into slow motion.

After a second, the spuck calms, wrapping its tail around itself, then sploots backwards onto the floor. It lets out a softer whimper.

"We're going down, Babe. Hold onto something."

I grab onto Murry, the más solid weight inside the transport, and brace my face against his supple scales. I let out a shuddery breath.

As we whirl towards the ground, boxes shift around us, thuds echoing through the hull. We rip through foliage before finally jolting to a stop.

I squeak out a noise and open my eyes. Brill looks back at me with concern. The transport's front window is intact, and he doesn't look injured, Gracias a Dios. We're pointing at the plantation wall, just visible through the trees. "Wow, mi vida. Even crashing, you hit the landing point."

Brill follows my gaze and smiles. "Close enough."

I unclench my hands from the spuck. It lets out un gigante snore.

Brill's eyes go wide with wonder. "What did you do?"

"I called for backup. Kayla's singing to him." I put the collar on the spuck. The plantation has lots of lethalriffic things inside, pero at least he won't be target practice for the drones.

Brill goes outside and inspects the damage to the transport. After a while, the spuck wakes up and climbs out of the transport. It unfurls the wing, examining the damage.

Brill's handheld says, "Well, this me won't fly any time soon. How's the transport?"

"It's seen better days. But it will limp back to where Frank hid it." Brill examines the Murry worm's shoulder to see if the muscle is damaged or just the wing's surface. "You diay, tegen?" Meaning *friend*.

The spuck makes an unhappy noise. Brill's handheld says, "The fight is over. We're dead, and they are leaving. The one of Awn that escaped says they're taking our bodies with them."

I gasp. "The Evevrons turned on you? Por qué?"

This is muy malo. If Murry stops feeling safe on Evevron, he could flee and become a mindplague again.

"No. The Evevrons are our friends," Murry insists.

"Maybe it was a hunting party from the other side of the river," Brill suggests. "They don't know about Murry, so they wouldn't think anything of hunting a couple of spucks for food." He grimaces.

"No," Brill's handheld says. "Relations are improving between my creators and their neighbors now that I have helped get more water into the region. There is a fragile peace. No one would cross the river just to hunt and risk destroying that."

"Then who?" I ask.

"Offworlders. Big game hunters. They took us as trophies."

"Su!" Brill looks horrified. Krom are vegetarians – though Brill's a little less strict about it than most. He'll eat some varieties of fish or eggs, when he knows the planet of origin. Pero the idea of hunting for sport sickens him. Me too, un poco. "The Galactic Court has sanctions against that."

"But in order to file a complaint, I would have to admit that I exist."

Y if the Court finds out he exists, he would likely be executed for being an illegal mind-controlling parasite. Ay-ay-ay. "Is that why you didn't attack the hunters?"

The spuck shrugs its massive shoulders. "All of our memories remain intact. Nothing we are was truly lost. You proved to me that individuals care about other individuals. Someone who cares about the hunters would come asking questions I can't answer."

It really isn't fair. Murry never asked to be made illegally, any more than I asked to be injected with the Invincible Heart.

Chestla calls my handheld. Her jaw is tight and her slit pupils have dilatated until they are almost round. She's on a ship. "Someone here wants to talk to you, Bo."

"That's not what I said, Stala." Leron appears at the holofield's edge. His eyes are a softer green than Chestla's, his hair dark and wavy. His claw-nails are evenly manicured, as meticulous as everything else about him. "I said I'm worried about Murry's mental state, and I wondered if Bo was in contact with him during the attack."

"Why don't you talk to Murry yourself?" I ask Leron. "He's been trying to contact you for days."

Chestla seems too busy flying the ship to participate in the conversation.

Leron shrinks away, and part of his face disappears from the holo. "I have nothing to say to him."

The spuck, which had started to move into the capture field, hesitates, then sits down, watching from the side.

"Oh, come on, mijo," I tell Leron. "You owe him."

Leron licks his lips, then bares his predator's teeth. "I said no." Then some of the aggressiveness leaves his posture. "Just – tell him we're doing our best to catch those hunters before they get too far with the parasites."

I freeze. The muerto Mindhuggers inside the spucks would be evidence of both Murry's existence and Leron's crimes. "Oi! I didn't even think about that."

"Expired parasites take a couple of weeks to dissolve. If these guys butcher the spucks … let's just hope they cut off and discard the heads."

"Ewwww." I shudder. "Who would want to eat spuck brains?" Pero, someone might. Murry said the dead spucks were taken as trophies. Would a taxidermist notice the parasite? And if so, what would they make of it?

"That won't be an issue," Chestla growls. "We're going to catch that ship."

"And do what, amiga?" I can't imagine that Chestla would destroy it, killing even more people to keep Murry's secrets.

Chestla bares her teeth. "Charge them with illegal hunting in protected grounds. And confiscate the poached animals. They're still in our space, and as a Guardian Companion, I'm technically a cop, with the full authority to enforce Evevron's global laws."

"Where's Nellet?" I ask. Chestla doesn't usually leave her charge. Pero, I doubt she would have told the young princess about the dark secrets we uncovered in her peoples' past.

"She is with her oldest sister's Guardian. The girls were going shopping together today anyway, and Shina owes me a favor."

The image in the holofield rocks. Chestla manipulates the controls. "Nav's been hit. And propulsion."

Leron says something in loud, angranxious Evevron. Then he looks at the camera. "We'll never catch them now."

"That engine has no registration, either, and the ship has no identifying features." Chestla bangs her fist on the control panel. "Which means we can't track these jerks."

"They're poachers," Brill says. "Even if they notice the parasites, they won't say anything to the authorities."

He's right, no? Pero, that doesn't calm the anxiety in my gut. Sin razón to believe anything will come of this. Nada. Except that my life has basically turned into a novela, uan something probably will.

Leron taps on his phone. "I've arranged for a tow. But it will take a while. We have time to get our story straight."

"We already have one spuck that shouldn't be here," I tell Leron. "Cierto, we'll support any story you tell."

Earth has a vested interest in backing us up. It's called Serum Green. When Evevron gave HGB assistance during the first contact war, their price had been that HGB would include Serum Green in the chocolate it exports. The Evevrons had been using the resulting chocolate to prevent the spread of mindworms in case their geneflipped experiment got off planet. Which, claro está, it did. If anyone tells the Galactic Court what the Evevrons did, not only would Murry be exterminated as a potential plague, a number of Chestla's people – including Leron – could be executed for mindhacking or for taking part in the coverup.

Leron asks, "Is Murry really learning at the rate you implied? I've seen the results of the civil engineering projects he's done for Ekrin's civic works group. But his emotional development, his morality. Is there something redeemable out of all our mistakes?"

I tell Leron, "You should talk to him, mijo."

CHAPTER ELEVEN

"That bionet's lethalriffic. Make sure you dig low enough." I adjust Murry's collar. On the hike from the downed transport to the wall, Murry's been agitated, both from the fight with the hunters and because Leron still won't talk to him. "And watch out for harvester robots. They carry hunormous knives."

"I'll be careful." The voice comes from Brill's handheld, even though the spuck's chompcrushing another box of carob bars. "If this me dies, it would be difficult to get another me all the way from Evevron to Earth."

Murry starts digging under the wall. I worry about his injured wing. Brill patched it for him using the transport's medkit. Pero, the wound apparently doesn't affect the spuck's ability to dig.

As the back end of Murry disappears into the hole, Brill holds up the walkie. "I hope Eugene hasn't given up on us. We took longer than expected to get here."

I laugh. "Eugene is nada if not stubborn."

The walkie crackles to life. "I'm still at the coordinates you specified," Eugene says. "It has been fifteen minutes since my last attempt at communication. I am very bored."

I take the walkie from Brill. "Oye! We're here! Once Murry tunnels under the wall, por favor come back through, and we can talk."

Moments later, Eugene emerges from the hole Murry dug. He's pretty buff from hiking and hacking through the rainforest for his work. Pero, he's pale and shaky now that he's been up close to a spuck, the trembling obvious even in the moonlight. "When Chestla sent me that message about an assistant from Evevron, I hoped she was playfully referring to herself. Or even that Leron guy. But not one of those giant monsters. What am I supposed to do with that thing? I can't even talk to it."

"Murry can talk, using your phone as an interface." I point to the outline of Eugene's phone in his front pocket. Only – Eugene's handheld won't work inside the plantation's no-call zone. "Eh. Maybe just use the walkie."

After a clomping noise, the spuck crawls back out of the hole.

Brill nods at Eugene. "Eugene, meet the being in the galaxy that knows the most about Pure Rot. Murry, this is Eugene, the su on this planet that's been studying the disease the hardest."

Eugene blinks. "Why does he know about an Earth-based disease?"

We've discussed the risks. While Murry has to confess that he bio-grammed Pure Rot, he still won't tell Eugene that he's a bio-engineered being.

Brill says, "I'll let him explain that one."

Eugene squints, pero, he lets the question go. Surprising, porque he's usually dogged about getting answers. "Can I talk to you for a second?" Eugene pulls me aside. "Look at those teeth. Those creatures are natural predators on Evevron. Chestla claims they're civilized now. But how do I know it won't get hungry enough to eat me?"

I put a hand on his arm. "Murry wants to make amends por todo. If he can't catch food, he'll eat fruit."

Eugene changes the subject. "So how's Chestla?"

Chestla is one of my closest amigas. She was my RA back at cooking school, and she served as my bodyguard until recently. Pero, she plays her love life close to the vest.

At one point, Chestla was interested in Eugene, when they'd been trapped together in the Brazilian rainforest. At the time, he didn't seem to notice. I assumed the predator pheromones and the sharp teeth scared him away from the prospect of dating an Evevron. Pero after she left, he started calling her. No sé – maybe he'd shown interest all along, and his signals were too subtle for her to pick up on. Chestla would be the first to admit she's no good at reading romantic signals.

After she left Earth, Chestla reconnected with un amigo de la infancia back home on Evevron. Ball, a half-Evevron, half-Krom tewakelle, was severely injured in a hunting accident. And when Ball came a breath from dying, he confessed to Chestla that he'd been in love with her since they were niños. Chestla promised to help Ball with his physical therapy.

The last time I'd talked to Chestla, she still hadn't made up her mind which guy she wants to be with. I think she's leaning towards Ball, pero I don't know if she's told Eugene that Ball exists. También, I don't think she told Eugene that we discovered the Evevrons created Serum Green.

I give Eugene a careful smile. "Chestla's doing great, no? She's happy as Guardian Companion to Princess Nellet. She worked so hard to pass the test."

"I know." Eugene's voice sounds tight.

"What, mijo?"

He frowns. "Is it selfish that I wish she'd failed? I have to be here, working to save Earth. And she has to be on Evevron, where that dude is trying to woo her away from me. He nearly died, trying to save her friend. How can I compete with that?"

By Chestla's friend, Eugene means me. And sí, selfless heroism is super-hard to compete with.

"This all has something to do with Serum Green, doesn't it?" Eugene demands. "And those cryostasis pods?"

I'm not sure what to tell him, porque I'm not sure how much he knows.

Eugene sighs. "I wish someone trusted me enough to tell me what's going on."

"I will tell you Murry is grieving. The people in those stasis pods were muy importante to him. He can use a little sympathy, no?"

Eugene studies the spuck. "Cryostasis has always been about the illusion of hope. Take the frozen seed bank HGB keeps in each plantation. So far, I've made no progress at unraveling this plant disease. It's ravaging every plantation across the globe. I doubt there are any uninfected trees left. The fruit is ruined, so we can't work from that, and HGB made sure these things turn to mush if you clone them. That seed bank, which has retained chocolate's full biodiversity, is intriguing as a potential solution. But without a way to revive the beans – it's just impossible. No one can figure out a way to revive the dead – be they plant or person."

I step closer to Eugene. "Murry's past false hope. They're about to lay to rest the dead in those cryostasis pods." My handheld rings. It's Kaliel. He's blushing pero his skin is too dark to show more than just an impression of mortification. I walk away from Eugene before Kaliel can say anything Eugene's not supposed to know. "You okay, mijo?"

"Yeah. Just Bo, honey – I need a favor." It's muy extraño that he'd call me that. He may be using it as a safe word, letting me know someone may be listening.

"Anything. Honey." I smile into the camera. "You know that, after all we've been through."

"The guys holding Stephen are fans of yours. They said the chocolate isn't enough to get his release, but if you say on camera that you're Team Kaliel now, and you shout out to them in person, they will call it even and tear up the paperwork."

I glance at Brill, who's behind the holo, out of sight. "They're looking for a gritclip to virafizz, no?"

Another round of media flurries tying me to Kaliel will hurt Brill. Not to mention Kayla.

Kaliel's smile is tense. "I know you wanted to keep our relationship private. But Honey, the punishment for stealing on this planet is death. You don't want Kayla to lose her brother, do you?"

"Dios mio!" Stephen's a moron, pero he doesn't deserve to die. I hate being manipulated for a media blitz, so even more people can make judgments about me. But there's no choice.

"Fine. Pero, make sure they have their camera set up right, because I'm only doing this once."

Brill steps toward me, gesturing at my phone and giving me a nod then a head shake then a shrug to see if I'm okay. I wave at him to stay where he is. So while mi vida stands watching, I tell the cameras that I'm done mourning my Krom, and that mi amor por Kaliel has grown, since he comforted me in my time of need. Brill folds his arms across his chest, that ridiculous hair and the tee oddly intimidating.

When I hang up, Brill raises an eyebrow. "Team Kaliel, huh?"

"Wait." Eugene points at Brill's chest. "You're supposed to be dead?"

Did he not know that? "Sí, and you can't tell anyone he's alive."

"Who would I tell?" Eugene throws up his hands. "If you trust me, maybe I can help."

"Maybe you–" My handheld rings. It's Tawny. Whelp. That didn't take long.

I move away again to talk to her.

"Bodacious! What are you doing outside the compound? And what happened to the tracker I put on you?"

I hesitate. "You know how my room has a microwave?"

"Yeah."

"I may have microwaved my clothes." Which is pretty much guaranteed to short out any electronics.

"Doesn't that melt a hole?" Tawny narrows her eyes. "You using the microwave for anything else?"

"No," I admit. She knows I prefer to cook from scratch. There's so not going to be a microwave in my room when I get back.

Tawny sighs. "I have given you a lot of leeway. You could have at least let me break the news about you and Kaliel. The way you spoke, it sounds like he's your rebound guy."

"Lo siento. It was a spur of the moment thing." And the way Tawny's about to latch onto the idea of me as part of a couple, something I'll regret for a long time.

"Since you're with Kaliel, I won't send anyone to retrieve you. Consider a private evening with him my gift to you. But that doesn't mean you can be late tomorrow, so don't get too carried away."

Um, awkward! "Gracias, mija."

Kaliel deserves any flak he gets over this. Tawny's about to make my life miserable. At least that should distract her from being mad over Janvier flirting with me.

Once we get Murry settled with Eugene and get back into the transport, Brill asks me, "Was that performance designed to distract Tawny from the fact I'm on this planet."

I explain about what had happened with Stephen. "Hanstral, mi vida. I have to play into this. I may have to spend time with Kaliel."

Brill shrugs. "I trust you."

Oi! This will test how much he really has changed.

My handheld rings. "Speaking of Stephen."

I move back a row of seats and angle my phone so Stephen can't see Brill.

Stephen lounges in the copilot seat on Kaliel's ship. He is Kayla's twin, with the same pale skin and dark hair. Now, he's got a bruised eye, and a sling cradles his arm. "Thank you, Bodacious."

"You owe me."

"Absolutely."

I say, "Que? You couldn't you overpower the guards with your telepathic feedback?"

Stephen blushes. "I still don't have enough control when invading a non-telepath's mind to be sure I wouldn't kill those guys."

"I admire your self-restraint." I'm being flip, pero I mean it. It's the first sign I've seen that finding out he's Nitarri hasn't made Stephen totalmente arrogant. I shrug. "Too bad it was all por nada. Kayla said she warned you not to get involved with these people."

"Who said it was for nothing?" Stephen pulls his arm out of the sling and starts unwrapping the bandages. A silver-toned cylinder's hidden against the underside of his bruised arm. He pulls it out and re-wraps the bandages, which aren't for show. "This is a duplicate of the gene database. It proves that Kayla and I are who we claim. And that we have the right to rule."

"To rule what?" Kaliel asks. "The diaspora?"

Kayla and Stephen's home world was destroyed when they were niños. They spent most of their lives in hiding, because some Nitarri fear the return of the true heirs, even though their people are scattered across la galaxia.

"Kaliel's right," I say. "What does it matter if you're a prince, if you don't have a kingdom?"

"My uncle has set himself up as king. He's working to find the Nitarri a new home world. And when he does, Kayla and I will take it from him." He makes a fist with his good hand.

"Have you asked Kayla about this, mijo?" I ask.

Stephen shrugs. "I haven't convinced her yet. She's more concerned with staying safe and in hiding. But when you look at how everything lines up chronologically, my uncle must be the one who took advantage of the eco-disaster that ripped apart Nitarri. He could have focused on saving our people, but instead he killed the royal family. Once I get proof of that, Kayla will see reason."

Kaliel says, "Kayla said if your uncle finds out you are alive, he will have you both killed. I think she gets it. She just doesn't want to fight him for power."

That's why Kayla has never been allowed to appear on camera, why her familia freaked out when HGB put her in a holomerical without permission. Pero now, Stephen's making the risk more immediate. "Oye! Whatever decisions you make, you should make them together. Kayla has to live with the consequences too, no?"

Stephen holds up the cylinder. "I will rally a following. And when she sees that people want us back, then she'll understand."

"You don't even have a fleet yet?" Kaliel asks.

Stephen blushes again. "I'm working on that."

Oi! As soon as I get off the handheld with Stephen, I call up Kayla's number.

Brill asks, "Babe, are you sure you have the right to interfere?"

I nod. "She's mi mejor amiga."

Kayla answers the phone in her PJs. When I tell her what Stephen's doing, she sighs. "I know. We keep fighting over it. I'm not looking for power or to fight to be recognized. I have a business now, and I'm getting to know my mom on a whole new level now that we have no secrets between us." Kayla considers me for a moment. "I hate to bring up a painful subject, but you spent a long time with Brill, and you read the Krom Codex before he died. Please tell Stephen to stop, with some of that Krom-know-the-history-of-pain logic."

Brill glances back at me, the shocked look on his face clear even without me seeing the shift in his eyes. I'm super surprised también that Kayla would respect Brill's opinion about anything – after all Kayla never acted that friendly towards him before his "death."

Keeping such un gran secreto from mi mejor amiga has been hard, pero I couldn't risk telling *anyone* that Brill's vivo. I swallow the urge to blurt it out. I redirect, back to her. "Stephen wants to understand who he is, now that he knows he's adopted. You're really not curious about your family, KayKay? After you spent half your life wishing you were a princesa, only to find out you really are one?"

Kayla rolls her eyes. "Why does everyone immediately assume that every adopted person has this innate need to look for their birth family? I've got enough issues with one family. No need to multiply that times two." Kayla laughs. "Besides, it's all too weird. Like, my real name is Shirazende Okkawashilede."

"I'll talk to Stephen," I say, "though I doubt he will listen."

After I let Kayla go, Brill says, "I wish I could talk to him myself. Being dead is getting tiresome."

CHAPTER TWELVE

The next morning, I'm back on set, preparing to holo the first ad spot on Tawny's roster. I'm up with the sun, despite the not getting back into my room until almost four this morning. I'm still not adjusted to the time change being on Earth, so on top of everything else, I have jet lag something fierce.

Y todavía, waking up without the shakes – this is the best morning I've had in a long while.

Brill calls my sublingual. *I'll check out that bar as soon as it opens.*

Don't go alone. Frío fear colors my bubblechatter. *After I'm done with filming, I can meet you at the Japanese place again, and we can go together.*

Ga. That's not a good idea, Brill bubblechatters. *The whole point is finding out who wants to kidnap you and why. If you walk in there, they'll just kidnap you.*

And what will they do to you?

I'll make sure they don't figure out who I am.

Tawny sits down beside me, with her headphones on, and starts doing something on a tablet computer. Probably perfectspinning holo about me and Kaliel. Tawny has a sublingual and I've exchanged crosstalk with her before. Without another word, I hang up on Brill.

Tawny pulls off her headphones. "What has you so jumpy?"

"I may should have gotten more sleep last night, no?"

Tawny pats my hand. "I hope it was worth it."

I look at the jraghite stone, shining on her finger. Those rocks glow with body heat, and this one is gorgeous in its setting. The styling on the crest is somehow similar to the one on my mourning pendant. "Do you know that ring's Krom?"

"Do you like it?" Tawny shows the ring off to advantage.

"As much as you disliked Brill, you choose to wear a piece of Krom jewelry?"

"I never disliked Brill. He was …" She searches for an acceptable word. "Inconvenient. I tried to warn you what you needed to do to keep him alive."

I look down at the ring again, not sure what to say to that. "Did you visit Krom?"

Tawny laughs. "Krom don't welcome human tourists on their planet. You know that." She nods down at her hand. "My grandfather was in Iowa during First Contact. He and my dad hid a Krom from the rioters and helped the guy get back to the ship. That Krom gave him this ring in thanks. My dad was just a kid, but he kept this ring all his life."

"Que? That's Jeska's family crest." It's a mega-small world. "Your grandfather might know Jeska. Though at least one other member of the familia was on board that ship." I take Tawny's hand, holding up the ring.

Tawny pulls her hand away. "My grandfather died before I was born, and my father died when I was very young. Just like yours. This ring is the only momento I have left of him. It's proof that he was a good person."

The air whooshes out of my lungs. "Lo siento. I didn't realize."

I have to tell Brill Tawny's story when he gets back from the bar. He still thinks Tawny's wearing this piece of Krom art is tacky. Pero, life is complicated. We're all so intertwined. I need to stop making assumptions. A cultural artifact or piece of art made by one species can be emotionally resonant – or have importante personal meaning – to someone from another.

Tawny taps her tablet screen. "We need to get some spin-holo of you kissing Kaliel. That clip you released yesterday has already made a noticeable impact on the polls." Meaning that less people want to see me dead, and more people want to see me kissing a guy I have no business kissing. "We can stage it so it looks accidental. Like the two of you were out hiking alone, and the celebarazzi just happened along with their cameras. If we release it today or tomorrow, it will ride the echo of the first bumpclip."

"That will be muy difícil," I say. "Kaliel took a side job and had to leave the planet."

I hope that won't get him in trouble. HGB can be picky about what their employees do.

Tawny sighs. "When will he be back?"

"I'll ask him."

"Maybe we can get something usable out of that conversation, even if you're not in the same room." Tawny rubs her temples, her expression turning serious. "Have you seen the feeds this morning?"

Fear sinks in my stomach like a ball of uncooked pasta. "Que?"

Tawny pulls up a holo. "It's about those creatures you tried to protect on Evevron."

Dios mio. I have un mal feeling.

She shows a flashback cast of Blizzard and Feddoink, mis dos favoritos newscasters. Blizzard's a Myska, like Tyson, with a diamond-shaped snake-like head and fists like a boxer, and Feddoink's kind of a blob.

Blizzard's spine is crunched down, so that he looks awkward in his jacket, and he's sucking his cheeks in so far his face looks inside out, sure signs a Myska is upset. "Just a warning about what we are about to show. These spucks look a little like my species. There's a lot of blood. I hope none of you are eating breakfast."

The gritclip starts inside what looks like a taxidermist's warehouse, filled with stuffed glass-eyed creatures from half the galaxy's worlds. The video pans over the specimens, the FeedCaster obviamente proud that this collection de muerte is getting it's virafizzed moment. Then the camera zooms in one a living humanoid with teal skin, wearing one of the purple-camo hunting habit so popular on Evevron. The muchacho's weird hat may be his planet's equivalent of a pith helmet.

He talks in a language of chirps and clicks, and the holo pops up subtitles in Universal. He boasts how brave he was on his recent hunting trip, how he never expected to uncover a galaxy-shaking secret. Ay! The camera zooms out to show a dead Murry dragon, the head tipped sideways, the tongue lolling out of its mouth.

I have a hard time pulling in a breath, and when I finally do, I dry heave. Dios mio.

The hunter draws a huge knife from his belt, steps behind the spuck and cuts the back of its cabeza open. That ball of dread inside me skyrockets, and I have to keep taking deep breaths, or else I'll puke right here on the floor. Tranquila y tranquila. This is only one of the dragons. That the one we let into the plantation is still safe. After a sickening *skuuuuuk*, the hunter pulls a fully-attached Mindhugger out of the spuck, bringing gore and brain matter with it.

The hunter holds up his grotesque prize. The subtitles translate, "I have proof that the Evevrons engineered Dragon supersoldiers to take over the universe. And who knows what will be next!"

Tawny shrugs. "I've spin-washed that this is holonique. But I don't know how many people will believe it's fake." She narrows her eyes. "Everyone told me this thing came to Evevron from outer space. Did they engineer it?"

My face feels hot. "Eso – I need a minute to think, por favor." I flee for the temporary safety of the restroom. Tawny's smart. My retreat is as good as an admission. Pero, at least she doesn't have me saying it on camera.

This is terrible. If people dig into Murry's nature, the secrets of more than one planet will be exposed in the most feo way possible. I check the stalls to make sure I am alone, then lock the outside door. I sit on the sofa near the sink and call Gideon Tyson. *Have you seen the news?*

Tyson's fluent in English and Universal, pero his reptilian jaw and lack of front teeth leave him unable to pronounce TH. *Not recently. I'm on te oter side of te galaxy, Bo. I'm on mandatory leave at a spa, pending medical clearance.* Tyson did, obviamente, have brain surgery a few months ago. I'm not surprised his superiors don't trust a venomous cop with a gun to be back on the beat until he passes a CAT scan. Tyson's sigh rolls through my brain. *I believe tey are waiting for me to finish my molt, so I won't look ridiculous trying to arrest people.*

I stifle a laugh, though that probably won't keep it from transmitting to Tyson across my sublingual. He *had* looked ridiculous the last time I saw him, with half of the gray-green scales missing off his face. Myska aren't supposed to molt once they reach adult size – except when they lose or gain a lot of weight – or suffer from certain neurological conditions. The neurological problems that came when Tyson was imperfectly infected with a mindworm nearly cost him his life. Pero, it's hard to remember how serious it was, since he's bounced back completely.

Tawny sends me a text. *I didn't expect you to get this upset, Bodacious. We should discuss this.* Which is really her saying, *What don't I know?*

I ignore her and focus on Tyson. *Poachers just found ejemplos de the Murry parasite. They're gritcasting all over the feeds, saying the Evevrons engineered a superweapon.*

Tyson's hiss echoes through my brain. *Dark night slime mold salad bar.*

I think Tyson's cursing has been influenced by the spa where he's staying. He's silent for a long enough that I think I lost the connection. I'm about to hang up when he says, *Flat heart closed eyes wilting flower. I looked it up. The Galactic Court is taking tese accusations seriously. Poor Murry. I will call and prepare him for death.* He hisses softer. He came out of the trauma of having been infected with enough sympathy to bend his firm moral code. He helped hide the hive mind's existence. *Maybe tey will get your Nitarri friend to execute him, since she knows his neural signature. If she sings her calming song first, it won't be so bad.*

Come on Tyson, I bubblechatter. *Where's the loophole for Murry? Eh? What should he be doing? Should he step forward and counter-sue the poachers?*

He should wait for te Galactic court to discuss tis with te Evevrons. Tey have to investigate te claim tat te parasite was engineered. Tyson sighs. *Te law is clear. Tere isn't a loophole for te mindhacking statutes.*

Tears sting my eyes. *You can't expect me to give up.*

Nobody would expect tat of you. I will try to tink of something. He bubblechatters a noise somewhere between a hiss and a sigh. *I don't tink te Court will be tat harsh on you, Chestla, and te others, even if someone proves you aided te Evevrons. Tose of us Murry infected can't be charged, as we might have acted under residual influence.*

My chest tightens. *Charged with what?*

Aiding te coverup. Te Court would be witin its rights to execute everyone involved, but likely you'll only get prison time — if tey even find out you were involved.

It's loco. When I'd decided to keep the Evevrons' secret, I never considered being implicated. Even considering the repercussions now: I'd do it again.

Jail time though, somewhere away from the treatments for the IH withdrawal. Con nada to do, y nada to fight and none of the people mas important to me. The Court might as well execute me. I'd wind up destroying myself.

I know wat you're tinking, Bo. Tyson's chatter takes on a warning tone. *And do me a favor. If te Galactics come to arrest you, tis time, don't run.*

When I make it back to the holo area, Tawny's left. Good. I don't know how to tell her Tyson thinks we might be implicated.

She's the one person who was with us on Evevron who doesn't know anything. If questioned, I'll testify to that fact.

I take a deep breath and start my lines – a bunch of drivel about how HGB likematches una familia. The words grind like sand in my mouth. Murry feels more like family than HGB, and Tyson is so sure that the Galactic Court will put Murry down that he is offering Murry grief counseling.

Janvier walks onto the set, and I falter mid-sentence. He holds a bouquet of flowers. For me. Oi! Maybe I can handle this before Tawny gets back. As I step out of the holocube, the director gives me a sour look, pero the take's already ruined, so what can he say, right?

"Shelly." I try to sound friendly, yet neutral. "Why are you here, amigo?"

He frowns at the word friend. Did he want me to call him mijo again? "Let's take a walk in the garden."

I follow him outside. It almost seems like *he's* avoiding HGB's security cameras. Which es estúpido, no?

Before I left my room this morning, I checked myself for bugs and found the one Tawny stuck on me. I popped it on some guy who stepped too close to me in the hallway. I want to check again now to make sure I didn't miss any surveillance equipment, pero that'd be difícil in front of Janvier. We walk through the tropical foliage and stop in front of an avocado tree.

Janvier hands me the flowers. "Is there anything I can do to make you trust me?"

I hesitate. "I don't know. Pero you could try. Have you heard the news from Evevron?"

Janvier nods. "Given the incidents with humans on that planet–" He's talking about me and Kaliel. "–the Galactic Court has asked me to give a statement."

"Then make a statement in the mindworms' favor. Trust *me*. Tell them your people returned unharmed, and that these creatures just want a place to belong. That they have a moral code. And a sense of humor." I know I'm talking loco. I can't expect mercy from Daschel Janvier.

"Okay."

"Que?" I clench my jaw to keep it from sliding open in shock.

If I didn't know better, I'd say he was wiping tears from his eyes. He clears his throat. "Have you considered what I said yesterday? I'm not asking for anything permanent – yet. But you responded by running to Kaliel. I don't want you to feel like you have to be with someone else to avoid being with me."

I blink. That's a bold assumption. Yet I can see that's how it looks. "You're right, mijo. That was impulsive. I shouldn't be with anybody right now."

Has Janvier given me the out I need, so I don't have to do a beso-holo with Kaliel while Brill broods in the shadows?

Nah … Tawny wouldn't let the media ball stop rolling that easily.

Janvier gives an ironic smile. "I don't want to miss my chance and have you bond with Kaliel before I make my case for you. I'm a businessman, Bo. I'm used to getting what I want, but I also know better than to pursue a bad deal. If you don't find me attractive, tell me and I'll drop this."

I wish I could tell him that. Pero with him standing so close with that serious face and chiseled physique, smelling of musky cologne – even I'm not that good of an actress. I give him back the flowers, then pluck one yellow daisy from the bouquet. "You don't want to be my rebound. That wouldn't be fair to either of us, no?"

"That's not a no."

I twirl the flower. "My heart's not ready for anyone new. Pero, I can use all the friends I can get. If you really want to take HGB in a more positive direction, let me help you as una amiga y an equal – without messy strings attached."

"We both know how this goes." He leans closer, his face angled towards mine, like he's imagining kissing me. "You can fight it, but if we spend all that time together, we'll wind up in each other's arms. So why play games?"

"I'm leaving for Zant in less than a week."

"No, you're not. Something will come up, to give you an excuse to stay."

I laugh, pero it sounds brittle, hollow. "You act like we're in a telenovela." Because in a cheesetastic dramacast, that's what would happen. "I've never been that girl. I had a chance to choose the rich Krom who'd been given a second chance to return to his society's good graces. Pero I chose Brill. He doesn't fit the script. But why shouldn't we write it whatever way we want?"

"I thought you were done mourning. You're talking about your Krom like he's still alive."

I try to steady my breathing y mi corazón. I promised Frank I would feel Janvier out. "What if he was? What if you didn't have the scenario all planned out? Would your offer still stand?"

Janvier hesitates. "I don't know. I've never had to fight for a girl."

He's discounting Kaliel's supposed bid for my affections. Muy presumptuous.

I press. "If Brill was alive, would you let him stay that way?"

Janvier pulls away. "That's not a fair question. That issue had nothing to do with you."

Anger bubbles through me. "Tu mientes." *You lie.* I take a deep breath, to get myself under control, before I say something that gets me, Frank or Brill killed. "Lo siento. You keep talking about a new direction for HGB. We should put the ugly past behind us, no?"

"Sure." Pero, he looks hesitant. "Can I just … I want to try something … see if we're both wasting our time."

Daschel Janvier, head honcho of the corrupt megacorporation that had my father killed and wants my true love muerto también, leans in and kisses me. The contact is warm and insistent, and as much as I hate myself for it, damn if there isn't chemistry.

I'm horrified to find myself melting against his solid body, at the same moment while Brill is risking his life at that bar to make sure I don't get ransomsnatched. And yet … I can't quite make myself pull away.

At a soft squeak behind us, Janvier breaks the beso. Tawny stands in the middle of the path, three pink-wrapped nutrition bars in one hand, and her phone in the other.

Her warm-toned cheeks are crimson. She looks from me to Janvier and back again. Then she zeroes in on him. "Do you care to explain this ad campaign?"

He looks at her phone, where a holo of dancing candy bars plays. "Surely they haven't released that. I told them to cancel production."

"Of these?" Tawny shakes the bars at him. "How could you, Daschel? I've been working on HGB New for years, and this isn't it. Who did you even get to do the promos?"

Janvier says, "I knew you'd be unhappy, so I hired an outside firm. People substituted carob for chocolate in the pre-First Contact days. It could have saved us."

Something about his unfocused eyes reminds me of several people, when they described decisions made while under the influence of the Mindhuggers. Además, the Mindhuggers were engineered to be susceptible to theobromine poisoning, so sí, Murry might have tried replacing chocolate with carob. Pero then, shouldn't Murry have known what the spuck was looking at in the transport?

"Why couldn't you have called it something else?" Tawny insists.

Janvier hesitates. "I honestly don't remember. But it doesn't matter. The product was a flop with test tasters, and the polls showed people found the packaging garish. I invested a significant amount of capital into this project, and now I'm stuck with tons of carob that nobody's buying. We can't show this to the galaxy as HGB's new product. We'll be the laughing stock of the worlds."

Tawny throws the bars at Janvier's feet. She jerks a thumb in my direction. "Then let her help you figure this one out. I'm done waiting for you to notice me, and I'm done cleaning up your messes." She turns to me. "I don't even want to imagine what

Kaliel would think. As soon as you're done here, I need you to put on a fresh coat of lipstick, go find your mourning pendant, and get in front of the camera. We have a planet to save."

Tawny stalks off.

Janvier stands there blinking. "Was she saying she's had a thing for me?"

"Are you blind, mijo?" I put a hand on his arm. "She's been sending out signals as bright as these candy wrappers."

"I never realized," Janvier protests.

At least he's not trying to kiss me anymore.

I call Kaliel to find out when he's arriving back on Earth. He and I have to put on a good show, at least until Frank has his meeting with Janvier. Loco, no? My heart is finally loyal to Brill, and I'm stuck pretending it isn't.

"We aren't coming back to Earth yet," Kaliel says. "Stephen wants to stop at the Moon. He's meeting some guy at Interface Station, to show the proof of his heredity."

Interface Station is where traders wanting to do business with Earth pick up and drop off goods. It's una town grande, with buildings sometimes visible from Earth, and a man-made ocean dotted with hotels levitating safely above the exaggerated waves.

Stephen leans into the holofield. "My contact's part of the group hoping to build resistance to my uncle's rule. I told you I'm working on getting a fleet."

It doesn't sound like this group has progressed very far. And it doesn't look like Stephen has any idea what he's getting into. "Mijo, Kayla wanted me to talk to you about Krom views on war."

"Okay." Stephen's listening at least.

I hesitate, feeling nerviosa. How much do I really understand about Krom, given the mistake I made in misunderstanding wevdaglarin? Kayla exaggerated – I've read parts of the Codex, not the whole thing. And Brill won't discuss the most uncomfortable parts of Krom history until I have. "The Krom feel it's wrong to take lives over land or commodities or power.

According to Povika, gaining power only puts lives in danger – including your own. Which means they have no desire to build an empire. And no desire to be king or president or CEO." I sound like a dictiwiki entry. I try to make it more personal, pero this is Brill's culture, not mine. "Becoming a leader on Krom is a mild punishment, where you get weighed down with extra responsibilities. Most of their laws are based on families policing their members, and on cultural shunning of people who violate Krom beliefs about neutrality and hoarding commodities."

"In English, Bo."

Had I slipped into Universal? No. He means to make it simpler. "They pursue peace, because peace prevents pain. And that's what Kayla wants."

"What happens if the Krom get attacked?" Stephen asks.

"Non-lethal defenses surround their planets. And they look to the Galactic Court for protection."

"That must be nice." Stephen scowls. "But the courts failed my family. I've spent my whole life in hiding, because I have no protection. And I'm tired of it."

I look to Kaliel. "Are you okay with this?"

Kaliel shrugs. "I wish Stephen and Kayla could agree. But I'm not ditching my girlfriend's brother on the moon."

Afterwards, I call Brill to check in and tell him I understand Krom a little better. He picks up – pero then hangs up without saying anything. Oye!

He obviously can't talk. And I can't sneak away from the holoing to check in on him. Pero, what if he's in trouble?

CHAPTER THIRTEEN

I send Tawny poseclips of me and Kaliel pretending to be all coo-ey in our holocall. I know she received the feed, pero when I see her, she doesn't acknowledge it. She just walks in and says, "Get back in that holocube and get your head in the game. You're still the star at dinner tonight, so this has to wrap up in time for you to get dressed."

Three hours later, we finally have a break in holoing. The minute recording ends, Tawny stalks out of the studio. The production assistants are leaving too. Nobody seems to care what I'm doing between now and dinner. I pull up the Dead Fish for a quick search on my handheld. The bar doesn't have a web site.

The director nods at me. "Try and get more comfortable in the holocube, if you want. Turn out the lights when you leave, okay?"

Eh? He trusts me alone in here?

Bueno esta bien. I call Brill on my sublingual. Again. For the thirtieth time. He's still not answering. The worry's been building in me for hours.

I call the bar, asking if any underage goth-ish teenagers tried to get in. The guy who answers laughs in my ear. As he's hanging up, I hear him say something about stupid moms. I'm un poco offended. Pero it's better than having him suspicious.

I call Gavin and tell him Brill's missing. "He hasn't been answering his phone, not for hours."

"Give me a minute to make some calls." It takes him a lot more than a minute. He really is a good amigo to Brill, sacrificing both potential trading deals and personal time to wait for mi vida. Gavin's married and has niños, pero I doubt his wife is with him. When he comes back, he says, "Ga, su. Nobody's heard anything that suggests a Krom's been seen on Earth. I have a name at the Dead Fish of someone who might be sympathetic. Call and ask for Mac, the piano player."

Forget calling. I'm going down there. I have hours before my speech at dinner. Plenty of time. And If I'm late, Tawny and her touchy attitude will have to deal.

Pero I need a disguise. The props room door isn't locked. And I doubt Tawny had the forethought to bug the clothes in there. I stroll past an entire rack of evening gowns, touching the satiny fabrics. As much as it feels like I've fallen into a novela, why have I not had a single occasion to wear one of these? Tawny's bound to have me wear an estúpido power suit to the dinner.

Sabes que? If Brill can pull off the pale, blush-incapable eternally-young goth look, I can hide in plain sight as the novela diva. I choose a deep blue, sleeveless gown with a swirl of gold glittering down the front. I take it to the work table, grab a pair of scissors and a box of safety pins and cut the dress to knee length.

While I'm pinning the hem, Chestla calls. She's agitated, showing her teeth. "Galactic Enforcers came to question me. Cesuda ma, I think we might both get arrested!"

Ball is with her. His hazel eyes have the slit pupils of an Evevron. His brown skin shares the same warm tones as mine. His face is more angular and thinner than I remember. Recovering from his injuries is taking a toll. He puts a hand on Chestla's shoulder. "Stala. It will be okay."

"I'm sorry, mi amiga," I say. This isn't Chestla's fault. She uncovered secrets about people she cares about – pero I convinced her to help us cover them up, to protect other secrets, ones that might destroy my planet. "If you get arrested, you'll lose your position as Guardian Companion, no?"

"No. I mean yes." She bows her cabeza. Chestla nearly died proving herself fit to be a Guardian Companion. It's what she's always wanted, to the core of her nature. "But that doesn't matter. I might face disgrace and imprisonment, but all the researchers, and half of the council of elders will be tried for more serious crimes. They could face execution. I – we're a social race. These people mean a lot to me. What should I do?"

"Proceed with the ceremony of salt," Ball tells her. "Give everyone as much peace as possible, so if they are condemned, they can consider the meaning in their ancestor's deaths before their ashes mingle. And let the Enforcers see their remorse, even as they wait their turn to be questioned."

"The Court just started this investigation, right?" I say. "So how come everyone is giving up? No entiendo."

Ball says, "I'm just preparing for the worst. That's what happens when Krom philosophy meets Evevron practicality."

"Ay!" I stick myself with a pin.

Chestla focuses on the dress in my holofield. "What are you doing to that thing?"

"Not giving up." I explain my plan to go undercover at the bar, then I let them go.

Once I find Brill, I may need to run, and this island's covered with rocks, sand and uneven terrain. I'm not loca, so I pass up the selection of high heels and find some funky boots. Then I pull my hair up under a cloche hat and go to work on my makeup, using contouring to change the shape of my face and painting on una muy grande swathe of blush that should distract most facial recognition software.

Once I leave the facility, I need to travel to the other side of the island. I pull up a hover-bus map of Maui on my phone. No one would expect me to travel by that, no?

Pero as I walk towards the bus stop, the hairs on the nape of my neck stand up. I'm being watched. I whirl around. A flash of motion melts into the oleander. Ay! I swallow a lump of fear.

I walk faster, trying to look behind me without being obvious. I wipe my sweaty palms on my dress, trying to ignore the anxiety building in my chest.

Another flash of motion. Sí. Someone is definitely trailing me.

Are people loitering around the HGB facility, waiting to collect the price on me? And is my disguise really that sad?

Brill's still not answering his sublingual.

I try Frank. *Someone's following me.*

Duh. Frank bubblechatters. *It's me. At least you noticed this time. There may be hope for you after all. But where are you going dressed like that?*

I keep walking for the bus. Frank will tell me not to go to the bar, that I shouldn't put myself in danger for my Krom's sake. He's never liked Brill, even if he did refrain from killing him. Pero lying about where I'm going won't help anyone. *Brill went to the Dead Fish to find out who wants me kidnapped, and now he's not answering his phone.*

Frank hangs up and melts out of the bushes. He quick-walks to catch up to me. "So you think you'll just walk in there? Because that's smart."

I reach the bus stop, sit on the bench and cross my arms. "What choice do I have? You won't protect Brill for me, no?"

Frank sits beside me. "If you want me to protect him, I should tell him that you kissed Janvier. That might actually make him leave."

Heat floods my face. "You know about that?"

"I've been keeping an eye on you since yesterday. Tawny's not the only one with cool surveillance equipment." He takes my arm, turning me towards him. "Janvier's young, and you probably find him pretty to look at. But he's dangerous. He's …" Frank takes a minute to choose his words. "Not for you."

"Porque now you realize Brill is," I say sarcastically.

"Maybe." Frank laughs. "I know that's ironic."

It's kind of sweet, when I consider how adamantly opposed Frank was to mine and Brill's relationship when he first met mi vida.

Then Frank adds, "But there's still a good chance the Krom dies before all this is over."

Cold spikes through my heart. "Viejo!"

He shrugs. "That's the hard truth. And if it happens, if you're really drowning in grief, don't let Janvier comfort you. Don't make the same mistake your mother made with me."

Frank loves Mamá. Even I know that. He's been doing his best to make her happy. "Was it a mistake?"

Pain scrunches his eyes. "I hope not. But I'm not free to be the man she deserves. When I run my hands through her hair, I can't believe that she doesn't feel how much blood there is on them."

"Ewwww, viejo!" I do not want to think about quiet moments between Frank and Mamá.

Frank says, "I've always put duty above all else. That hasn't changed. I went off script with the Krom. But that's because I believe he poses no threat to HGB, or to Earth. Or to you."

"Janvier wants to take HGB in a more positive direction. Move past chocolate." Ay, I can't believe I'm defending the guy.

"He's lying." Frank grip on my arm tightens a little too hard. I make a noise, and he lets go. "Sorry."

"People change." I dig in my bag and take out Frank's ID. Those cherubic cheeks y inocente eyes smile up at me with the hope of a future that didn't happen. I hold the card out.

Frank takes it. "Where on all the worlds did you get this?"

I can't tell him about the Murrydragon being on Earth. That would complicate what is already turning into a precarious situation for the mindworms – and another legal problem for me. So I keep it vague. "At the bottom of a shaft drilled into a mountain, in the arms of a girl who's probably been muerta as long as your backpack's been missing."

Frank lets out a soft, pained noise. He doesn't ask how I got to the bottom of said shaft. "We never found Rhonda. She must have starved down there, after the cave-in."

I put a comforting mano on his. He's right. It doesn't feel diferente than anybody else's hand, despite everything he's done with it. All the people he's killed. "One time, Tawny told me to ask you about weapons that could destroy a planet's core. I thought she was talking about Kayla's planet." The Nitarri home world was destroyed when the core erupted.

Frank's eyes widen. "Well, isn't she just full of surprises?"

"Tawny also said it's the one question that might push you far enough to kill me, with or without orders from HGB." My mouth goes dry as Frank stares at me, looking hurt that I'd think he might still shoot me. Eh? Have we *verdaderamente* reached the point where he wouldn't, even if HGB asked?

"I suppose you saw the spaceship and the bodies?" When I nod, he sighs. "They were part of a group of ecological ransomsnatchers. They find planets with a newly discovered resource or a source of wealth, and they drill into the planet's core to introduce a device to induce a planet-wide natural disaster."

"That matches up with–" I can't say it matches what Murry said. "–what we found inside the ship."

"You went inside?" Frank looks curious.

I nod. "They were horrible people. Brill destroyed some of their more distasteful cargo."

It's the first time I've seen Frank speechless. I can practically see him reevaluating the Krom. He believes, like most Earthlings, that Krom are greedy and don't care what effects their trading can have. Honestly, they're more about opensourcing everything so people can't fight over it.

I say, "You're the reason Earth didn't blow up, the way Nitarri did."

Frank nods. "After planting their weapons, these 'benevolent' aliens would step in and offer to help – for a price. I believe the Nitarri refused to ransom their world. They probably didn't think any species would be superior enough to fix a problem they couldn't handle on their own. Earth got off lighter – though I doubt we would have ransomed our world either."

"Pero *you* didn't get off light. It derailed your life." If all of this had happened in '92 – eight years before I was born – I would never have existed if Frank hadn't been there. If he – or someone with him – hadn't killed the planetary ransomsnatchers. Ni idea how to feel about that. "How did you get involved?"

"I was on a camping trip with a dozen friends from high school. We were near the caldera up on Haleakala, watching a meteor shower, when that alien ship streaked out of the sky. It was after the war, and in defiance of Earth's closed borders.

Maude, Rhonda, Xavier and I wanted to find the ship, photograph it, and report it to the authorities.

"It took us days to figure out where the ship landed. They'd already planted their eco-bomb and were collecting samples of cacao, in case the planet did detonate. They'd approached HGB and made their threats – which amounted to forcing Earth into a protectorate position to Gevexix."

"Greftash," I correct. "They're the ones who wanted the cacao."

Frank's lips make a thin line. "Never heard of them. The Gevexix are the planetsnatchers. Their home planet won't claim the ships officially, but the crews are of their species."

"Lo siento. The Gevexix." I gesture at him to continue. I cannot believe Frank's opening up like this. I'm afraid he'll remember who he's talking to and stop. I can tie in Greftash later.

"Some guys from HGB had followed the aliens to their ship, but got captured. We saw the HGB crew get taken. We'd been mountain climbing, so we had the gear to rappel down the shaft. By the time we caught up, the aliens were packing to escape the disaster – and arguing whether to kill the team or just leave them to die in the magma."

"You must have been terrified." What would I have done? No sé. Certainly not shoot all the bad guys. "You rescued the HGB team, at the cost of your innocence."

Frank nods. "The first person I ever killed was a Gevexix. He held a potted cacao tree against his chest with two hands while shooting at me with the other two. The bullet went through the pot, and blood, dirt, and cacao leaves exploded across the cavern. I'll eat chocolate, but it always reminds me of blood and death."

"Pero why weren't you hailed as a hero?"

"We hid the incident, both to escape retribution from the Gevexix and to avoid exposing Earth's vulnerable position. This proved a diplomatic mistake. When rumors circulated that a Gevexix ship had disappeared in Earth's solar system, the alliance the Gevexix belonged to nearly invaded."

Hope crunches up in my chest. "How was the crisis averted? Dios mio! Was it a legal tactic? Maybe we can do the same thing to stop the Zantites from invading us."

"Don't get your hopes up. Several chocolate-addicted civilizations, including the Zantites, stepped in to keep the Grevexix's coalition from damaging the cacao plantations. Garfex's father was king then."

"Oh." That crunched up hope goes flat.

This explains why Frank believes that holding onto chocolate is the only way Earth can win enough friends to stay safe. Everything with the Pure Rot and the cracks in Earth's choco-monopoly must be pushing on all of his anxieties.

"That's when HGB recruited you, no?"

Frank nods. "They recruited all three of us. I married Maude. A few years later, Xander became disloyal. The day I ended his life was the worst day of mine. Worse than the day my daughter and son-in-law got spaced. Or when Maude died."

"*You* killed him? I thought–"

"You assumed HGB had my friend killed, and that I'd be vaguely resentful. That maybe you could use it to drive a wedge between me and my employers." He gives a rueful smile.

"You give me too much credit." I need uno o dos minutos to absorb this. Frank killed his best friend in the name of HGB. It hurt him deeply. If everything that's happening now makes that sacrifice seem hollow, that could break Frank.

Maybe Mamá *has* made a mistake and Frank will break her corazón when he implodes – or turns on us to prove his loyalty. Pero maybe not. Maybe she's seen something truer in him than the rest of us can imagine.

The bus arrives, and I stand. "I am not abandoning mi vida."

Frank stands, too. "You are not taking public transportation."

"You're coming with me, viejo?"

Frank clears his throat, and holds up the ID card before slipping it in his pocket. "This reminded me that some things are worth fighting for." He smiles. "By which I mean your mother and you. Not necessarily the Krom."

That's fair. He has no vested interest in keeping Brill alive. And whatever Frank's reasoning, I need his help.

CHAPTER FOURTEEN

The driver stops out front of a run-down building that once might have been an IHOP. Surf boards frame the sliding glass doors. A neon sign proclaims The Dead Fish in bright yellow, next to a cartoonish picture of said fish, with x-es for eyes. The whole thing feels much more commercial than I expected.

Frank pays the driver and gives me paper money, in case I need to bribe the piano player. Los miro. It's been a long time since I've seen paper bills, but they still spend.

"Since you're young enough to be my daughter, might as well give them the wrong impression. Especially since I'm the distraction." He takes my arm in his. "Shall we, my dear?"

"As long as I don't have to kiss you." I wrinkle my nose in mock horror.

If anyone had told me yesterday that I'd be walking into *anywhere* arm in arm with Frank Sawyer, I would have said they'd gone loco.

It's mid-afternoon, uan the bar's not crowded. An open dance floor lies between a stage and a tiki-hut style bar. Tiny tables ring the edge. The stage is empty, and the lights are up. Canned music plays in the background. Ay! Where's the piano player?

Frank walks us to the bored bartender. "Whiskey for me and a glass of red wine for my niece."

The guy snorts and gives Frank a look that means *if that's your niece I'll eat this dishrag*. Pero he doesn't look closely at me.

I giggle. "Do you have any yewstral? I've always wanted to try it."

I figure that will sound like I'm trying to get something more expensive out of my date. It works – the bartender seems even less interesado in me as he puts two glasses on the bar.

He fills mine with bubbly rust-colored liquid. Moisture beads on the flute. I take a sip. "Oooooh. Yummy."

I do like yewstral, mucho, and this is a good vintage. I haven't had any this good since Jeska gave me some of his private stock aboard the *Layla's Pride*. Like many foods produced on Krom, this stuff's medicinal. It saved my life once.

Frank smiles at my glass. I wonder if he's remembering the phone conversation we had after I'd escaped him and went on the run. It had been surreal. Frank was the assassin who was supposed to kill me to recover the cacao pod I'd stolen. I spoke with him after Tyson had bitten me, and Frank'd told me a bottle of yewstral might counteract the venom long enough to buy me time to turn myself in.

Frank makes eye contact, and the smile fades. He's not happy that my contact isn't here, and he doesn't have much to go on for a backup plan.

I give him the tiniest micro-shake of mi cabeza. We'll have to improvise.

Frank turns to the bartender. "I've heard this is where Pitch hangs out." Pitch owns the place, and his name keeps coming up in connection with my potential kidnapping. Es aterrador. He's not exactly the person I'd wanted us to talk to.

The bartender freezes. "What do you want with him?"

Frank shrugs. "I have information. Might lead to something he's looking for."

I'm discovering I don't like it when Frank improvises.

The bartender gets that unfocused look, and the muscles in his jaw twitch, like he's talking on a sublingual. Finally he says, "Pitch is intrigued. Take a table, and he will come talk."

"You hear that, honeybunch? You get to watch me work."

"Excelente." I wave my glass at the bartender. "Another."

Frank chooses a corner table near the stage. The bartender pours me more yewstral. I take it and then follow Frank.

Mac the piano player finally shows up, coming in from a back room. The front of his clothes are soaking wet, pero he doesn't seem to care as he ambles to the piano, which is on the other side of the stage, near the bathroom. He's maybe thirty years old, with dark eyes and dark hair. He puts a vase of flowers on the piano. The canned music stops, and he launches into a pre-contact Jazz standard.

I let out a breath, hoping no one notices my relief. Todavía, before I can go request a song, Pitch comes out of the back. He's a thin, twenty-something white guy with sandy blonde hair, wearing a sedate-ish Hawaiian shirt and a cowrie shell necklace. He looks like he'd be at home on one of those surf boards.

Frank introduces himself as a bounty hunter with close ties to HGB. Using his real name, he places his ID on the table.

Pitch nods at me. "Who's this wahine?"

"My niece," Frank insists again. "I'm no space case. Those trips can get long, you know." Ewww. He's implying that I'm his traveling companion. I hide my reaction. Frank sets his phone on the table, displaying a pic of Brill from last night, sake cup in hand, ridiculous disguise in place. "I'm looking for this young man. The bounty on him is significant."

Pitch squints at the picture. "Never seen him."

"Are you sure?" Frank asks.

Pitch sighs. "I thought you had information to offer."

"I do. I understand you are interested in getting a certain girl off this planet. I have access to her media schedule, and I can tell you where she'll be at two p.m. tomorrow. In exchange for him. And fifty thousand dollars."

I really, really don't like it when Frank improvises.

"I'm afraid it's too late for that. He … well, he drowned." Pitch looks back toward the door Mac had come through. Mac, with his wet clothes.

My heart lurches, and I suck in air. Ay! Ay! The glass trembles in my fingertips. I drain the yewstral to hide the reaction, pero I'm not alchafuzzed.

It's almost impossible to drown a Krom. They have book lungs, similar to some Earth arachnids. The tissue will hold air for hours and hours, without them even needing to breathe. It *is* possible that, if Pitch and Mac didn't realize mi vida isn't human, and they didn't check too hard for a pulse, they might not realize Brill's faking muerto.

If he didn't die of something else. Tension builds in my shoulders. That grief pendant in my purse is making me feel claustrophobic.

Frank grins. "Even better. Saves me the trouble. I'll take the corpse now, and the cash when you have possession of the Princesa."

AKA me. The face of HGB. La Princesa de Cacao.

As the two of them negotiate, I roll my eyes, look bored. Inside, though, I'm terrified that Pitch is going to recognize me. I pick up my glass, saunter over to Mac, sitting by him on the piano bench.

He jerks back in surprise. I drop cash into the tip jar. "I'm here about the goth guy."

Mac keeps playing and whispers, "Take your money back. You're too late. The kid really did drown. I pulled him out of the lobster tank myself."

"Please," I lie, "I need something off the body."

Mac reaches the song's end. While he shuffles through some sheet music, he drops a metal key into my hand. He starts playing una cancion diferente – *a different song*. "Just be quick. Pretend you're going into the bathroom."

Frank and Pitch seem in deep conversation as I slide off the bench and head to the door. The key turns effortlessly, and I slip through into a large storage room behind the stage.

Outside, past an open cargo-sized door, there's a stack of boxes and bags – kitchen trash – with a clear leaf bag nestled among them. It holds mi vida. Mac bent Brill's legs so that his knees are near his chin. The bag's knotted tight. Mi vida's not getting air. Brill can go a long time without needing to breathe, pero his still chest freaks me out. With his wet hair plastered to his pale forehead, he really looks muerto. Brill's gun and pocketknife have been carelessly tossed into the bag with him.

Maybe he really is dead. And they're throwing mi vida out with the trash.

I stifle a sob, turning it into a mild squeak, when inside, I'm trying not to shatter into un millón pieces. The room doesn't appear to have any cameras or signs of trouble. I race across the room and reach out to unknot the bag.

A hand hits my shoulder, and a gun barrel pokes my back. A woman's voice asks, "What are you doing here?"

"Nada, por favor." I'd been so focused on Brill, I hadn't even register her coming up behind me.

"Riiiiight." The woman marches me back into the storage room, just as Pitch opens the door and gestures Frank in ahead of him. The gun moves away from my back, and the hold on me shifts to my forearm. The girl holding me bobs her gun, asking for permission to shoot me. Pitch gives a subtle head shake.

"Go ahead," Pitch tells Frank. "Take your corpse. But we'll take our Princesa now." Five armed guys charge through the open doorway.

Pitch steps close to me and swipes at the exaggerated blush with a thumb that comes away red with makeup. "Did you think that would fool our facial recognition software?"

"I hoped." I bat Pitch away. My nails scratch him, drawing blood.

He grumbles a curse and glares. I am so muerta.

"Por favor." I don't have to act to look aterrorizada. I move as close as possible to the door, without giving Pitch idea that I might bolt. I take un mejor look at the ominous bag. "Why did you kill that man?"

Please, please don't let Brill be dead. My chest squeezes at the thought of saying goodbye to him like this. Heat builds behind my eyes.

Pitch wipes the makeup on his jeans. "He was asking questions about our smuggling operations. Who we worked with, how we got things off planet."

Frank and I exchange a look. My chest goes cold. If this muchacho's being that open about his illegal activities, he doesn't plan to let Frank walk out of here either.

I play for time. "What happens to me now?"

"The Commodore didn't say. You get to live long enough to be transported onto his ship. But after that?" Pitch shrugs.

Pitch knows who this Commodore is. If I'm careful, maybe I can get him to tell me.

"Why would he want you to kidnap me?" The lump of fear in my throat is still more for Brill. I keep blinking, as I force myself not to look back at the bag.

Pitch shrugs again. "The Commodore doesn't like you. Something about a vapgun and his friend."

The only time I've handled a vapgun was aboard the *Layla's Pride*. I tried to shoot Crosskiss, pero only zapblasted his insignia and made him angry. Later, though – when Brill and I tried to sell the stolen cacao beans – I hit a space pirate with the back end of a vapgun, cracking open the casing. The blue goo inside burned the guy. Pero the pirates involved – including Jack Wolfe, their captain – are in prison. So ni idea who would be mad at me.

Unless Jack has escaped.

An automated trash truck backs into the doorway, and a pair of oversized drones starts tossing trash in the back.

Frank grabs me, pressing the frío barrel of his gun against my temple.

"Viejo!" I feel my panicked heartbeat in my ears, especially the one behind the gun.

Frank growls, "If I shoot her, your Commodore won't like it."

A half dozen gun barrels come up, trained on Frank's forehead.

"You wouldn't kill her," Pitch says.

"You sure about that?" Frank growls. He's muy muy convincing. "Better than me dying for nothing and you getting what you want."

Pitch warns them not to fire as Frank drags me into the truck's cab and pushes me to the driver side. He locks the doors as the drones finish loading. A hologram blinks, counting down from sixty, in time with a beeping alarm. A chirpy AI voice says, "Counting down to compacting. Please make sure all staff are clear."

"Drive!" Frank shouts. "I have to override the compactor function, or your Krom really will be dead in a minute."

Cold jolts through me.

"Vale!" I switch the steering wheel off of autopilot and punch the gas. I haven't driven a car in a long time, and this one's a lumbering monster. I jump two curbs, and smash the corner of a wooden fence, pero I get us on the road.

"Please drive more carefully," the vehicle tells me."

"Por favor," I tell the hologram. "Please. Deactivate."

"Command not recognized," the voice says.

"Turn off the compactor," I shout.

"Command not recognized."

"You are un estúpido piece of metal junk," I tell it.

"Command not recognized." The beeping stops, turns into a long solid whine, and I feel the mechanism in the back starting to move. Ay no! I suck in air, unable to make myself breathe back out. There's only a few more seconds. I force enough breath to say, "Con rapidez, viejo!"

"Right." Frank rips off part of the dash, and pulls out two wires and taps them against two other wires. A shower of sparks erupts. The noise stops.

In the silence, my hands tremble against the steering wheel. My limbs feel weak. Please, please let it have been in time.

I tell Frank, "If he survives, then I will forgive you for using me as a human shield."

A blush breaks across Frank's cheeks and nose. "Sorry about that. They needed to believe I might actually kill you to save myself."

I'd been half-joking to break the tension, but Frank really feels bad about it. "Oye. It's diay. At least you *didn't* kill anybody this time."

When we get far enough away from the bar, and I'm fairly certain we haven't been followed, I pull over on the side of a rocky stretch of road, with the beach on one side and an elevated area on the other. Between the two of us, we get the compactor to release and pry the back of the trash truck open.

"Mi vida?" Mi corazón feels fragile. I can't stop my hands from shaking. He so easily could be dead in there.

Trash rustles and moves. Brill's cut his way out of the leaf bag, and he's crawling out of the trash. He's still not breathing. The effect is eerie.

"Damn," Frank says. "Now I see why some people call Krom zombies."

Brill climbs down and moves away from the truck before drawing a breath. "You wouldn't breath in there either, Mr. Sawyer, if you didn't have to. Shtesh! I stink as bad as it does." Brill casts a longing look at the ocean.

Frank nods, and Brill races off to take a quick, fully-clothed dip. He dives in and disappears. For a long time. At least he's not wearing another leather jacket that would be ruined.

Frank shades his eyes, trying to find any sign of Brill. "He needs to stay out of sight. Those smugglers think he's human now, but they won't if they see him walking around breathing. And you need to stay inside the HGB compound. Out here, you're fair game."

"I laughed when Tawny said I wasn't to leave HGB unescorted – for my own safety." Dang if she wasn't right. Again.

When we get back in the garbage truck, Frank drives and makes me sit between him and Brill, who still doesn't exactly smell like a fevxaqil. I take mi vida's hand.

"I'll drop you within walking distance of your hotel," Frank tells Brill. "Then I need to ditch this truck on the other side of the island."

"Hanstral to be so much trouble, Mr. Sawyer," Brill says.

Frank rolls his eyes. "At least tell me you learned something."

Brill nods. "Wal. After they thought they'd drowned me, they pulled me up out of the water, snapped some pictures of me and started making phone calls. Those su's aren't Earthlings. They're from Greftash. And their Commodore is too."

"So not Jack, then," I say. Jack is from Earth. "Pitch and Mac looked and talked like Earthlings, right? And that contract we found was written in a form of English."

Brill says, "Maybe it's like when a stalker gets obsessed with particular holostar. You've become the face of HGB. If they could get you to betray Earth with enough camera feeds rolling, that might scratch the itch they're looking for."

"Or they might still want to use Bo to force the Zantites into war," Frank says. "Like they hired Jimena to do."

"We don't know that was them," Brill points out.

"Maybe they're loco FeedCast fans. Or think they can trade me for cacao trees. Or something." These are all unsettlingly viable possibilities. "We know they want to ransomsnatch me, and that they're trying to–"

Frank slams on the brakes and pulls into a little parking lot near a boarded-up sugar cane juice stand. The momentum throws me off balance, and fear sparks through me. I'm starting to trust Frank won't hurt me, pero it's such a secluded spot. And his face has an icy expression. Mi corazón hammers, even though he just rescued me. Brill's body language goes stiff and nervous también.

"Give me your hand," Frank says. He reaches into his jacket and Brill sucks in a short breath. Frank pulls out a thin case, a little bigger than my hand. He cracks it open, revealing several vials of liquids, a rubber-banded wad of cotton swabs, and a digital display.

"Su. You carry DNA processing equipment?" Brill leans over to get a closer look.

"Sometimes HGB thinks it's important to verify that we eliminated the correct target. Or we want to keep someone on file. There's a whole database that gets crosschecked for all sorts of things. My DNA is in there." He gives Brill a rueful grin. "I also sent them yours."

As proof of death. Brill swallows visibly. "I never could figure out why you picked that loose hair off of my seat."

I hold out my hand. "You want to prove that Pitch isn't human, no? To give us leverage?"

Earth's borders remain closed. Unless Pitch has a super-rare special diplomatic visa – like the temporary one Brill had once – Pitch could be executed for just being on this planet. That would give him un muy buen incentivo to rat out his employers.

"And enough evidence to get HGB actively involved in protecting you and unraveling what these Greftashians are up to." Frank runs a swab under my nails. He swishes it in a vial of the liquid, and then dips in a paper strip, which he places into the machine.

The machine beeps. Frank looks at it, then looks closer. "This can't be right."

"Que?" I ask.

"The sample shows two distinct DNA sources. One is you and the other is an unknown human male."

Eh? "So Pitch isn't a Greftashian?"

"It could be Greftashite," Brill says, trying to lighten the mood.

Frank shoots him a glare. "He's an Earthling. But why would he lie about that?"

We leave Brill in another empty parking lot, close to his hotel. Frank's agitated and seems in a hurry to ditch the trash truck before someone tracks it, so I don't get out. Which means I don't get to kiss Brill goodbye – let alone tell him I'd accidentally kissed Daschel Janvier.

CHAPTER FIFTEEN

Frank has access to the garden gate, so after we clean up at a gas station and Uber to the compound, I don't have explain to anyone where I've been.

Frank pulls the gate closed a little harder than necessary. "I need to walk Botas before he makes a mess on the floor. He's a good dog, but he has his limits." Frank heads into the compound. He must have a room in the same building as mine. He's not the only one on a time crunch. I'm cutting it close to make the dinner Tawny set up, so I can continue my diplomatic duties.

And yet I pause and look back at the gate Frank locked behind us. I'm trapped inside HGB. For my own safety or no, that makes me itch. And I've been pulled away from Brill again, right when I want to hold him and reassure myself that he's okay. That he's *breathing*.

Gravel crunches. Janvier is walking through the garden. It seems to be one of his favorite places. Janvier catches sight of me. "Bodacious, that dress looks stunning."

"Gracias, Mr. Janvier." I want to put emotional distance between us. I'm terrified he'll kiss me again, that just by being here, I'm leading him on.

"Call me Dash." He flashes the full wattage of his smile – and those dimples.

I blink. "You said to call you Shelly."

He hesitates. "Oh, that's right. Depends on my mood, you know? So, are the holomercials close to wrapping? I can't wait to see them, and you must be eager to get back to Zant."

"Mijo. Didn't you ask me to stay?" I'm confused.

He blinks. "I – well …"

"You thought I would say no, even after you tempted me with these treatments? You have no idea what it's like to live with IH, no? Leaving will be agony for me now."

"But you have to, eventually. Zant won't wait forever."

"I know. And I will. Por favor, I have to get ready for tonight." Janvier's smile returns. "I will see you at dinner."

"Cierto." I leave the garden. Pero, before I head to my potentially-bugged room, I need to chat with Murry. This Dash–Shelly business worries me. And now Janvier wants me to leave, instead of staying to change the course of HGB by his side. In short, he's acting like someone under the influence of a mindhug.

I find a quiet corner of the grounds and call Chestla on my handheld.

"Are any of Murry around?"

"Several. I've been explaining what a ceremony of salt means. He's trying hard to understand that mingling an individual's ashes with those of their ancestors is different from becoming part of a hive mind." She sighs. "Why?"

"I need to talk to him, and I want to see one of his faces."

Chestla takes me outside, where a spuck lounges in the sunlight. Chestla holds up the holo of me, and the spuck sits up and waves a claw hand. The phone says, "Hi, Bo!"

I ask, "Do you have a hug on Daschel Janvier?"

The spuck shows its teeth, managing to look offended. "I did. Over a year ago. But after about two days, someone needed him to test chocolate, and I couldn't figure out how to make him not do it, so the hug died."

"So you didn't influence him to make HGB New?"

The dragon looks embarrassed, dropping its cabeza almost to the ground. "I whispered to him that carob was just as good as chocolate and might be a direction to explore. The idea probably didn't fade after the hug disconnected. But that pink packaging he did on his own."

I suck in a breath. Janvier made a statement to the Galactic Court and a separate one to the press in defense of Murry. He might recant if he found out he'd been infected with the parasite.

"Mira. Honest that wasn't you I just talked to in the garden? Daschel sounded a lot like Kaliel did when you were in his brain."

The dragon flips over, looking at me upside down. I swear he picked up more from being Frank's corgi than he realizes. "The only me on your planet is the one with Eugene."

If Janvier isn't suffering from the influence of a mindworm, what *is* going on with him? There must be some record of Janvier's activities in his office. Pero how would I get in there to look?

"I think Murry's telling the truth," Chestla says. "I've gotten pretty good at telling when he's lying."

"I hope they believe that when they try me for my life. I could use a character witness." The spuck shows its teeth. "Now that the Galactic Court has questioned all my friends, it is sending special investigators to examine me. They will be here in a couple of days."

He's scared. My heart hurts for him. "How are you feeling, mijo?"

"Tired. Tired of running, and tired of hiding what I am. That's one thing I learned from being Kaliel Johannsson, and then watching him face a Zantite execution squad after the hug died. I did the things he was accused of, when I was him." Murry forced Kaliel to set that bomb on Minda's set, and then to run and to do things to save Kaliel's body that went against Kaliel's moral code. "And when I wasn't him anymore, he didn't run to save himself. As long as they don't find out about Awn, I won't run either." The dragon scrunches up its mouth. "Probably."

The mindworms hadn't understood that before. Murry has learned something from every person – and Corgi – that he's been. Cierto, he has made such strides, becoming a beneficial species on Evevron. He doesn't deserve to be destroyed.

Even if the law says he should be.

No sé what to say, and forcing Murry to dwell on his probable fate seems cruel. Which leads to an awkward silence.

Murry pushes a holo-link to my handheld. The preview shows a still of Chestla's abuelita, standing at a podium, her dark hair pulled back from her determined-looking face. Murry's voice breaks. "My creators stood up for me, even though confessing they made me puts them at risk of death. They're outraged that I was hunted, and they're bringing counter-charges. This is part of the pretrial debate."

I play the CastClip. Grammy's reflective, slit-irised golden eyes glint with protectorangeation. "Evevron is *not* a Class 082 planet. People cannot land illegally and hunt without a permit. Murry is a sentient species, and we chose to share our region of Evevron with him. That hunting party committed murder."

"But this is a hive entity," a guy of the same species as the hunters says from a podium in a different room, possibly a different planeta. "Killing a few members of it barely damages the whole. While my clients admit to trespassing, and disabling a pursuing ship, they can barely be held liable for bodily harm, let alone fourteen counts of murder."

Grammy growls and looks like she's about to leap over the podium, pero since these feeds are patched together, it's not like she could attack the smug lawyer. "Every individual in this hive has unique experiences. At what point is it damaging? What minimum number would you name to consider Murry whole?"

The lawyer looks discombobulated. "That's a question more for philosophers than the courts. It's also relevant to consider the complaint your neighbors on your own planet lodged. They claim that your illegal experimentation occurred without their knowledge, and they never agreed to share the planet with another alpha-predator species."

Oi! The Galactic Court does its best to respect each planet's internal laws. That's a more damaging argument than anything offworlders might say. Murry said Chestla's people had achieved a fragile peace with their neighbors across the river. They'd ceased hostilities over agua – because Murry's been re-shaping the water table. Ay-ay-ay! Wait until the neighbors learn that the five individuals making up Patient Zero were from their side of the river. Disagreement over Murry's right to exist could dip them back into war.

Grammy smiles, showing her predator's teeth, and even filtered through the holo, it's chilling. "That is a purely internal matter. This court has little to say on the circumstances of civil war, as long as atrocities are not committed."

"Such as the use of genetically engineered bio-weapons?"

"Murry is not a weapon."

"Have you seen those teeth?"

They're both leaning over their respective podiums, breathing heavy.

That's una gran acusación.

The clip bounces to the judge, who holds up seven of his tentacle arms in a beseeching manner. "Perhaps we should all take a moment to calm down."

I take a deep breath, too.

The camera shifts to Leron, at a different podium. Behind him, a group of terrified Evevrons sits in a row, their hands in their laps – his fellow scientists and codefendants. Producing and then covering up the Mindhuggers – with the original intent of mindhacking other people – is one of the few offenses the Galactic Court itself holds punishable by muerte.

"I still can't get Leron to talk to me," Murry whines across the feed, as Leron speaks to the judge.

At the podium, Leron accepts the blame, doesn't ask for mercy. He confesses to putting the five Evevrons that made up Patient Zero into the cryostasis pods, knowing they could not be revived. Pero at the end, he stretches his fingers and says, "Everything we did was wrong. I can't deny that. But if I could undo it? A few months ago, I would have, without hesitation. But I've watched holo of the spucks' accomplishments, and they are astounding. I've read reports on Murry's psychological progress, and I for one wouldn't be prepared to destroy that, even to undo my own mistakes."

One of Leron's coworkers takes the podium, briefly grabbing Leron's hand as they swap places.

"Dios mio, Murry, can you believe he said that?" I wipe tears from my eyes, watching the Evevrons defend Murry with every bit of their collective alpha-predator protector/nurturing power. Absolutamente. They made him, and they're finally taking responsibility for him.

Murry shuts off the courtroom holo, appearing in the field again. "You once said that the Zantite court showed Kaliel mercy because they realized he was not a threat. Because he was sorry for all the pain he caused. Won't the Galactic Court do the same for Leron?"

"Oh, mijo." I wish I could tell him the answer es sí.

"I don't expect they will find the same of me. I'm a parasite. And a science experiment. I can't prove I deserve to live. I lied to the court when I said I didn't have any parts of myself outside of the Mountainous Continent on Evevron. If they find out that I'm also on Earth, helping Eugene, it will be worse."

"How's the research going?" I ask. "If you can solve this problem, the court might decide you're a beneficial species.

The spuck sits up. "You know how I said the plant disease has no cure?"

"Sí."

"Yeah … there's still no cure. I've been watching the feeds. People are starting to suspect something's wrong with Earth's chocolate supply."

I sigh. "I know. We're running out of time."

The dragon gestures with its cabeza at Chestla. "Eugene keeps asking about her. Should I tell him a me is with her?" He addresses Chestla. "I don't mind passing messages, even love notes."

Chestla's fair freckled cheeks turn bright pink.

I look at her. "Eh, amiga? Should he give Eugene hope?"

She looks at her glitter-polished claw-nails. "I've never been good with guys. I never thought I'd have to choose between two of them."

I smile. "I've watched enough novelas to know that in a love triangle, you're choosing between two futures."

The spuck nods. "Because as an individual you can only live one life. Bo told me that's why you watch holos in the first place – to see the other choices."

Chestla shrugs and looks hopelessly lost. "But they both fit."

CHAPTER SIXTEEN

I call Gideon Tyson. When the holo comes up, Tyson is in his saucer. His face is still missing scales.

I try not to laugh. "I thought you weren't leaving the spa until you finished your molt."

"I need to be with Murry, after te trial. If I can make it in time." Tyson holds up his manos with their missing scales. "Not tat tere's much I can do for him."

"I know one thing you can do, amigo."

"What's that?"

I explain about Murry's reaction to Leron's testimony. "Leron was forced to freeze those people. If he didn't, six people would have gone into those cryostasis pods instead of five. That's enough of an extenuating circumstance to justify something other than his death."

There's a pause, as Tyson watches the CastClip. "He doesn't tink so. He trew his lot in with te rest of te defendants. I can't be his lawyer, Bo." Tyson made some errores malos in his past that barred him from pursuing his passion for law. "But I will testify for him. Tell him to call me. Even if it is virtual, I'll be tere for Leron, when te time comes."

"The enforcers haven't come to talk to me yet," I say. "They've been gathering testimony from everyone else. You said not to flitdash, pero should I be getting nervous?"

"Hold on." Tyson types something into a keyboard attached to a display. "Tey haven't approached you because someone filed an intercession request. Tat has to be dealt with first."

"Who would do that?" I ask.

"HGB."

My brows furrow in shocked puzzlement. Is HGB afraid of what I'll say? That I might somehow implicate them? Or are they honestly trying to protect me? More of what Tawny said about HGB taking care of their own?

No sé. I've never been more conflicted about how to feel.

Before I see Janvier at dinner, I need to know what's going on with him. I want to search his office – pero breaking one of the floor-to-ceiling windows would be imprudent, y getting caught going through the ceiling ducts would be difícil to explain. Mi plan es simple. After Janvier showed up at the filming yesterday with those kalltet flowers, everyone here must know that he's attracted to me. I'll play along with their assumptions. No lasers. No bionets. And if the guards turn me away, I won't even be in trouble.

I stop at the employee store, looking for a gift for Janvier. I find a hunormous teddy bear with a chocolate bar sewn to its paws. Es perfecto.

I head to the main building and tell the two guards, "I want to leave this in Janvier's office."

"Wait here," one guard says, while the other takes the teddy bear. He looks me up and down, stopping at my legs, bare between my boots and the short formal dress. "Our CEO has good taste."

I roll my eyes. Pulling this off rests on unwavering confidence. "Will this take long?"

The other guy scans the teddy bear for bugs and explosives, and feels it to make sure nothing solid is inside. "Nah. You're good, Miss Bodacious."

"Gracias!" I smile at him as I take the teddy bear. "I'll just be a minute. I need to write him a note."

I walk down the hallway, through the thicker and thicker doors. Nobody stops me, even when I open Janvier's office door. I close it behind me, set the teddy bear on the floor and flick on the lights.

I open the drawer where Janvier had tossed the data stick I brought. It's not there – he must have followed up after all and sent it to someone who could understand that data. Muy bien, no? Pero the drawer holds a stack of paper file folders. The top folder contains una gran colección de death threat letters, some printed out – y some creepier ones that must have come through the mail. A few with drawings of guillotines. More people still want to see me get shaved than Janvier, pero he has a real number of haters.

One of the creepiest hand-written ones simply says, *In retribution for the pain of the people of Greftash, your world must burn.*

The terrolting emotion in the handwriting's uneven letters sends piel de gallina – *chicken skin* – prickling down my arms.

Someone wrote on the bottom of the letter. *Greftash? Never heard of them.*

The glass in front of the chocolate fountain slides open. I jump. "Dios mio!"

The security robot comes out of a hidden alcove. "Found what you're looking for?"

It has a hand on the gun at its hip. Ay! I assumed the bot would be shadowing Janvier. It draws the gun. I squeeze my eyes shut, expecting to be shot.

Pero nothing happens. I open one eye and then the other. The robot is waiting for an answer. Did I find what I was looking for?

"Not really. I want to know why Shelly is acting so strangely." I hold up the letter. Mis manos tremble, so the paper shakes. "But this is just a bunch of death threats."

"You want to help, right? And we're good to just talk," the robot says. "I don't have to shoot you to protect him."

"Absolutely. Por favor." My mouth has gone dry, though I'm feeling less in immediate danger.

"You're looking for this." The robot holsters its gun and detaches a tablet screen from its chest. The tablet is showing a classified-looking file on Greftash. "Don't dig through anything else."

"Vale." I take the tablet. "You're worried about him, too."

It shrugs. The face is an impassive mask. "As much as a robot can be. His behavior has changed, and I find that unsettling."

I scroll past the title pages on the file to the abstract. I read through the first paragraph, and my understanding of Earth's history shatters like a dropped blown sugar bubble. "Dios mio, robot. Have you read this?"

"No. That data is irrelevant to my duties."

Right. Robots have no natural curiosity. "The Krom First Contact wasn't really our first First Contact. The planet that sent Shelly the threatening letter – Greftash – their populated continent started out as a prison colony. From Earth."

The robot doesn't get why I'm upset. Pero almost forty years before the Krom landed, another group of aliens came and offered to take Earth's worst undesirables off our hands – for a price. They made clandestine deals with many of Earth's pre-HGB governments and shipped people off to help colonize un nuevo planeta. Something went wrong, and the Greftashians had revolted. Part of the power that would become HGB – a part that had nada to do with chocolate companies – came together after so many people secretly went missing. They worked to prove aliens existed, and to close Earth's borders. Even when, after the Greftash revolt, the aliens stopped taking people. HGB had had good intentions and a righteous beginning.

"Does this explain why they are angry with Mr. Janvier?" the robot asks.

"Sí y sí. It explains todo. Why they poured everything they had into the space race. Why they tried so hard to get chocolate. And why Pitch's DNA scan came back as human."

"Who or what is a Pitch?"

I ignore the bot's question. "This isn't Oceans 11. This is E.T. again. Sort of. Mixed with a bit of Blade Runner, and maybe a touch of Iron Man."

The Bot is silent. It probably doesn't know my movie references, or understand the fascination with recycled pop culture that results in those films being remade over and over – or treated as too "classic" to be touched. There's no time to try to explain. I need to finish up here before the guards come to check up on me. I return the tablet.

This revelation explains a bit about Janvier's changed attitude towards la galaxia. He must have examined this information and found out that HGB wasn't originally what even he thought. I put the folders back in the desk drawer. Eh? At the back lies a bottle of medication, stripped of its label. It could be antidepressants, or some other mood-leveling medication. Could that be enough to explain Janvier's inconsistent behavior? Maybe?

I've made it outside the building when Kaliel calls my sublingual. I start to tell him what I've discovered about Greftash, when he bubblechatters, *This was a mistake, Bo.*

Que? Is Tawny making your life miserable too since you told her you love me?

Not yet. Kaliel laughs. *Look, I never should have landed on the moon. I lost Kayla's brother.*

Ay! How?

We were at a restaurant. He left with a bunch of rough-looking people just as I was coming back from the bathroom. I thought he might have gone voluntarily, but then I found that DNA cylinder under the table.

That's Stephen's proof of his heredity. He never would have forgotten it. *Why call me? If Stephen's conscious, Kayla can communicate with him.*

I hoped you had a better idea. Kaliel's sigh rolls through mi cabeza. *She's already mad at me for helping Stephen, but you know how stubborn he is. I thought if I helped him, I could keep him safe. Because you know me. I always have to be the hero.*

Sí, he does. And that's what I liked about him.

Lo siento, pero this time you have to ask Kayla for help.

I was afraid you were going to say that. He hangs up.

I picture Kaliel. I can still acknowledge that he's hot, but now, doing Tawny's beso spin-clips would be uncomfortable. I told

Chestla that the trouble she's having choosing between two guys relates to her trouble choosing a future.

Pero now that I'm not at the mercy of the IH withdrawal, I could turn that question back on myself. In a 'verse where Kayla and Brill didn't exist, I could have fit with Kaliel – the one who didn't run to save himself at the risk of others, even when facing a Zantite execution squad. Para esa materia, I could have fit with Jeska, the Zantite diplomat cast out of his society for following his conscience instead of putting other people at risk. And as much as it galls me, I've sparked with Janvier, who seems to be embracing change to improve people's lives.

Uan, what makes Brill the one guy I can't live without? He's risked himself for me. And he has a heart as big as the others. Maybe bigger. I doubt any of them could have stopped Murry from fleeing in terror and spreading as a plague. Pero there must be more to it than that. Brill's complicated and flawed in a way the others aren't. What does it say about me that I want a future with him? And what does it say about me that I'm selfish enough to think I deserve one?

CHAPTER SEVENTEEN

I haven't even reached the residence building when two HGB goons in dark suits stop me. One says, "Mr. Janvier needs you in his office, now."

My heart jolts. Oi! Janvier said he would talk to me after dinner. He must have been notified that I snuck into the office. How mad is he? Tawny said he wouldn't shed blood on that plush carpet. Pero Janvier's made several exceptions for me already … What's one more?

The two goons escort me across the compound and into the main building. The guards who let me in earlier barely look up, like they expect me. The goons stand chatting with them, leaving me to continue on solitaria down Janvier's private hallway.

When I open the office door, Janvier's smiling, focusing on a camera drone hovering in front of him. Que sorprendente. *Amazing.* He laughs and waves me to a chair beside his massive desk. The teddy bear still lays on the floor where I left it.

Thoroughly flusterfused, I sit down.

"Bodacious is here now," Janvier says to the drone. "Let's get started."

"Good." A low, grumbling voice speaking clipped universal comes through the room's wired-in audio system. "Please state that you both give this testimony freely, without coercion or hope of monetary gain."

"I am." Janvier looks over at me.

No sé what we're talking about. Surely, Janvier's not suing me for breach of contract because of the nanites. I did his holomercials – except for that one. Pero I do my best to hide my ignorance. "Sí. I am."

"Good," the voice says. "For the official record, in exchange for your freely given cooperation, you are not being charged in this matter."

Are we talking about Murry? Is this HGB's intercession?

Janvier says, "The Court will confine its case to the Evevron scientists and the thing they engineered, as long as you and your friends aid the investigation."

The pride when he says it implies he negotiated this little trade.

Uf. Relief pours through me. I won't wind up isolated in jail.

Y then I feel selfish. Murry's fighting for his right to exist. I swallow hard. "Why are you testifying también?"

Janvier shrugs. "You asked me to."

This is a step or two more than I'd asked. Maybe I misjudged Señor Call-Me-Shelly.

The voice says, "Mr. Janvier, please state your interest in the entity collectively known as Murry."

Janvier smiles shyly at me. "Several citizens of my planet recently visited Evevron, where they interacted with Murry." He continues through the dry formalities of his testimony. Then he says, "How is it fair to hold a creature at fault for the circumstances of its birth? Murry did not choose to be created as a parasite, and he has done his best to satisfy his need for a host without damaging sentient beings. The spucks he now occupies were a pest species. Limiting himself to that form is a sacrifice he made as a gesture of goodwill. He may have started life as a science experiment, but that doesn't mean he doesn't have genuine humanity beating in his primitive hearts. After all, aren't all of us just searching for acceptance?"

Janvier's eyes have softened, like on some level he's talking about himself. Daschel Janvier, the cold-hearted CEO of HGB feels kinship with the geneflipped monster. Extraño, no? Porque why would Janvier feel out of place? And why would he want people seeing the truth en his corazón? Aren't too many secrets nestled there for him to want light shone in on it?

When Janvier's done, the voice asks me about my experience with Murry.

Es imposible to recount fully, not without making Murry sound so peligroso the court wouldn't dare let him live. The first time I met Murry, he'd killed, kidnapped, infected or threatened most of the people close to me. I sigh. "Think of Murry as a child, por favor, one who was abandoned, and abused. A child who experienced violent death, who saw people fear him. A child who is finally coming to understand what it means to love."

I talk for a while after that, pero Janvier's affectionate looks distract me.

Afterwards, when the camera drone settles on a shelf, Janvier says, "That was a beautiful statement, Bo. I hope it helps. How many people do you think can look past Murry as a scientific freak to see the hearts of gold inside?"

I bristle. "Don't call him a freak, por favor."

Janvier smiles as he stands up from his desk and takes those few steps to where I sit. He takes my hands and pulls me up so that I stand facing him. He moves in like he's about to besarme again. Instead he says, "Not everyone would say that. Like not everyone would have brought me a teddy bear. You must be coming around."

"That was meant as a thank you," I improvise. Though when his smile crumples in response, I see I've accidentally hurt him.

When I don't lean forward to be kissed, he steps back. I feel conflicted, wanting to like Janvier as un amigo – uan he still wants something more, something I can't give him. And he seems almost okay with that. Which makes him even more likeable. Pero he's still HGB. And he's the guy who ordered a hit on my boyfriend. Where is the ruthless puppet master who would be so easy to hate?

As I leave Janvier's office, one goon still stands near the door. He walks with me to the main hall.

"Where's your friend?" I ask.

"There was a disturbance on the grounds. Ever seen this guy before?" The goon flashes me a stillholo of the bartender from the Dead Fish, his eyes wide in terror, as the other HGB goon stands on his back while wrenching the bartender's arms behind him. Two other HGB hombres stand in the background of the image capture.

"No, mijo," I lie. "Is he dangerous?"

The goon shrugs. "Not anymore."

Oye! A chill goes through me. Pitch's men tortured Brill, and they're trying to ransomsnatch me. Pero sthesh! It's horror-heavy to think one of them just died out on the lawn.

And I'm no closer to figuring out who's asked them to kidnap me. It has to be Jack Wolfe, the pirate named for the twentieth century painter. I told Brill as much. Pero it can't be Jack the Earthling. Or can it? It's possible that the Greftashians are backing Jack for their own reasons, and Brill misunderstood what Pitch and his friends said about their Commodore.

Brill is, ahora mismo, following up on what we uncovered at the bar. He promised to work from his room, out of harm's way. He discounted my theory on Jack, but he's trying to find another lead.

As I head back to my room, I send a text to Gavin, Brill's mejor amigo and my benefactor. I still don't understand the limits of mine and Gavin's nueva relationship. When the Zantites had had Brill slated for execution, Brill made me a promise on Gavin's behalf. I became Gavin's trevhonell, which is a socially binding thing on Krom. It's a bit ironic, because Gavin isn't a fan of Earthlings. And now he has to look out for me.

I ask, *Is Jack Wolfe still in prison?*

The Galactacops don't advertise the locations of their prisons or prisoners. Gavin's muy bueno at getting information. If anyone knows the whereabouts of the space pirate with a grudge against me and Brill, it will be him.

Gavin texts back. *Brill just asked me the same thing.*

So Brill hadn't discounted my theory after all. Bien, no?

Gavin adds, *Jack and his crew escaped while the Galactics were bringing them in. He called me the other day with a recruiting message. You remember Jack set me adrift once in the cargo hold of my own ship. To die of heat exhaustion. Sthesh! Why in the molten heart of Krom would that kek think I'd work with him now?*

I laugh, trying to picture how that conversation went. *Did he ask about his jacket?*

Back aboard the *Layla's Pride*, Brill stole Jack's leather jacket, after his own got ruined. It's una minúscula, pointless obsession, pero Jack seems to want that scratched-up brown leather back. Up until Brill donned his layered-tee disguise, mi vida had still been wearing it. Despite the patched bullet hole from where a different pirate had shot at him.

Frank's right. I keep putting Brill in danger. He's almost been killed on my account at least three times. Four, if you count the pressure plate down in the cave. As much as I love my Krom, at what point should I let him go?

Gavin texts back, *Jack did mention that jacket. Which was in extremely poor taste, considering Brill's supposed to be dead. I told him we buried Brill in it.*

My phone shows Gavin's typing something else, and then deleting it. And then he sends, *Are you sure you can't renounce citizenship of Earth? Your people keep doing kalltet things, and it would be better for Brill's family honor not to be associated with that.* After a pause he adds, *Avell.* Please.

Oye! Frustration builds in my chest. *Like what, mijo?*

Like intentionally limiting the genetics of your cacao trees to one variety that turns out to be highly susceptible to disease. Do you know the Nilka are just outside the Sol system, investigating the rumors that there's a problem with chocolate? Su's are bound to panic. Rumor is that Admiral Alabaster himself is demanding to see Earth's cacao plantations, but Earth's representatives keep citing closed borders and that the Nilka were once part of the coalition threatening to invade.

Dios mio! I did not know that. How am I supposed to face all those people tonight, with this new danger at our door? What can I say? For once, I need Tawny. And ni idea how to find her.

How do I not have Tawny's phone number? En serio?

I let Gavin go and make a beeline for my room. The phone there has a direct line to the concierge. When a woman picks up, I ask, "Can you put me in touch with Tawny Kamaka?"

The woman hesitates. "Miss Kamaka left the facility. She requested that no messages be forwarded. She assures everyone that she will be on time for dinner tonight."

Oye! Tawny's still mad at Janvier for co-opting her project and at me for kissing Janvier. I bet he's been calling her. Tawny built her life around her job. For her to turn her back on that – that beso must have hurt her deeply.

On my bed lays a dress, another formal gown. This one's red and slinky, with gemstones on the bodice and a slit halfway up the thigh. I'd begged for a chance to wear something like this. Pero now the dress will make me shimmerpop negativo, on so many levels. Beside it, a box holds a couple of chunky glass bracelets, and one tight, elaborately-patterned metal one.

Brill texts that he wants to meet on the beach outside the complex, before the dinner starts. I haven't decided what to tell him. He's my life. Pero he keeps risking his life for mine. I'm hazardous to his health. Pero can I bear to let him go?

I put on the red dress and do my makeup and hair. There's no way I'll find all the bugs Tawny's put in with the gemstones, and I'll have no time to change later, so I cover the bodice with a thick, sound-muffling shawl.

Frank helps me leave through the garden gate.

El no está feliz – *He's not happy* – with me leaving the complex, pero the beach isn't far, and he seems to understand that I need to talk to Brill.

In one hand, I carry the basket of the remaining picnic food for Brill to take to his hotel, to make it easier for him to stay out of sight. In the other I hold my shoes, so I can walk barefoot across the sand. The basket still holds lots of goodies, most unopened. Including that can of Surströmming. No es sorprendente. *Not a surprise.* Brill and Kaliel are the only people I know who like fermented fish.

Mi vida's still in disguise. The brown contacts, the boy-band hair and the jewelry overload are the same, pero he's ditched the layered tees in favor of swim trunks and water shoes. Krom are superhumanly hot – slightly mas grande and somehow more imposing. The sheer sight of Brill's washboard abs makes me lose my resolve to give him up.

I run to him across the sand. I put down the basket and the shoes.

"Sthesh, Babe! You look amazing."

"I could say the same about you, mi vida." I laugh, running my fingers through his dark locks. "Though I still can't get used to the hair."

"It makes for a solid disguise, revwal?" He kisses me gently, just a quick brush of lips that won't mess up my makeup. "I can't believe those su's though I was human, even after they tried to drown me. I was sure they'd feel my heartbeat when they pulled me out of their lobster tank."

I shudder at the horrible image. "Just be glad they didn't shoot you instead."

He shrugs. "They weren't done questioning me. I didn't want them to get around to shooting me, so I let them think they'd gotten carried away and left me under too long." Now *that* image sends ice through my veins. He smiles and adds, "Ni idea what I was going to do if you and Frank weren't there when that trash truck showed up. Uan, if I'd had to fight my way out, they'd have known for sure I'm Krom."

"How'd they even catch you?" I ask.

"I was distracted. The bartender hit me with a stunner from behind." The look on his face – still vulnerable and scared – makes my mind up for me. It's muy estúpido for him to be on this planet, where everyone wants to hurt him.

I swallow a lump of sorrow. "I can't take this anymore. Looking at you muerto like that … Tu mamá was right. I am going to get you killed."

"What are you saying, Babe?"

I take a deep breath. "I want you to leave. Por favor. Before Frank has his meeting, and you wind up back in HGB's lasersights."

"Ga, Babe." He traces a finger along my jawline. The touch is electric, like I'd never worn that mourning pendant at all. "I came here to protect you. That's what I mean to do. Up to my last heartbeat."

"I'm not worth that." I feel my bare feet sinking into the sand as the wind whips the edges of my red dress. "Eschucha mi bien. You have three hundred years of life ahead of you. I'm just a blip on that graph, no?"

"Don't say that. I told you, we'll look for the fountain of youth plant. And if that doesn't work, I'll deal. I'll–"

"I kissed Daschel Janvier." I hurl the sentence at him, intending to hurt him – the same way he's hurting me. He still thinks that for our relationship to be fair, he has to find a way for my lifespan to match his. Pero I need him to love me for what I am. I see the pain in his eyes. Y I keep going. "I kissed Daschel in the garden right over there, under an avocado tree, and sparks flew that left me breathless."

"I know." Brill looks straight at me, and I would give anything for him not to be wearing those contacts. "That's one reason I'm not leaving. I've learned that love is worth fighting for, and I won't step aside and let some kek pull you into a future you'll regret."

I blink at him. "And what kind of future are you promising me?"

Brill's lips take on a serious line. "I'm not in a position to promise anything. I wish I could, Babe."

I suck in air. Que? Is there some reason Brill *can't* propose? Some of the things he's said, about happily-ever-afters. The depth we've achieved to our relationship. It's felt several times like he wanted to propose – but he always stopped short. "What does that mean?"

He shrugs. "I haven't made my fortune or my reputation, so my family wouldn't let me choose my own future on Krom. And I certainly wouldn't be accepted here. Even if I tried, it would mean giving up every connection I've worked to build back home. How could I provide anything for anyone else? Not for years."

The air rushes from my lungs. I thought he'd hesitated porque I'm not Krom, porque I'd embarrass his parents. Pero it's because he doesn't think *he's* good enough.

Brill is so much more than he knows. He deserves a future, a chance to take care of someone who won't implode the minute the IH shakes come back. "Frank doesn't think you'll live through all of this, so if you stay, you won't get the chance to find out what you might accomplish. Please, mi vida. Don't die for me."

"I intend to save us both. If I left now, I couldn't live with myself." Brill tangles his fingers in my hair. "And if I stay away from you much longer, I'll start to lose something that means more to me than anything ever has."

I touch his face. "Te amo." *I love you.*

Brill blinks, and the edge of his contact slips. His iris is the color of naked jealousy. "How many sparks flew between you and Janvier?"

Before I can answer, a beach cruiser vrooms to a halt, and Tawny steps down onto the sand. My heart freezes. If she's found out Brill's alive, an HGB assassin won't be far behind. No, por favor.

She frowns. "I asked you not to leave the facility. And you risk your life just to meet up with some beach bum?"

I guess my shawl covered the cameras – pero did nada about the tracker. Still, is it possible that she hasn't recognized mi vida?

Brill turns away, hiding his face.

It's too late. Tawny does a double take. She circles around to take a good look at Brill, reaching out to turn his face towards her. "How are you not dead?"

"Freak chance, a lost dog, and a heck of a lot of healing foam?" By which mi vida implies that said dog found and dug up the shallow, sandy grave Frank claimed to have left him in back on Zant. Frank drove Brill out to just such a spot, a beautiful cove full of thick plants and sandy soil, before changing his mind – in part because of the Mercy is a Gift campaign.

Brill brings a fist to his chest and double-taps the massive, mostly-decorative scar Frank gave him to simulate a messy gunshot wound. It's muy muy convincing. At the time, it felt like overkill detail, pero now it could well save Frank when Tawny turns this information over to HGB. It even matches Frank's report – that he shot mi vida en el corazón.

"A massive gunshot wound? In a Krom?" Tawny looks skeptical. She knows that Krom don't bounce back well from blood loss. She was there when Brill nearly died over a nicked vein in his wrist.

Brill shrugs. "I'm as shocked that I'm alive as you are."

"You okay down there?" the Asian muchacho driving the beach cruiser asks. He's got thick hair and intelligent eyes, and fills out his long-sleeved tee respectably well.

"I'll only be another minute." Tawny turns to me and bites her lip, genuinely fizzbounced. She drops her voice to a whisper. "Hosei's one of our transport drivers. He's been pestering me for a long time to go out with him. I've been aiming a little higher, but he's cute, don't you think?"

This would be adorable if Tawny didn't have mi vida's life in her hands. I say carefully, "Sí, chica. He has a certain charm."

There's a pause. None of us want to return to the real subject.

Finally, I say, "Tawny, por favor–"

"Be glad this didn't happen yesterday, when I wasn't mad at Daschel." She scrunches her nose. Then she turns to Brill, holding out her hand for him to shake. "Hi, Bo's new boyfriend. I'm

Tawny Kamaka, Bo's publicist. I don't think I caught your name."

"Ricky," Brill blurts. "Ricky McGillicuddy."

Tawny scrunches her nose again. "Someone's been watching a little too much *I Love Lucy*."

Brill shrugs. "You put me on the spot."

"Well, Ricky, make sure Bo gets back into the facility in the next twenty minutes. After all, the dinner is in her honor." She climbs back into the cruiser. Her face appears next to Hosei's. "We're getting ice cream at this place down the beach. I'll be at work when I'm scheduled and not a minute before."

"Pero, Tawny," I say. "How should I handle tonight?"

But Hosei's put the cruiser in gear, and they're off in a peel-out cloud of sand.

Brill steps in front of me, shielding my dress. "Did she say that su's name is Jose? I thought that was a Latin name."

"Ho-se-i. It means bird. Perfect for a pilot, no?" I pause. Brill tilts his cabeza, obviously curious why I know that. "I, eh, dated an actor with that name for about a month. A long time ago."

Brill frowns, but lets it go. "So did Tawny just agree out of the kindness of her suddenly romantic heart not to tell HGB that I'm alive? Or will there be strings attached?"

I shrug. "Your guess, mi vida, is as good as mine."

CHAPTER EIGHTEEN

We're still on the beach when Chestla calls. I pop up the holo. Her face is very close to the phone, giving the impressing that her green catlike eyes are ten times normal size. I flinch away.

Frantically, she asks, "Have you heard from Nellet?"

"No. Why would I?" Princess Nellet is Chestla's kaenn – *person she has sworn to another to protect with her life*. Which es muy diferente from the relationship Chestla and I had – as her cesuda ma I was her employer, and while she did protect me, I made choices and she had to adapt. Uan with a kaenn, the job is as much nanny and mentor as protector.

After the ceremony where Chestla became Nellet's Guardian Companion I met the girl a couple of times before I left Evevron. She's Earth-equivalent seventeen or eighteen and kept asking questions about becoming a media star on Earth. She wanted to know all about mi planeta. Especially current fashion and music. Pero when I asked questions, she was reluctant to answer. Especially when I asked what happened to her previous Guardian.

Chestla says, "I'm afraid she's with that boy from the other side of the river. He came over here with a peace delegation, and he marked through his entire dance card for her. They were limiting security forces, so I couldn't attend the ball, so I never even met him."

Ah. Amor a primera vista. "They've kept in touch, right?"

Chestla nods. "Via holo, all the time. She keeps talking about how their love will unite the region. But the war's heating up now that the secrets about Murry have been blown open. Several members of our last hunting party have gone missing." Chestla pulls the phone back. She's wearing a simple white top with a square neck and decorative edging. She'd worn it before, to introduce me to her council of elders.

On a planet where amethyst dust stains everything, white garments are a status symbol that Chestla wouldn't wear every day. She probably just left the ceremony of salt. I hope Murry's found some peace, now that those parts of him kept on ice for so long have been burned to ash and given respectful rest.

"Nellet probably took advantage of the distraction of the ceremony to call her hermoso again, no?"

Chestla bares her predator's teeth. "I spoke with the prince's Guardian down at the riverbank. He was looking for his kaenn. On his side, there's a missing starship. He believes they're heading for a planet that will do a legit marriage ceremony with few paperwork requirements. I thought Nellet might have called you, since you're the only person she knows with experience traveling on the run."

"Oye! It's not like I was muy successful, right? I got bit by a Myska and addicted to the Invincible Heart."

My phone beeps, signaling another incoming call. It's Nellet.

"Let me call you back, amiga."

The girl, flushed with excitement, asks for a list of safe spaceports to stop at for fuel and food between Evevron and Praxion 5. Which, if you want a quickie wedding and a stunning backdrop for a tropical honeymoon, is just about perfect.

She looks pleadingly. "You won't tell Chestla, will you?"

I sympathize with Nellet's passion and hope. Pero she's young, and mi amiga is her Guardian. I shrug and say noncommittally, "Mira, why would I do that?"

Tawny must have felt like this, standing on the sand watching me and Brill, deciding whether our amor should have a chance. But more is at stake than just love. There's peace. And family. Chestla's from the side of the river known as Pendosha. Patient Zero consisted of criminals from Curtsar. And that geography line is the only real difference between them.

When I call Chestla back, I ask, "Could Nellet's plan actually unite the region?"

Chestla nods. "It's possible. Nellet's a minor princess, but the guy she's with is his region's crown prince. Their marriage would force people on both sides of the river to consider each other family again. Sort of like an anti-Romeo and Juanette."

"Juliette," I correct. Though I'm impressed she knows the story. Chestla hates tragedy.

"Romeo and Juliette. Those two could have solved everything by just going, hey ma, we got married, now deal with it. The fallout from that would have made a much more interesting story." Chestla sighs. "Evevrons sometimes get married as young as Nellet and Watae are. But if I let that happen, I'll get sacked as Guardian Companion. Besides, I've never met this guy. How do I know he's worthy of my kaenn?"

"Maybe you should meet him and give him a chance."

"I may not get a choice about meeting him. If he's put Nellet in danger, he'll be lucky to escape with his life!" Yet Chestla hesitates. "With Murry's help, we have started repairing the ecological damage from the changed course of the river, decades ago. If the courts order him destroyed, we won't be able to finish the project. Getting Curtsar to drop their complaint about our research would go a long way to saving Murry's life – and maybe even some of our scientists." I know she feels guilty that HGB's deal included her and Ball, pero not her otros amigos. "But I can't allow my kaenn to sacrifice her future for such ideals. Our culture doesn't believe in marriages of convenience."

"Maybe she loves the muchacho."

"Then she needs to do this right." Chestla bares her teeth. "And that means I get to vet the guy and his family. And his parents and hers have to agree to the match."

Which won't happen.

An hour later, Chestla sends word that a party of Evevrons are pursuing the runaway couple. The Guardian guy from across the river insisted on going, and Ball said that if some strange hombre was taking off in a starship with Chestla, he was going too. Leron somehow got dragged into it. It's surprising that the Galactics are letting him leave the planet, pero he's been chipped, so they can track him.

I tell Brill, "Part of me hopes they don't catch up to Nellet and Watae in time."

Brill laughs. "See? I told you love is worth fighting for."

Then Brill kisses me, deeply, no longer caring if he's smearing my lipstick. The hesitation en mi corazón's still there, pero that layer of distance between us grows thinner. Tal vez it's because he finally explained why he hasn't proposed. It makes sense. With a Krom lifespan, they probably don't feel the need to marry as early as Earthlings. But that's another mismatch between us where something will eventually have to give.

Pero, in this moment, I can push the future away and just appreciate that Brill is vivo, with warm lips to kiss me and strong arms to hold me, no matter what happens.

There's a series of whistles and shouts. I open my eyes. A jeep full of teenagers passes us on the sand, and they're cheering us on. Embarrassed, Brill pulls away. Krom are shy about public displays of affection. Brill may be less traditional than most of his familia y amigos, pero his culture is still part of who he is.

My lipstick is smeared across his cheek. He says, "You should get back. We need you on Tawny's good side."

I wipe the lipstick away. Then I look at that faked scar on his chest. Part of me still wishes he was leaving. And part of me couldn't bear to see him go.

Once I'm in the complex, lipstick back in place, I head towards the building that houses the ballroom.

A guy near the main building is kneeling down, examining the wall. I'm guessing he's paparazzi, fizzbounced for the rare chance to look around inside the HGB facility. Ni idea how he got away from his chaperones, pero it seems like all bets are off today, since Tawny's abandoned her hyper-vigilant post. The pops have never been kind to me. Nada y nunca. Pero I won't tell on him to HGB.

"Hola!" I say, walking past him.

He jumps, then tries to cover the motion by picking a dandelion. He doesn't think I'm buying that, does he?

He goes with it. He moves onto the sidewalk, looking uncomfortable as he tucks the dandelion into the buttonhole on his suit coat, like that's what he planned all along. He's six-foot-three, with brown eyes, black skin and a fade haircut.

"Are you lost?" I ask.

He shrugs. "I'm supposed to report for a debriefing."

"Nobody's in the office this late."

"I know I'm late." The guy looks even more nervous. "I'm Kaliel Johannsson, pilot and former fugitive from justice."

I muffle a laugh, turning it into a cough. That is not Kaliel Johannsson. This muchacho bears a passing resemblance to Kaliel, pero Kaliel's eyes are gray-green. And he's not nearly that tall.

This imposter's not another would-be kidnapper. If he's trying to pass himself off as a guy everyone knows I've kissed, he has no idea who I am. Todavía, even if this guy doesn't know me on sight, he's probably heard my name linked with Kaliel's and will realize I've seen through his disguise.

I call Frank on my sublingual as I say, "Monica McGillicuddy."

Curse Brill and his I Love Lucy reference. The fake last name slipped out, thanks to the way my neural patch holds onto language. And my subconscious admitting how badly I want to marry the su who calls himself Ricky.

Frank bubblechatters, *What's wrong now?*

"You don't look like a McGillicuddy," Not-Kaliel points out, studying my Latina features.

"And you don't look like a Johannsson," I reply. Over the sublingual, I tell Frank where I am, and that I may be in trouble. I smile sweetly at Not-Kaliel. "If you're looking for someone to report to, they're all at dinner. The building isn't far. I'm headed there now."

I hold my breath as I walk past him. This guy won't try to pass himself off as Kaliel in front of half the HGB staff.

"I'll wait," he says. "It's rude to show up at a function uninvited."

"Vale." I hurry away, pero I feel him watching me. When I glance back, he's shadowpopped.

As I enter the ballroom, I spot Tawny at a corner table – and she's brought her pilot. He cleans up well and looks just as at home with a champagne flute in hand as he did behind the wheel of that cruiser. Tawny could work with that.

I head towards her. I need to find out what she expects me to say. Are we even acknowledging that the Nilka are in the neighborhood and that when the butterfly people are angry, they make the Zantites look like minnows?

I freeze. Mi hermano está sitting solo at a front table. He pulls nervously at the knot in his tie. Mario is not usually a tie kind of guy. I cast a dirty look at Tawny, who gives me a beatific smile and gestures me towards Mario. He's got a speaker placard in front of him on the table.

Anger floods through me. Mario was only supposed to be here to visit the archive. Now they're putting him on stage. Which is exactly how they started with me. Mario's got a wife y niñas. What if something happens to him?

"Hola," mi hermano says. "Looks like I'm your opening act."

"Bo!" Someone waves at me from deeper in the room. Someone with gobs of dark curly hair, pale skin and wide-set eyes. Someone who's secret Nitarri royalty, masquerading as a newly graduated, human culinary arts student. She's dressed in chef's whites.

"Kayla!"

She rushes to hug me.

"Stephen?" I ask.

She grimaces. "I can't find him. I'm staying busy, to try to stop thinking about it. I'm teaching my assistants how to make galaxy sundaes, like we used to at Snedik's."

Kayla and I worked there our second year in culinary arts school. The choctastic sundaes were their showiest desserts, using edible nanites to make the ice cream spheres float up in a spinning representation of the Larksis planetary system, with a rippling fudge ribbon for the asteroid belt. Ay. Nanites again.

I force myself to sound feliz. "Does the sundae still become Larksis?"

Kayla grins. "They wanted us to do it with the Sol system. We're trying to make everyone feel good about Earth's prospects. You'd be amazed how much chocolate they allotted for this dinner. It's in every course."

When choco-prices are skyrocketing.

I ask Kayla, "You got Fenzet-pau's chocolate syrup recipe? En serio?"

"I made up my own. The test-tasters said it was even better than Fenzet-pau's."

We share a laugh, pero suddenly the humor falls away. Kayla's finished school, moved on, started a business, while making peace with her past. I'm still stuck in the mess I've made of my present, still at odds with my past, and unable to picture the future.

Finally, Kayla says, "Why haven't you graduated? I keep checking the alumni boards for your name. Wasn't the show with Minda supposed to be your final exam?"

"Minda's set got destroyed before anyone could evaluate my edible nanite project. And I haven't had time to schedule another final." Which is a lie, no? I could have found time.

Janvier comes up to me. "May I speak to you?"

I give him a tight smile. "Have you met mi amiga Kayla? Her new company is catering tonight."

"Charmed, I'm sure." Sparing Kayla barely a glance, he pulls me away to an empty spot near the stage. Porque he's used to ignoring anyone dressed for menial labor. Which is annoying, even if now he's standing just a little too close, looking all handsome in his suit. "Have you seen Eugene?"

"No. Why?"

"Because he's supposed to be here. I sent word today that he needs to give an update. I need that information by eight o'clock, and if it's good news, I need him to give a speech."

I sigh. Janvier doesn't know Eugene. Nada. The botanist doesn't trust HGB, and he doesn't like people. Demanding he show up is probably the easiest way to be sure that he won't. "Mijo, you should have sent a transport, or had me go talk to him."

"There's no time for that now." Janvier forces a smile, like nothing importante is going on. Pero, eight o'clock is a very specific time.

He clasps my hands in his, and it's obvious from the warmth of his touch and the way he runs his thumbs across my palms that he still wants me, even after I responded to his beso with bafflement and hesitation – despite the sparks. "Not a hint of the shakes. It seems the treatment has been effective.

"Sí. I–" I feeling the effect of those dimples all the way to my toes. I wish he hadn't kissed me. Because if I didn't know what his lips felt like, I wouldn't have so much trouble not staring at them. He seems muy, muy sure that the soap opera trope will work if he gives it time – that if he keeps showing up and being devastatingly handsome and charming, eventually I'll be the one kissing him. I focus on his eyes, which are warm and kind and that flusters me worse. I swallow, hard. "Gracias. I haven't felt this well in a long time."

I catch Tawny staring at us. Only this time, her eyes are laughing. Of course, Tawny thinks it's fun to watch me awkwardly rebuff Janvier's advances, now that she knows I won't give up Brill for Daschel.

Is she fizzbounced Janvier's still available? Or is some lingering crush smoldering in her corazón, despite everything he's done to her and her project? Or maybe she's still angry at him, and anticipates his reaction when I finally tell him no. I don't care which, as long as it gives her a reason not to tell Janvier that Brill is alive.

Mario scowls, obviously having caught the interchange between me and Tawny and the intensity between me and Janvier. El no esta feliz.

"I'm almost glad the treatment isn't permanent." Janvier releases my hands, but doesn't step away. "It gives you a reason to stay here. Though I don't want to see you suffer. Or lose you to needless self-destruction."

I still feel his touch on my palms. "You ask me to stay. You tell me to go. I'm not sure you know what you want. You're not who everyone says you are, no?"

He looks flusterfused, then turns up the wattage on his smile. "You mean I'm not ruthless and cold? I assure you I can be, if the situation warrants. But this thing with the cacao disease has shaken me up."

It's more than that. And if his problem's not a mind worm, then I need to figure out what is. Frank comes in, giving me an excuse to turn away from Janvier. Pero Frank supposedly assassinated my love. It wouldn't be natural for me to go up to him or to ask him questions. And Tawny doesn't know that Frank knows Brill's vivo. She seems to have bought Brill's story that Frank left him in a shallow grave, without knowing Brill survived the assassination attempt. Uan I can't call Frank on my sublingual and risk Tawny picking up the crosstalk. And Frank doesn't know that Tawny knows about Brill still breathing. Ay-ay-ay. It gives me a headache.

Frank gives me un minúsculo head-shake, meaning he found no sign of Not-Kaliel. He strides over to Tawny, asks her something I can't hear.

Janvier is responding to a text. *Contact Eugene again and make sure he has left the plantation.*

Whatever is going on with Eugene es importante, after all. I almost forgive Janvier for dissing Kayla.

I walk over to Tawny, who sits alone now that Frank and Hosei have moved a little distance away, and are in deep conversation. Eh? They know each other. Does that mean Hosei is something more sinister than just a pilot? I sit by Tawny. "You've been watching the news underneath the news."

Tawny downs her champagne before answering. "For once, I haven't."

"For once, I wish you had." I whisper. "The Nilka are near Earth, porque they've heard rumors our chocolate is ruined. When these chicos here find out the truth, they'll panic. You always have something scripted for me to say. How do I diffuse the situation?"

Tawny points at me with her champagne flute and whispers, "Pretend you know nothing about it. Be your usual charming self. Tell them about being on Zant and about culinary school. Show off Kayla and her nanite sundaes." Tawny rolls her eyes and brings her voice back to normal levels. "That's advice anyone could have given you. Gawd. I'm not even sure anymore why I'm here. Daschel takes me for granted, thinks he can replace me with a firm run by two twenty-year-olds."

What to do with this version of Tawny? I can't let her spiral out of control. What if she changes her mind and tells Janvier about Brill? "I don't think Janvier wants to replace you. And if you want to show him how much better you are than these other publicists, maybe I can help you figure how to sell all that carob."

"*You* want to help *me*?" Tawny looks taken aback.

"I owe you. For today."

Tawny laughs. "And someday, I may well collect. It's nice, holding something over you that actually has the power to keep you in line."

"How can I show you I'm grateful?" Whatever it is, bien, I'll do it.

"Check in with the gossip feeds tomorrow. I shipped you and Daschel using the holo I got walking up to that kiss. Nothing personal. It just embarrasses him to have a private moment shared, while at the same time making HGB look more human. It was also very satisfying at the time."

"Vale. I'm sure it was." I'm not seeing the favor.

"Painting you torn between Team Kaliel and Team Daschel without making you seem fickle and ruining your approval rating will be a lot of work. Your cooperation will help." Tawny sighs. She has dark circles under her eyes. "But right now, I just want to think about Hosei and what he looks like with his shirt off."

"Are you just playing with the poor boy?" I ask.

"No." Tawny shrugs. "Not entirely." She looks over at him, her expression somewhere between amusement and affection. "I haven't decided. But I'm tired of not getting to decide things like that, because I've put my job first. I signed on with HGB when I was fresh out of school. It felt perfect, right here on the island where I grew up. And then one night, I met a guy, a rich rancher who was on the island for a conference. He wanted me to marry him, but I would have had to move the mainland, and HGB was in crisis … again." She flags down a waiter, who gives her another glass of champagne. She drains it, then says, "Looking after the fate of Earth is tiresome."

As I head back to the table, I catch snippets of talk. People are dressed up like tonight is something special, pero they're still absorbed in the same old conversations, unaware that anything is going wrong with their world past Janie's bad grade in school and Javier's delayed promotion. Mario gestures Frank over to sit with us.

Frank asks Mario, "Why are you here?"

"Janvier found out I was in the compound and sent me a request – and a suit – a few hours ago. He said it would be a way I could support mi hermana."

Frank and I glance at each other. That doesn't sound bien. Janvier is definitely up to something.

Frank asks, "And HGB hasn't asked you for anything else? Not information, not to say something to Bo, not to join their writing staff."

"No. They just want me to give my canned book speech." Mario points at Janvier. "You think he has an ulterior motive?"

"Not necessarily," I say, at the same time Frank says, "Yes."

I exchange looks with Frank again. The hardness he sees in Janvier – it's like we're talking about two totalmente diferente people.

I change the subject. "Hermano, when you were looking through the archives, did you run across anything about the planet Greftash?"

"Greftash?" Mario squints. "Never heard of it."

CHAPTER NINETEEN

Mario's first libro is about choco-history. He gets up on the stage, adjusts the microphone at the podium and talks about Earth's accomplishments for a few minutes, then embarrasses me by showing some historyholo of us as niños. There's even one of me in a diaper and tee-shirt, holding a churro, while Mario y Papá work on a go-cart. Frank smiles at that one – though he killed one of the people in that image. It has been so long since my father's death that Papá's face in my mind is fuzzy. I don't remember him looking this young. And I certainly don't remember the outline of a gun in his pocket. There's a lot about mi papá I still don't understand.

When Mario passes me to sit back down, I whisper, "Those holos better not be part of your standard speech."

"Of course not, Pequeña." He grins at me. "But how often do you get to introduce a hero who's also your little sister?"

I make a face at him, then head for the stage.

I keep my own speech short, and then I answer a lot of questions like, "How did it feel to be inside a Zantite's mouth?" and "What's the grossest food they made you eat on Zant?" and "How did it feel to watch a Zantite officer execute one of his men with his teeth?"

I answer diplomatically, pero they're the morbid questions of people who believe they are about to be invaded and want to paint their enemies as faceless, grandes monsters.

I finally ignore the hands and talk about Minda, whom I consider una amiga. I tell everyone how Minda thought I was beautiful because of the way my hair moved. And how, while she – like all Zantites – was bald, I found beauty in the way light gathers to her skin. And that I'd used goggles that simulate Zantite vision to see Minda as another Zantite would – and the whirls and points of her heat lines were the más spectacular thing I've ever seen. Biologically, I have little in common with Minda. Pero I think of her, if not exactly a sister, as una muy eccentric aunt. Porque what binds us together, what makes us family, what makes us "human" isn't biology or geography. It's something noble in our hearts.

My audience looks blankly back. No sé if it's because I'm not doing justice to the experience, or if they're not prepared to get my point. We don't have to be enemies. I've risked my life trying to convince the Zantites of that. Pero I hadn't realized that someone needed to tell my people the same thing.

It's like what Chestla said about the Evevrons who had been frozen in the cryostasis pods. They weren't really criminals – they were desperate people trying to save their children and abuelos from dying of thirst, who blew up a dam to reroute the agua they needed. Pero instead of recognizing that and finding a way for everyone to have enough agua, those five were arrested and experimented on. I can't tell my audience that, and if I could, I doubt they'd understand.

Janvier comes to my rescue, escorting me down from the podium. I realize I'd been standing for a couple of minutes, looking out at the audience, seeing them as just as alien as the Zantites or the Evevrons or the Krom. As Janvier helps me into my seat at Mario's table, I wonder if I can belong anywhere after this. Even though Mario's family, I'm not sure even he would get what I've become.

Sympathy shines in Janvier's eyes. "Are you okay?" Even after I nod, he hesitates. Then he says, "I have to go back up there."

I thought I'd come so far, pero this feeling is the same one I had after committing treason and then having Brill abandon me. I don't quite fit on any of the planets I love. And Brill's not going to propose, which means Krom won't be mi tierra either.

Kayla sits in the empty seat next to me at the table. No one seems to notice. Their eyes are on Janvier. Kayla puts una mano on mine, y at first I think she's comforting me, pero she activates my sublingual without it even ringing, something only a telepath could do. A megastrong telepath. Even Murry has to wait for me to accept the call.

Bo, we have to help them.

Help who, amiga?

Bo? Kaliel's in mi cabeza también. He must be talking to Kayla via his handheld. *I found Stephen. I'm on the roof of one of the levitating hotels, hiding behind a closed margarita stand. The guys who took him from the restaurant are torturing him, to get him to tell them where Kayla is. They keep saying if he reaches out to her, they'll find her neural signature. And then they'll let him die in peace.*

Dios mio! I look over at Kayla. *How can we help?*

I don't know. Kyla's face has gone bone white. *It's not like with Murry. His hosts have a standard brain, connected to the telepathic parasite. The standard brain is what I could attack. I can't incapacitate fellow telepaths with telepathic feedback.*

It's too late, Kaliel bubblechatters. *Kayla, they shot him and threw him off the roof. The water's like ink down there. He's gone.*

Kaliel's words punch me in the chest. Ay, no! Kayla's hand trembles in mine.

I squeeze her hand. *He didn't tell them where you are. That's noble.*

She pulls her mano out of mine. *Don't try to make me feel better about this. We were supposed to stay in hiding.* Tears glitter in her eyes as she turns to focus on Janvier.

She pulls her mano out of mine. *Don't try to make me feel better about this. We were supposed to stay in hiding.* Tears glitter in her eyes as she turns to focus on Janvier.

Janvier's finished his introductory remarks, done his best to set the audience at ease. Now his face takes on a serious expression.

"Many of you may have heard rumors that something is wrong with Earth's cacao trees. I am sad to tell you that this is true. We had hoped to find a cure for this disease before it became common knowledge offplanet. Unfortunately, that did not happen. The Nilka, with whom HGB shared chocolate, are demanding quarantine of this disease before it spreads to their plantation."

I let out an indignant squeak. Shared? I'd nearly been shaved for handing those cacao beans over to the Nilka.

Janvier continues, "They're giving us the option of destroying our cacao plantations. Otherwise, they will file an emergency injunction with the Global Court that could lead to our planet's destruction as the center of a galactic plague. We have chosen to destroy the plantations. Our workers and robots have spent much of the last twenty-four hours moving the seed banks, research, biological records, and equipment to areas outside the bionets. Don't give up hope. We live on a large planet. Unaffected cacao may be growing somewhere in the wild, and if so, HGB will find it." Murmurs build in the crowd, and Janvier makes downward gestures with his hands to quiet them. "If you cannot leave the island, please stay indoors for the next few days, and whenever you must go outside, move to your cars as quickly as possible to avoid inhaling undue amounts of smoke."

Cómo? Por qué? My mind refuses to process that they're really burning the diseased trees. Janvier had been stalling, hoping Eugene would help him find a way out of this. Pero Eugene never showed.

My heart jolts. He and the Murry dragon are still in the plantation. Shtesh! The Murry dragon. Whether we get it out, or someone finds a roasted spuck corpse in the plantation ashes, how can we explain that? Both here on Earth and to the Galactic Court?

Tawny stands up, looking pale and shaky. "Daschel, how could you not tell me?"

"I tried to call," he protests. Pero she'd gone off the grid.

I look at Janvier. "Eugene?"

He shrugs.

Ay, no! I'm on my feet, running for the door in my spiked heels before I even think about what I'm doing. "Eugeeeeeennnnne!" It takes a second to realize I'm the one shouting it into the night, like he could hear me from inside the plantation.

Frank runs beside me. "Stop, Bodacious."

He'll tell me to go back inside, that the edge of the burning plantation is un primo spot for me to get ransomsnatched, that there's nada I can do. And he's probably right. Still, I take a deep breath, preparing to defend my decision to go.

Frank holds out his hand. "Give me those shoes. You'll break your neck as soon as the path gets uneven." He breaks off the heels and gives me back improvised flats.

"Pequeña!" Mario calls from inside the room. He looks like he's about to ask to come with us.

I don't want him to. I've become very protective of my older brother. I hurry back to him, taking the opportunity to grab my shawl off the chair, to cover up Tawny's cameras if we do find the spuck.

Kayla is standing next to Mario, still looking devastated.

Kaliel's voice rings in my head, via the link Kayla hasn't closed. *What's going on? What do I do now?*

Kayla needs a real ally. Someone who can protect her, not a ragtag band of rebels. And I realize who is close enough for Kaliel to reach, who might be sympathetic to someone whose hermano was just killed in an attempt to snatch power – and who even the Nitarri assassins won't dare mess with. *Bring the evidence about Kayla's heritage to Admiral Alabaster on board the Nilka ship. Tell him you know me.*

No! Kayla's bubblechatter's whiney. *I want to stay in hiding.*

Haza. She needs to get off the grid. I look at Mario. "Por favor, take Kayla back to your house. Don't let anyone see you together at the airport."

"Vale, Pequeña." Mario sounds confused, pero he moves protectively closer to Kayla.

I hang up my sublingual and dash after Frank, who lets me catch up.

As we race back towards the garden, I say, "You have to tell Mario you killed our father. It isn't fair that he's the only one en mi familia who doesn't know." To the rest of el mundo, mi papá died in an accident, during the course of his job as a firefighter, not in an HGB coverup.

"I know." Frank's barely breathing hard. He's in excellent shape for his age. "I just haven't figured out how. If he tries to retaliate, I won't hurt him. I promise."

Frank takes off through the garden. I'm slower, porque I'm flabbergasted. If Frank can't find a nonviolent way to defend himself, would he really let Mario kill him? What makes everyone want to protect Mario?

I try to catch up. Only, I spot Janvier, standing under an avocado tree. How did he get outside? And ahead of us? He'd been on the podium, getting ready to answer all those hysterical questions.

"Bo." Janvier blocks my path. He's taken off the jacket and bow tie, leaving just a crisp white dress shirt and suit pants. He takes my arm. "I need to talk to you."

"Later." I scowl. If I stop to talk, I'll lose Frank. "You should have made sure Eugene was out of the plantation before you let them set fire to it."

Janvier blinks. "Who's Eugene?"

"Oi!" I slap him across the face. How dare he pretend not to know the man he just left to die?

Janvier lets go of my arm. "Bo, please. I need your help. You know smugglers. I need to get off this planet, quietly."

My mouth drops open. "You just told everyone you're burning Earth's last hope, and now you're running? Cierto? I never took you for a coward."

"I did what?" Janvier sounds alarmed.

I'm muy tempted to send him to Pitch and the goons who water-tortured Brill. They're smugglers too, no? "I'm tired of the

Jekyll and Hyde routine, mijo. You're Dash or you're Shelly or you're cold or you want to kiss me."

"I'm Dash." Janvier claps a hand over his mouth as though that's a horrific secret. He recovers, dropping his hands to his sides. "Look. I can't explain."

"And I don't have time to listen."

"Tomorrow," he insists. "Meet me here at sunrise tomorrow. Please."

"I'll think about it."

Frank waits by the garden gate. As we step through, he grumbles, "I told you not to trust him."

CHAPTER TWENTY

We take an HGB jeep to where Murry dug under the plantation wall. Felizmente, Brill's already there. We get out and survey the destruction. The acrid smell of smoke is already heavy in the air.

Frank lets out a low whistle. "What kind of equipment did that?"

Brill holds the walkie talkie up to his ear. Without looking at us, he says, "Ga. No equipment. Just a spuck."

Frank pinches the bridge of his nose, like we've given him an instant headache. "When will I learn not to ask?"

The fire inside the plantation is already devouring the area to the left of where we're standing. The heat from the crackling feels dangerous, even though the destruction won't pass through the wall. The conflagration reflects against the bionet, highlighting the blue-light grid that rises until darkness absorbs it. The full moon now feels ominous instead of romantic.

There's a soft scrabbling noise inside the tunnel, too small for a spuck. About right for a human.

"Eugene?" Frank asks.

Brill moves towards the tunnel. "Ga. The spuck said Eugene's unconscious. Too much smoke, given Eugene's lung issues from prolonged exposure to Pure275. Stocks of the herbicide were stored where he worked in Brazil."

Ay, su. Pobrecito Eugene.

Pero – no one else should be in the plantation. Brill and Frank flank the tunnel. Frank pulls a gun from his coat.

Brill, still sticking to his layered-tee disguise, pulls his gun out of a boot holster.

Frank motions me behind the jeep. I duck down, peering over the open top.

I catch the reflection on the whites of a pair of eyes. Not-Kaliel climbs out of the tunnel. He wears a black sweater and black jeans, with a hard plastic backpack strapped over both shoulders. Frank and Brill let the hombre walk past, then close in, bringing a gun barrel up to each side of his cabeza.

Seeing them work together feels surreal. Frank pulls a zip tie from his pocket. Brill takes it and binds Not-Kaliel's hands behind his back. The guy doesn't resist. They pull Not-Kaliel to the front of the jeep. Brill gestures for me to turn on the headlights.

The imposter blinks. His wide eyes look terrified.

"Who are you?" Frank asks.

"Kaliel Johannsson."

"We all know Kaliel," Brill says. "Try again."

"You do?" Not-Kaliel squints past the lights at me. "You're not Monica McGillicuddy then."

"Afraid not, mijo. Bodacious Benitez."

He groans. "Well, that was a stroke of bad luck." Pero en serio, how has this guy never seen a holo of me? "Then again, everything is bad when it comes to you. I didn't get a clear look at your face that day, but I killed that Galactacop because I thought you passed him something before you ran."

"You killed who?" Brill asks.

"The short guy with the cop who shot her." He turns to address me. "Not only did he not have what I was looking for, but what you stole from HGB was just chocolate. Not even the pink pods. I mean, how stupid are you? Throwing your life away for chocolate?"

When Tyson confronted me and Brill in the park on Krevia, he'd had a partner. And he didn't have one when he captured me later. Galactacops don't break up partnerships lightly, so we'd conjectured that Tyson's partner either screwed up so badly he got kicked off the force, or he was injured or killed.

Now I know. The muchacho's muerto. And it was my fault. I never considered that there might be a connection between my choco-theft and Tyson's partner's death. In part because I never got close enough to Tyson's partner to pass him anything. Not-Kaliel's loco. Or he mistook someone else in that park for me.

I'm a bit in shock. "Didn't have the pink what?"

Not-Kaliel laughs. "Don't tell me you haven't been down in the basement? You sucked face with Daschel Janvier, and he still doesn't trust you?"

Frank leans in closer. "What basement? This island is made of lava rock. Nobody has a basement."

"You know," Not-Kaliel says. "The vault for HGB's biggest secrets. Where Janvier hides everything that guarantees war with the Zantites. And the hope for this world."

"So you mean a myth." Frank looks to me. "There's no basement."

"He's doing that whole 'I have information you need so you have to keep me alive' thing," Brill says. "I've done that myself. It works, because your captor can't risk that you're not lying."

"Guys?" Murry's voice comes from the walkie-talkie. "I hate to interrupt, but I still need a plan of action."

Brill says, "He's gone to ground to get Eugene out of the smoke. But they're close to the center of the plantation, and he's not sure Eugene will survive the heat if they tunnel out under the fire."

"But if I go the other way," Murry's voice says, "I'll come up inside the walls of the HGB facility. There's no hiding that. Or me."

And the injured spuck can't fly, so going over el fuego isn't an option.

Shtesh! That's just perfecto, no? "Por favor, Murry. Bring Eugene to the facility. He's important to Chestla. We'll find a way to deal with the consequences."

"He's important to Chestla, and Chestla's important to you, and you're important to Frank Sawyer and Frank Sawyer's important to Lavonda Benitez. All of you are about two steps from being a hive mind. Even Brill Cray. Even though I never could infect a Krom." I hope the spuck is digging while Murry's talking.

"De prisa." *Hurry!*

"I'm digging as fast as I can."

"Hest! Why couldn't you infect me?" Brill asks.

Murry makes an unhappy noise. "The iololla in Krom blood functions as natural antifreeze for you. For me, it prevents the pearl from unfolding. Why do you think I decided you had to die instead of hugging you, to use your abilities?"

"I never considered it," Brill says softly. Back before the hive mind became Murry, it thought Brill had uncovered evidence of its existence. The hive arranged to have the Zantites execute him – only to give him a last-minute reprieve.

While Brill and I are focused on Murry, Not-Kaliel gets a knife out of somewhere and cuts the zip tie. He lunges at Frank, the knife heading straight for Frank's chest.

Brill, moving as a blur to human vision, dashes between Not-Kaliel and Frank and knocks the knife from la mano del hombre. The long sleeve of Brill's tee flutters where the knife sliced it as it flew. Brill hesitates, making sure he's not cut.

Not-Kaliel fires up his backpack, which turns out to be a jet pack. Brill stops. He can't grab onto the back of a guy wearing an active engine. Not-Kaliel takes off.

Frank aims his gun at the light from the jet pack, then glances back at me and lowers his weapon. "I'd like to interrogate him more. Can't get information from the dead." Todavía, I think Frank chose not to kill Not-Kaliel because I'm watching. He steps closer to Brill and says, "Bo and I need to get back and mitigate the fallout from this. And you need to disappear."

"Just so you know," Brill tells him. "Miss Kamaka knows I'm alive."

Frank grumbles out an unhappy noise.

"Pero she thinks you believe you killed him," I reassure Frank. "It's una muy realistic scar."

"I'd like to stay close, in case Eugene needs to reach medical assistance fast." Brill says. "I'll wait outside the compound walls."

"Fine. Get in the jeep." Frank looks over at me, then tells Brill, "But don't blame me if you get hurt playing the hero. You probably wouldn't walk away from that med facility alive."

I swallow a lump of foreboding. "Mi vida, maybe you should listen to Frank."

"And let Eugene die, if I can help?" The Krom code permits self-defense, but does not demand self-sacrifice. So this is Brill's own choice, and not one he would have made when I first met him. Brill's grown so much, earned my respect as well as my love. That's why he's the guy I can't give up. "Hest. What's this?" Brill picks up something Not-Kaliel dropped in his urgency to escape.

It's a glass vial with something white inside. I say, "That looks like the Pure Rot Eugene was working with. This muchacho was in Eugene's lab. He was looking for something else, though, no?"

"Maybe." Brill studies the glass as he climbs into the jeep. "Or maybe he's working with whoever got that disease sample off your planet and freaked out the Nilka. If the disease shows up on their planet, the consequences to Earth would be disastrous."

This all keeps coming back to Greftash. And I still don't know what we can do about it.

"It doesn't matter now, does it?" Frank says. Still, he takes out a white handkerchief and picks up the knife. Dark blood stains the blade. "You sure you're not bleeding?"

"Ga, su. My blood is bright orange."

Frank says, "Which means we can identify our Kaliel after all. Assuming he's in any of the Galactic DNA databases."

Brill says, "If you get a match, Tyson'll want that information."

"Obviously. This imposter's brought the wrath of all the Galactacops down on him, now that we have his confession." Frank sounds like he regrets not shooting Not-Kaliel out of the sky when he had the chance. He finishes processing the DNA off the knife, doesn't look surprised at the result. "But right now, we have to get back to headquarters."

Brill shrugs. His ridiculous hair falls into his eyes. "Losing chocolate could be the best thing that could have happened to this planet. Now that you don't have the resource the invasion coalition wants, they'll lose interest in forcing open your borders."

"You said the threat of the plant disease would catapult us into war," I say.

"The threat of it, wal. Because the armada would be desperate to get the commodity before it was too late. But actually destroying it? It's the same as sharing it." Brill points at the plantation wall. "No one would have believed you'd destroyed chocolate to stop the war. But now – you may get a few vultures hoping Janvier's right that chocolate survived in the wild. But nobody will send soldiers – who have families back home – to die to find out."

Frank says, "You're really tempting me to shoot you right now."

He doesn't mean it. He's just not ready for mi vida to talk logic in the reflection of that blaze in the bionet. Pero I can't begin to understand what's going on inside Frank, with everything he fought all these years to protect turning to ash before his eyes.

I climb into the back seat, put a hand on Frank's shoulder. "You okay, viejo?"

Frank shrugs. Pero his shoulder muscles are tense like rocks. "HGB will have some plan. We nearly lost control of chocolate a couple of dozen times over the years. Somewhere, there's an untainted grove, or a secret lab, or cloneable trees. Hell, maybe the basement is real. Janvier wouldn't have burned the groves without a plan. He may be a monster, but he's not stupid. We just need to hold the course steady."

That's hard to believe, as we drive away from the crackling destruction. But I hope it's true, for Frank's sake.

Brill tears off the ruined sleeve of his shirt.

Frank nods at mi vida. "If I hadn't let you live before, I would have died back there."

Brill shrugs. "Mercy is a gift you give yourself as much as the other person." He glances over at Frank. "I never have properly thanked you."

He means for letting him live, back on Zant.

"You did," Frank insists. "At the spaceport. You were a bit incoherent, and it was in Krom, but you said it. And wished me a safe something. I didn't understand most of it."

"Did I?" Brill smiles. "I can't remember. I just kept touching my chest, because I couldn't believe my heart was still beating and I wanted to feel it. I must have looked like a total kek."

My phone rings. It's Chestla. She studies the entire holofield before speaking. We're pulling onto the street outside the garden gate. "Cesuda ma, are you heading somewhere safe?"

I'm not Chestla's responsibility anymore, pero she looks so freaked out, now's not the time to correct her. "I have to take care of something first."

"Hurry. Please." She closes her eyes and takes a deep breath. "The shadow news is already spinning out the early polls. Public opinion on Earth is that you are single-handedly responsible for the destruction of chocolate. You can forget being put back in line for the shave. If you don't get off that planet, you'll get lynched in the streets."

"Dios mio!" I picture all those blank faces at dinner. They couldn't grasp anything I tried to do for them. It's not hard to imagine them turning on me.

And what of Mamá, still on Zant amidst Earth's would-be enemy? I call her on my sublingual, while still on my handheld with Chestla. Mamá doesn't answer.

My chest is frío y sparkly, my heartbeat echoing in my ears.

"I've talked to the others on board my ship." Chestla gestures behind her, outside the holofield. "They're willing to change course. We can come and get you."

Which would mean giving up their pursuit of Nellet and Watae. Part of me wants to say sí, because I'm rooting for the young couple to bring peace to their world. Especially since that moment of possibility seems to have passed for mine. No matter what Brill says, I can't believe the Zantite's coalition will call the war off without punishing Earth for destroying chocolate.

"No, por favor, amiga. You're days away from here. Whatever happens will play out well before you could get here."

"I've talked to Gavin," Brill says. "He's trying to get us a ride off of this rock, so we can meet his ship."

"Pero stay by the phone," I tell Chestla. "Eugene is trapped in the plantation."

Chestla's flinches. She does have feelings for Eugene. Her eyes widen into reflective pools of worry. "What happened?"

"We don't know much yet," I say.

"He's conscious now," Murry's voice announces from the walkie. I assumed we'd gone out of range – pero Murry's been traveling parallel to us. He's had the connection open, listening the whole time. "Still wheezing pretty bad, but I brought the pack he takes for field excursions, and it held some canned coffee. He said caffeine helps sometimes, but he's out of medicine. I'm still dragging him, which makes the digging slow."

Chestla watches the walkie. Her expression obviously means *what digging and what dragging?* "So really all Eugene needs is his inhaler?"

"I should be able to handle that," Brill says. "I've made friends with the pharmacist near my hotel."

Frank gives him a sharp look. "Packing your suitcase with a few Krom 'discoveries' even while people are trying to kill you?"

Brill unbuckles his seatbelt. "On the off chance I still have a future, I need to keep building my reputation." He glances back at me. As a moment of feliz giddiness bubbles through me, despite all the terranguishment, I blush. He is thinking about *our* future. "Because that's all a su has, revwal? But don't worry. It's just analgesics and antihistamines. For my legacy, I don't want anything shalshiset." *Dangerous*. He sighs. "I'll keep in touch with Murry, see where he's at when I get back. I'll be quick."

Frank looks too gobsmacked to reply before Brill races Krom-fast into the night.

"See," Chestla says, dropping her voice so that the people on her ship can't hear. "When you have a hero like that, it's not hard to choose."

Eh? Then why is she still crushing on Eugene, who is more the dude in distress than the hero type? When Ball and I got pushed off that cliff on Evevron, Ball wrapped his solid body around me to cushion my impact. If we'd hit the ground instead of being stopped midair, he would have died. So that I could live. I whisper back, "Amiga, if you're looking for a hero, you have your own half-Krom, no?"

She blushes and her voice gets even softer. "Ball's a great guy. But it's a bit intimidating how long he's had a crush on me and how tied he is to Evevron. And you know – if he gets super attached, but then it doesn't work out, or I decide to leave the planet again, it could literally kill him. Eugene's fun. And he doesn't mind that I'm not ready to decide yet. At least, he doesn't mind much."

It sounds like she's leaning towards Eugene. I can see why. Krom have been known to die of broken hearts, due to their weak cardio systems. It's supposed to be ita ita rare, rare enough that I've not even worried about it with Brill. Pero I can see how that risk would make being with Eugene seem simpler, even though Eugene's from a different planet.

CHAPTER TWENTY-ONE

The walkie crackles from the seat where Brill left it. "You guys know the basement you keep talking about?"

"Sí, mijo," I say.

Murry says, "I think I found it."

Frank tells the walkie, "Give us a way in, then stay down there out of sight until we find a way to sneak you out."

Frank's helping Murry. Muy bueno, pero I wonder how helpful Frank would be if he knew that Murry made the disease responsible for choco-destruction. Mi corazón wants to trust Frank. And that keeps making me forget how complicated all of this is. And how dangerous for everyone.

"I wish I could help," Murry says, "but it's dark, and Eugene and I are on in a room with a locked door."

"That's good," I say. "Stay in the dark. HGB's bound to have cameras everywhere."

"We need to get Eugene that medicine soon. If you can't find access, I may have to break through the door." Murry pauses. "Wow! I just found the motherlode of carob bars Janvier's been hoarding. This me's so hungry." Murry goes quiet.

"Well, he won't be any help for a while," Frank grumbles.

Thath calls my handheld from a fixed ship's com. Ni idea how he got my number. He runs both hands through his hair, pulling it away from his face, giving me a glimpse of the seriousness in his three orange eyes. "Many apologies, Bodacious."

"Que?" I blink, still worried about Murry and Eugene. "I mean, apologies for what?"

"I was wrong." The curtain of hair hides Thath's face again. "I am in a teleconference discussing the invasion of your planet. Many of our most ardent constituents have pulled out, some saying this has become the Nilka's business, but that isn't true. The Nilka will do nothing for you – or against you – since you complied with their demands."

I stop myself from doing a little happy dance. I keep my voice neutral. "So without chocolate as a prize for this war…"

"The coalition is crumbling. There will likely be no attempt at resolution of your antisocial behavior." He points at the holofield with a thin finger. "As I said, not everything is fair."

Brill was right. Losing chocolate was the best thing that could have happened. I say, "Maybe we're not so uniquely flawed after all."

"Perhaps you are right. I am seeing bloodthirsty traits in several other species here, as this conference proceeds. Alliances in the galaxy will never be the same."

I'd taken Thath for a giant hypocrite. En realidad. he's as naive as I'd been when I took that cacao pod from HGB, thinking one fruit, shaped like the human heart and just as heavy, could change mi planeta entero. I feel some sympathy for him, having to rethink where he fits in the worlds. I ask, "What convinced you that humans are so bad, Thath?"

Thath shudders. "Your science fiction and horror films have become underground classics throughout the galaxy. No other species has anything like them."

"I know. You muchachos like to laugh at how much we got wrong."

"My daughter–" Thath is so visibly shaken that he has to start again. "My daughter had a slumber party. Her friend brought a dubbed version of the Earth classic *Friday the Thirteenth*, the original. I have never been so – the disturbed minds that created dream-killers from beyond the grave – what is wrong with you people? I understand that film has 127 sequels, each gorier than the last. Art can create so much beauty. Why delight in violence and death?"

That question isn't easy to answer. Especially because I'm not into horror. I say, "Not all Earthlings are fans of horror. I'd say most of us aren't. And those who are often age out of it, once they see actual violence in the worlds." How to put this in a way that won't make us sound as mal as he already thinks? "People like to prove that they are brave. Most lead small lives, with little problems they're powerless to solve. Seeing people face hunormous, unstoppable forces and fail makes them feel that maybe failures in ordinary life aren't so bad."

"What an unusual perspective," Thath says.

I nod. "At the same time, fear gives an adrenaline rush. Adrenaline makes humans feel stronger, more focused, decreases sensitivity to pain." Por supuesto, that's how you feel while high on the Invincible Heart. Without the fear. Plus pure exhilaration. And oh so much stronger than anything your body could do naturally. I miss that feeling to my core. Janvier's treatment stopped the shakes, pero can't quiet the memory.

"Bodacious, are you okay?" Thath asks.

"Not really. The real horror is that my world is burning." I hang up.

Frank is watching me. I don't have to tell him I was thinking about the IH. He says, "You don't need comfort that comes out of a syringe."

I swallow to wet my dry throat. "If I could get a dose right now, how could I not take it?

"You're stronger than this." Frank looks worried. Cierto. He doesn't want to have to shoot me.

CHAPTER TWENTY-TWO

I clutch the walkie as we head into the garden. As Frank closes the gate, locking us inside, it clanks too loudly. This whole area feels abandoned. Everyone's either inside the ballroom, out watching the flames, or glued to the feeds.

Frank heads towards the main building. "If everyone's calling it a basement, then logically, it would be under here. But I've been everywhere inside this place, and there isn't an elevator or a staircase headed down."

"Not-Kaliel was poking around out here. Allá. On the far side of the building"

Frank follows me.

Not far from where the fake Kaliel had picked his dandelion stands a row of bougainvillea bushes. And when I look closely, there's an odd gap between two of them.

Mario calls my handheld. He's in some kind of library or records room. "Are you okay, Pequeña? I have Kayla down in the archive. She's safe here if you want me to come help you."

"Don't leave her, hermano" I move closer to the bushes to examine the gap. "Her brother just died, and the people who killed him are looking for her. Pero they have no reason to think she'd go to Brazil. Uan, if you can get her off the island, the danger to you is slight."

"I don't care about danger. I just want someone to tell me what's going on. Why are people after her?"

I look over at Frank and back at holo-Mario. I don't see Frank turning Kayla over to HGB for being an alien improperly on the planet. Not when he's helping Brill hide here. "Kayla's an alien princess."

"The lost Nitarri twins," Frank says. When I nod, he looks incredulous. "They were on Earth all the time?"

"And someone just killed her hermano." Mario looks concerned.

Frank asks, "Is Carl still in the archive room today?"

"Sí." Mario looks over his shoulder, deeper into the room. "He's the one that let me bring Kayla in. Is he dangerous?"

"Tell him to show you the stuff from the aborted Gevexix invasion. Clearance code 17756. And also everything about the Gevexix first contact that may be of interest to a Nitarri." Frank grimaces. Mario will see some things in there Frank didn't want us to know. "Now that the Zantite invasion is off, if Kayla can speak for us, the Nitarri's allies might be willing to help us deal with the fallout of this ecological disaster."

"If she acknowledges who she is, that will tell the people trying to kill her *where* she is." I point at the ground. "Oye! Mira."

A dent in the dirt outlines an access panel. It is easy to reveal the edge of the metal hatch and pry it up, and by the time I'm done, Frank's finished giving Mario instructions on the archive.

If it wasn't obvious by the way the bushes had started to grow over the hatch, the dusty staircase below proves that this entrance isn't used often. And to think, if I hadn't interrupted him, Not-Kaliel would have found this hatch and gotten inside.

Frank types a number off the inside of the hatch into his phone. "That should shut off the bionets and cameras in this area."

"You couldn't do that for Murry?" I protest.

"He didn't have the code. And I've never been in this section of the building, so I couldn't even guess." Frank steps down onto the staircase. "Besides, I want him staying put. Either you can tell me what that spuck has to do with all of this – or he will."

I say, "There's no point in torturing a spuck. Nada. Murry will suicide the hug, and then you're left with a rampaging terrangerated animal."

As I descend, I pull the access panel closed. There's no way to smooth the dirt back on top of it. Not when we're both inside, climbing down the stairs, which lead into a hallway. There's only one direction to go.

The hall's overhead bulbs light up a section at a time as we pass. If anybody's down here, we won't stroll past unnoticed. Still, we move quietly, trying doors and backtracking to explore different branches of hallways.

There's muchas locas stuff down here. Experiments involving giant wheels and blown glass, a room full of cages holding alien animals, an area that smells of ginger and flowers and seems impenetrable to light, racks ad racks of weird-looking weapons. Nothing down here seems to relate to chocolate.

In one room, a glassed-in rack of giant translucent pink pods fills the back wall. Human-looking forms float inside, their features indistinct, like not-quite finished statues. A tube pumps viscous yellow fluid into each pod.

"Is this what Not-Kaliel was talking about, viejo?"

Frank studies the apparatus. "I can't see him imagining you secretly passing along something as big as a person."

I turn to the counter along the side wall, which is scattered with test tubes and vials filled with many different colored liquids. "Maybe they start out smaller."

This is cloning gear. Why would this stuff be más importante to Not-Kaliel than chocolate? And how could this force a war? Is HGB creating a clone army?

I know nada about the ethics of cloning under Galactic law. I do know it's frowned upon on Earth.

I move to the door across the hall. We need to find Eugene and get him to where we're supposed to meet Brill. Then we can worry about the implications of what we see down here. Frank follows me.

"Mr. Janvier?" a voice calls from farther down the hall. "Are you alright? The cameras went out, and I was afraid–"

I turn, and there's Daschel Janvier, standing in the hall. I don't see whoever spoke to him. Eh? Was he talking to himself? Janvier sees my hand on the knob, and his eyes widen. "Bo, don't."

"Don't what? What's in there?"

"Please. Go back upstairs, and we can pretend this never happened. You and I can continue falling in love, and one day, when we trust each other completely, I'll explain all of this over strawberries and crème fraiche in a little villa off the coast of Italy." He studies my face. "So not Italy. How about my hometown in France?"

Either Janvier's gone loco, or he hasn't paid much attention to who I am – just who he wishes I was. That's probably it – he's wishing out loud, what might have been.

Not sure what to expect, I turn the knob and peer into the room. I blink in confusion. Behind a bionet that spans the width of the space, a second Daschel Janvier stands in his pajamas, his beard grown full, microwaving a heat-and-eat meal while reading a stack of paper files.

He looks up. "It's about time someone came."

"Daschel!" Frank pulls his gun on the Janvier in the hallway and looks for a way to deactivate the bionet.

I turn back to my unbearded Janvier. A lot of things make sense. "That's how I talked to you in the banquet room and then seconds later in the garden. You're a clone."

Shelly nods. "1.0 over there needed someone to hold down the fort when he goes on vacations and to serve as a decoy in dangerous situations. Several of us have died in such service. One of my co-genes had enough and shot 1.0 in the stomach. Only, do you have any idea how hard it is to let yourself die? He brought 1.0 to the med facility. And that's when I stepped in. No one's supposed to know we exist. So after the surgery, no one suspected that I took 1.0's place. Afterwards, I just said I was visiting a private doctor for follow-up appointments. Even the clone that shot 1.0 doesn't know about the switch. He's been living in fear of his life."

"Then why hasn't he left Maui?" I ask.

"Because if I really was 1.0, I'd have flagged all the airports and spaceports to be on the lookout for an imposter. Everyone knows our face, and HGB has enough funds to find anyone, anywhere. Even if he did find a way off this island, If I wanted to hunt him, it wouldn't be difficult. So he has to be looking for a way to either disappear secretly or to patch things up with 1.0."

I think about the desperate guy in the garden. Who had asked me to introduce him to smugglers. It's another novela trope – the twin who takes over his hermano's life. Aunque in this case, there's more than just the two of them. And the reality is more complex than the trope could ever hope to be. Usually, in a soap opera, it's an evil twin. Pero Shelly doesn't seem evil. "So you're Shelly and he's Dash."

"That's the shape of it. Though officially I'm 2.4 and Dash is 2.9." Shelly smiles, and the effect his dimples have on me hasn't changed. He's the same person, with the contradictory sweet side. "Just because 1.0 was born first, does that make him the real Daschel Janvier? We started with the same memories, didn't diverge until less than a year ago. Finding out I was a clone made me think differently about life. I wanted to do better than my original."

"Born is the key word," Janvier says. "You were made."

Shelly ignores him. "Bodacious, would you rather have the guy who put an assassination order out on your boyfriend, or the guy who wants to take HGB in a more positive direction? Could you leave 1.0 down here and learn to love a clone?"

I say, "I never promised to love you." Though it hurts to say that, porque I realize now that part of me wants to love him.

From inside the bionet, Janvier says, "Oh, come on. Make the inevitable pod people joke and move on. He's not denying that I'm the original. I can prove it, using scars and dental records, even if my microdot has been cut out." He pulls up his pajama sleeve, showing a dark, circular punch scar on his forearm.

Frank turns to me, still keeping his gun on Shelly. "Only the highest-level HGB employees get those, and that they have to be

re-dotted every year. The dots let the bearers walk through all of
HGB's doors without a passcode."

"You don't have one?" I ask.

Frank looks at me, sympathy in his eyes. Finally, he sighs.
"We can't let this stand. Say goodbye to your friend and go
upstairs."

My heart suffuses with ice. Frank's telling me he doesn't want
me to watch him take another life. Shelly's life. "Por favor. No."

Shelly sighs. "You never have had an imagination, Frank. If
there's a problem, kill it, right?" He reaches into his pockets and
pulls out a gun with one hand, and a boxy device topped with a
single blue button with the other.

Frank's gun makes a soft, anticlimactic click. He pulls the
trigger again and again, with the same effect.

"Are you done?" Shelly smiles, and I see his frío original in
him, after all. "I've always been good at sleight of hand, and I
was afraid, being this close, that you'd figure something out, so I
took your bullets when we talked at dinner." He holds up the blue
button, which he's depressed with his thumb. "If you drop me,
and I let this go, it sets off a biosweep of this whole section of the
basement."

A cracking noise comes from up above us. A ceiling tile
crumbles and Brill spills out of the air ducts. Ay! Por que now?

"Shtesh!" Mi vida pushes himself up to his feet.

Shelly looks at me. When he realizes that Brill's been vivo all
along, heartbreak fills the clone's eyes. Along with accusation.
"You let me kiss you."

"I told you my heart wasn't ready for someone new, mijo." I
can't look at Brill, not with the shame of my latest disloyalty.
Pero I need to be honest with Shelly. "That beso set off fireworks,
and I wished – if we could live more than one life… You had to
see how conflicted I was when you tried to get me alone again."

"Do you mean that?" Shelly looks from me to Brill. And back.
"Then come over here before I push the button on the bionet.
Come back upstairs with me, help me sort the mess HGB is in."

"After I watch you kill two people I care about – and the original you couldn't bring yourself to destroy before? Gracias, pero no. The sweet side inside you would be dead too, no?"

Brill squeezes my hand, and whispers, "I'm proud of you for being honest." Then he pushes me towards Shelly.

I stumble. Shelly catches me with his gun arm. The momentum of being off balance, being caught against the clone's strong, solid body makes me gasp.

Brill flashes over and grabs the button, and before Shelly can get his balance, Frank grabs the gun from his hand. Estás jugando conmigo. *You've got to be kidding me.* They used me as a human shield. Again.

Though maybe Brill didn't plan to – just saw a chance to take the button.

After Frank forces Shelly at gunpoint to release Janvier from his prison, we all move to the next section of hallway. Brill releases the button, allowing the biosweep to harmlessly pass through the room we were just in. We continue down the hall. Brill lags behind, examining things in the hallway. Maybe he doesn't want to look at me after he used me to distract Shelly. Or maybe he doesn't want to think about how I'd looked *at* Shelly.

Janvier takes Shelly's phone. He does something to the device, and a web of bionets comes on, dividing this hallway into the same sections as the fluorescent lights.

"Oye." I jump, startled.

Brill is stuck in the section behind us. Each partition of the bionet has no doors, just smooth sections of hallway. We're trapped here with Janvier until he tells us what he wants. I assume it's a list of things we're not allowed to say once we go upstairs.

Janvier waves a hand at Frank. "You know what you have to do, Sawyer."

Alarm spikes through me. Frank has one job for HGB – making people muerta.

Shelly goes pale. "Mr. Janvier. Please."

Janvier frowns. "I can't let you out there with my face and my genetics. I can never trust you again."

"He's right." Frank shoots Shelly with the clone's own gun.

"No!" My shout echoes down the hallway, echoes in my own ears. Panic sparks through me, jolting my chest.

Blood blooms across Shelly's shirt, and as he sags towards the floor, I catch him. He's bigger than me, and heavier, and I collapse to the floor with his head and torso in my arms. He's not muerto, pero he's bleeding fast.

He wheezes, "You killed the wrong one." He glares down the hallway at his original. "I was going to save us all."

"Lo siento." Tears shimmer in my eyes. "I didn't mean for this—"

Hidden from the others by the angle of my body, Shelly gouges his forearm, scraping out the microdot he stole from Janvier and embedded under his skin. He touches his finger to mine, passing me the dot. Still in shock, I stick the dot to the inside of my bracelet.

Shelly whispers, "All HGB's secrets kept close, where they couldn't be stolen …" At first I think he's gone. Pero he rallies. "Proof HGB exported huge chunks of cash off Earth. It's enough for the Global Court to take the company apart …" He closes his eyes, speaks even slower. "The combination to my – his – personal safe is on here too … and he's afraid of caterpillars."

I almost laugh at that last one, pero Shelly goes slack in my arms.

"No," I whisper, heartshattered.

Brill's still got those contacts in, so ni idea what he's thinking as he watches me kiss the dead clone's forehead. Janvier rolls his eyes, obviously misinterpreting the exchange between me and Shelly as a last-minute confession of love.

Shelly asked me to take that microdot to the Galactic Court. Which, considering the burning cacao plantations, makes mucho más sense. With the invasion off, why keep HGB's secrets? Imagine Earth without HGB. No more secrets. No more assassinations. I need to think about—

"That one too." Janvier points at Brill.

"No." Shock jolts through me again. I lay Shelly on the floor, and I jump to my feet, moving towards Janvier. "No y no."

Janvier scowls at Frank. "Why isn't he dead already?"

Brill pulls his shirt up, showing his scar. "Miraculous recovery from a near-fatal gunshot wound."

Janvier raises an eyebrow. "In a Krom?"

"Doubly miraculous?" Brill pulls his shirt back into place.

Frank's lips form a hard line. "This guy just saved your life, Daschel. He gets a pass."

Janvier snorts. "Don't be ridiculous, Sawyer. He's a problem." Janvier pushes me towards the bionet separating us from Brill. Oi! If he pushes me through it, I'm muerta. Brill's got his gun in hand, pero, if he shoots Janvier, the kek could probably still push me into the net. "Besides, the only thing the Krom cares about is whether Bo gets to walk out of here. Right?"

"Wal." Brill drops his gun and kicks it across the bionet. The blue light shimmers and sizzles, pero the field isn't disrupted. Janvier releases his hold on me and picks up Brill's gun.

Mi vida is trapped behind the bionet, pero it won't stop a bullet. There's nowhere for him to run. Waves of sparkling terror sink into my core.

Frank is a weapon for HGB. He killed his best friend for HGB, was prepared to kill mi mamá. Letting Brill go was one thing, with the assumption that Brill would shadowpop and Frank's employer's intent would be honored. It's quite another for Frank to deny a direct order to Janvier's face, right after he killed another man at Janvier's request.

And yet Frank hesitates.

"Please." Frank looks at the floor. "Tell me what he's done that makes this right. One thing beyond you testing whether I'll follow orders."

Janvier counts points on his fingers. "He's in this secret facility. Who knows what all he's seen? Two, he remembers everything that the original kill order was supposed to blow out of his head. Three, his visa expired months ago, so he's on this planet illegally and could be executed for that alone. Four, he's corrupted Bo, which has led to the destruction of chocolate. If he was a citizen of this planet, we'd have him shaved. Do I need to go on? Or can you remember who gives the orders around here and why?"

"No. I understand." Frank's eyes remind me of his picture on that old ID, of the niño he was before he became HGB's hired gun, steeling himself to do something he's not ready for. Frank has his sense of justicia. And if he kills my Krom, he can forget a future with mi mamá.

Still, Frank has to kill Brill or break with HGB entirely. And I'm the one who put him in this position. I rock slightly, the motion comforting, though it doesn't lessen my guilt. "Por favor."

I say it under my breath, pero Frank hears. He turns to look at me.

"La! Frank." Brill says. It's the only time he's ever used Frank's first name. That gets Frank's attention. "We're wasting time. Help Eugene."

"What did you say?" Janvier looks shocked.

Brill ignores Janvier. He takes the inhaler from his pocket and holds it out to Frank, then sets it on the floor at the edge of the bionet. He's accepting his fate, facing Frank square on, with his hands at his sides. Mi corazón breaks as I stand there watching Brill trying to keep his dignity instead of begging for his life, which he knows won't work. "Just, like I told you the last time, not in the face. Ga, avell. Not with Bo here. I don't want her to remember me like that." He pauses and actually smiles at Frank. "Thank you for the extra time. Every breath has been a kindness, su." He looks at me. "Suavet ita hanstral." *I'm so sorry.* "Reveet haetenla nallshiset neb quenell dadaiset, suavetta neltal." *Safe journey and true heart, my love.*

His way of saying goodbye. Why are we always saying goodbye? And this time, there's no hope, no use fighting Frank for the gun. I shatter.

Brill looks levelly at Frank and half nods. Then he holds up a hand. "Wait." Brill takes out his contacts and drops them on the floor. His irises are solid black, pero he blinks a couple of times and nods, stronger this time. "Diay."

Frank turns to Janvier, a pleading look on his face.

Janvier's face is unyielding. "Don't make it personal. You swore your loyalty, just like your friend Xavier did. And look what happened to him when he broke it. Don't think you'd be exempt from the same consequences."

Threatening Frank is the wrong move. Especially using the amigo HGB forced him to kill, an act that haunts him. Janvier wasn't even part of HGB then and likely never met Xavier. Which means he has no right to talk about what happened.

Frank's eyes harden. "I've proven my loyalty. And if you want to keep it, the Krom gets a pass. Permanently. I've never asked you – or Foster – for anything else. Not even the one time I should have." He looks over at me. I think he's referring to the leverage HGB put on me by having him threaten to kill Mamá back when I was on the run with that cacao pod.

Though he doesn't raise the gun, Frank's finger tightens on the trigger.

Janvier steps back. He seems to have forgotten the gun in his own hand. "You wouldn't."

Frank gestures towards Shelly's corpse. "We can just go three doors down and clone a new one that hasn't seen Brill alive. But Brill would still have to pretend to be dead. And I'd have to live with shooting my boss. It would be better if we could reach an agreement."

I can't help but ask, "If we made a new one, would he even know he's a clone?"

Janvier gives me a sour look. "He'd remember requisitioning the cloning system. And realize significant time had passed since the memory upload his mind's built on. But he'd be me, so he'd adapt. But that's not going to happen. Right?"

Frank nods. "I know you, Daschel. You're going to want to have one of my colleagues show up at my place in the middle of the night tonight, or tomorrow or the next day. But please, show mercy for once. I'm the kind of asset you can't replace. And with everything else stacked against you now that the plantations have burned, you don't want to lose someone with as much influence as I have to keep my colleagues loyal. Not over a life as insignificant in your scheme of things as his." He gestures towards Brill.

Mi vida is not offended. Cierto, he nods along enthusiastically.

"Nice speech." Janvier does something else to Shelly's phone, and the bionets disappear. Then he types a message. A second later Frank's phone dings.

Frank shows me the memo that Janvier sent to anyone who would find it relevant: *Elimination order rescinded on Brill Cray. Said Krom to enjoy HGB protection while on Earth, without visa or paperwork for up to one month.*

Meaning that Brill better get his info in order. He was issued a temporary visa once before. With HGB's backing, he can get another one.

CHAPTER TWENTY-THREE

I turn to tell mi vida how relieved I am. Brill's already scooped up the inhaler and ran to find Eugene.

A minute later, he runs back. Eugene, who's pretty grande, is draped over his shoulder in a fireman's carry. Eugene sucks on the inhaler. His color's not great, pero he looks better than I expected, considering how long it took for us to reach him.

Janvier starts to say something – probably wondering how Eugene wound up in the basement –then he closes his mouth.

Frank nods. "Better not to ask."

Brill's eyes remain an anxious gray. "Is anyone at that facility Bo went to for her treatment? You don't want to lose one of your last chocolate experts. Eugene says he needs something called a nebulizer."

Janvier taps on his phone again. "I'll arrange for a technician meet you there. Be careful, though. Probably not everybody's checked their messages."

Brill takes off, carrying Eugene towards help. I force myself not to look back, to wherever Murry is no doubt hiding, waiting for a chance to tunnel to where no one will find him.

Janvier smirks at Frank. "I didn't think you liked Krom. Funny you're risking dying for one."

Oye! He's threatening Frank while Frank has a gun. Someone has to stop this horrible hombre. The microdot's safe against my wrist. Mira, maybe Janvier shouldn't be so smug. I have all the evidence now of how HGB keeps hurting people.

I gesture in the direction of Shelly's body, which Janvier is leaving for someone else to take care of. "Shelly had a honey cowrie shell. If you find it, I'd like to have it."

Janvier shrugs. "Wouldn't mean anything to me. I stopped collecting seashells after I left France."

Walking ahead of Frank and Janvier, I go up the main stairs leading to an entrance on the back side of the facility.

Frank asks, "So what is the plan? How do we save chocolate?"

"There is no plan," Janvier says bitterly. "I told that nincompoop not to burn the trees. Now we have to steal our own chocolate back from another planet."

Porque Janvier can't just let chocolate go. And Frank can't let this just be over. A leaden weight settles into my chest.

By the time we walk around to the front of the building, Brill is already on his way back. When he sees me, he rushes over and wraps me into a hug. "Babe! I was so worried. I'm sorry I left you downstairs."

I blink and pull away so I can really look at him. "You left to save Eugene."

"And you're not mad I prioritized someone else above you? Like I did before? You were still in danger, if Mr. Janvier-"

"I got mad before when you prioritized yourself over me, after putting me in danger." That had been a long time ago. "Saving someone else makes you un gran héroe."

His eyes shift to gold. He takes my hand, and walk fast, to catch up to Frank and Janvier. "You finally think I'm a hero, huh?"

"Escucha. I'm proud of the way you faced Frank." I squeeze his hand. Brill could have tried to hide his fear behind blue irises, or left his contacts in as a mask. There was something authentic in him not wanting to die wearing them. He wanted me to remember him for who he is, even if he looked vulnerable.

And I'd seen the change in Frank because he did that. Dropping those contacts on the floor, acknowledging that he wouldn't need them anymore, trying to make the situation easier for Frank, even though it meant Brill's death – those things changed something inside Frank. And are likely what saved Brill's life.

A soft moan comes from my right, in the darkness. Tawny's up against the wall, kissing Hosei. She opens her eyes, looks at us, and squeaks her shocked protest into his mouth. He pulls back and looks around to see what is wrong. Tawny's wide eyes are fixed on Brill – still vivo and walking two steps behind Frank and Janvier.

Frank tells her, "Check your e-mail."

I'm grimy and my dress is stained with blood. As the adrenaline fades, my aching feet abruptly inform me that I'm wearing mi mundo's most uncomfortable shoes. Janvier says something to Frank, then turns towards the garden. Janvier's still holding a gun. I hope it's to make him feel safe, and not because he's hunting Dash.

Frank turns towards the housing unit. I'm shocked that he's staying inside HGB. Pero maybe leaving would be worse.

"Hey, viejo," I call.

Frank turns. "What? I got to go check on my dog."

"You going to be okay?"

He walks back towards us. More softly he says, "Probably. Maybe." He jerks a thumb in Brill's direction. "Your Krom has a guarantee in writing that it's supposed to be hands off. Janvier can't take that back without looking weak at a time when he needs to look strong. But if he puts an elimination order out on me, no one will question it. They'd just assume I did something disloyal. And they wouldn't be wrong."

"You're staying here, knowing that?" I protest.

"If I ran, Janvier would have to put out that order. I still hope that, given the circumstances, he will see reason."

Brill gives Frank a double-tap, close fisted salute. "Safe journey and true heart, until we meet again." He smiles. "And thank you. Tanyaliesh. Thank you soooooo much. Uan, I am sorry my actions put you in danger."

"I don't blame you," Frank says. "But if Botas made a mess, I'm calling you to clean it up."

My handheld rings. It's Mario. Frank waits while I answer it.

Mario is still in the archive room. "You keep saying you want us to be close, Pequeña, but you've been hiding more than I realized. Carl – en serio Carl the archivist just told me that Brill's vivo. You couldn't trust me that much?"

"Lo siento, mi hermano. It was a risk."

"Did Mamá know?"

"Eh … sí."

"Did Frank?"

Frank holds out his hand for the phone. "Here, let me talk to him. I need to say some things, and I might not get another opportunity."

Because, you know, he might be dead by mañana. "You're going to tell him about Papá, no?"

"What about Papá?" Mario asks.

Frank grimaces. "His death wasn't an accident."

"I suspected as much. You killed him, right?" Mario doesn't look nearly as upset as I expected.

Frank nods. "You knew?"

Mario says, "No. But I watched you kill a man in our garden shed, and I know you threatened my mother. I'm not stupid. Assassins just don't randomly show up in people's lives."

"And you've come to terms with that?" I ask. Mario never believed Papá's muerte was an accident. "Cierto? After all that stuff you said when we were niños about how if you ever found whoever hurt Papá you'd kill them?"

"Teenagers say a lot of stuff. And we Mexicans have that machismo thing going on. You know that." He sighs. "That's why you didn't tell me it was Frank?"

Heat floods my cheeks. "I thought you might get hurt trying to get revenge. You couldn't stand up to Frank without getting yourself killed."

"You think I don't know that? Pequeña!"

"I told you I wouldn't hurt him, even if he tried something," Frank protests.

"Now," I say. "Pero not when you first met us, not when you didn't care so much what Mamá thinks. What good is Mamá's opinion if you stand there and let Mario kill you? Or let HGB?"

Mario says, "I don't want to hurt anybody. But I would like to talk to Frank alone."

"I'll call you on my phone," Frank says. "Once I get back to my room."

I hang up. "Por favor–" No sé how to finish that sentence. It sounds stupid to say, *please don't die.*

"You need to get off this planet." Frank puts a hand on my shoulder. "Stay safe out there."

"You sure you don't want to come?" I ask.

Frank chuckles, pero then his jaw tightens. "I've never been the kind to run."

We're at the med facility, waiting for Eugene. This place feels desolate without the holo playing in the corner, or sunshine streaming in through the glass door. It's late, and I'm slypered. I've cleaned up as best I can, pero my dress is still too gross for me to lean against Brill and fall asleep.

I nudge Brill. "What will you do first now that you're vivo again?"

"I need to tell my family. My mom will be ita, ita mad at me for letting her grieve this long. I have to get my hair back to normal before I call her, though. Or I will never hear the end of it."

I put a hand on his arm. Mis manos are clean, though blood coats the microdot on the inside of my bracelet. "Wait. You need to contact the Galactic Court and let them know you'll testify about Murry."

"Wal. Shtesh! The last thing I want is a Galactic Enforcer showing up thinking I'm hiding something."

I should tell Brill about the dot. Pero I'm not sure yet what to do with it. And I'm not sure he'll understand why I took it. Krom don't have power struggles. Mi planeta is in a fragile place. Those fires are still raging. And so far, my plan amounts to blackmailing Janvier into liquidating HGB. Which hardly seems likely to succeed.

My handheld rings. It's Chestla. Ay! I forgot to call her.

Chestla says, "I just got off the phone with Eugene. Thanks, you guys, for helping him. He feels awful for being so much trouble."

Brill's eyes shift bright green. "Are you two together now? As in together together?"

She did just speak for Eugene like they're a couple.

Chestla blushes. "Not exactly. I don't know. I think he'd like to be. What do you guys think?"

"You had a good conversation, right?" I smile, despite the blood and the stress of the night.

"He told me my teeth are beautiful."

Which sounds like an odd compliment. Pero Chestla is touchy sometimes, because many people find her teeth frightening. So it was kind of the perfect thing to say.

Later, Eugene comes out of the treatment room, typing on his phone. "What kind of idiot planned this evacuation?"

"You're welcome for saving your life," Brill says. Pero his eyes are lavender.

"Thank you. I'm sorry." Eugene holds up his phone. "But look at this. They removed the seed bank, which is stupid. Once you freeze a cacao seed, it's dead. And even though the seeds should be cloneable, a coating on them disrupts the process. We still had a chance with the pods, and the live seeds, and nobody thought to harvest any. Sample pods could have been isolated, without the rest of the galaxy knowing. Murry had some great ideas about manipulating the cell walls to introduce an antifungal agent he'd whipped up. We were close. And now, kpffffkkkt!"

I have never seen Eugene so passionate. He looks back down at his phone and types angrily.

I tell Brill, "If Shelly saved the seed bank, he probably had a plan for it."

Brill shrugs. "If so, that plan died with him."

"Shelly?" Eugene asks.

Apparently, he *is* listening.

"Where are you staying, su?" Brill asks Eugene, changing the subject.

So we still aren't telling Eugene what's actually happening.

Eugene looks at his phone again. "Nowhere, I guess. My quarters and all my gear burned with the plantation."

I stifle a yawn and stand up. "Oye. Let me see if the technician can get ahold of the concierge. Maybe HGB will spot you a room."

As I head for the exam rooms, Eugene tells Brill, "They gave me medication specifically to help with my condition. The guy said he was surprised I didn't come in earlier, either here or in Brazil. That it's a commonly available drug now for HGB workers. But my primary doctor had never heard of it."

No sé whether to be horrified that enough people got sick from Pure275 that HGB worked out a treatment – or shocked that they care enough to invest in it.

My phone dings with a text from Jeska. *Su, how could you not tell me Brill's alive? Many apologies for overstepping my bounds,*

I finally get to go back to the residence building, and Brill heads for his hotel. All I want is a hot shower. Only – somebody has left a threatening note on my door. It says, *You burned chocolate, now we burn you.* Then there's a crudely drawn picture of a basket on fire, with a guillotine in the background. Meaning they want to cut off my head and set it on fire.

Standing in the hall, a shiver runs down my spine. There was a bit of chaos earlier. Things are probably under control now, but if someone got into the facility and found my room – it's mejor not to go inside.

I call Brill. After he arrives driving a newly rented car, he goes into the room and packs my bags, gets me into his hotel without anyone seeing, then goes out for supplies. Hopefully, no one knows where I'm hiding – except Tawny, who has a tracker on my dress. Pero if she'd wanted to turn my location over to the people who want me muerta, she'd have done it already.

Almost as if she heard me thinking about her, Tawny calls my sublingual. *We need to talk about how to handle Brill being alive. He can't hint that fear of HGB caused him to fake his death. Otherwise, Brill could wind up in a cell somewhere.*

Brill's not estúpido, I tell her.

Tawny chatters, *I've already released the first perfectspin. It's vague, but implies that Brill was injured in an accident on Zant. And may have been wandering around with amnesia. Until he saw an image of you and remembered his one true love.*

Oi! We're back to the novela tropes.

I've been avoiding the polls, pero I cave and selfiesearch. Six hours ago, the people who want me dead had decreased to less than 25%. Tawny's will-they-won't-they between me and Kaliel was doing awesome things for my ratings. Since the fires started, the hater factor's jumped up to 67% thinking I deserve to be shaved.

It's not as bad as I feared. I assumed it would be close to 100%.

A couple of articles about me and Janvier float the rumor that he's trying to steal me from Kaliel for publicity reasons. When I find the holo of mi vida's face, it's attached to a number of articles, many of them sympathetic. Most assuming that Brill has returned too late, and he's lost me to Kaliel.

CHAPTER TWENTY-FOUR

At about three in the morning, I make an emergency call to
Valeria, my former stylist. She stayed with Mamá y Minda, to
work on the show on Zant. It's daytime there, and things on Zant
are relatively tranquilo. Tawny managed to perfectspin the images
of all those burning trees to gain a grande amount of sympathy for
Earth. According to Minda, no one's enthusiastic about invading
a diseased planet. That's on fire.

The emergency is Brill's hair. I tried to bleach it. It didn't wind
up anything near his original strawberry blond. It looks like pale
straw – with a light lavender overtone. That tanto black dye must
have had a purple tint. At least he's gone back to his brown
leather jacket and tee combo, so he looks a lot more like himself.
Just a punk-rock version.

Brill's holding a plate of vegetarian stir-fry I whipped up using
ingredients he brought back from the 24-hour megastore – along
with a single pot and a hot plate. I can do genius things with food
and understand the chemistry behind baking and candy making.
Por qué can't I get Brill's hair to a normal color? Por la verdad,
we're still talking organic material and chemistry.

Valeria sighs. "Take him to a salon. If you keep putting
chemicals on it, the hair will break, and then he'll be half bald."

Mamá comes into the room. "I am just glad we can tell people
he is alive. Está bien, no? Holding onto that secret was so hard,
Bee." She crowds in closer to Valeria, getting bigger in the
holofield. She raises an eyebrow at my ill-fitting clothes. "Frank
is not sure where he stands with HGB. He went for a late-night
run on the beach with Botas, and I am afraid by the time Frank

burns off all his nervous energy, the little corgi's legs will be all tired out." She really is worried – and not for the dog.

"What he did for Brill last night was amazing, Mamá." Tears bite at my eyes. And not just because I haven't had any sleep. I feel estúpida, feeling this grateful to someone for not doing something horror-heavy. Especially because I had to watch him *do* something horror-heavy first. "Por favor, thank him for me. Porque no sé how."

"It would mean more if you tell him in person," Valeria points out.

"She can't." Brill tugs on strands of his hair, trying to get a better look at the damage. "Ga. For the same reason Bo can't go with me to a salon. People are making threats against her life."

"And someone is still trying to kidnap her." Mamá looks at me. "You cannot come back to Zant, Bee. And you don't need to – Minda is cancelling the cooking class. Most of the students backed out."

"Oye!" How can I suddenly be this useless, this irrelevant – this hated?

"We're leaving Earth in a couple of hours," Brill says. "We have a ride coming to take us to the planet where I left my ship." He means Gavin. We're going to take the half-crashed shuttle out of atmo to meet him, out past the range of Earth's defensive weapons. "Then we can go somewhere safe until this blows over."

"Oye! I said I wanted to regroup, not hide out." I put a hand on Brill's arm. "There's some things I haven't told you." Y I still have a lot to sort out, in mi cabeza. Frank texted us Not-Kaliel's stats sheet. And there's that microdot. Brill and I make tense eye contact. The frustration inside him's boiling over into an orange tone in his irises. I look at mi mamá. "I have to call you back."

Brill moves to the window.

I hang up the phone and follow him. "Que?"

"Chocolate is gone. The threatened invasion has been stopped. I get to be alive again. It feels like a win to me. Uan maybe it's time for you to take your graduation exam and then find a kitchen you can run or a school where you can teach."

Sí, that is tempting. I've rarely even gotten to cook for myself since Mamá took my spot on Minda's foodie friendly show.

Though somehow, I'm not sure if I'll be feliz cooped up in a kitchen. Maybe that's part of my reluctance to graduate. Porque if I do, I'm locked into a future that might be boring, after all the adventures I've had.

I sigh. "My planet is still in ruins, mi vida. I can't abandon it."

"Even if it's abandoned you?"

My shoulders tense, and my hands ball into fists. I force myself to relax. He's right, of course. Over the last few hours, the comments in the polls have grown truly feo – *ugly* – with haters bragging that if they got the chance, they'd murder me in the street. The polls may be divided – and some commenters support me – pero, it only takes one kek with a knife who's willing to do worse than comment.

I can't stop an anguished sound from escaping my throat, and a few frustrated tears from falling. Before I even register he's moved, Brill's cupping my face in his hands, wiping the tears away with his thumbs. "Hanstral. I shouldn't have said that."

"What am I supposed to do? Run and hide forever? No y nunca. I'm not built that way." I'm echoing Frank. Eh? I never thought there'd be ways I likematch Frank. Pero, the more I think about it, the more I realize that in some ways, Frank and I need the same things, psychologically. "I need somewhere to belong. I was never more miserable than when I isolated myself on Larksis 9." I lean my forehead against Brill's chest, hitting something solid in his jacket's upper pocket. I think it's the Surströmming from the picnic basket. I move to the other side and snuggle in closer. "Mira, I need to ask Gavin for news, so I can be smart about my next move. Now that you're free from HGB's shadow, I understand if you and Gavin keep your distance. It's not your planet."

He tenses, like I've said something hurtful. Pero he's hiding his feelings behind fizzbounced blue irises.

"Que?"

"Nothing, Babe. You're right. It is your planet." He shrugs.

I sigh. "Remember how you said that for our relationship to work, I need to be open with my feelings?"

Brill's trembling, still holding something back. Finally he says, "Why can't you accept that I've vowed in my heart to fight for *you*. You keep pushing me away, telling me to leave you in danger – and now, to let you go back to danger. Sthesh! I was willing to sacrifice my life for someone you care about. What more proof do you want that I love you?"

It would be petty, no, to tell him I want a permanent commitment, proof that even if I have nowhere else to belong, that I'd belong to him, for always. Proof that I have a right to ask him to risk himself for me. "Mi vida. Por favor."

He studies me. "I just can't help wondering if you'd be coming back for Janvier."

"Que?" I pull away, defensive tension knotting my shoulders. How can he say that, when the blood of the man Janvier killed is present in this room?

The blue slips and the deep yellow-orange shifting into his eyes says he's jealous. "I realize there were extenuating circumstances, but I can't help but wonder if you'll develop a relationship with every attractive single guy you meet. It's a big galaxy. If you stick with me, you'll meet a lot of guys."

"Oye!" Heat floods my chest. All Brill ever asked from me is loyalty. And I don't have the best track record. I *was* falling for Shelly – and that won't be easy por mi vida to deal with. "I wasn't going anywhere with Shelly, no matter what I felt. Nada y nunca. I'm loyal to you. Pero you know I care deeply about people. I'm always going to lead with my heart. If you can't handle that, mi vida, you should walk away right now."

"I probably should. And believe me, I've tried. But I can't." He sighs, exhaling far longer than an Earthling could. "That corazón of yours is what I love about you. You deserve better than a screwup like me, though. And I'm afraid that in one of these guys, you'll find it."

I point at my ruined dress. "Don't worry. This one's muerto."

Tears spark to my eyes, unbidden. Porque it makes sense now, why Shelly would be captivated by me while trying to make peace with his own tenuous position inside HGB.

"I'm not talking about the clone. I mean 1.0. The one who– Hest!" Brill sees my tears. and sympathy colors his irises apricot. "Lo siento, Babe. You're really grieving." He puts a hand on my cheek, then pulls me to him. "What did Shelly say to you, there at the end? Or is it too personal to ask?"

How could something en mi corazón be too personal to share with mi vida? He thinks there might be – that's how deeply I hurt him. Again.

"I need to show you." I pull out of his arms and step over to the desk, and pick up my metal bracelet. I tap the underside of the bracelet, getting the dot Shelly gave me to stick to my fingertip.

"What's that, Babe?"

I'd wanted to think about the implications of this minúsculo dot before I shared it with anyone – even Brill. Maybe that was a mistake. "Shelly gave me all the answers."

Brill sucks in a breath – in and in, a gasp that seems to last forever. "Is that what I think it is?"

I nod. "HGB's accounting records. Everything the Galactic Court needs to take them apart. We couldn't risk disrupting HGB's power when the invasion was coming. Or when they were the only thing propping up Earth's economy. Pero now everything's changed. This dot could help us mold a new future. Maybe the Court would help us restructure HGB."

"Jrekt!" Brill's irises go black. I'd expected a shade of deep green – interest and excitement – or dark purple concentration – not terror. "La! Anvet shonre bep sawa."

He asked me to destroy the microdot. And he's so upset, he couldn't say it in any language other than his own.

"Shouldn't we at least think about this?"

Brill squints at me, like I'm just not getting it. "Think about finishing destroying your world? That dot holds more than accounting files. Details of HGB's illegal activities. Maybe even kill lists. If you brought this to the Galactic Court, Earth's Global Court couldn't deny its own laws. Frank, Janvier and Tawny will get shaved for sure, and who knows how many other su's? Who knows what would happen to all of Janvier's clones? And what other secrets might come to light? If you're right about how your mom wound up on HGB's payroll, that might constitute bribery for keeping quiet about your father's death. In a wide enough sweep, she could get executed too. HGB wouldn't be restructured. It would be put to death."

I'd never pictured Tawny and Frank in line for the shave. They've both become amigos of sorts. And while they've done some bad things, they aren't evil.

I remember watching that reporter get shaved, the way her executioners strapped her to a board and tilted her forward, the stark terror in her eyes as her neck slid into the dangerous circle of the guillotine. I can't imagine that same fear in Tawny's eyes – or mi mamá's.

The tension in my shoulders cranks even tighter as I project the implications. "And with HGB gone and our Global Court still weak, Earth descends into war over the power vacuum. Ay-ay-ay. Even without the monopoly on chocolate, we can't expect HGB to just go away, and everyone to be fine."

"You know that," Brill says. "So why did you take that dot?"

"Because I want Janvier to pay for killing Shelly." Heat floods my cheeks. "I tried to convince myself it was a good idea. I should have realized it wasn't when I didn't want to tell you about it. Shelly at least had a plan, would have taken HGB apart quietly and replaced it with something mejor. He gave me that dot as he was dying, because he was frustangerated. And anger made him estúpido. Yo también, apparently."

I had never thought past getting justicia por mi papá, whom HGB had murdered for uncovering their secrets. And my angerzentment over their ordering a hit on Brill.

Brill says. "I can see how that might be tempting."

I sigh. "Then you think we should give the dot back to Janvier?"

"Ga! Ga y ga. You can't get close enough to him to do that. Now that the polls have turned on you, you 're a liability. If Janvier believed you could destroy him – he wouldn't wait to hire an assassin. He'd shoot you himself."

I consider breaking the dot between the nails of my thumb and forefinger, like one of Tawny's bugs. I hesitate. "Oye. What if Janvier figures out that I took this? They're bound to find the gouge in Shelly's forearm, and it's not a huge logic leap. He would never believe I destroyed it."

"Sthesh!" Brill paces, fast enough that he's making me un poco dizzy. I've never seen him so agitated. "We need to get out of here. Before we discover the limits of Frank's mercy and HGB's protection."

I tuck the dot inside my phone case. "La! I hope–"

Brill's handheld rings, and when he answers, even from across the room I hear Frank's angeriffic voice.

"Ga," Brill says. "She didn't know what it was. Not really." Frank says something else. Brill swallows visibly. "I'll return it. And accept the consequences. But before that, I'll make sure Bo disappears."

Why does Brill keep volunteering to die for me? Taking that dot was my mistake, not his.

"No!" I stick the phone in my pocket. "Tell Frank I took it, and I'll give it back. And then you and I will shadowpop together. If he lets me."

Brill doesn't look happy. Pero he relays the message. Then he and Frank speak more softly. Finally, Brill hangs up, then sends a quick text. He gets an immediate response.

"Frank wants to meet us on the beach. Like right now." He hesitates, his eyes shifting through a dozen conflicting colors. "Or we could run. Actually take that dot to the Galactacops. Your mom's offplanet. She could stay on Zant."

Part of me still thinks that's a good idea. Por qué no? Frank and Tawny are resourceful. If Janvier pulled in enough favors, even he would probably escape the shave. Wouldn't he? "How would we get the dot to the Galactacops?"

"Gavin's already in orbit. He's texted that your planet's shut down their defense system – probably Shelly's last act – uan Gavin's willing to risk running the border and landing on the beach."

"Where Frank will be waiting, no?" I feel bitter and dry inside.

Brill shrugs. "Frank knows about the transport we used to move Murry, uan he's probably already secured it, and the spaceport will be crawling with people would love to turn you in. My rental car's GPS can be tracked. Gavin's ship's too big to put down anywhere else in walking distance. Frank's good with a gun, but if I run full speed, carrying you on the beach, he probably couldn't hit me. You could contact Gideon Tyson. I'm sure he'd be happy to escort us. We'd probably make it, too, before HGB's guys could space us."

I consider it. "No. We have to give the dot to Frank. That's his chance to prove he's not switched to our side. HGB would owe him enough to keep him breathing, right?" Though if I'm this terrified of what HGB might do to Frank, is giving them back the dot the right thing to do? What choice do we have? "Besides, you said contacting the Galactics would be a mistake."

"Wal. But it's your planet. And you suddenly have a great deal of power over its future. I tried to change Earth's future by pushing you to steal chocolate – and ever since, I've regretted not letting you make your own decision."

Tears blur my vision. "Even if I'd never wound up on Crosskiss's ship, that conference to invade Earth would still have happened – and I wouldn't have been there to talk to Garfex. You weren't wrong. Holding onto chocolate was dangerous. Eso es –

I've never been on a voyage of discovery. And I haven't finished reading the Codex. So I could use some Krom insight."

He smiles at my acknowledgement of his value. Pero his words are somber. "Without chocolate, Earth is in trouble. Those fires are destroying your ecosystem, in ways you won't understand for decades. Earth needs resources. That means an organization that people galaxy-wide are familiar with, that has legal power to trade for the things you need. From the Krom point of view, you need HGB." That sounds reasonable too. "Whatever we do, we need to get out of this hotel, soon."

"Oh, mi vida." I'm crumbling, pero Brill's arms hold me together, hold me up. He kisses me, and the distance between us vanishes. His hummingbird heartbeat steadies the rhythm of my panicked corazón.

When he finally breaks the beso, Brill says, "It will be diay, Babe. Somehow."

I run my hands through his unnaturally pale hair. It feels like straw. "Why would you think I'd give you up for Janvier? Did I miss something? Porque he practically slammed me through a bionet. I didn't get the impression he liked me."

Brill's eyes go an embarrassed pink. "He sent you a gift. It came while you were drying your hair." He hands me a small box. Inside, there's a honey cowrie shell.

Brill has no idea what that means, and he doesn't pry – pero he can see how upset I am. And he has to be worried too. He says again, "It will be diay."

It probably won't. Because maybe when Janvier sent it, he was being kind. Pero he knows exactly where I am, and that I was likely awake to receive a delivery. I'm surprised the assassins haven't showed up already.

I call Tyson to ask for sanctuary. I don't tell him about the dot, just the threats to my life.

The sunlamps on in his ship surrounded him with a halo of light. "Here's te ting, Bo. Te Galactic Enforcers have been busy in oter parts of te galaxy wit te pirate attacks and riots over te limited supply of chocolate. And now tis ting wit Murry. I don't tink anybody's close enough to Eart to escort you."

Fantástico, no?

CHAPTER TWENTY-FIVE

It's time to head for the beach. In the time it's taken for Brill to get everything coordinated with Gavin, and me to get us packed, no one has showed up to kill us. So Janvier must trust Frank, after all.

I tell Chestla again, "I have to go."

Calling her for advice was a mistake. She's too far away to help, y it is driving her loca. She's been rapid-firing questions and offering self-defense techniques for five minutes straight.

"Consider taking a gun," she says. "Or at least a can of pepper spray."

I roll my eyes. "I am not going to shoot Frank. After everything I've told him about how much I hate violence, I won't give him the satisfaction."

"I doubt he'll come alone, cesuda ma."

"I have to take the chance." Though my palms are sweaty, and the room feels too hot because I'm nervous. I redirect her. "So have the niños made it to Praxion 5?"

"Not yet. Or at least they haven't landed at any registered spaceports."

"I hope they make it." I hope we make it, too. I'd love to be breathing long enough to congratulate Nellet and buy her a wedding gift.

"Hey!" Chestla says. "You want me to fail?"

"Not exactly," I say. "I just want peace to win, for once."

Ball, leaning on a cane, limps into the holofield behind Chestla. The edges of his hazel eyes flash lavender. It's the only shift color his half-Krom irises can produce, the gift of laughter. "Chestla can't fail."

"It's time to go, Babe." Brill says.

"You should take a gun, Bo." Ball gestures at his injured leg. "This won't feel worth it if you die without a fight." He puts an arm around Chestla.

She blushes, pero when he squeezes her shoulder, she doesn't move his mano.

Brill says, "I don't even have a gun, su. Janvier took mine. I–" Brill hesitates. "I wasn't supposed to need it anymore. Frank was kalltet to let me live, given the circumstances. I almost wish he'd – I just don't want to see him dead."

"Would you have killed him, had the circumstances been reversed?" Ball asks.

"Set, Ga," Brill says. "Even if I'd die as a consequence, it wouldn't have been self-defense. Uan, that's my moral code, not his."

Ball gives Brill a meaningful look, and Brill's eyes shift an embarrassed pink. I don't understand what passed between the two of them.

It is still a good hour until dawn. Brill and I are in an area near the beach that offers some cover, a thick stand of trees and foliage. Pero, the trees end in an abrupt line ahead of us where the sand takes over, so we've got a decent view of the beach-side sky. The Murry dragon is here, somewhere, waiting for this interaction to be done and Frank to leave before he shows himself.

I keep glancing tristemente toward the HGB compound, towards the garden where the other clone, Dash, last spoke to me. I have no way to contact him and let him know we are leaving. The sun will come up, and Dash will be left waiting. Which leaves me bitter and dry inside. I couldn't save Shelly. And I can't save Dash either.

"La, Babe!" Brill points at the sky.

Gavin's ship comes in fast and hot, arcing towards the beach. It lands a good distance to our right, so we creep through the trees, as quietly as we can. Pero if Frank's on the beach, I'm sure he can hear us coming.

My nail polish suffered massive damage last night, and the puce green shows through the cracks and chips. I swallow a lump of painful emotion. I'm flying away from the machine that eased the symptoms of my IH addiction. In a week or so, I'll be back to fighting the shakes and trying to convince myself that I'm strong enough to deny the need.

The trees in front of me thin. Frank's moving between me and Gavin's ship, like he's afraid we might sneak past and fly away. Pero no. Resolve sits warm and heavy like melted chocolate in my chest. If Frank goes back to Janvier with the dot, Janvier might keep him alive.

"Wait here, mi vida." I set my bag at Brill's feet.

He starts to protest at being made to wait in the trees. Then he looks out at Frank, and back at me and nods. "Be careful."

As I step out onto the beach, Frank turns towards me. He's not holding a gun. Which gives me hope.

I call loudly, "Por favor, the Krom gets a pass, remember?"

No matter what happens to me. I force the tension from my shoulders, force my breathing to slow.

"With another Krom for backup, I wouldn't dare." Frank gestures at Gavin's ship, where the hatch is now open. I can't see Gavin, pero chances are he's got a weapon trained on Frank. Gavin's ideas on the Krom philosophy of self-defense are quite broad, considering how traditional he is about everything else.

Gavin comes down the ramp. The irises under his lightly hooded eyes are pale gray. Uan he's nervous, not afraid. His aim never wavers from Frank's cabeza.

"La! Por favor, Gavin." I relax my hands again. "We can all keep breathing today."

"That depends on this su." Gavin tells Frank, "Open your jacket."

Frank does, and Krom quick, Gavin snatches his weapon.

Frank smiles with what looks like genuine humor. "Bo might be right. Now, if you shoot me, it wouldn't be self-defense." He looks over at me. "And that makes it your call. Do you want to burn it all down?"

"Shelly already did that, no?" Pero he's not talking about the literal incendios. He's talking about dismantling HGB. "Shelly wanted me to finish the job. And sí, I was tempted." I take out my phone and hold it out, even though I'm a good twenty feet away from handing it off. "Brill convinced me that's not the answer. If you hadn't saved him yesterday, I can't imagine I'd have reached the same conclusion on my own."

Frank says, "I'm beginning to appreciate that his life's not as insignificant as I told Janvier."

Brill walks into the open, burdened with all our luggage, and in a flash of movement stands beside me, his eyes light gray in the moonlight.

I walk towards Frank. "Why'd you come alone, viejo?"

"Because it's the best shot at getting the dot back. It's like what you did with the mindworm plague at the aquarium on Zant." Frank is ita ita good at getting information, no? Few people know what happened that night. Maybe he talked to Kayla when he'd called Mario. "Violence would have put the parasite beyond your grasp, and it would have spread destruction as it fled."

I smile. "And Shelly said you had no imagination."

Frank frowns. "Speaking of that. I'm not exactly alone."

My heart squeezes. Have we walked into a trap?

"Bodacious?" Gavin asks uncertainly.

"Wait," I tell Gavin, though I'm nervous también. "Frank, what do you mean?"

"Don't freak out. Please." Frank smiles tentatively at Gavin, then gestures towards the bathroom building, farther down his side of the beach. "Mr. Gern, the man about to step out here is not Daschel Janvier. He's a clone, and he wants nothing more than a ride off this planet. When I went for my run with Botas a few hours ago, he and I had a long talk."

A frightened-looking Clonevier peeks around the doorway. He's wearing a Hawaiian shirt over khaki pants.

"Dash." An intense wave of relief flows over me. Janvier hadn't hunted him down after all.

A shadow passes over the moon. Somebody's flying silently above us in a hang glider.

Gavin cries out. I turn back toward him. He's trying to pull a dart out of his face. I move to help Gavin. I've seen these darts before. They're designed to exploit the way Krom bodies handle electricity, making the victim too dizzy to move. As long as this sand is dry, I should be okay if I touch a darted Krom. Pero being shot with a dart would likely kill me.

"Viejo!" I scold Frank. He said it wasn't a trap.

Frank shakes his cabeza. "Don't look at me."

Brill, who had also been moving towards Gavin, leans heavily against me, reacting to a dart in his hand, and then a second later Frank groans and collapses to the sand.

My muscles tense at the shock. "Frank!"

"Shtesh!" Brill stops trying to get the dart out of his hand, and lurches to Frank's side. Four men from the hang gliders come out from behind Gavin's ship. Brill shouts, "You keks, this one's not Krom."

I move to help Frank también, pero one of the men grabs my arm. He's got a gun. I'm smart enough not to fight him.

Brill gets Frank's dart out, scraping a gouge in Frank's neck as he angles the shaft to get out the electricity-disruption chip too. Brill's moves as though through water and looks like he might throw up. He makes one more try at pulling the dart from his own flesh, pero it's lodged between the bones in his hand. Brill puts a hand on Frank's chest and says a couple of harsh Krom words I've never heard before.

Frank's not breathing, and because my brain's loco, all I can think is that if Frank dies, who'll take care of his corgi?

A voice comes from the earpiece the guy holding me is wearing. "Take the stick guy and the girl." He means Gavin, who is almost unnaturally thin. "And get my jacket back from the other moron."

Jack. He must have a camera on us.

One guy pulls Gavin to his feet, as the other two henchpirates approach Brill. Mi vida takes off the jacket and tosses it to them. Then he leans over Frank and starts CPR.

The henchpirates look at each other, and one shrugs, like *should we shoot him*? And the other one gives a little head shake. Gracias a Dios.

Frank sucks in a breath. Relief floods through me, even though I'm still about to be kidnapped. By space pirates. Again.

Brill meets my gaze, and his irises are shifting back and forth between gold and brown as the emotions inside him boil between love and anger. His jaw is tight with resolve. He knows he can't stop them from taking me. He glares at the hombre holding his jacket. "Tell Jack this isn't over."

Why isn't the spuck coming to our rescue? I'm worried something might have happened to it. Pero to be found on Earth, right when Murry promised he wasn't expanding, would have horrific consequences. So I can't blame him if he's watching as the pirates take me and Gavin right off the beach.

I drop my phone into the sand, hoping to leave it, so Brill can give the dot to Frank. A henchpirate notices and scoops the phone up.

Well, that's just crudtastic.

CHAPTER TWENTY-SIX

I'm sitting across from Gavin, on matching cots that line both walls of a small cargo hold. A clear tub holding laundry supplies sits on a shelf above Gavin's cot and a portable toilet is against the back wall, between us. Someone must have used this room as temporary quarters. There's no door, just a transparent bounce field across the open doorway.

I move over to sit beside Gavin. I need to get that dart out of his face. His reacción to the electrical disruption seems mucho peor than Brill's. *Much worse.* "Mira. Let me see."

Gavin angles his face so I can get a better look. Now that the emergency is over, I'm more careful about doing this right.

"Lo siento," I tell him. "I don't know how to make this not hurt."

Gavin shrugs, just a quick bob of his dark denim jacket. "I don't think there *is* a way to make this not hurt."

Gavin and I have never been this close to each other. He's in his Earth-equivalent fifties, pero due to Krom delayed aging, he looks like a human my age. His skin is perfectamente smooth.

I grasp the dart, as close as I can to Gavin's skin, I flinch inside. The first time Brill got hit with one of these things, it broke off, leaving the chip in mi vida's flesh. The darts are designed to do that, to keep the darted Krom from being able to remove them. I pull as carefully as I can.

The dart breaks.

Gavin lets out a soft, "Grnmh."

Sympathy sparks through my chest. "Hanstral. Ita, ita hanstral." Somehow, apologizing in his language feels more sincere.

It does get me a chromashift towards lavender, pero with that extraño orange tint, ese es un color feo.

"Por favor!" I say to the henchpirate standing with his back to us in the hallway. I hold up the broken dart and gesture towards the edge of the chip protruding from Gavin's cheek. "It's making him sick."

They haven't given us any agua. Krom don't do well with dehydration. Gavin's eyes are deep gray with an orange undertone, like he's flushed and his iron-rich orange blood is bleeding through the worry

The henchpirate scowls. "I'm not coming in there. And I'm not giving you pliers to use as a weapon."

"What am I going to do?" I ask. "You have a gun."

The guy looks with sympathy at Gavin, who is pulling the portable toilet over to him. Gavin's already thrown up once, when they put us in here. He throws up again.

These darts are supposedly an alternative to lethal weapons. Yet Gavin could die from the side effects. Pero that would negate whatever reason a group of pirates chose non-lethal weapons in the first place.

Gavin's vomiting puts a grimace on the henchpirate's face – pero even more sympathy in his eyes. "It'll be a couple of days before we reach Jack's ship, and that guy won't last. Hold on." The guy disappears down the hallway.

"When he drops the barrier, don't try to escape," Gavin warns. "It won't go well."

I huff. "I know."

So as the pirate puts the pliers on the floor, I stay on my cot. Before I even move to pick them up, he reactivates the field.

I step quickly over to Gavin. I take a deep breath. Vale, Bo. I can do this. I set the pliers against his cheek and use my fingers to press the skin down. The pliers grab an edge and, as the chip comes out, a smattering of bright orange blood splatters my hand.

Gavin presses the cuff of his jacket against the wound, trying to stop the bleeding. I place the bloodied pliers on the floor and retreat to my bunk.

"Don't expect bandages or anything," the hombre says as he grabs the pliers and leaves.

With the energy barrier in place, I can do nada pero stand by Gavin. "Diay, su?" *You okay, dude?*

His eyes shift more lavender. "That hand gesture looked so Krom."

Que? I didn't realize I made a hand gesture. Apparently I've picked up a lot from mi vida without realizing it. "What do we do now, mijo?"

Though he still looks ill, Gavin laughs. "Brill called *me* mijo the other day. You su's really have grown on each other. If he's not careful, he'll form a–" His eyes shift to an embarrassed orange-pink.

"A what, su?"

Pero if for a moment he forgot he wasn't talking to another Krom, that moment has passed, and using his language won't bring it back.

He shrugs. "Forget I said anything. It's not like we're likely to live long enough for it to matter. Brill either. He's become the most honor-bound Krom I know. And that's your fault. He'll come for you, even if it's a trap."

"You think kidnapping me is just a trap?" It seems muy elaborate.

"Wal, su. By taking back that jacket, Jack called out Brill. He wants your boyfriend to come and get you. Otherwise the goons would have taken him too. Or he'd be lying dead on the beach."

I shudder, picturing Brill's face dusted with sand, his chest as still as when he'd played dead in that trash bag. "Why?"

Gavin rolls his eyes, which are turning light orange. "Jack's the kind of petty being that wants payback because Brill stole his jacket. And then the first time Jack tried to get it back, he wound up prison bound. You know he blames Brill for that, and not his own crimes. The su was still mad about it when he thought Brill was dead. I think Jack wants to kill Brill himself and can't return to Earth because he's still a wanted criminal."

I picture Jack's deceptively friendly face and warm brown eyes. "Jack tried to kill *me* more than once. Uan, why does he suddenly want me alive?"

"He must have a plan," Gavin says. "But are you bait, and he wants to make Brill watch you die? Or does he have something else in mind that makes you valuable?"

Eh? We've assumed someone wanted to kidnap me because of my connection to the Zantites or HGB – or even because I might represent Earth to Greftash. If I'm just bait – that's muy, muy humbling. Pero it's a valid possibility to add to the list. Jack could have lied to the Greftashians, claiming his goals aligned with theirs, just to get me off Earth – just to get to mi vida.

"Brill knows that? And he'll still come?" I don't quite dare to sit beside Gavin again. It's been awkward between us, from the first time we'd met. He refused to eat food I prepared because he'd learned about Earth's Victorian-era lack of hygiene. We had un gran fight over it. Pero I feel muy estúpida just standing here. I start to move back to my bunk, pero Gavin moves down, so I can sit closer if I want. He takes the high-tech sick bucket with him.

I sit on the bunk and sigh. "Sthesh, su. I keep telling Brill I don't want him to die for me."

Gavin smiles. "He really had better be careful."

He means it as a compliment – Gavin sees something of value in me now. Pero he's also alluding to whatever he didn't tell me earlier. Which es muy frustrating. Brill isn't supposed to form a whatever-it-is. Which means Gavin still doesn't approve of something about mine and Brill's relationship, and I wish he would be open about what. It's like with that mourning pendant. I'm not Krom, so I don't deserve to know. Pero pushing Gavin won't get me anywhere.

Instead, I ask, "How can Brill be the most honor-bound, if he's not into tradition? He's dating me, no?"

Gavin leans back, looking like he might throw up again, pero much of the orange tint has left his eyes. "If Brill didn't care about honor, would he have made a parvbada for his alien girlfriend, who wouldn't even know what it means?"

I try not to bristle. "Doesn't that make you the most honor-bound? Uan, you're fulfilling that promise even though he didn't die – and you don't like me."

Gavin shrugs. "You're growing on me." He gestures first to the blood on his sleeve and then to the portable toilet between his feet. "Hest. A lot of people wouldn't have just taken care of somebody sick like you just did – either because they don't care if someone's in pain, or they would have been too grossed out."

I wrinkle my nose. "Puaf! You have seen cleaner days."

His eyes shift lavender at the irony. Then they settle back towards gray. "We can't stop Brill from coming."

"Frank will come too. He wants–" I can't say it here. Jack's bound to have surveillance on us, and ni idea if there's audio. Pero if Brill's coming for me, Frank's coming for that microdot. Well – and maybe a little for me.

"I know what Frank wants." Gavin glances around, probably checking for visible cameras. "And wal, that makes sense."

My sublingual rings. I gasp. I assumed they'd have us signal-blocked. If this kidnapping is a challenge to Brill, then maybe the pirates don't care. Maybe they want me to talk to him.

Pero, it's not Brill. It's Gideon Tyson. He must have found a Galactacop close to us after all. Hope builds inside me.

Party happy dance flips, Bo. I don't know how you guys did it. But te peace that comes from having identified te guy who killed Mrigweck is profound. Now all you have to do is catch Anton Conrad and bring him to justice.

I sigh. Supongo que no. He's talking about Not-Kaliel. Gideon must have just received the information Frank forwarded to him hours ago. *That's un poco difícil. We're about to be murdered by space pirates.* That's a minor exaggeration. We'll be alive at least a couple of days. *Is there anything you can do?*

"Who are you talking to?" Gavin asks. "Brill?"

I mouth, *Gideon Tyson.*

Gavin's eyes go green with sudden interest. "Is he close enough to help us?"

I shake mi cabeza.

Tyson chatters, *Maybe you can call your friend tat.*

Okay. *My friend that what?*

Tat. Tyson hisses again. *T. H. A. T. H. Tat. He wants to start a GalacticFundster to help put out Eart's fires. Don't ask how he got my contact info.*

He's not the type to stand up to space pirates. Pero it's nice to know we have a start towards allies en la galaxia.

I hang up on Tyson and then try calling Brill, then Frank. Neither answers. I don't know anyone else close enough to help us.

I tell Gavin, "Tyson called to see if we could help capture his partner's murderer. Conrad's loco and killed Mrigweck because he thought Brill and I passed him something."

Gavin's eyes go an excited green. "I wish they hadn't taken my handheld."

"Como?"

Gavin looks confused.

I repeat it in Krom. "Fwa?" *Why?*

"Uan if Tyson knows where Conrad's going, I could have him stopped. Capturing a cop killer means a significant reward. I know guys who'd take the risk, some as close as Praxion 7."

Of course Gavin knows people on Praxion 7. He does business with pirates and killers. If Praxion 5 is the Pleasure Moon, where Nellet and Watae are headed to get married, Praxion 7 is its darker cousin that nobody talks about.

"Could you get your people to talk to me?" I ask. Being both an Earthling and a civilian, and all. Pero one with the benefit of a sublingual.

Gavin's eyes cycle through several shades of purple. "Maybe. And it's not like we can do anything else from in here."

"We should try to escape, su." I say.

"How?"

The room has no hatches, and the ventilation system consists of fist-sized vents in a line along one edge of the ceiling. "Ni idea."

Gavin shrugs. "They have to bring us water eventually, and we can try to change the equation then."

He pulls that laundry box off the shelf. The supplies include an indelible marker. En serio? Whoever had this space before us worried about writing his name in his underwear?

Gavin says, "Get Tyson to give you the coordinates where Conrad was last seen."

Gavin moves to a cleaner part of the floor and lowers himself, bringing a hand to his forehead like he has un gran headache. Sitting cross-legged, he writes a list of phone connections directly onto the hard flooring. I'm surprised he realizes how my sublingual works. It's easy for my brain to process a written-out number directly into my neural patch.

I get the relevant information from Tyson, and Gavin adds that to the chart he's making, so I won't have to remember it.

While Gavin's writing, Brill calls. *It took a little while, but we hotwired Gavin's ship, and we're exiting atmo. We have a bead on your trajectory. Babe–*

Don't come, I interrupt. *Gavin says it's a trap.*

I know it's a trap. That's why we have a plan. He hesitates. *I have a few other calls to make, but I wanted to hear your voice, know that you're diay.*

I'm fine, mi vida. So's Gavin. He's so confident that we'll get out of this, that we're planning out how to help Tyson catch Anton Conrad.

Thank the Codex. Brill's relief is like warm honey in my mind, sweet and comforting. *If anything happens before we get there, play for time. Beg for your life – Jack likes to feel in control – but not for Gavin's. Jack might kill him just to prove he can. Promise Jack anything he asks. Shtesh, kiss the kek if you have to.*

Ewwww, mi vida, no. Y no.

Brill's laugh echoes in my brain even after he's hung up.

Gavin spends ten minutes coaching me on what to tell his amigos to keep them from hanging up on me.

"Why don't we ask these su's to come save us instead?" I ask.

Gavin grimaces. Then his eyes dip towards black. "If enough people chase them, this crew will space us, to make the pursuers stop to keep from running over our bodies. I might survive long enough to get picked up, but you …"

I shudder. If I have to die, being spaced is at the bottom of my list. Well – right above being shaved. The shave is humiliating, porque it's so public. Pero dying in space would be the opposite – muy frío y sola.

Besides, I'm supposed to die of the Invincible Heart before Brill has a chance to form a whatever-it-is.

I try to shake off my sense of defeat. Brill and Frank could save us. Or Gavin and I could escape. And even if that crashbangs, I don't know for sure that Jack wants us muerto. He specified that I be brought to him viva. At least it seems less likely that this situation has anything to do with Jimena and her conspiracy.

I call Brill to check in. Pero he's gone communications dark.

I start calling Gavin's friends. By the time I'm halfway through the list, they're calling *me* back. They want more details on Not-Kaliel. And every one of them asks whether the bounty stipules bringing him in alive. When Tyson assures me that the Galactacops don't care – as long as the DNA matches the blood on the knife and the guy is still identifiable – I feel un poco sorry for Not-Kaliel.

I didn't realize at the time, pero Frank recorded Not-Kaliel's confession of killing a cop. The viejo records all his little chats in his official capacity. Then, when he's sure the recordings won't be needed, he deletes them. Which means he captured mi papá's last words – and then threw them away.

In this case though, the recording is solid evidence – and has brought comfort to Tyson.

Gavin smudges the list of contacts on the floor into una gran black smear. He then starts coordinating the other information using indecipherable abbreviations so we can track his friends' progress. Gavin keeps adding information to his chart as more calls come in. I'm not sure how to feel about working this close with him. It feels comfortable. Only – if not for my sublingual, he'd never include me in a project like this.

At one point he says, "Your sublingual comes in handy. Only–" He sort of studies my ear. "If Jack knows you have it, aren't you afraid he might cut it out?"

"Dios mio! You think he's that cruel?"

Gavin shrugs. "He comes from a pretty nasty family,"

"I thought Jack was named after a 20th century painter."

Gavin snort-laughs. "That's possible. His grandmother was an artist. But the Wolfe family's been involved with Earth-based crime for generations. I looked into it after Jack started targeting Brill. They were responsible for a massacre in the late 2050s that made them outsiders even in the crime syndicates. Supposedly, other criminals tried to kill the entire family, but Jack's ancestors survived in hiding."

My sublingual rings again, and I'm certain one of Gavin's amigos is calling back for more details. Pero it's Chestla.

We didn't make it. Yet her voice sounds cheerful as it bubblechatters. *They're married.*

Then why are you fizzbounced, chica?

Because they're safe. And Watae's Guardian Companion bought them this ridiculous cake, since Nellet said that's a tradition on your planet, and she felt like you made this possible. It's shaped like a giant shoe. Which I don't think is quite right. Chestla's babbling. Which she does to cover when she's nervous.

I stop her. *You know we're in trouble, no? It's okay. It's a sublingual, and nobody's close enough to pick up crosstalk.*

Chestla sighs. *We've spoken to Frank and Brill. We're on our way to intercept your ship, in case they can't catch you first. Thank goodness I put a tracker on you.* She still sounds fizzbounced. She probably really had been eating cake when she found out pirates abducted Gavin and me.

Que? I thought Tawny was the only one who bugged people. And I haven't seen Chestla in a long time. *How do I have a tracker I don't know about?*

You swallowed it. It's nanite-based and looks for the nearest way into the bloodstream. After the last time you got kidnapped, I wasn't taking chances. When I don't say anything, she says, *What? I'm Evevron. Tech is what we do.*

She doesn't sound the least bit embarrassed. And she has a point. Porque who manages to get kidnapped by pirates – twice?

CHAPTER TWENTY-SEVEN

Mamá calls me, chattering, *Would a Zantite warship be of any use to you, Bee?*

Que? She must have been talking to Frank. It's nice to know that this time, Mamá's taking the initiative to help. Even if she's too far away to do any good. *No, Mamá. It would take weeks to get here and the pirates wouldn't surrender, porque they'd be executed by the Zantites.*

And since Zantites execute criminals with their teeth, it's a muy, muy vivid image.

Mira, Alex Crosskiss and the Layla's Pride are at the edge of the Sol System. Now that the invasion has been called off, he might be willing to help. Of course, that's only because mi mamá es amigas with his mamá.

I blink. Wait. *Eso es imposible. He was on your show a few days ago. On Zant.*

Minda's voice bubbles into mi cabeza. Mamá must have me on speakerphone. *When he was in the Sol system the first time, Crosskiss discovered a wormhole leading close to your home world. He argued it would make the invasion cheap and easy. Nobody told me, because they knew I'm sympathetic towards your planet and would have warned you. But now that the invasion is off, King Garfex doesn't think it needs to stay a state secret.*

Mi corazón goes cold. Earth had come closer than it knows to being overrun by alien warships. Brill was right – losing chocolate has saved us. We can worry about trade with la galaxia and not being a pariah planet later – while we're all breathing and enjoying not being a Zantite protectorate.

I'll ask Gavin if he can think of a way that Crosskiss could help.

Mamá gives me a number for Crosskiss, in case we decide to contact him. As soon as I hang up, I get another call – from Murry. *Bodacious Benitez, are you alright?*

Sí, Murry. We've been on this ship for a while now. Y Murry saw us get abducted. *It took you long enough to get worried.*

Murry stays silent for a long time. *We were afraid you wouldn't want to talk to us after we abandoned you on the beach to save ourselves. Kaliel Johannsson would not have done that. Even Botas would not have done that. I have learned that it is noble for individuals to risk themselves for people they love. I have a form of love for you.*

He's apologizing. Uan I try to make him feel better. *Sometimes individuals risk themselves for each other. Sometimes they even die for people they care about. Pero sometimes that doesn't make sense. Sometimes you have to trust that the other person can take care of themselves.*

Murry bubblechatters, *Understanding individuals is complicated. You do not think I should feel shame and guilt, as Kaliel Johannsson would have?*

No, mijo. Other individuals are coming to rescue me. When I fled Earth for a culinary school as far away as possible, I would never have imagined having so many amigos willing to put themselves at risk for me. It kind of blows me away. Without even thinking, I bring a loose fist to my chest, a gesture that that feels both human and Krom. *And even if they fail, it's not your fault. Vale?*

Murry verbalizes something. It's not words, exactly, more the audible version of his thinking process. It sometimes takes humans most of their lives to realize the bad things that happen around them aren't their fault. And they haven't been hunted and told they were a plague since the day they were born. And they probably don't have nearly as many bad deeds to actually feel guilty for as Murry does. Finally, he bubblechatters, *I will try to believe that. But I prefer if you keep yourself safe. Okay?*

I'll try. I wish I could hug Murry. We both need it. Pero he's just a voice en mi cabeza. A voice that I suspect has something else to say.

Finally, he bubblechatters, *I wouldn't have called at all, except ...*

After a second, I prompt, *Except what?*

I've been helping dispose of the cryostasis pods on Evevron – and I found a device attached to one. It's flawed, but suggests interesting work on overcoming the cryostasis barrier. Leron was trying to wake us up. Remember what he told the court? Someone else decided to sample the brain tissue from Patient Zero, which made us too damaged for his research to do any good. Leron just ran out of time.

Oh, Murry. Now I really wish I could hug him. *Lo siento mucho.*

Murry bubblechatters, *I'd like to thank Leron, only he left with Chestla. It is so confounding being unable to talk to individuals like I talk to parts of myself. You understand – your sublingual is part of you, but you can't contact just anyone.*

Murry's profound ability to forgive brings moisture to my eyes. *I'm sure Chestla will give you Leron's phone number, no?*

What good would that do? He won't answer. Murry's whining. *I need to ask Leron where he got the tech. Some parts of me that were Zantite – before I released all those hugs –were working on something similar. Mertex Makanoc remembers one of his first tasks after he volunteered to crew the Layla's Pride was as maintenance assistance to a team working on that same problem.* So Mertex's gig on the kitchen crew had been a promotion – likematching Jeska getting promoted out of laundry duty. Maybe chefs on a Zantite ship have more status than I realized.

Murry asks, *Why are you laughing?*

I wasn't, out loud. Pero my neural patch registered it. *Lo siento. Go on.*

We tried cloning the frozen cacao beans, but the plants didn't come out right. And none of the other techniques we tried could overcome the fact that the frozen beans are dead. If only we had access to that lab Mertex worked in maybe Eugene and I could ...

This time I do laugh out loud. Gavin, who'd had his eyes closed, resting after being darted, looks up at me. "You are aware that sometimes you telepaths just look crazy."

I start to protest that having a sublingual doesn't make me an actual telepath, pero what's the point? I nod and laugh even harder. My life really has become a telenovela. Those cheesetastic productions are known for super-convenient timing. And not five minutes ago, Mamá offered us access to the very lab Murry needs.

I say out loud, for Gavin's benefit. "I think I can arrange to get you on board the *Layla's Pride*, Murry. Pero you have to get offplanet first. You and Eugene need to raid one of the seed banks to get enough frozen cacao for your experiments. And then you'll have to steal a ship."

Murry makes a startled noise in my mind. *Eugene couldn't fly a drone! Should I ask Kaliel Johannsson? He's here, to see Kayla Baker. Which is sweet, him making sure she is okay after the fire. He just left with her and Mario Benitez. I was too shy to approach them.* He hesitates. *Do you think he's forgiven me enough to want to ride in an enclosed space with me?*

You respect him, don't you, Murry?

Of course, Murry chatters.

Murry needs Kaliel to forgive him, the way he's forgiven Leron. *Mira, I will talk him into flying you. You talk with Eugene about how to get those cacao beans. If they thaw improperly, you lose your window to experiment with them, right? And bring some of that carob, so you have something to eat that isn't your crew.*

Kaliel's the easy call to make. I tell him, *I hear you've made it back to Earth.*

His bubblechatter's somber. *The fires are vivid from the moon. I'm getting Kayla and your brother out of here. I have a friend who runs charters with a couple of jets who will take us. Very discreet. Though I assume the smoke will be just as thick around Rio.*

That thought sits like lead in my chest. *Would you consider letting them go alone? I have a favor to ask you.* I explain about the spuck, the cryostasis lab, and the hope of saving chocolate, even though it doesn't matter anymore to the rest of la galaxia. *I know you wanted Murry killed for what he made you do, those people he forced you to kill when he was inside your mind. I hope–*

I'll take him, Kaliel interrupts. *If he's really trying to help. Borrowing a ship should be no problem.*

Kaliel, por favor. You shaped a lot of what Murry is now. Be nice to him, okay?

I won't be rude, Kaliel bubblechatters. *But we are not friends.*

That's the best I can ask for. I'm feeling more productive from this cell than I had been the whole time I was stuck on Earth.

Gavin's eyes are green with interest. "Now what are you doing?"

I give him a recap. "And now I'm about to call the Zantite that once tried to use me as a murder weapon."

Gavin gives me a close-fisted salute. "True heart, su."

I nearly fall off my bunk. That's the shortened version of what Krom tell someone who's leaving on a long or dangerous journey, or about to undertake a difficult task. If that person's a close friend. And he said it so casually. I'm glad my own eyes don't give away as much as Gavin's or Brill's, because they'd be whirling through colors right now. I manage a soft, "Tanv." The informal word for, *Thanks.*

Then I call Alex Crosskiss, whose Crosskiss's flat-nosed face had starred in many of my nightmares over the last several months. It is easier not having to see him.

Before I can speak Crosskiss grumbles, *Pirates don't have a habit of surrendering to Zantite warships. I'm as likely to get you killed as help you.*

I know that.

Then what do you want? He's still grumbling, pero sounds curious.

Por favor, there's a researcher from Earth and a spuck from Evevron—

This sounds like the start of a joke.

I wince. *If you take them on board, all you have to worry about with the spuck is how to dispose of his poop.*

Who said anything about taking them on board? Crosskiss's voice rings through my brain.

I realize I hadn't quite gotten to that yet. *They need your cryoresearch lab. It's a long shot, pero they may be able to revive chocolate.*

Crosskiss snort-laughs into his end of the connection. *Why would you want it back?*

I see his point. Chocolate is gone, so the invasion is off. *Because when this is all over, Earth will need a muy grande gesture of goodwill to find a place in the galaxy.*

So? Am I supposed to suddenly believe all the Mercy is a Gift nonsense mother and her friends keep spouting?

I knew that interview was staged. *You should believe it, mijo! You tried to murder your father. Garfex could have had you executed instead of making you the royal heir. If that's not mercy, I don't know what is!* I take a deep breath. Losing my temper won't make him want to help. *I apologize thoroughly. You could benefit. You could get credit for bringing chocolate back from the dead, to be shared with all the worlds.*

The Krom and the Nilka already have it, Crosskiss counters.

I wince. *I can give you money. It's in Earth currency, but I can transfer—*

He interrupts. *I've got more money than I know what to do with. Like you said, I'm heir to a multi-planet empire.*

I don't know what else to offer. Crosskiss has everything he wants – and apparently his mother only stipulated that he offer assistance in rescuing me from the space pirates. *Mijo, I don't have anything left. Unless you want me to come back aboard your ship as a personal chef.*

I expect him to laugh again, pero there's a profound silence. *You serious?*

I guess?

You have no idea how often I think about that banquet you prepared. It was some of the best food I've ever eaten. He sighs. *That's the only thing I hate about captaining a starship. The food is uniformly awful.*

The complement gives me an unexpected confidence boost. I smile, lightening my chest. *You help my friends as much as you can, and if I survive whatever these space pirates have in mind, I'll come cook for you. I still want to graduate school – which is just one project away – and make sure my planet is safe. Then I'll make mi mamá's choctastic cake for you again.*

For a year. Crosskiss sounds gleeful.

My breath catches. I should have known he wouldn't be happy with a week or two of good meals. *No. No y no. Six months. I can't take being that close to the Invincible Heart for longer than that.*

We work out a few more details. I agree not to tell anyone I bribed him. Crosskiss seems pleased that his mother will think he's doing all of this out of kindness.

I tell him, *If the researchers are successful, I'm sure Minda will arrange for all the PR stuff to take place aboard your ship.*

After I hang up, Gavin gives me a curious look. "You look like you just made a bad deal."

"Wal. I probably did." And if I wind up having to spend six months aboard a Zantite warship, ni idea how I'll explain it to Brill.

After that, the sublingual falls silent, and I realize just how much the flurry of activity had distracted me from my predicament. I'm stuck in this room with Gavin, with no handheld, no householo to watch – not even a book to read.

Gavin pulls out a deck of cards. "Fancy a game of Varan?"

"You know I'm horrible at it." I sit across from him on the floor, where he can lay out the cards next to his chart for keeping track of Tyson-related information. It's a complicated game, with aspects rooted in Krom history. "But if you don't mind winning."

CHAPTER TWENTY-EIGHT

Hours pass, and the pirates still don't offer us food or agua. I keep an eye on Gavin, even though he looks less ill. Eventually, the same henchpirate who took pity on Gavin comes to get us. Another hombre comes with him, and both have guns drawn.

Gavin's irises are bright blue, covering another emotion. Like stark terror. He whispers, "Not the time to try to escape. Unless there's no choice."

The two of us, against two armed guards, in an unknown ship? Um, *sí*, he's not kidding. I don't want to think what *no choice* means.

Gavin's troubled gaze turns to Pity Guy. "Where are we going, su?"

It's not a hunormous ship. And we didn't hear any of the typical noises associated with docking. Uan I share Gavin's fear that they might be transferring us out the nearest airlock. Only, wouldn't it be simpler to shoot us in the cell than risk an escaped Krom running lose on their ship?

The new guy groans. "Why'd you take the dart out? Now moving him will be a pain."

Gavin holds his hands up submissively. "Don't dart me again. Avell. I want to talk to Jack as much as he wants to talk to me." When the two henchpirates hesitate, he adds, "Look." He takes a zip tie out of his pocket – they didn't bother to take it off him when they took his gun, pocketknife and phone. "I'll attach myself to her." After I nod, he binds our wrists together in a figure eight. His pulse against my skin is a little high – even considering Krom normal. "Now you don't have to worry about me going anywhere."

"Fine." New Guy deactivates the field. "Jack wants you on the bridge, so you can be visible on the com screen. But if you try anything funny, he's authorized us to shoot you both, no matter what that does to his plan."

"No jokes then," Gavin says, deadpan.

New Guy gives him a cross between a glare and an attempt not to laugh.

I'm still trying to figure out Jack's plan.

Once we exit the storage area, we walk through a short hallway and emerge on the bridge.

New Guy says, "Stand over there."

He points to a spot away from the pilot's seat, and from the galley, where the fourth henchpirate is opening a beer. That muchacho's got a bag of cved chips, like he's about to watch a good holo or something.

We move to where they want us to stand.

The henchpirate who had given me the pliers moves to the weapons station. "Cray's ship is on the radar. If you want me to focus on hitting it, I need sustenance."

The guy with the chips tosses him a bag. Weapons Guy opens them with a loud smack. I can't stifle an outraged noise. What happened to his human empathy? He's acting like this is a video game. Even though he plans to blow up Gavin's ship with mi vida y Frank inside.

I have una buena vista de nav and of the external closeup cameras. A ship's blipping closer, moving faster than this one.

Gavin's *Boundless Hope* appears on the externals, a sleek white ship with fins, the same model as Brill's. I wonder if Jack took into account the kind of speedy, lithe ship Brill flies when challenging him into pursuit.

Brill maneuvers the *Boundless* up behind the ship I'm on. The pirates can't fire on the *Boundless*, because Brill took an angle that keeps him clear of this ship's weapons. The helmsman dances the ship about, trying to get flipped around to an angle where they can fire, only to have Brill's faster ship arc back around behind them. While the pirates discuss changing tactics, the *Boundless* Hope launches a grappling hook.

I give Gavin a skeptical look. "A legit trader, eh? Brill's ship doesn't have anything like that. Just a few basic defensive weapons."

Gavin shrugs. "They're handy for things other than piracy. For instance, rescue missions."

The grappling hook bites into the hull, rocking the pirate ship. As the ship changes trajectory to escape, I get knocked off balance. I fall, pulling Gavin down with me, since we're attached at the wrist. At the visual screen's top edge, I glimpse something traveling next to a second grappling cable, which hits even harder It must have been a reinforcing cable. Or something.

Gavin and I get untangled and sit up. Gavin motions for us to stay seated, since we'll likely just get knocked down again.

A com request flashes. The pirate in the pilot's seat answers. "Here's the proof of life you demanded. What's your move now, Cray?"

Brill's face appears huge on the screen, his eyes a bright, happy lying blue. Frank stands behind him. Brill says, "You give up the hostages, and we pretend this never happened. You can even give Jack that jacket back. All I care about are the two lives at stake."

"Not happening," the pilot says. "You should have disabled this ship as soon as you had us immobilized. But you're not the type to strand somebody to die."

The pilot nods to the weapons guy, who fires his weapons as additional thrusters. Between the two of them, they flip the ship around so fast they break the grappling cables, and they are able to get a shot at the *Boundless*. Ay!

Weapons Guy says, "We disabled one of their thrusters. Want me to blow it up?"

A jolt of terror sparks through my core. I suck in a startled breath.

"No," the pilot says. "He's no threat anymore."

I let the breath out and tension seeps out of my frame. Gracias a Dios por the kindnesses people instinctively show. When the pirates resume their course, the cameras rotate, showing the *Boundless*, limping along behind. At least the pirates didn't stall it out entirely.

Brill's face remains on the screen, his eyes sinking towards a frustangerated maroon. Dash is just visible in the galley. Muy feliz they got the clone off planet with them, before he wound up back on Janvier's radar.

Gavin smiles at the viewscreen.

"Qu–What?" I whisper.

"Tell you later." He touches my hand with his. On purpose. "I knew my best friend wouldn't let me down."

"What's Jack's game here?" Brill demands. "If I can't catch up, why hold onto Bo and Gavin? And why let me live? Twice?"

The pilot and the weapons guy look at each other and crack up laughing.

The pilot says, "You think this is about you? Jack didn't realize you were alive until we darted the others on the beach." Jack must not have bothered to look at the pictures of the *drowned Earthling* from the bar. "He's just playing with you, because there's no way you can stop his plan. And he doesn't like you."

Without dignifying that, Brill hangs up.

So this is about me after all. Y these hombres know what Jack wants with me. If they are as sympathetic as they seem maybe–

The pilot turns to the weapons guy. "If Cray shows up on the scanners again, blast him."

–or maybe not.

New Guy gestures us up off the floor with his gun. "Show's over. Back to your cell."

"Por favor. Can I use the real restroom first?" I'm pushing my luck, pero I'm desperate to pee.

"And water," Gavin says. "I could really use some water, avell."

He must look sick enough, they take pity on him. The two armed pirates walk us down to the head. Clearly they expect me and Gavin to go in there together.

Gavin shrugs. "What else can we do?"

I really do have to pee. And everything that just happened made me so nervous. "This is embarrassing." Still, I walk through the door in front of him. Nothing looks amiss – a human-friendly toilet and a shower with an opaque glass-like door – pero as soon as I step inside, the hairs at the back of my neck stand up. And now I really, really have to pee.

I suck in a breath. The sensation is familiar – my immediate reaction, not blunted by IH residue, to Evevron predator pheromones.

"Chestla?" I say hopefully.

The shower door pops open. She's holstering a short sword. "It's you guys. I was afraid I'd have to kill someone in here."

"You may, if you want to get us off this ship," Gavin says. "I caught a glimpse of a spitpod bay on the far side of the bridge."

"Por favor." I raise my hand towards her, pero it's still bound to Gavin's, y he wasn't expecting the movement, which stops with a jerk. "They showed us a little kindness. Can we find a way out that doesn't end with corpses?"

"I brought my own spitpod. I had to get here somehow, you know." Chestla gestures at the zip tie and takes out a small knife. "Let me see."

One swipe later, my wrist is free.

That second thud we heard earlier must have been her pod landing. And Gavin realized it. No sé how he could have communicated that to me, pero I still feel out of the loop.

Gavin moves towards the shower. "Let me give you some privacy. Your need seemed urgent, and we have to leave this room together."

"Vale." When I'm done and I've washed my hands, I ask that shower door, "How are you resisting drinking from the tap?"

Gavin makes an unhappy noise from the other side. "I'd rather die of dehydration than dysentery. I can't imagine this water's potable."

He's right. I still splash my face with it.

"How many?" Chestla asks Gavin.

"Two right outside this door. And two on the bridge. If there are others, they're keeping out of sight."

Chestla nods. "Stay behind me, Bo." She points with her knife. "What's that?"

Gavin holds up the pipe that had been screwed into the shower. The showerhead is still attached to it. "I'll try not to hurt them too badly, then we can make a run for it."

"Wait," I say. "The muchacho at the weapons station still has my phone."

"Can't be helped," Gavin says. "We'll get you another one when we get to civilization."

I put a hand on his arm. "The microdot I was supposed to hand off to Frank is inside the case. If I don't get it to him, a lot of people could die."

His irises spark through five colores diferentes, settling on deep gray. "At least the su's on the bridge don't know the dot is there."

"We can try to capture one of them and trade him for the phone." Chestla says. "But it had better work. There's no way to negotiate without them figuring out what they have."

I gulp around a dry throat. Like Gavin, I don't dare drink the agua.

Chestla pulls open the door, hiding herself behind it. Gavin steps through into the hall, acting like his wrist is still bound to mine.

"You still want water?" New Guy asks.

"You are kinder than I would have thought," Gavin says. "Sorry about this."

What happens next is literally a blur. New Guy hits the floor, landing hard on his butt after Gavin hits him.

Chestla punches the other guy. He falls backwards, shooting randomly. There's un aterrador high-pitched sucking noise somewhere out of my line of sight. An alarm goes off.

"You idiots aren't using space safe rounds!" Chestla shouts.

The pirate Gavin hit crawls up the hall, yelling, "Hull breech! Seal off the back of the ship."

Gavin makes sure Chestla took the gun from the other guy – who seems half-conscious – then turns to go after New Guy. Solamente – A wall slams down between us and the retreating pirate.

"Well, that's just perfect," Gavin says. He moves to pick me up and dash for the spitpod, pero Chestla has the same idea. She's closer, and he's faster, so they arrive at the same time. They both hesitate, staring at each other. Then Chestla grabs me, and we race for the hatch where she left her pod, as more panels start closing around us. Gavin could flash ahead, pero he stays with us.

A panel slams down in front of Chestla. She hands me off to Gavin, who sets me on my feet. She hacks through the panel with her short sword and her knife. The air already tastes a little thin – pero Gavin and I can do nada to help.

The metal gives, and she kicks in the weakened part, and we rush through it to the hatch.

Chestla's moving slower than she should be. I feel un poco lightheaded myself. Gavin's already unscrewed the hatch and climbed up inside the spitpod. He reaches for me. Chestla pushes me up – pero then she collapses to the floor. Her oxygen concentration requirements must be higher than mine.

"Jrekt!" Gavin looks like he wants to shut the hatch and flood it with oxygen before I pass out, too. After all, I'm the one who's his responsibility. He takes one look at my distressed expression and nods. "Haza." *Fine.*

He climbs down and scoops up Chestla. He tries to push her up over his cabeza, pero he's having trouble getting her high enough to tip her into the spitpod. I'm too weak to help. I search for a rope ladder, or anything inside the pod we can use. A box marked Nebdnal Silla, *Emergency Supplies* is pushed up against the back of the pilot's seat. My limbs feel leaden, but I pry it open. Inside, I find a collapsible grappling hook and a length of cable – and under a bunch of other stuff, a mask attached to a small tank. I'm pretty sure the gas mix is breathable. I get the mask on and the gas flowing. Almost inmediatamente, I feel more alert.

I loop the wire around the pilot's chair, then drop the grappling hook down to Gavin. He wraps the cable around Chestla a couple of times, securing it with the grapple pointed outwards. I pull on the cable y Gavin pushes on Chestla, y together we get her into the spitpod.

Gavin gets the door closed and the atmo flowing. I take the mask off.

"Quick thinking, Bodacious." Gavin's eyes show a greenish-yellow tinge. Shtesh, I think he's proud of me.

CHAPTER TWENTY-NINE

The three of us crowded into the spitpod is claustraziety inducing. Chestla's still unconscious, pero she's combing her hair in her sleep, using those claw-nails. Space is so tight that she's pressed against me and making a noise in her throat that I'd almost call purring. I'd never dare mention it to her when she wakes up, nunca – comparisons between her species and Earth cats is a touchy subject.

I smile at Gavin. "Tanyaliesh," I croak. "This is above and beyond your responsibility to look out for me." My throat was dry before. Now it's like a sandstorm on Chestla's planet.

"Don't talk," Gavin says. Pero the blue shift in his eyes says he's pleased. "And try not to move around too much. We have a limited supply of oxygen and no idea how long before Brill rescues us. At least with the hull breach to deal with, the pirates aren't chasing us."

"They'll be okay, no?"

"Probably not the one guy." Gavin only breathes enough to talk. Since he has book lungs that can hold oxygen for days, he's leaving the oxygen for us. Which is kind of him, considering he's the most likely to survive.

Chestla opens her eyes. "Why do you two look so grim?"

Gavin breathes enough to say, "I need water and you two need air, and this pod was meant for one person, not three. It could take Brill longer to get here than we have."

Chestla waves a dismissive hand. "It won't be as long as you think. I have a ship out here too."

I hug Chestla, "Muchas gracias por coming to save us. Lo siento you had to leave Nellet behind."

Gavin looks exasperated that we're still talking, pero he doesn't try to stop us as Chestla hugs me back.

"I didn't leave her. We found Nellet and Watae in their honeymoon cruiser. We interrupted a rather personal moment, and embarrassed the heck out of them, but that's the worst punishment they can expect. Well, and that we hijacked their honeymoon. Their ship was the only one big enough to hold everyone. They haven't had another minute solo with all of us on board." As she emphasizes the Spanish word, she breaks into a smile. "This marriage is best for everyone. I couldn't officially condone it, but now that the vows have been exchanged, and I've met the guy, he's earned my respect. The way he protected Nellet when he thought we were trying to take her away from him …" Chestla runs a finger across the back of her hand. The skin is foamglued together in a line running halfway up her forearm. To get a hit like that on her, this guy must be quite a fighter.

I put a hand on her arm, above the injury. "You respect him enough to be okay with losing your job?"

Chestla's handheld rings. She answers it, and the holo opens on a scene in the basement cave where the Evevron council meets. The spuck claw across the bottom of the image shows that one of Murry is precariously holding the phone.

Murry's voice sounds nervous. "Do you see this? Oh, hi Bo!"

Obviously, he didn't expect me to be with Chestla. "Hola, mijo. How did the flight go to the Zantite ship?"

"Fine. We're there now, helping Eugene. But we're also here. See those guys? They think because I can't talk I'm stupid. Otherwise, why would they say horrible things about me right in front of me?"

The guys in question stand on the far side of the council chamber, where three other Murry dragons lie splooted backwards, staring at the cave floor. One of muchachos looks like an Earthling. The other is a blocky orange guy.

"Who are they?" Chestla asks.

"Oxygen, you su's," Gavin says.

I can't not talk to Murry when he's in this much distress. The amount of oxygen it will take to comfort him won't make the difference in whether we survive.

"They're representatives of the Galactic Court, here to study me. I had to bring three of me here, and now they want to take these me's apart for research."

In the holofield, Grammy moves forward. Her voice carries clearly. "I don't care that it's a hive mind. Killing these three spucks would cause Murry pain. And each of those deaths would leave a psychological scar. How would you like it if we cut off three of your toes? You have seven or eight more, and can still function without them."

"Is that a threat?" The blocky orange representatives asks.

"Not unless you choose to take it as one." Grammy's eyes flick towards the stairs. Her smile is especially predatory. "Although the civic services unit headed this way might take it personally if you kill some of their number. They have been working with the spucks to create improved irrigation for the city and consider Murry part of their squad. When they aren't leading our hunting expeditions."

Ekrin's elite warrior squad marches in, all wearing that black body armor and carrying bo staves. They form a menacing line in front of the Murry dragons.

It's probably all those predator pheromones hitting him, pero the guy says, "On second thought, it will be sufficient having a telepath who is also a psychologist communicate with him. Preng?"

Preng gives him a look like *Why me? You picked the fight.* Pero he approaches the line of soldiers, which parts for him. I'm guessing Preng's a Nitarri, porque he looks human. He asks questions out loud, for the benefit of his boss. Murry must be answering.

I ask Murry, "Are you okay with what he's asking, mijo?"

Murry makes an unhappy noise. "There's nothing inappropriate in the questions. But now that we're communicating, this individual will have no problem locating our neural signature, if the Court does decide to execute me. Which could well happen before we solve the cryostasis problem."

Murry goes silent for a long time, then he says, "He keeps probing me for more about Kayla." Telepaths can't read minds, so he's only getting what Murry's willing to communicate. "He wants to know if I trusted her. If she was kind. If we're still in touch. I think he admires her."

"Tell him those questions aren't relevant to his investigation," Chestla says.

"I won't hide more than I have to. I want him to let me live, so I can fix things." Murry sounds desperate. "I caused Bodacious Benitez's world to burn. I now consider her one of my closest friends. How can I let them destroy me before I make amends? It would be so easy to eat this guy and pretend none of this ever happened."

"No, Murry!" I sit up, expending more precious oxygen. "Wait! If you do that, you will be executed. You'd deserve it."

The spuck loses its grip on the phone, which lands face down giving us a holo of nada. "We wish we had had a hug on Leron, back before you helped us see how wrong it was. We could use the information in his head to help solve the problem. His insights could be the key."

"How about we bring you Leron?" Chestla asks. "And I'll come too. You need a biochemist."

"You're taking us all to a Zantite warship?" Gavin splutters, breaking his own prohibition on excessive oxygen use.

"It's more of a risk for me than for you," Chestla says coldly. Porque the Evevrons have had two recent wars with the Zantites, and still-simmering animosity could lead to violence.

Gavin reaches over and hangs up Chestla's phone. "I hate to be a pessimist, but the point may be moot. There's a ship on the radar. We have no weapons, uan if it's hostile, we're toast. I suggest you contact your respective ships and let them know what's going on."

"That probably *is* my ship." Chestla holds up her phone, showing off a stillholo of a heart shaped vessel, painted fluorescent pink, proclaiming itself the *True Love*. Someone scrawled *Just Married* on the side. In the holo, it's docked with a space station. "The inside is absolutely hideous."

I think the outside is hideous también, pero I keep that to myself.

There's a com request, and Gavin answers, "Wal, su?"

Porque, por supuesto, he hopes Brill's on board.

"Kaveram." The more formal Krom word for *Hello!* comes over the com.

Gavin looks taken aback. He mutes the com.

"It's Ball! Gavin, we're saved." I poke Chestla in the side. "How has it been traveling with someone who's loved you your whole life?"

Chestla looks uncomfortable. "I still haven't decided how I feel about him."

Gavin asks, "You're in love with a Krom?"

"Ball's a Duracell," I say. The name is slang, pero it's not an insult. Half-Krom, half-Evevron bloodlines tend to lead to tewakelle offspring that have the long lives and book lungs of Krom, with the teeth and claws of Evevrons. Which makes them más o menos – *more or less* – unstoppable. Though, as Ball's injured leg proves, not invulnerable.

"Right." Gavin nods. "The one Brill mentioned, who nearly died in his arms."

I nod. Then I point to Chestla. "She saved him, when it shouldn't have been possible."

"Then it's a good thing we didn't leave her behind when I almost couldn't get her in the pod."

"You what?" Chestla gives Gavin a sharp look. It's not even directed at me, pero I still nearly wet my pants.

Gavin shrugs. "Nobody wants to be on a Duracell's bad side."

I give him a glare, también. "Leaving someone who just rescued you to die is horrible, no? You saved her because you're a good guy."

"*We* saved her," Gavin reminds me. "You thought of the pulley."

Chestla purses her lips. "Would you have left me if you'd been alone? I know Krom have a do-no-harm philosophy, but what about the opposite?"

Gavin straightens the cuffs of his denim jacket. "The Codex doesn't require us to help people. But that doesn't mean we don't know when something's the right thing to do."

He navigates towards that radar blip. We meet up with it fairly quickly, pero the air's already so stale inside the pod that when the hatch opens, it feels like someone's opened a window on a spring day. After a moment, I realize the air isn't just fresh. It's also scented with flowers.

CHAPTER THIRTY

I climb down into an open area with two red vehicles that likematch Jet Skis parked in it. Ball waits for us, balancing on his cane, his limp still pronounced. Cierto, considering his leg was shredded by a spuck's teeth, it's a miracle he can walk.

"Thanks, su." Gavin says, offering Ball a close-fisted salute.

"Don't thank me. Thank the pilot." Still, he returns Gavin's salute. His eyes, a steady hazel, don't betray even a hint of chromashift. He must not feel much like laughing. So while his manners match a polite, well-raised Krom, he looks all Evevron. "Besides, we haven't escaped the pirates. You disabled the ship that captured you, but they won't give up trying to take you back."

We follow Ball into the main part of the ship, where two young Evevrons sit on a heart-shaped velvet-ish sofa. Nellet's black dress is on the short side, and Watae wears a long-sleeved tee-shirt thrown on over what looks like silk pajama pants. He's barefoot, the claw-like nails on his toes blunted, but still intimidating. He doesn't look injured. He got a blow on Chestla and escaped unscathed. He must be un muy buen fighter.

I hold out my arms to Nellet. "Congratulations, mija!"

She jumps up and hugs me in a suffocating wave of predator pheromones that freezes me to the spot. "Are you really happy for me? I was worried that even you wouldn't understand."

I take a few deep breaths, and when I can speak, I whisper, "Tell me what you love about him."

She whispers back, "He's funny, charming, and wants to help people." Then she giggles. "Besides, look at him."

Watae has even features, reflective yellow slit-pupil eyes, and thick wavy dark hair, on the long side but not unkempt. His skin tone is light, pero sun-kissed. And even for an Evevron, he's built. So sí, I see the appeal. "Good for you, mija."

"There's cake," Watae says. He hasn't moved from the sofa, but it feels like he's taken over the situation. Turning towards Gavin, Watae speaks in heavily-accented universal. "And sparkling water. I'd offer you wine, but Ball said you're probably dehydrated."

"Thanks, su," Gavin says. "Water sounds great."

Nellet moves toward the bridge – which on this ship is in a separate room – to get us cake. Gavin follows her. I arch an eyebrow at Watae. He's the crown prince. "So, mijo, have you told your parents the good news?"

He grins. "They just about exploded. But what's done is done, and the only wedding gift I requested is that they drop their complaint about Pendosha sharing space with the Mindhuggers."

"And they will do that?" I ask. Watae's confidence amazes me, considering he's Earth-equivalent of eighteen or nineteen years old.

"They already have." He gestures to the far end of the sofa, and when I sit, he asks, "What does Murry have to do with my people? I heard Chestla tell Ball that something connects the mindworms to Curtsar. But when I walked into the room, they clammed up."

Watae acts so mature, and he just married his enemy to bring peace. Pero he is still a teenager, whatever that means for an Evevron. Can he handle learning the origins of Patient Zero? Will he be angry at Chestla for hiding the truth? Maybe even at Nellet?

Todavía, how will lying to him help? So I tell him the truth. "Murry's original consciousness *is* your people. Five individuals from Curtsar went to prison in Pendosha for blowing up a dam to try and bring you water. As part of an experimental rehabilitation project, they were injected with the first Mindhuggers. Everything went wrong, pero the parasites survived. They infected the scientists that created them and eventually the Mindhuggers became Murry."

Watae blinks in surprise. "I see. You're saying he ties us back together. All those wrongs on both sides turned into something beautiful?'

"You find Murry beautiful?" I blurt.

Watae nods. "Have you ever seen a spuck in flight? Those wings – man, they're gorgeous."

"I've ridden one, mijo."

"Shut up!" Watae shoves my arm. And for a second, he really is a teenager. But then he regains his composure.

"I could talk Murry into letting you ride one." My mouth goes dry. The predator pheromones already hang thick in the air, pero now I have a distinct feeling someone is watching me. I have trouble keeping my breathing even.

Watae notices my sudden discomfort. He glances at the door leading into the galley. "What's up with you and Leron?"

"That's a long story." I get up and force myself to move towards the galley. Towards Leron. It's hard enough traveling in an enclosed ship with six Evevrons on board. If one of them is sulking and staring at me, I won't be able to take it. Esto es tonto. When I enter the galley, Leron looks cornered. I make eye contact with him. "Are you afraid of me?"

Leron sucks his bottom lip between his teeth. "I can't take any more recriminations."

"I don't have any." And then it clicks. Obviamente. "You came on this mission so you wouldn't have to face Murry."

"I won't let him eat me. I already face probable execution for my crimes. He will have to settle for that." Leron shrugs. "Though Chestla wants me to help with the cryostasis project when we get to the warship. If we make it in time."

"You should talk to Murry when we get there. You might be surprised at what he says. He knows you tried to reverse the cryostasis."

Leron's mouth slips open, revealing his predator's teeth. "Lot of good that did. There's no way around the barrier between life and death. Which I'm sure I'll experience for myself soon. They say execution by hendenket is painless, but they haven't asked anyone who's been through it, have they?"

The haunted look in Leron's eyes reminds me of Kaliel, back when Kaliel was facing the shave. I force myself to put una mano on his arm, though his fear makes the predator pheromones even stronger. "Don't give up hope. I have seen strange things happen in desperate situations."

He laughs. "I'm not Kaliel, Bo. I don't have a defense. I'm guilty." Leron shakes his cabeza. "But it feels good to have everything out in the open."

"There are possible sentences other than death," I insist. "Gideon Tyson says the extenuating circumstances could weigh in your favor. You can call him, if you want."

Now Leron looks gobsmacked. "You talked to him? For me?"

"I saw the CastClip where you defended Murry. It touched my heart." I tell him, "Tyson was part of Murry for a while. It gives him a unique perspective, and mucho empathy for you."

Moisture glitters in Leron's eyes. He runs the back of his hand across his nose. "Empathy's fine and all, but don't expect me to get my hopes up. Quick and painless. That's what I'm holding onto."

I get a call on my sublingual. It's Xevik, one of Gavin's friends. She chatters, *Give me somewhere to push Gavin a holo. We're closing in on the bounty.*

A second later, Gavin turns the corner into the galley. Someone's found him a change of clothes and patched his cheek. He says, "Bodacious, come check out the media viewing room. This ship has everything –including a VR gaming range and a hot tub. Su, my wife would love this place. We could lock the boys in the VR area and not have to worry about them for days."

I can't get used to Gavin willingly asking me to do anything with him, pero I guess I'm the most familiar face aboard the *Just Married*. I relay the information Xevik gives me, and transmit Gavin's response to her, and shortly después de esto, I'm sitting in a three-row theater, preparing to watch the capture of Not-Kaliel.

Leron comes into the room and walks over to us.

Gavin's eyes sink towards a sullen gray. "Su, I'm not sure you want to watch this. Not considering your … predicament."

Leron sits by me. I steel myself not to flinch away. Leron looks stoically across me at Gavin, two seats to my other side. "You can say it. My impending death."

They gray in Gavin's eyes takes on a hint of angranxious orange-brown. "No. And you shouldn't either."

Leron blinks. "Isn't it morbid for you two to be watching them space a guy?"

I say, "They might bring him in alive, no?" Either way, I need to see this, to get closure. This muchacho killed Tyson's partner because of something he thought I did.

"Ga." Gavin's irises turn solid gray again. "I thought you understood what it meant when everyone kept asking if Conrad needed to be brought in breathing. He's a cop killer. Even if the Galactics had captured him, this wouldn't go well for him. Maybe you should leave."

I shake my head. "What is the heart that doesn't have hope?"

Leron's hand tightens on his armrest so hard his claw-nails scratch the leather.

In the actioncast, a ring of ships surrounds Conrad's vessel. A camera mounted on Xevik's ship shows the action as Conrad starts to run, trying to slip through a gap. Suddenly, the ship loses momentum.

"They hit it with an EMP blast," Gavin says. "Seriously, Bodacious. You should go. Now."

With the ship disabled, Conrad has few options left. Pero even if I wanted to go, I couldn't leave Leron.

Xevik's voice comes over the com. "You're drifting, Conrad. Surrender now, and we'll do this the civilized way. I'd prefer you breathing to see trial."

"All you care about is the money, bounty hunter," Conrad replies. "And I won't give you that satisfaction. Stop underestimating the resourcefulness of people from small planets."

"Jrekt!" Gavin shouts, as Leron gasps. Gavin leaps up, holding out a hand like he can somehow rearrange the ships in the holo. "Xevik! Naramoosh. Get out of there!"

I remember the one rule about bounties on criminals: the Galactics won't pay up over for a smear of DNA. They need a body intact enough to identify. This guy intends for there to be nada left of himself – or his ship.

Xevik wanted to take Conrad in alive. I was right – sometimes people offer mercy and hope. But offering mercy doesn't make you immune from being hurt.

"It's alright," Conrad says. "There are plenty more to finish this."

A chill dances down my spine and settles into my core. Conrad's just said the same exact words as Jemena Duarte's final ones. Y they are his last también.

The explosion is massive. The fireball from Conrad's ship's engine flares until the oxygen is gone, as pieces of the ship fling like weapons at the pursuers. A huge piece of metal comes flying towards the camera on Xevik's ship, sending the camera bucking before everything flashes white and then goes dark.

"Dios mio!" Conrad repeating Jimena can't be a coincidence. The muerte de Tyson's partner – the intrusion into Eugene's lab – they're tied together somehow with Jimena's mission to have me killed on Zant.

"Xevik?" Gavin asks plaintively. Pero there is no answer.

Leron tries to hide his face, which looks near tears.

I force myself to put a hand on his. "Conrad had a chance, if only he'd taken it."

Leron's voice sounds leaden when he says, "Instead, people got hurt. I froze five people, Bo. Not a day goes by that I don't remember their faces, their protests from inside those cryostasis pods. I stayed with them until they died."

"At gunpoint–" I protest, pero Leron cuts me off.

"I could have said no. I knew it was wrong. Don't make excuses." Leron pulls his hand away. Then he stalks out.

I stare por un minuto at the empty holofield thinking how Conrad's situation likematches my own. Destroying everything around you only works if you don't care who gets hurt. En serio, I'm not prepared to do that. We have to get that dot back before it unleashes something I can't control.

I turn back to Gavin. "You going to be diay?"

"Wal," he says hollowly. His eyes are deep mahogany. "Xevik was a friend of a friend. I met her maybe once. But she did things the Krom way, even though she wasn't Krom." He gives a closefisted salute to the empty holofield. "Damn, I need a phone. I need to call Tyson and tell him his need for justice has been fulfilled. And I need to find out how long it will take to retrieve Brill."

He leaves, walking faster than I could have run.

"Gavin!" I call.

He stops, already on the far end of the hallway.

"I want to be there when you talk to Tyson, avell. I have something to ask him."

In the holo, Tyson stands near the giant track ball that serves as the controls to his ship. His manos are balled into solid fists, and he tips his diamond-shaped cabeza up towards the ceiling. "Tank you! Tank you both!" The molted scales are growing back. "I never tought to see justice for my friend. How can I repay wat you have done?"

"You probably didn't mean right away," I say. Tyson dips his cabeza, looking intently at me, the angle of his head and glint in his iris-less golden eyes hitting every nerve inside me that still fears snakes. I keep going. "We're gathering information on a conspiracy led by the planet Greftash. Has anyone from there been arrested for trying to harm someone from Earth?"

"Greftash?" Tyson blinks. "Never heard of it."

CHAPTER THIRTY-ONE

When Brill comes aboard, I rush into his arms. His eyes turn gold, and he kisses me. I lose myself in the intensity of his lips, in the feel of his strong hands at the small of my back.

I hear a snort. Startled, I break the beso. Frank's walking past the red Jet Ski things, carrying a box that must be from Gavin's ship. "Glad to know I let him live to do something truly worthwhile."

"Kissing the girl is always worthwhile," Brill insists, pulling me even closer, so that I feel his hummingbird heartbeat against my shoulder.

I laugh. Brill is shy about public displays of affection. That he's still holding me says something about how things have changed between the three of us after Frank forced HGB to leave Brill breathing. Muy bien. It's a nice moment. I'd like to hold onto it.

Frank sets the box down and holds out his hand. "The microdot, if you please."

I force myself to maintain eye contact. "The dot's inside my phone case. The pirates took my handheld."

Frank looks pale. "That's unfortunate. Do they know what they have?"

I shrug. "I don't think so. Last I saw it, the case was still sealed."

Frank huffs. "I'll have to have a little chat with them."

A chill runs down my spine. Most of Frank's "chats" end with someone's muerte. "Por favor. They let me take the dart out of Gavin's face."

As a plea for leniency, it isn't much.

Frank says, "I can't save everyone for you, Bo. Janvier has agents hunting you. And soon they will be hunting me."

Somewhere in all the tension, Brill dropped his arms. I wrap my own arms protectively across my chest.

Footsteps sound on the metal grate at the threshold of Gavin's ship. Dash passes through the coupling between the two ships, onto the plush carpet. He looks more confident than when he was stuck inside the HGB compound. He flashes me a smile, and those dimples are sexy, just like with Shelly. I smile back.

Brill frowns and makes a soft, unhappy noise. I drop my smile a few megawatts, and Dash looks flusterfused and maybe hurt. Ey! Do I look angerated now? Why would he think I'm upset with him? I hardly know him.

Dash hurries past, looking down at the floor, all shy nervousness again. En serio, what happened to the original Janvier that made him so much colder than his clones?

Frank takes in the jealous deep orange-yellow in Brill's eyes. He shakes his head. "After everything, you still think that guy has a chance?"

Brill's irises go an embarrassed pink. "I'm working on it, su."

Frank studies Brill's face. "We should talk about your plans for the future. If things were more settled, you wouldn't feel so insecure."

Is Frank offering to help Brill make new economic connections? Or pressuring him into proposing to me? Does he feel responsible for Brill after saving mi vida's life? Or protective of me, because he's dating Mamá?

Brill's eyes shift to black – probably remembering his and Frank's last little chat – and then push back to gold. "Wal, if you want."

Frank nods. "As soon as we make sure I even have a future left."

I never expected see Frank Sawyer scared. Pero now my heart hurts for him. I can't imagine him facing the shave. Or dying from an assassin's bullet. "Lo siento, Frank. When I took that dot, I wasn't thinking about you."

He gives me an ironic smile. "You were never vague about what you wanted, Bodacious. I just never thought you'd get it."

I study his face, his brown eyes. He loves mi mamá. He's said more than once that he'd love for me and him to be on the same side. "Viejo, you kept asking me to come home to HGB. What if I asked you to leave it?"

Frank considers the question. For a long time. Finally, he says, "I promised Janvier my loyalty. He needs help salvaging Earth's environment and our reputation in the galaxy. So I'd tell you that we could use your help now more than ever. Consider it? You want to *be* HGB New?"

I say, "I'm tired of being manipulated."

Frank sighs. "If it's your choice, it's not manipulation. But if we don't get the dot back, it's a moot point."

My heart squeezes. "We have to, viejo."

"If we don't, and I do face the shave, I blame Shelly. And myself. I should have made you leave before I shot him, no matter how attached you were to that clone. And I should have talked to Shelly first. I always talk to them, when there's time. Though if I had made Janvier wait, I doubt I could have saved your boyfriend." He looks over at Brill. "You basically told Janvier I let you keep breathing on purpose the first time. I'll have to smooth that over, if HGB's operatives don't kill us."

The three of us look at each other with recrimination and regret. And yet … something's clicked into place, and we fit together now.

Chestla walks in. "You need help with Gavin's tech gear?"

She hesitates, and takes a step back toward the door.

"Why don't you and Bo sort the rest of it?" Brill puts a hand on Frank's arm. "Let's go give the pilot the last known coordinates of the pirate vessel."

Frank grumbles, "This would be so much easier if Bo just left the trackers Tawny keeps putting on her stuff. Then we'd know exactly where her phone is."

Chestla coughs. And suddenly looks guilty.

I ask, "Something you want to tell us, chica?"

"I may have coated your phone with a layer of nanites that burrowed into the case and created an undetectable tracker." She moves on into Gavin's ship. "Kind of like the ones you ingested. It seemed like a good idea when you started sharing your phone with Brill."

I squeak in outrage. Even Tawny was never that devious about placing her tech.

Brill exchanges a look with Frank and says, "La, she's good."

My phone is in the vicinity of where we left it. We're too far away to tell whether it's stationary. It will take us mucho tiempo to catch up to the pirate ship.

I head to the kitchen, looking for something productive to do. Nellet and Ball are there, making dip and slicing vegetables. Brill leans against the counter, talking to Ball. Mi vida doesn't cook.

Nellet says, "This is my honeymoon, according to your planet's custom. I plan to have at least a little fun. Watae's turning on the simulated sun and beach. There's even a hvexa court. You should come hang out."

I groan at the thought of any sport that involves jumping when I'm this tired and achy. "I'd rather check out the hot tub."

"Me too," Brill says. The look on his face is wistful. It's been a long time since we've done something normal together.

I sigh. "I don't have a swimsuit or a change of clothes. We left all our stuff back on the beach."

Brill smiles, "After Frank recovered enough to remove the dart from my hand, I grabbed everything."

"Cierto? Muy chido! I'll go change." I can't believe I'm this excited over something so ordinary. Pero … I get to sit in a hot tub instead of stressing over some new problem. I head for Gavin's ship, which is still attached to the *Just Married*. We're towing it while Gavin works on repairs with Dash's help.

According to the feeds, Daschel Janvier got a degree in mechanical engineering before being tapped to join HGB. And Dash inherited all those skills. I walk through the ship, towards where Brill stowed my clothes. Dash, busy pulling out a piece of machinery from inside the wall, looks up from his work, then looks away.

"Hola," I say.

He looks up again, surprise in his eyes. He points with a soldering gun. "So you *are* talking to me."

"Lo siento." I'm apologizing to everyone today. "This has nothing to do with you. I paid a little too much attention to Shelly, and I don't want to make that mistake again."

"Well, you don't have to worry about me. You remind *me* a little too much of a girl who broke Janvier's heart. And I'm too concerned with escaping 1.0 with my life intact to want any strings attached." He swallows, hard and as his knee shifts it hits the panel he's removed to get into the wall. "Should I be worried about Brill, though? Is he dangerous?"

I laugh. "Not to you, mijo. Krom believe violence should only be for self-defense."

He turns back to soldering bits onto the machine piece. "Good to know."

I watch him work, trying to see how this multicolored jumble of tubes and wires, and metal grids and plastic bumps the piece connects into helps make Gavin's ship run. I've got nada. Pero, Dash obviously knows what he's doing. "How did you go from engineering to running the most powerful corporation on Earth?"

"*I* didn't do anything. I wasn't even alive a year ago." Dash deftly slides the mechanical part he's been working on back into the wall. "HGB needed an engineer to untangle a piece of alien technology, in case Earth ever needed a secret weapon. 1.0 was just the right combination of ruthless and ambitious to get promoted out of the engineering lab and groomed for bigger things."

Dash looks like Shelly, which tugs at my heart. Pero Dash es diferente enough that I feel like I could tell them apart, if Shelly was still alive. "It must be hard knowing you're a clone."

"It's hard knowing I'm Daschel Janvier." Dash makes a face. "I don't have an existential problem with being a clone. Or that I share my memories with someone else. But do you know how many people hate me? For things I actually remember doing, before I diverged from 1.0? I can't blame them – some of it is despicable – but I can never be anonymous. I'll always be looking over my shoulder for HGB agents not wanting a rogue loose *and* for people who want Janvier dead."

I sympathize. "None of us have a certain future right now."

Dash says, "It's a good thing you took that microdot. You saved Sawyer's life."

"Que? I thought taking the dot put Frank in danger."

"Back at the compound, I was sleeping in one of the pool houses. I adapted the entertainment system to tap into HGB communications. 1.0 sent out a kill order for Sawyer – and then fifteen minutes later, he rescinded it. Which means 1.0 decided to eliminate Sawyer for disloyalty – until he started looking like the best shot for getting the dot back."

Ay-ay-ay! How did everything get so complicated? "Gracias por telling me."

"Well, don't tell him. Sawyer's had enough blows to his confidence."

Leaving Dash to his work, I find my luggage in the spare cabin. I clean up and change into my swimsuit, un precioso red polka-dotted two piece.

When I get back to the other ship, Brill's already in the hot tub. We're alone for the moment, although we will have company soon.

When he takes in my polka dots, his eyes go a flirtatious tea green. "You keep telling me to give you up, and then you wear something like that."

I slip into the agua and sit next to him. "I was afraid. I still am. I can't handle the thought of una galaxia without you in it. Krom are supposed to live to be three hundred years old. It wouldn't be right for you to die before you turn thirty."

I lean back against the jet. The water massage is nice against the old shoulder injury where Tyson shot me.

"But I *am* still alive. Uan I, for one, would like to celebrate that fact." He pulls me close and me besa brevemente. "I'm a trader. My life will always be dangerous. At least half a dozen times before I met you, I came as close to dying as I did in HGB's basement. I told you somebody tried to space me once–"

"Let's not talk about that." I watch own hands clench under the water's surface.

Pero he's not done talking about it. "Look at Gavin. He has a wife and kids, and they could have lost him today. If I can't risk as much for you as he did – then what kind of a relationship do we have?"

"Oh, mi vida." I kiss him, and his lips are hot and his hands tangle in my hair. I'm over whatever the pendant did to make me feel apart from him. My heart changes rhythm, beating with love and joy. We are both alive, able to feel the heat of this beso.

Behind us, Gavin clears his throat.

Brill breaks the beso and inches away. He looks a lot more discomforted than when Frank caught us kissing.

Gavin's eyes shift from worried gray to amused lavender and back again. "I hate to interrupt, but you su's need to see the news."

Brill jumps out of the hot tub. As the splashing subsides, Gavin whispers, "Wen canar vetnash sen. Ranvetta quequen shalnall hes." *That shade of gold. Careful of your heartbeat.*

Brill's irises turn an orange-tinted gold. He whispers something even more softly. I'm not sure I hear him right, pero I think it translates as, *I don't care if it is one-sided.*

Que? What's one-sided? Shtesh! I can't join a conversation they didn't intend for me to hear over the hot tub jets.

Gavin puts a hand on Brill's chest, like he's checking mi vida's quequen – *his heartbeat.* Brill pushes the hand away. Does Brill have something wrong with his heart? Surely not. He told me when he'd bought the Paladzian pendants that he wasn't an invalid. My own heart lurches.

Brill turns and looks at me, like somehow he noticed. He's smiling, pero his eyes have tinted towards gray. "You diay?"

"Sí, pero mi vida–" My sublingual rings. After what Gavin said about the feeds, dread fills me as I answer.

It's Mamá. *Bee, who is that feo man who answered your handheld?*

It's a long story, Mamá.

Can you find a holofield somewhere? she bubblechatters, tension in her voice, edging towards fear. *I want to talk face to face.*

Cierto, Mamá. I slide out of the agua and wrap myself in a fluffy towel.

"What's wrong, Babe?" Brill asks.

"I don't know yet." I turn towards Gavin. "I need you to put a holocall through in the media room."

CHAPTER THIRTY-TWO

I should have taken time to change, pero I'm so worried that I just followed the guys into the little theater still wrapped in that towel. So now I'm freezing. Gavin's setting things up. Frank's here, talking to Chestla. No one pays any attention to me and Brill. He slides an arm around me, even though I'm getting his tee-shirt wet. He's still wearing his swim trunks.

Gavin says, "I got the system in here running off my phone."

Mamá stands in her hotel room, a half-packed suitcase on the bed behind her. She glances at my bare shoulders and Brill's arm. Brill pulls away and sits up straight.

Minda leans into the closet, sorting through Mamá's shoes. She turns and throws half a dozen pairs into the suitcase. Her normally bright yellow skin looks pale green. "I'll mail you the rest later. We can't send you with an entourage to the spaceport."

"Que?" My chest jolts in alarm. "Mamá, why can't you have an entourage?"

Mamá always has an entourage, or a cloud of press, or at least un hermoso who's helping her escape the press.

Minda says. "It's about to get ugly. We need to get all humans off Zant before the news spreads. The invasion is back on."

I gasp. "Ay! My planet isn't worth invading anymore. We're in the middle of an ecological disaster."

"That's true," Minda says. "And ordinarily, you'd be in a position to ask for assistance. Only – members of our Royal Academy examined the samples of the cacao disease the Nilka presented in their demands against your planet, and the researchers got sick. They determined that the plant disease was engineered out of Pure275."

"That makes zero sense," Frank says. "Pure275 is the herbicide HGB used to prevent the spread of cacao outside their plantations. It's not a disease."

I can't look at him. Or anyone in this room. I can barely make myself breathe. Cierto, I can't tell Minda that Pure275 was created on Evevron, sold to Earth, and then used in a weaponized form to turn the tide of the First Contact War in HGB's favor 40 years ago. Both Evevron and Earth would wind up in trouble with the Galactic Court. Y I can't tell Frank that Murry bio-grammed the plant disease, porque Frank would ensure Murry's execution.

Minda smiles aggressively, showing most of her feartastic teeth. "The neurotoxins in both substances are quite specific. The chemicals attack certain plants, sure. But they also target the Zantite nervous system in a way that doesn't look accidental. It looks like Earth created a bioweapon to hit back at Zant – and then it got out of hand and ravaged your own planet."

"Ay! Dios mio." My shivering worsens, and not just because of the damp towel. "If you take these accusations to the Galactic Court …"

Then we'd be in the same boat as Murry and Evevron. Probably because HGB got Pure 275 *from* the Evevrons. I glance at Chestla. Who has an odd expression. She's been digging into her own planet's history. Ey! Realmente … the Evevrons sold Pure 275 to Earth shortly after the first Zant-Evevron war. Pure 275 must have been a holdover from research the Evevrons did during that three-year conflict.

The Zantite researchers are half right. Pure275 was designed to attack the Zantites. Only—Evevron, not Earth, created it. When the war ended, they sold us chemicals they no longer needed – because they no longer wanted to destroy the entire population of Zant. And the Zantites happened to likematch cacao trees in some unexpected way. So when the second Zant-Evevron conflict broke out, the Evevrons couldn't use Pure275 in their war, porque it would be easy to trace back to them.

The strength goes out of me. Even if we recover the microdot, key members of HGB could still face punishment for war crimes.

Leron said the Galactic Court's method of execution is quick and painless. I can't imagine Tawny or Janvier taking comfort in that.

Minda asks, "Are you okay, Bo? You look ill."

Mamá sits on the bed next to her suitcase. "This won't go to the Galactic Court, Bee."

Minda nods. "King Garfex is angry. But consider how our justice system works. Zantites don't often get other people caught up in legal complications, because if things escalate, we have to watch the executions – or even be called to participate. If an offense is too big to ignore, we challenge the person to a duel, instead of fighting them in court." Zantite duels are bloody, because their main weapon is their shark-like rows of sharp teeth. Zantite executions are horrific, for the same reason. Brill had come close to taking the Invincible Heart – resulting in instant death for a Krom – rather than have his near-executioners eat him alive. "We duel, because if we kill enemies with our teeth, we prefer it to be on our terms. And that's about to happen between my planet and yours."

This isn't *Independence Day*, and it isn't *War of the Worlds*. Or even *Mars Attacks*. All of those were about invaders coming to Earth for mysterious and nefarious purposes. I don't have a movie to likematch this to. This invasion is personal – and we kind of deserve it. It's not *The Day the Earth Stood Still* either. That was a morality play, not a bloodbath. This is almost like *The Count of Monte Cristo* with a touch of *Tinker, Tailor, Soldier, Spy*.

Brill's eyes go mahogany with concern. Gavin scowls at us. It's not disapproval his black irises are showing. It's fear – not for my planet, pero por mi vida. The minute he catches me looking, his irises bounce back to blue and his expression relaxes. He really is a better liar than Brill.

Chestla stares at her hands. The only thing that could turn the tide of Invasion away from Earth, would be for me – or Chestla – to reveal the true history between Earth and the Evevrons – pero I have no desire to single-handedly start a third Zant-Evevron war. Nunca. Zip.

I turn to Frank. "Can't you convince them this is a coincidence?"

Frank opens his mouth, pero Minda interrupts.

"The investigators cataloguing materials from the crime scene after Mertex's death discovered that the chocolate from my show was poisoned with Pure275."

My chest goes heavy. HGB had once stored a batch of tainted chocolate on Earth. Murry brought it to Zant, where – before becoming a good guy -- he had intended to use it to poison the audience at Minda's show. After Brill and I stopped that plan and took a temporarily infected Tyson in for neurological help, Frank showed up at the hospital, sent by HGB to determine if the doctors there had discovered one of their patients had a brain parasite. Frank may not know about Pure Rot, pero he knows enough about everything else for me to be worried.

"We have a little time to figure this out," Frank insists. "Let's go after Bo's phone, put out a few fires, and then formulate a response. I'll talk to Janvier. If this ends in a duel, maybe we can turn it into something that doesn't involve the whole planet."

Gavin says, "You don't suppose King Garfex would be appeased by a bribe?" Everyone in the room turns to stare at him. He shrugs. "What?"

Mamá starts crying. Which rachets me into panic mode. Mamá never cries.

Minda sits beside Mamá and puts a giant yellow hand over hers. "This will happen faster than you guys think. That wormhole we discovered can get a warship from Zant to Earth in roughly thirty-six of your hours. They're stocking and organizing now, but it won't take long to launch the armada."

I gesture to the suitcase. "Where will you go?" Mamá can't go back to Earth.

"Minda and I are going to Larksis. I connected with a couple of the teachers when I was there for the honorary degree ceremony. They are offering us a place to stay and facilities to keep FeedCasting."

Not that it's likely to matter. This whole thing will be decided before they even get there. A chill settles into my chest. We fought so hard, and now we're out of time. Mario is still on Earth – with Kayla, at his home in Rio, where Mario and his wife have been taking care of my younger sisters alongside his own niños and Frank's granddaughter, for the duration of Mamá's media tour.

"What about Mario and the girls? Y mis abuelos?"

"They are packing for a flight that leaves in a couple of hours. A SeniorLeisure tour vessel." The same type of ship Kaliel blew up. Sí, the irony's painful. "It will take them halfway to Larksis, then they will pick up a connecting shuttle." Mamá holds both hands out towards Frank. "You will meet us there too, right Papi?"

He smiles back. "As soon as I can."

First off, eww. I do not want to think about mi mamá calling Frank by a pet name.

More importantly, they're all giving up. Verdaderamente. After everything, how can they just accept defeat? Just because Minda cancelled the cooking class where I planned to talk to Garfex doesn't mean he isn't still intrigued by me.

I stand up. "Por favor. Let me talk to King Garfex." I look around the room. Given their personalities and communication styles, none of the people here will help get Garfex into a good mood. "Alone."

Minda nods. "I can arrange that. It may take a few time segment partitions. In the meantime, tell everyone you care about to evacuate the planet, before there's a rush at the spaceports. And you should to change into respectable clothes. I doubt anyone has ever addressed our king while wearing swimwear."

"Entiendo." She doesn't speak Spanish. "I understand." Mi mamá is carefully folding a dress into her suitcase. "You be careful, Mamá."

She wipes a hand across her eyes. "You too, Bee."

I send a quick message to Kayla, who responds that she's already left Earth. En serio? She's supposed to be hiding out with Mario. Not only will she not risk using her influence to help us, she left the planet before she even found out there's a new issue. I start to send her an irritated reply, pero no. I defended her choice to stay in hiding to her brother. I shouldn't be dissapointangerated with her for sticking with it.

I head into the hallway.

Chestla follows. Once we're out of earshot of the others, she whispers, "I'm sorry my planet got yours involved with this."

"You're not responsible for what your people did before you were born. We're still amigas, right?"

"Of course, cesud – mi amiga." She crushes me with a hug.

When she lets go, I rush to change. In the middle, I get a call from Tawny. She bubblechatters, *Wear the mauve blouse with the pansy brooch. That's got my best camera.*

I dig the shirt out of my suitcase. *I thought you didn't care anymore, chica.*

Of course I care! Tawny's sigh rolls through my brain. *I took my eye off the ball for one minute, and it all came crashing down. It's too late to ask for more mercy, and it's too late to make deals. I'm out of my depth, but I'll collect feed of you and Garfex and try to spin something out of it. Hurry, though. HGB has figured out roughly where you are and is sending operatives to collect whatever you stole. Even with Frank to protect you, it likely won't go well, for you or for him.*

I wince, though the news is not surprising. Interesante que Janvier hasn't been forthcoming about my stealing the microdot. What do the HGB guys think they're coming to take off me?

Without waiting for my answer Tawny makes an annoyed noise. *I'll take you out in a second. Don't you dare pee on my floor.*

She's not talking to me. And I assume her nuevo hermoso, Hosei, is housebroken. *You have company, chica?*

Frank asked me to take care of his dog. I have never been a pet person. But he asked me not to kennel it, and I owe him a favor or two.

Botas has been in the shelter at least twice, when he lost his first two owners. So sí, I can see Frank not wanting the dog to fear he's not coming back. Pero what does the fact that she's doing this herself say about Tawny?

Did you tell them my location? By which I mean, am I wearing a tracker as well as a camera? And is she spinning me into HGB's hands?

Tawny's huff rolls through mi cabeza. *I don't want our best hope for salvaging this situation to die, now do I? And I have no idea where you are. I'm just lucky you pulled out that swimsuit, or I'd have no idea what's going on.*

I find myself smiling. *You just think it's too much work to update my eulogy.*

When I get back to the theater, Brill is waiting by the door. He's changed out of his swim trunks and into jeans and a dry tee. "If you need anything, call me on your sublingual."

"Sí." I give him a quick hug, then step into the theater and move close to the holofield. I'm nervous, fidgety. Pero less than I would have expected, given who I'm about to talk to. I guess porque, with the situation this desperate, I can't make it worse.

Minda asks, "Are you ready?"

When I nod, the holofield shifts from the hotel to a blackstone-walled room, dominated by an elaborate throne chair. The floor is raw cement, angled downward towards a drain outside the capture field. Garfex's throne room doubles as an interrogation chamber, used for executions and duels, and the drain makes it easier to clean up the blood.

Garfex, short by Zantite standards, and a bit rounder than most, has his legs casually hooked over the arm of the chair. When I appear, he sits up properly. "Bo Benitez, the Merciful, Bearer of the Invincible Heart, Spuckslayer and Champion of

Kaliel the Mindworm Murderer. It is an honor to make a new impression of you."

He sounds serious, not mocking, no matter how mad he is with mi planeta.

"And I likewise, King Garfex, holder of the Trident of Awe." There's a lot more to his title, pero I can't remember what. Y mine keeps getting longer. It's hard to believe I've done that many things the Zantites find title-worthy. I get to the point. "I am here to beg for mercy for my planet."

Garfex leans forward, his cold, tight smile revealing far too many feartastic teeth. Tranquila, yo. He's just a holo-him. He can't bite me in half. I still back up. Garfex says, "I am well aware of the Mercy is a Gift campaign. My wife is constantly wearing those ridiculous rubber bracelets instead of proper jewels. Ordinarily, I give her whatever she wants. But your people have directly attacked mine. I cannot let that stand."

Which is almost exactly what Frank said before murdering Shelly. It wasn't right then – and it's not fair now.

"I apologize thoroughly on behalf of my planet." I swallow a lump of frustangerated mourning. I'm not sure who all I'm sad for. "Much of this problem is simply a misunderstanding. I don't think anyone meant to attack you directly."

"Do you have proof of that?"

I actually don't. Murry sent that poisoned chocolate to Zant, back when he was the cold version of the Mindhuggers – pero I never found a shipping receipt or any records. And even if I had, I couldn't prove Murry was testing me and me alone, without regard to the collateral damage. Murry used humans he had hugs on to engineer the Pure Rot disease. Pero some of those humans are muerto, and the others bear no physical marks of having been infected.

I have trouble keeping my voice steady. "Por favor. Please. What can I do or say to convince you to show leniency?"

"Bring me an undiseased chocolate tree, and I'll call off the invasion." He's being sarcastic and flip, and his gravelly voice sounds angry.

I force eye contact with him. "Can I hold you to that?"

His eyes widen. "What do—"

My sublingual rings. It's Frank. *What are you doing, Bo?*

I say, "For full disclosure, media on my side of this call are recording it, hoping I'll give them a soundbite they can use. And they will share what you just said."

"Do you have an undiseased chocolate tree?" Garfex asks.

"No." I step closer to the camera. "We're working on it." Now here's the dicey part. "We've been conducting research with a joint team, aboard one of your vessels. If you want to honor your wife's participation in the Mercy is a Gift campaign, let us continue our efforts. At least let us try to accomplish your impossible task."

Garfex's mouth slides open, revealing even more feartastic teeth. Then he gives me a smile, close-lipped and small. Pero it's a real smile this time. "I have always liked you. So I hope, after the invasion begins, you stay aboard that particular warship. You can only be talking about one vessel, and it will not be participating in the fighting. I will give you sanctuary afterwards."

"That is very generous." I swallow again, yet my mouth's even drier. *Afterwards.* After mi mundo becomes a Zantite protectorate. Or gets jangleblasted trying to defend itself. Garfex doesn't know that I promised to stay aboard the *Layla's Pride* for six months. I'm not going to tell him. "Pero you haven't answered my question."

Garfex puts his hands on his knees, leaning down closer to my height. "My armada will arrive at Earth in roughly two of your days, and I will be aboard the flagship. If at that time Daschel Janvier himself gives me an authentic, whole cacao tree, along with an apology, I will turn around and go home. Kesvesk, I'll even leave a couple of ships behind to help with your ecological disaster. The rest of the invasion coalition has pulled out, so if my armada leaves, you have nothing left to worry about except what your people have done to themselves."

Janvier won't go for that, Frank bubblechatters. *If you come up with a cacao seedling, he'll want to keep it for Earth.*

Pues, I'll burn that bridge when I get to it, no? I smile gratefully at Garfex. "That's not much time." And then I half-quote Brill. "But every moment is a kindness."

Frank lets out a string of less than kind words en mi cabeza that ends with, *and now you're quoting the damn Krom.*

Garfex frowns. "I'm not sure that it is. I'm just loaning you false hope and desperation, and for that I apologize thoroughly. But it is what you asked me for, and all I can give."

"And I will do my best," I tell him. "With all my might."

The proper Zantite reply to that is, *Then your success is assured.* Garfex doesn't say it. He just stares at me for a moment, and then says, "Goodbye, Bo."

Then the holofield goes black.

Frank's bubblechatter sounds urgent. *We need to talk about this. Right now.*

Later, viejo. I need a minute to regroup. Porque it's all become way too real. Garfex is talking about the invasion like it's already been accomplished. And Earth won't surrender. There'll be more environmental damage and loss of life. And Garfex won't be careful, because he doesn't want the planet anymore.

I bow mi cabeza and close my eyes. No wonder the others have given up.

The holofield lights up again. An amused-looking General Crosskiss stands in the middle of a hallway, selfie-holoing at an angle that leaves one side of his face outside the capture field. "You know my stepfather is just playing with you, right?"

I walk back to front and center. "What did he tell you?"

"To expect you on board my ship soon. And to keep you here, along with your crew, so you don't get any crazy ideas that might mess up the invasion."

I laugh. "That almost sounds like a compliment, no?"

"I guess you could take it that way. So who is this crew? What sort of quarters should we prepare?"

I can't help but glance at the door. "Mira. I'm traveling with a group of Evevrons. A couple of them have a background in cryogenics research and chemistry. Will that be a problem?"

Given the recent war, and all.

Crosskiss adjusts the phone. "Holding a grudge after a battle has ended is a luxury best suited to civilians. As long as your Evevrons don't start trouble, they're safe aboard the *Layla's Pride*."

CHAPTER THIRTY-THREE

Brill's still waiting when I leave the theater. It may be the lighting, or the extraño purple tint still in his hair, pero he looks pale. I take the brooch off my blouse and place it on a ledge in the hallway. I want to talk to mi vida about something he hasn't been ready to share, and I can't do that with Tawny watching.

I pull Brill into the main cabin. The only place to sit is that ridículo heart-shaped sofa.

We sink onto it, our knees tilted together. "I'm so proud of how you handled yourself with Garfex." He tries to run his hands through my still-damp hair.

I stop him. "Is there something about your heart I need to know about? Are you sick?"

Brill looks confused. He brings a hand to his chest. "Babe?"

"Then what is it? Nobody will say why wearing that pendant makes me feel numb. Or why–"

His eyes go green with curiosity. "Feel numb how?"

I shrug. "Like there's layers of cotton between you and me. Now that I've stopped wearing it, the sensation's faded. When I beso your lips, I can feel the heat again."

He swallows visibly and grabs my hand. "Go on. Avell. You said, 'or why.' What were you going to say?"

He still hasn't told *me* anything. I huff. "Gavin said you needed to be careful about not forming a something, pero then he remembered he was talking to an Earthling and stopped mid-sentence. It was like for a minute he had accepted me and you as a couple – then he remembered something. What won't anybody tell me?"

Brill laughs, and his eyes tint back towards gold. "You've almost put it together by yourself. I didn't want to hurt your feelings, because I never imagined it might be returned – you really felt numb? Not just comforted or steadied?"

I arch an eyebrow. "Mi vida."

His face goes serious. "Gavin was saying he was afraid I would develop a heart bond with you. It's the kind of way you tease someone who's with their paqunell, when they're too young to get married. Babe, he really is getting comfortable around you."

"Fantastica. I'm winning over your species, one Krom at a time." Jeska once called me Brill's paqunell. The words literally mean beginner's heart. Brill said I was more than that to him.

Brill's eyes shift towards lavender. "Gavin had to be joking, because heart bonds are supposed to take decades in a committed relationship to form. He couldn't have known– Shtesh, Babe, you and I have been through some intense things together, which can jumpstart it. That's rare for Krom in general, practically impossible with crisscrossed hearts like ours."

Is he saying that's what's happened? "So that's why Gavin freaked out when you and I were in the hot tub. Something about the color of your eyes."

"Told him that I had bonded with you, wal. It's a distinctive shade of gold, but you couldn't tell it apart from the other shades of love unless you knew what to look for. I realized a while back I'd formed a bond, but I thought it was one sided. I'm still not sure – seriously, most Krom in crisscrossed relationships know they're giving up the hope of forming a reciprocal bond. Half the time, we never even pick up the energy from a compatible heart. Let alone incite a reaction in return."

"Mi vida." I stop his babbling with a finger against his lips. "That still doesn't explain what a heart bond is. It's a part of Krom culture I've never heard about."

Brill takes my hand in both of his. "Ga. Not culture. Physiology. You know that we process electricity differently than most of our compatible species." He glances at the healing foam patching the dart hole in his hand. "Uan, two Krom can form a biological bond where energy from our heartbeat syncs with that of our life's love."

"Why haven't I heard about this?" I'd read notes on the Krom Codex, and saw nothing about bonds of any sort.

"It's not something we talk about. It's personal and private – and could be exploited to cause pain. So many people hate my species." He squeezes my hand. "Even though I thought it was one-sided, I started to tell you about it back on the beach, but then you asked me to leave. And said you kissed Shelly."

Mi corazón jolts with anguish. And the color in Brill's eyes shifts towards pain. Could that be a reaction to my feelings? The thought elevates my heartbeat.

Brill touches his chest again. "Even if I'm wrong, and you can't feel the bond, I'm diay. But the longer we're together, the stronger a bond gets. A bond is a risk and a responsibility. It makes you vulnerable to the other person. They hold your life in their hands."

This explains so much. "Pero acknowledging this bond is not the same as a proposal."

He looks taken aback. "No. Hanstral, Babe. I told you, I can't."

Because he doesn't feel prepared to support me. It doesn't matter to him that I'm rich. It needs to be his dinero, his accomplishments. Ni idea what happened to his half of the bounty we got for turning in Kaliel and then Jack. Or maybe even that wasn't enough of a nest egg.

My mind works out lots of little things he's hinted at over the course of our relationship. "Is this bond why Krom can die of a broken heart?"

He half shrugs, half nods. "Sometimes. Sympathetic death is rare, though, unless the Krom is old or weak. Our cardio systems are always our downfall. We're more likely to die from the stress of other types of grief, such as the loss of a parent or a child, or later after losing a bond, from the stress of loneliness. But if the two of us are in proximity, there's still a chance that when you die, I'll die too. Isn't that comforting?"

"Mi vida!" My eyes widen with shock, and my heart skips a few beats. He's serious. For him, that *is* comforting. Which gives context to his obsession with making our life spans the same. It still doesn't fix the problem – nada, nunca – pero I don't feel like he still considers me biologically inferior. I blink. A couple of times. "How do you know you've bonded with me?"

"Our heartbeats synchronize dramatically from time to time. It happened in the hallway, where you were talking to Frank. I felt your fear for him, and how much you care about him in the way your body responded to his words. My heartbeat changed too, prompting my body to feel the same things." He clears his throat and looks away. "It's how I sensed you were developing feelings for Shelly. What happened with your heart when he died in your arms was so strong it overrode my jealousy. I hurt for you, instead of fearing for myself."

Tears fill my eyes. He's held so much back, desperate not to hurt me. Porque he didn't want me to feel inferior. If only he had told me … "I've imagined several times that our heartbeats matched, that you've steadied my staccato bass with your hummingbird rhythms." I wince at the cheesetastic poetry. Pero that's how I've thought about it. "It seemed too silly to even mention." It almost feels too strange to be a real biological phenomenon. "Your heartbeat's so much faster than mine. How could your system handle going that slow?"

Brill brings his face in close to mine. His eyes are solid gold. "I hit two beats for your one. But you can feel the rhythm."

He pulls my hand to his chest. As my heart races with the excitement that I haven't just imagined that feeling of connection, his heart speeds up a little to match.

Which, despite everything going on around us, makes me feel like I've been broken open and flooded with joy. It could be that joy, or the steadying influence of his heart prompting a response in me – pero my heartbeat slows to normal. "When did this happen?"

Brill runs a hand through my hair, playing with the ends of it. "I first noticed it on Zant, when we were sitting in the van, waiting for your mamá's ship to land. But then you started wearing the Paladzian, which disrupts a bond. It took a while to return. You have no idea how much that distance hurt."

I arch that eyebrow again. "Don't I?"

His mouth drops open. "Maybe you do. Hanstral, Babe. I'm taking a bit to wrap my mind around the possibilities. It's like, you grow up believing that someday you'll meet someone and look forward with them to sharing the special moment when you both realize you've bonded. Then you fall in love with someone who isn't Krom and realize that moment will never happen, but you want to be with them anyway. And now – to realize it's possible after all. It doesn't feel real. Like, when will I wake up from this dream?"

I pinch his chest, hard.

"Ouch!"

"Nope. Not dreaming." I lean towards him, and he kisses me. At the touch, hope washes over me. No matter what happens, I have this – my Krom – to hold onto.

When we break the beso, he looks at me with golden love. Then he gets serious. "I told you the bond isn't a proposal. It shouldn't have happened this fast. We should have had decades to figure things out. I'm too young to have established what I need to in life. It feels like we're always going at things backwards."

That stings. "Oye."

"Babe. Ga. I didn't mean it that way. I mean, what we have is intense. And that's cool, right?"

"I guess so. Pero with my shorter lifespan, I need things to happen faster."

He considers that. "Sorry, Babe, but that seems unlikely."

"I can accept that," I say. For now. I feel totally connected to him. Which is muy chido. And completely overwhelming. "Will I feel this way all the time?"

Brill says, "Mostly, you won't even notice it. From what I've heard. Obviously, this is my first time experiencing it. But you're not stuck. Bonds can fade – though Krom don't often bond more than once. Supposedly, it hurts too much getting over it uan your body protects itself. If you can't handle the weirdness – or if you can't handle dealing with my mother – and decide to leave, I will live. And if something happens to me, you wouldn't likely die either, even if it's a truly reciprocal bond. But the longer a heart bond lasts, the deeper it gets, so that it can bind us together despite the distance and time necessitated by space travel. It's part of why Gavin never so much as looks at another girl, even though his wife is back home half the time. And they've only been bonded for a couple of years."

I think about the dark terror in Gavin's eyes. "Then why is Gavin afraid for you?"

Brill hesitates. "His sister died sympathetically when her husband was killed. She was from a previous generation, when Gavin's parents first got married. She and her husband lived together for about a hundred and thirty years, uan that bond was super deep. She'd always had weak health, and they were holding hands when it happened. Plus, he died instantly of a gunshot wound. That's a lot of things to have line up, no? Gavin's afraid that with your lifespan being so much shorter, I'd be his sister's age when I lost you. Uan more risk. But Babe, someday our kids might be able to form bonds with other Krom."

Y given the look on his face, for Brill, that changes everything. He looks like he's about to propose. Even though he keeps saying he can't. His longing expression shows that he wants niños. With me. I don't understand how he can want that so badly and not make the commitment I need. We'd find some way to handle the economic issues and the prejudice between our families. Pero if I push for a vow he's not ready to make, I could ruin this special moment.

"What's wrong?" Brill asks. "Is this too much for you? I understand if you want to back off. While the physical risk to you is slight, there *is* some risk. I–"

How can I tell him that I just want to be even closer to him? I put my hand back on his chest. "I'm not going anywhere, mi vida."

He crushes me to him and rests his chin on mi cabeza. He's crying a little as he whispers, "Avell, don't let this be a dream."

Brill and I get to enjoy holding each other for a whole two minutes before there's thud, like something's been dropped. Frank's standing in the doorway, holding his phone upside down, which causes a weird angle on the holoprojection of Feddoink from the news who, without the volume, still looks like he's shouting. Frank shuts it off.

Brill's irises go pink. "Su. How long have you been standing there?"

Frank smiles. "Long enough to learn a few new details about Krom biology. I didn't want to interrupt, but it was too damn interesting to walk away from."

Brill snorts out a laugh. "Then I should be glad you're known for being discreet."

Frank steps closer. "You overestimate how much people care about retribution for Krom discoveries. And how creative they are when it comes to torture. Why hurt someone's bond mate instead of hurting them directly?"

Brill shrugs. "People have tried it. You can't keep something that innate to your species a complete secret. No one can empirically prove that a heart bond exists, uan it's not in the wiki entries. But there are rumors, which get lumped in with all the lies about us other species have come up with over the centuries."

Frank gestures towards me. "I guess this changes the estimation Krom have for Earthlings?"

"If we could convince them Bo isn't faking? Wal. But not enough for the Homeworld to intercede for your planet. Krom don't do war. We make sure no one ever has the legal right to start one with us."

Frank sighs. "It was worth a shot." He looks at me. "Chestla said we're heading for a Zantite ship after we retrieve the microdot. So what vessel and what research team are we pinning our hopes on?"

"The *Layla's Pride*."

Frank looks like he just bit into a skelhted. "Crosskiss's ship? Didn't he try to use you as a murder weapon?"

"Sí. We worked out a deal." My cheeks burn. "You can't tell anyone. It was part of the deal."

"What deal?" Brill's eyes go purple with concentration. I have his full attention.

I rush the words out fast. "I told him I'd be his personal chef for six months."

Both Brill and Frank say at the same time, "You what?"

I jut out my chin. "I needed him to take Eugene and Murry on board and let them use the lab. Garfex gave them permission to keep working."

"Uan what are they working on, Babe?"

I hesitate. They'll think I'm loca. I squint my eyes and shift away. "Cryostasis."

"What?" they ask in unison.

I shift back towards them, standing straighter, trying to look confident. "Leron was working to overcome the revival barrier for Patient Zero. Eugene thinks he hopes to use the tech Leron was developing to reverse the freezing process and sprout cacao beans from HGB's seed bank."

Brill puts his hands on my shoulders. "You threw away six months of your life over the galaxy's biggest snake oil con? Babe, why?"

I move his hands off my shoulders and squeeze them. "Mi vida–" Suddenly, he looks like he might cry again. "What?"

He squeezes my hands back. "It's just – that's what some heart-bonded couples call each other. Suavetta quenell os suavetta av. My heart and my life. That's why I've always loved it when you call me mi vida."

"And why you called me your corazón in the van when–"

We glance at Frank. When Frank took Brill with the intent of killing him.

Frank rolls his eyes in exasperation. "Can we please get over that? I didn't kill him, okay?" He looks back at me. "If there's any possibility Leron could help Eugene succeed, we need to get him to that ship ASAP." He turns towards Brill. "How are the repairs coming on Gavin's ship?"

"Dash said it should be flight-ready within the hour."

"Good." Frank puts a hand on Brill's shoulder. "Then you, Gavin and I will take it and go after the microdot." He pauses until Brill nods his willingness to help. "Bo, the clone should stay here with you."

Brill's eyes shift towards yellow-orange.

Frank pokes him in the shoulder. "You have this special love bond with the girl and you're still jealous?"

I stifle a giggle. Frank's getting good at reading chromashift.

"You're right." Brill breaks into a huge grin. "I have to trust her. She's my heart."

And his life.

Frank's phone rings. "You two be quiet." He answers it, and a holo of Daschel Janvier floats above Frank's mano. Frank's turned so that Brill and I are out of the capture field.

Janvier says, "Tawny just streamed me some interesting footage."

"Bo has given us a chance," Frank says. "I advise you to at least consider it."

"The Aztecs associated cacao pods with the human heart. Life and blood. It's an important connection. One you might be losing sight of." Janvier takes a cacao pod shaped stress ball from the bowl on his desk and squeezes it until it looks crushed. "You told me you could be an asset, Sawyer."

"And I'm attempting to do so," Frank says. "I've chased down Bo, like you wanted. She's still breathing, because she's being helpful."

"I want you to shadow Miss Benitez, figure out where she's getting this sample tree, and take it." Janvier throws the stress ball back into the bowl. "We can salvage this. If we prove we have chocolate on Earth again, the Zantites won't dare attack us."

That is not true. My hands ball into fists. Pero I can't protest, or Janvier will hear.

"I'll take that under consideration," Frank says. "But it's not likely to happen. She's put all her eggs in a giant basket labeled cryostasis."

"Cryostasis?" Janvier laughs. A loud, deep belly laugh. "I guess I have to keep working on the problem myself."

Heat flames into my cheeks. Am I that ridícula to him?

Janvier says, "I don't understand anything surrounding Bodacious Benitez. You know Shelly had a crush on her? Tawny linked Bodacious with me in the polls. So now my news alerts keep giving me status updates on Team Janvier, Team Kaliel and Team Brill. And I'm losing to Kaliel. How is that possible? He's been disgraced, twice."

Frank sighs. "Perhaps focus on diplomacy with the Zantites."

"I have been." Janvier brings a hand to his forehead, as though rubbing away worry – or a mental image of King Garfex. "Where are we on the item Miss Benitez took?"

"I'm still trying to recover it. I assume a few of my colleagues are on their way to make sure I'm on task?"

"I'm not heartless," Janvier says. "Their orders are to help, not kill you. Unless you give them reason to believe you are hindering our interests. And I'll respect the memo I sent about the Krom. But Miss Benitez has put us in a vulnerable position, and they will question her – however necessary. I advise you to find the item soon."

Frank hangs up. He opens his mouth to speak.

I say quickly, "Let me pack you some food. Vale?" My face flaming with embarrassment, I head for the galley.

Frank follows me, as Brill heads towards Gavin's ship to make sure it will be ready to separate. I sigh. I have no choice but to talk to Frank now. I expect him to say something about Janvier. Instead he gestures after Brill. "You heard the poor guy say he only gets one chance to bond like this, right?" I nod. Frank adds, "Don't break his heart."

"I don't plan to. I want him to marry me." I scrunch up my nose. "Why do you sound like you're mi padre or something?"

Frank's face goes crimson, and suddenly I don't feel like teasing him anymore.

I stare at him. "You said Mamá made a mistake being with you. Now you plan to propose?"

He turns away and opens a cabinet, then pulls out a box of snack crackers labeled in indecipherable writing. "I'd like to. But I doubt Lavonda would have me until we get all this settled about me and HGB and the fate of Earth, and she knows where you and I stand with each other. You have no idea how much I love your mother. But one of the things I love most is her devotion to her family. She'll always love you more, and I'm okay with that."

I bring Frank a tote to put the cracker box in. "And if Earth is destroyed two days from now? Or it's broken and HGB dismantled?"

He bends the box a little as his hands try to make fists. "Then we'll all be homeless, and it won't matter anymore. And if I have your blessing, I'll ask if she'll make me her home, and we can wash away the past on Larksis, or wherever she wants to go."

He wants me to tell him whether I support him marrying mi mamá. I'm so flustbarrased, I can't make a rational decision right now. "Ask me again in two days, viejo. If I'm still alive."

"I'll do what I can to convince HGB that you're acting in good faith." Frank drops the crackers into the tote. "I have the easy part. All I have to do is retrieve that microdot and talk Daschel Janvier into giving the Zantites the thing he's held onto the tightest. And to apologize to them. Which will be harder than getting him to give up the new cacao tree – assuming you can even sprout one. Now you – you have to take a bunch of Evevrons onto a Zantite warship."

"That war is over, no?"

Frank shrugs. "Are wars ever really over? Chestla took a big risk coming to Zant to find you. A lot of Zantites resent the concessions they were forced to give to end the fighting. She could easily have disappeared down a dark alley."

As if on cue, Chestla's voice comes over the ship's com system. "Can everyone please report to the bridge? It's rather urgent." She says it like she's calling us to a party. I believe her words rather than her tone.

Frank drops a can of vegetables into the tote. We exchange a *what-the-heck* kind of look and then head for the bridge.

CHAPTER THIRTY-FOUR

Despite having been in the other ship, Brill and Gavin beat us to the small bridge. I didn't even see them blazebang past us, pero the two Krom are both leaning against the wall, arms crossed over their chests, looking all litoll in their denim jackets. Brill must have raided Gavin's closet. The jacket looks tight, porque Gavin's thinner than Brill. Traditionally, Krom don't wear animal skin. While Brill's not a mega traditional guy, he still embraces much of his culture. I hope he never takes on that particular tradition. Maybe it's the denim's ill fit, pero I like Brill better in leather.

Dash comes up behind us. "I'm an engineer, and I still don't understand how Krom can move that fast."

The bridge area has two seats, for the pilot and navigator. The Evevron I haven't yet met – Watae's minder – sits at the controls, with Chestla at navigation. She introduces him as Jewndel. He has ash blonde hair, reflective green eyes, and a dark scar across the bridge of his nose.

"Greetings," he says in formal, awkward universal. I bet he only speaks Evevron.

"Greetings!" I reply. "Ensa ucon anma." *So nice to meet you.*

The conversation doesn't get much farther than that.

During our awkward exchange, Chestla said something to Frank.

"What?" he shouts. Frank's reddening face looks like it might explode. He turns to me. "The signal from your phone disappeared over an hour ago. We've been following the ship's last known trajectory, and nobody bothered to tell us."

"To be fair, Bo was a little busy with the diplomacy." Chestla flexes her fingers. "So, either the phone got destroyed – yay, mission accomplished – or it got moved somewhere with thick layers of signal shielding.”

Ay! No wonder Frank looks like he's going to pop.

Chestla waits for the other Evevrons to join us before she says anything else, though the tension in her jaw betrays that she's got more bad news. When we're all present, she points at the screen. "That ship is closing fast. The *Just Married* is a party barge. It wasn't meant to outmaneuver pirates."

"How do you know they're pirates?" Leron asks.

"Because they sent this message." Chestla punches a button.

Jack's face appears in the holofield, mucho, mucho larger than life. I tense. The pimple on his chin, that wouldn't be noticeable except for the magnification, doesn't make him any less intimidating. "I guess you can see me coming on your radar. This doesn't have to be a fight, and I don't have to disable your ship. Just send Bo Benitez out in a spitpod, and I'll pick her up. Her boyfriend won't want to give her up, so subdue him first. If it's easier, you can send him too."

Gavin mutters a couple of Krom words I've never heard before.

"Wal, su," Brill agrees. "He's always been a kek."

"He's crazy if he thinks we'll give either of you up," Chestla says fiercely. Todavía, her gaze flicks to Watae and Nellet. Watae has a protective arm around his bride's shoulder. Pero even he can't fight a gang of pirates if they disable our ship and wait for us to run out of air.

They just got married. They're their entire planet's symbol of new hope and a blank-slate chance for peace. They don't deserve to die protecting me.

"We have two ships," I say, though dread coats mi corazón and dries my mouth. "Gavin's ship's faster and more maneuverable. I've practiced flying Brill's ship, and the *Boundless* is the same model as the *Fois Gras*. I can take it now, before Jack gets here."

"Babe!" Brill flashes over to me, clasps my face in his hands. "Ga. What would be the point?"

"The point is they get to live." I gesture over to Nellet and Watae. "And their lives have a purpose that needs to be fulfilled. Muy bien. Jack just wants me. So if he has to choose targets, he'll follow the ship I'm on, and the other one will have time to escape."

"That's noble." Gavin pushes away from the wall and makes an open-palmed sweeping hand gesture denoting respect. "But I refuse to send my trevhonell on a suicide mission. If you want a chance of outmaneuvering Jack, you need a real pilot. And I assume Brill's coming too."

"I have to." Brill grins at me. "She's my heart and my life."

Gavin's eyes go bright green. He knows what Brill meant – only he's probably got no clue that I feel the heart bond too. Or any idea whether Brill's told me about it.

Frank opens his mouth to speak.

I stop him. "No, viejo. If this goes badly, el corazón de mi mamá won't be able to take losing us both."

Frank looks like he's about to protest. Then he nods. "Thank you, Bodacious."

"Don't worry, viejo," Brill says. Frank raises both eyebrows at mi vida's use of the nickname. Brill cracks a smile. "When we get close to Jack, we'll do our best to get that microdot. I'm getting attached to you breathing, revwal."

I think Brill says that to make Frank feel better about staying behind, choosing to live when our odds of doing so no es bueno.

Frank brings a hand to his ribcage, which Brill probably bruised when he did CPR. "Yeah, I get that idea."

After all, Brill could have justified letting Frank die so Brill could save me from the pirates.

Everyone starts talking and planning – except for Watae's Guardian, who has watched in silence, looking increasingly frustrafused, up until Ball hobbles over to him and starts translating. Jewndel says something emphatic to Watae.

Watae says, "He is grateful for your compassion towards me. I am to remember this day and learn much. But he hopes – as do I – that I will not have to learn how it feels to lose a friend."

Ball says, "If anyone can survive a crisis, it is Bodacious Babe Benitez. I owe her my life." He then repeats himself in Evevron.

Chestla looks upset, pero she manages a brief smile when he starts translating. Ball's the kind of guy who does the right thing too, who takes everyone into account. He makes eye contact with Chestla. She looks away, a blush flooding her cheeks. He looks disappointed. Rather than deal with that, Chestla follows me into the hallway. "How can I let you do this, cesuda ma? I swore to protect you. This ship's weapons are limited, true, but–"

"Because I'm not your cesuda ma anymore." I put a hand on her arm. "I'm Gavin's trevhonell. And Brill's heartbound love. You have Nellet to protect. She needs you more now than ever before. Let the guys do what they've promised."

Chestla trembles. I've never seen her look vulnerable. Nunca. *Not* springing into action might be the hardest thing I'll ever ask her to do. "But what if there are too many pirates? Sometimes one extra fighter is all you need to change the outcome."

"Por favor, mi amiga."

Chestla draws me into another crushing hug. "Forget everything I taught you about fighting. It's totally different in zero g. If you guys can't outrun Jack, put on an environment suit and sneak out of the ship. Jewndel and I will get our kaenns out of radar range, but we won't leave the area. Even if you're drifting, I can pick up your signal."

True, though by the time Jack gave up and she could safely return, I'd have run out of air. The two Krom might survive, pero I don't want to picture Brill having to watch me suffocate.

A shiver runs through me. "Let's hope Gavin's the mejor driver."

Brill puts a hand on my shoulder, "Hanstral, Babe, but we have to go."

Because every second I waste saying goodbye gives Jack that much time to catch up.

When Chestla lets me go, her face is resolved. "If that pirate hurts you, he'll regret it."

Leron waits near the red Jet Skis. "I'll help Murry, when I get to the warship. Even though it means having to talk to him."

That's as close to a touching farewell as I'll get from the Evevron. I wrap him in a hug.

Then Brill and I hurry across into Gavin's ship. I go straight to the sofa, which converts into a row of crash chairs, and strap myself in. I don't want Gavin to have to worry about me.

Brill sits beside me, just looking at my face, like he can hardly believe I'm real. My acknowledging the heart bond has made him affectionate in a way I've always wanted. I lean in close to him. How can we have found this nueva profundidad – this *whole new depth* – in each other, just to have a pirate try to take it away?

Now that our ship's set a course, Gavin sends a com request to Jack. When Jack's face appears in the holo, he's at the bridge of his own ship – the *Shimmering Pearl*. Porque that's the kind of hombre Jack is. Named for a painter, he took his ship's name from a movie and considers himself clever for twisting it. He's never had an original thought in his life. Uan, I can't believe he thought up this pirate coalition.

"You want to explain what this is all about?" Gavin asks. "First you try to recruit me, and now you're trying to kill us?"

"I'd prefer not to kill you. I still have a business proposition for you. If you survive," Jack says. "But my priority is Bo, and I will kill to take her. I need her alive, so after I disable your ship, I'll give you time to get her into an environment suit."

"Why her?" Brill asks. "HGB won't pay a ransom."

Jack laughs. "I wouldn't ask them to."

I say, "I'm not helping you."

Jack laughs again. It's a creepy sound. "Oh, you won't have a choice."

Though Gavin flies at a tremendous speed, the dot representing Jack's ship on the nav is catching up at una tasa alarmante.

Gavin waves his hand at the holofield. "I can't figure out how Bo plays into any scheme of yours. She's not worth much dead, to anybody. And alive, she's only important as a liaison between Earth and the Zantites."

I sigh. Jack really never has had an original idea. The kek. "You plan to blame me for killing one of the Zantites, no? And leave my body at the palace. I'm guessing you planned to make me kill Garfex at my cooking class and threaten to kill Gavin if I didn't cooperate."

Jack looks at me curiously. "Not entirely correct. But you get the gist. And don't worry – I know your event got cancelled."

I say, "If you want to start a war between Earth and Zant, you're too late, mijo. It's already happening."

Jack shrugs. "I've heard this Mercy Is a Gift campaign might still work. Why take chances? Earth could have made a graceful First Contact. It's not my fault they screwed it up. And disowned their own people."

Oye! Dios mio! Jack's got the microdot, whether he knows it or not. And the people he works for – this prison colony vengezentful at their origin planet – would use it to hurt us. And Jack is so angerated at Earth turning its back on him for going pirate, he doesn't care what happens to his home world.

I gasp. Jack looks over at me. "What?"

"De nada." Something still feels off, though. If this is about fueling war between Zant and Earth, why was Not-Kaliel looking for the HGB basement?

"Uan now that we know your plan, what's to stop us from calling the Galactacops?" Gavin shifts the controls and the ship banks sharply, sending us at a ninety-degree angle away from our previous course.

"You see," Jack says. "When I said you could live, I meant if you accept my business proposition."

Which won't happen. Nada y nunca.

Whatever Gavin hoped to do, it's not enough. As soon as Jack's within shooting range, he hits us with an EMP blast. The lights go out inside the cabin, and the subtle hum of life support shuts off. We keep moving in the direction we were going – until a grappling hook hits our hull.

I squeak in fear.

A tiny light comes on. Gavin lies under the control deck, using his phone – which must have as much shielding as my sublingual – to see by as he tries to reboot anything in the system that's not fried.

Brill unclips my seatbelts. "Come on, Babe. Jack's right. We need to get you into an environment suit. He'll pop the doors eventually."

Waves of fear echo through my core. How can Brill be so calm?

We head for the cargo bay that houses the spitpods and maintenance equipment. Brill must have environment suits on his ship, también, though I've never been inclined to take a spacewalk, so I'd never looked.

Halfway down the hall, I pull Brill to me in the dark and kiss him, fear and hope and this newfound closeness mingling into something electric. Our heartbeats synchronize. He's right – it's something you hardly notice, except as a feeling of closeness, of rightness. So if one of us doesn't make it through this, the other will feel the wrongness of a heart ceasing to beat. Tears spring to my eyes again. "Mi vida, I can't do this."

"Lo siento, Babe." He hands me the suit's helmet. "I'm sorry that I couldn't protect you. And that I spent so much of our time together being jealous and unsure." He kisses my forehead. "Mi corazón y mi vida. Incluso en la oscuridad." *My heart and my life. Even into the darkness.*

It's a Krom saying, pero he said it in Spanish. For me. He's talking like we're about to die.

"No, mi vida, no." And then I realize – he isn't putting on an environment suit. I gesture with my helmet. "Where's yours?"

He pulls at the collar of his shirt, showing a swath of shiny black fabric. "This is a super-insulating layer." He pulls up the cuffs of his jacket. Bracers outline his arms. "And a simulated gravity rig. Gavin and I can't afford to lose our only advantage in this fight – our accelerated speed. A full environment suit would slow me down to match Jack." He pulls out a crushable head covering that is mostly clear, reinforced with strips of black fabric that matches what he's wearing under his clothes. "Now put your helmet on, so that I can make sure it's sealed."

I do as he says. Then I gesture that he should put on his plastic bag. He gestures back that he's going to wait. He wants to keep breathing as long as the atmo lasts. I can't say I blame him.

I've thought it odd that the Krom, with their fragile cardio systems and wide range of allergies, became a spacefaring race. Pero with his book lungs, Brill doesn't need to worry about depressurization or lack of oxygen. Scientists have theorized scorpions – which have similar lungs – could survive for three days in a jar in space. Y Brill's got antifreeze in his blood. If you wanted to design a being capable of surviving even in open space, for at least a while, Brill's not far from ideal. He doesn't need an environment suit because he doesn't need an environment. Just a way to keep from getting too cold, too fast. He even survived being thrown inside a giant chocolate mold and run through a blast freezer.

CHAPTER THIRTY-FIVE

It's quiet inside the suit. Brill takes my hands in his, and we sit, waiting.

My sublingual rings. I assume it's Chestla, checking in, pero it's Murry.

How's the research going? I bubblechatter. Even if I don't survive to see it, I hope they make a breakthrough that could save mi mundo.

We are going to die on this warship, Bo.

Murry must not be getting along with Eugene, or maybe he did something to upset the crew. *Ya basta, mijo. I'm sure you're overreacting. What did Eugene say?*

Not Eugene Giles. The Court passed its verdict. They believe I am still too dangerous. I am to be executed, along with all the Evevron scientists. The council members face sanctions, a few of them prison, but the rest of us will die. My lawyers have filed an appeal with the court's board, but they expect it to be rejected. All that we are must be lost within just a few time cycles.

Oye. I'm so sorry.

I'm the one who's sorry. I wanted to set things right before I died. Solve this disease, find another way to help your world. And now, there's not enough time.

I doubt anyone's told Murry about the time limit Crosskiss gave us. Earth may be in ruins before Murry even dies.

A pounding noise comes from outside mi cabeza, loud enough to hear through the muffling of the suit. Jack, as predicted, is breaking through the hatch.

I have to go now, Murry. I'll call you back later, if I can. If not, remember I love you – a lot of people love you.

Bodacious –

I hang up on him.

Brill gestures for me to grab onto a bar that's bolted to the wall. I have a hard time getting my gloved hands around it. I've barely found my grip when the ship depressurizes with un gran sucking whoosh that pulls me off my feet and sucks at me until the atmo's gone.

The artificial gravity fails, and I'm floating, weightless. Brill has shadowpopped. I push off from the wall and peer out of the cargo hold, down the hall at the patch of stars revealed by the ship's open hatch.

A giant spotlight, brilliant and temporarily blinding, flashes through Gavin's front door. I bring my hand up to shield my face. Seven pirates lumber in, clad in suits just as heavy and clunky as mine. They have partial grav – and vapguns. One hole in this suit, and I'm muerte. And therefore useless to Jack. Brill said they'll be careful.

A blur of motion flashes through the shadows at the spotlight's edge. Two of the pirates fly backwards out the hatch. The environment suits all look the same. Was one of those muchachos Jack? No lo sé. The remaining five pirates circle up, backs to each other as they advance through the cabin. Several pirates fire at another rush of blurred motion. I can't see well from where I'm at, pero I don't think they hit their target. I edge a little closer.

One pirate spots me, and heads towards the cargo hold. Ay de mi! The blur of motion streaks towards him, and I glimpse something heavy and metallic in the blurred figure's hand. The pirate falls forward, firing randomly. He doesn't move again.

Brill appears at my side. The lethal blur must be Gavin. And even though it's self-defense, I'm glad it's not mi vida hurting people.

Two of the four remaining pirates try to corner the blur. The other two advance towards me. Brill steps in front of me, pero over his shoulder I see Jack's face through one of the faceplates. Everything feels like it is happening in slow motion as the pirates deal with the constraints of their suits. Jack fires the vapgun. Brill dodges, pushing me out of the way. The gun vaporizes a hole in a structural piece of wall, which flips forward, crashing into the other pirate. The muchacho's gun goes flying and he backs away. Jack grabs for me, and I shove him, then aim a kick at him. I don't know how to move effectively without gravity, and Jack steps back to safety.

Brill dashes between us again. Jack punches Brill in the face, a move that would have fractured a faceplate.

Brill punches Jack's chest. Por un momento, nothing happens, then Jack starts flailing. Has Brill ruptured something inside Jack's suit? Jack's hands rip the plastic covering off Brill's cabeza, then Jack falls backwards, floating y spasming.

Brill motions to Gavin, who grabs two of the prone pirates and starts hauling them out of the ship. Brill retrieves the head covering, pero it's torn. I gasp at the sight of mi vida's face bare in the open vacuum of space. How long does he have, before he gets too cold to move? Before the exposure stresses his cardio system too much for him to recover?

Jack seems to be in trouble himself. Brill grabs Jack's shoulders, and gestures with his chin for me to grab hold of the unconscious guy half floating near the outer hatch. Untethered, Gavin pushes off from the hull of his ship, arrowing towards the *Shimmering Pearl*, hauling his two pirates with him.

Brill follows, pushing Jack with one hand and holding Jack's vapgun in the other.

I grasp the floating pirate's shoulder with my awkward gloves. This guy could be muerto. I close my eyes, then force myself to push the pirate over to the open doorway.

I've never been this close to open space. The sheer magnitude of stars takes my breath away. An unfamiliar planet lies beyond Jack's ship. It's so beautiful, and I'm so relieved to be alive, that at first I can't move. Then my pirate stirs. And I realize, we only brought the ones that might be vivo. The two Gavin threw out of the ship are floating away, their cracked faceplates visible in the ambient light from Jack's ship. And one more dead pirate remains aboard the *Boundless Hope*. Shuddering, I push across, and we all glide into an airlock into Jack's ship.

As soon as atmo hisses into the small chamber, Jack rips off his helmet. The funk of fermentation fills the air. "Good night, Cray, what did you do to me?"

Brill shivers, and his lips are blue. Through chattering teeth, he says, "I remembered I left a can of fermented fish in that jacket pocket. Seemed better than killing you."

"What *are* we to do with these su's?" Gavin asks. He pulls the helmet off one prone pirate and sets two fingers to the muchacho's throat. His irises go mahogany, and he places the helmet slowly onto the floor. He pops the second pirate's helmet off. This guy is breathing. Gavin pulls off the rest of the environment suit, to make him more comfortable.

"We don't have time to wait for the Galactacops," Brill says. "And if we start spouting conspiracy theories, nobody will believe us. Let's get Chestla to tow them to the nearest planet with a police station." He sweeps his arm towards the hallway leading deeper into the Shimmering Pearl. "In the meantime we can search this ship."

"Looking for what?" Jack asks.

Without missing a beat, Gavin says, "You took my favorite knife. I want it back."

Jack runs a hand across his still-watering eyes. "The crew who took you kept it."

Brill and Gavin exchange a troubled glance.

The pirate I'd dragged in here sits up. Gavin gives him a stern look, and he lies back down again.

Gavin says, "Why don't I look around anyway, while you two secure these su's?"

"Stay out of my dresser drawers," Jack protests. "I don't want the mental image of Brill running around the galaxy in my boxers."

"I'll settle for this." Moving as a blur, Brill pulls Jack's jacket off and binds the pirate to a bolted-down table leg.

Jack jerks his chin towards the jacket. "Take it. You'll never get the fish smell out."

Still inside the environment suit, which I haven't figured out how to take off, I lumber over to Jack. I manage to take off the helmet. "The muerte de Tyson's partner – the intrusion into Eugene's lab – they're tied together somehow with your mission to have me killed on Zant. Conrad was looking for something dangerous, no? To use as a weapon."

Jack snort-laughs. "There are several ways to ensure a war. Taking weapons tech is one of them."

Weapons tech? I'd meant something like the plant disease, or evidence of HGB's activities. Was Not-Kaliel looking in the basement for whatever weapon the Gevexix brought to Hawaii? To use against us, or to make sure HGB couldn't use it to save the Earth? Somebody has to tell HGB. If they still have that weapon, they need to make sure Jack never gets his hands on it.

Brill tells me, "I'll ask Dash when we get back. He's bound to know how to discreetly contact HGB."

CHAPTER THIRTY-SIX

When we get back to the *Just Married,* Brill, Gavin and I agree to meet up in the living area, after we each clean up. We need to discuss Jack's ship with the Evevrons on the bridge. My new room is in a different wing of this spacious ship from either of the Krom. As I head down the hall, I hear Brill tell Gavin, "It isn't one sided."

They're walking the other direction, so I can't quite hear Gavin's reply.

We didn't find my phone – or much else of use – on Jack's ship. The interior was surprisingly neat – and completely devoid of personality.

Fifteen minutes later, Brill and I meet back together in the living area. Gavin doesn't show.

We wait. Brill looks worried, pero finally says, "Vamos, Babe." *Let's go.*

As we head for the bridge, Brill and I meet Leron coming from the other direction. I'm sure he never expected to see us again, and this is the first time we've seen him since the Court condemned him to death.

"Murry told us the trial's outcome. I am so sorry, mijo." I try to put an arm around him, pero he shrugs me away.

"I don't want pity. I want to be doing something."

Mahogany deepens Brill's eyes. "We will be back underway soon. Skadish is close, and they will hold Jack and his friends for the Galactacops."

"We lost so much time dealing with the pirates," Leron protests, "If we make a pit stop on a planet, we won't get to the *Layla's Pride* soon enough to help. Even if the Zantites run late,

I've only got a little time left until The Review Board decides my appeal."

Ay! I wince. Leron is taking this blow so calmly. How isn't he screaming about extenuating circumstances and demanding to keep his life?

"I am sorry, su," Brill says. "For what it's worth, I don't believe you deserve to die."

Leron huffs. "Yet you won't honor my last request. I know Krom are all about money and reputation, but I didn't think you'd to sell out your girlfriend's planet for a few pirate bounties."

"Oye!" I protest. "That was uncalled for. Krom aren't–"

Brill interrupts, "This has nothing to do with money. I refuse to leave three men stranded in a disabled ship to asphyxiate, and if we leave the ship functioning, they'll try to kill us again. And we're not stupid enough to take them with us. I'm advising Chestla leave Jack on the *Shimmering Pearl* while we tow it. Uan unless you have a better option . . ."

Suddenly deflated, Leron shrugs. His anger isn't really at Brill. "I'll find some way to help without being with the research team on the warship. Surely the lab has holographic capabilities." He checks his phone and stalks away down the hall.

Oi! Poor guy!

"How long will his appeal take?" I ask Brill.

Brill shrugs. "The court doesn't publish that. But they'll have told him. A few days? Maybe less."

I call Tyson. He's no help. He and Leron spoke, and Leron refuses to name those who forced him to put those people in the cryostasis pods. Without that information, the court won't consider his case separate from his colleagues.

"Bo," Tyson says. "Try to get Leron to talk. Murry would appreciate it."

Sí, Murry would. Pero I have no right to push Leron to make that decision.

Two hours later, I'm sitting with Brill on that heart-shaped sofa again. We lean towards each other, somehow both deciding to bring our foreheads together.

I tell him, "Before Jack showed up, you talked like we were going to die. I guess he underestimated dealing with Krom in space."

"We shouldn't have survived. Not that I'm not super-happy about it. To discover a heart bond and then lose it in the same day – that'd be worse than dying in that kalltet basement." He touches my shoulder, like I'm the mas especial thing in all the worlds. "Those pirates focused so much on not hurting you, they ignored the most effective fighting tactics. They shouldn't have grouped in the center of a room. Jack isn't a good tactician, but sthesh. He got four people killed today."

"And he wants to be king of the pirates." I slide my hand into Brill's, lacing our fingers together. "All the other pirates would be loco to listen to him."

Gavin walks past, heading towards the galley. "That's the scary part."

Banging comes from inside and then Gavin pokes his cabeza back around the door. "They have every kind of alcohol in here except yewstral. How could they not stock yewstral?"

"Maybe somebody already drank it," Brill says.

"Jrekt." Gavin disappears back in the kitchen, then stalks past us with two bottles and one very large glass.

I give Brill a questioning look.

"Gavin *killed* four people today. His definition of self-defense may be broader than most Krom, but he still believes in the Codex. Not finding a peaceful option carries tons of guilt."

"Because it's considered a personal failure. I remember reading that." Though Gavin won't face legal repercussions – the law is clear on who's at fault in a spacejacking – he's punishing himself. Interesting, considering back when Murry was a mindplague, Gavin had wanted to sacrifice all the innocent hosts.

It doesn't likematch Frank, who doesn't second-guess his actions, as long as he feels they were justified. Frank, who I still haven't seen since we got back. "Where is Frank, anyway?"

Brill's eyes go ash gray. "He's in the VR studio, inside a simulation of Earth, staring at what the rainforest looked like before everything burned. Dash is with him. They've been there since Gavin told them we couldn't find that microdot. I think Leron went in there, too."

I haven't looked for Leron, after what he said in the hall and what Tyson told me. I'm embarrassed to talk to the doomed Evevron. I had tried to give him hope, which seems cruel now that I know he's trying to hold onto his moral code by not naming those who'd forced him to his crimes. And we're taking him to a Zantite warship, to spend his last days among his enemies. He hasn't refused to go. Cierto, he stated the opposite. Pero it still feels selfish.

I change the subject. "How'd you get the fish smell out of that leather."

Brill's eyes tint lavender. "Ask Nellet. She took the jacket and did something to it. She said she could smell it from the other end of the ship, and it was sense-blinding every Evevron on board. Then she set off one of those pine-scent tabs, which made *my* eyes water."

"I'm glad she could fix it for you, mi vida. It suits you ita ita better than denim." I've cleaned the brown leather jacket for him too, removing Brill's own blood before the stain set.

He touches the patched bullet hole. "Even with the patches and the scratches?"

"Even so." He may have to replace it eventually – because sí, working as a gray trader is dangerous, even without the peril I've brought him. He once offered to sell his ship, find work that I'd find más aceptable. Pero I've come to love him for what he is – not, like back then, when I loved what I hoped he'd be. And the Krom I've heart-bonded with is an adventurer, a pilot, a romantic, a prude, an open-minded optimistic, and a good son. His morals have some gray areas, y he's made mistakes – pero he doesn't keep making the same ones.

And what I want more than anything – more than running my own kitchen, more than teaching – is more adventures with him. How can I reconcile those two futures?

The planet looked beautiful from space. It's not impressive up close. We put down on a run-down spaceport connected to a shopping mall. Behind us, a brown-ish ocean churns.

In the hallway, Brill checks his nueva gun, a gift from Ball. When he sees me, he pockets it. "Don't worry, Babe. The pirates are already subdued." He pats his pocket. "This is just a safeguard."

"I know." I brush my lips against his. He knows I dislike guns, though he often carries one when transporting expensive cargo. "I'm going to the mall while you guys get these guys processed. I need to pick up a new handheld. And I want to buy a wedding gift for our happy couple."

"Give them something from Earth. They're obsessed." Brill's eyes tint violet. "Weddings are about the only occasion where Krom don't give gifts. The person you marry is the gift, freely giving themselves to you. Wedding guests competing with that would be considered tacky." His eyes shift towards an embarrassed pink. "But I was wondering … I still don't understand the Earthling protocol on gift-giving … and I've messed it up in the past … but are you diay with exchanging heart bond sealing gifts?"

Elation bubbles through my chest. "Of course, mi vida. Something like this should be celebrated."

He grins at my use of the endearment. I feel giddy, too, at the added layer of meaning. He crushes me to him, and we stand that way for a long time. Long enough for me to realize I'm supposed to get him a gift, también.

I say into his jacket, "So how expensive are we talking? So that I don't get you a paperweight and you get me a hovercraft. Or vice versa."

He laughs, loosening the hug, pero not letting me go. His lips brush my forehead. "It should be the first thing you think of when you think of me. It doesn't have to be expensive. I know you don't equate cost with worth."

Oye! So no pressure, right?

He squeezes me close one more time. "Don't go by yourself, my heart. I doubt anyone realizes that Jack's in no position to pay them for your kidnapping."

"Vale." I go look for people to come with me.

I knock on the door to the room where Leron is working. When he comes to the door, I ask, "You want to get out of here for a bit? See the planet?"

He shrugs. "Sure. I'm getting nowhere with this project, because I keep feeling sorry for myself. The body is an amazing thing, and I've taken mine far too much for granted. I pick up an empty sevrekkt can, and …" He crushes it in his fist and sets it on the table. "But tomorrow?" He shudders.

"And you're sure you'd rather face execution than tell the court who ordered you to put people in cryostasis?"

"So they can die with me? Or instead of me?"

Sympathy and respect for his sense of honor stir in me. "I won't say anything else about it, mijo."

"Good. In that case, let me get my jacket."

I glance down at his mano, picture those powerful fingers gone slack. No sé how to comfort him. I hope the distraction helps.

"Can I come too?" Watae has walked up behind me. The predator pheromones are so thick in this ship that I didn't even notice. "Chestla has Nellet practicing self-defense for the next couple of time segments. My bride wanted to do everything like on your planet, so we researched the customs and found the Earthling idea of spending time alone together after the wedding very pleasing. This hasn't been much of a honeymoon."

"Sure, mijo." That means that Watae's Guardian Companion will come, too. "What about Ball?"

Watae shrugs. "He's helping Chestla. I'm not sure he could walk that far anyway. He's still undergoing massive amounts of physical therapy."

So the four of us leave the ship. Now, what to get Brill? The first thing I think of when I think of him is an expensive bottle of wine, pero this gift should be something he can keep. I walk past a shop selling wall-sized paintings. Brill's into art, too, pero he lives on a spaceship. Everything in that store is too grande to be practical.

Leron drops a hand on my arm, and I realize I've wandered off from the group. He scrunches his nose up at the art gallery. "They said there's an open-air bazaar on the other side of the complex. It's bound to be more interesting than this."

"Sí, sure." I guess wandering around a mall is a sad way to spend some of your few remaining hours. When we get outside, the sky has a green tint to it – no sé whether naturally, or from pollution. I spot a booth selling spices. They have stacks of rectangular spice boxes with little compartments, like a masala dabba. It could make a perfect wedding gift. I glance at Watae. "On your planet, does a prince like you ever cook for yourself?"

Watae nods, starts to say something, then he looks past me at a purple-skinned guy with four arms pulling a gun from his jacket. He's not alone. A half dozen people from that same species form a spread-out formation around us, standing far enough back, that had Watae not been paying attention, we might not have noticed. Ay!

"The Commodore's been arrested," I shout. "Kidnapping me won't be worth it."

The one girl in the purple group points at Watae. "She said that one's the prince. Grab him."

Eh? This isn't about me?

Watae assumes a fighting stance, and a knife appears in his hand from somewhere inside his clothes. Pero these muchachos know better than to get within hand-fighting range of an Evevron. The guy across the square levels the gun. Watae's Guardian steps between his prince and the danger.

"Jewndel, don't!" Watae's voice is commanding, far beyond his years. Pero his Guardian wouldn't be a Guardian if he'd listen.

Jewndel whips out a gun and fires at the guy who dared attack his charge. His other hand draws his shortened sword from its sheath. The projectile punches into his chest. Jewndel crumples. Across the square, the other guy does too.

Despite the danger, Watae, eyes wide with shock and panic, squats beside to his fallen Guardian. "No. Please. Jewndel."

I step towards him, but another guy's pointing a weapon at me. He makes a subtle shake of his cabeza, and I freeze. Leron, a few feet away, does the same. Shouting erupts all around us, and a siren blares as a security team approaches. Pero they'll be too late.

The spice merchant whips out a daser from under the table and hits Watae with it from behind. Despite obvious pain, Watae whirls and knocks the merchant out with his fist. Woozy, Watae stumbles backwards.

Another purple guy draws a weapon. The girl shouts, "Don't kill him! We need him to call to his sister. Princess Shirazende can't be far."

My brows furrow. Que? I mean … que?

With Watae disoriented, the group close in and throw a net over him. They drag Watae into a waiting ground vehicle.

My mouth hangs open with shock, and I haven't moved, though no one is holding a gun on me anymore. "Shirazende!" I splutter. "They mean Kayla. They think Watae's the secret Nitarri prince."

Leron wrinkles his nose, revealing his upper teeth. "What kind of morons can't tell the difference between an Evevron and a Nitarri?"

"Those kind, obviamente. Besides, Stephen's dead." Although, people are still looking for him … and I'm basically living in a novela … and they never recovered the body. I take a deep breath and get ahold of my imagination. Nah. Kaliel said Stephen got shot in the cabeza. And Stephen never contacted Kayla after the attack. He's definitely muerto.

"Come on. As soon as they realize their mistake, they'll kill Watae." Leron grabs my wrist. He glances at the dead Guardian, and a complicated look passes over his face. He's looking at poor Jewndel's hand, which dropped the sword onto the pavement. That mano, so powerful, and yet so easily stilled.

Leron blinks and taps a finger against his lips. "They said they didn't want Watae dead." Leron leans down and rolls Jewndel onto his back.

Para mi sorpresa, Jewndel groans. He's pale and doesn't open his eyes, pero he's breathing. And despite a small hole in his shirt, he's not bleeding. Leron hefts Jewndel into a fireman's carry.

Then Leron pulls me towards another vehicle idling nearby. He yanks the driver out of it, and we climb in. Like a Jeep, it has a windshield, pero no top, so the ride is loud and bouncy.

I'm in the back, cradling Jewndel against me. I pull up his shirt. A bruise is forming at the top of his abs, with a red mark at the center. Ni idea what they shot him with. Either Leron doesn't think Jewndel is in immediate danger, or he cares more about the prince.

We careen along the street in pursuit. We're circling back towards the spaceport. Do they plan to take their "Nitarri" prince offplanet? Pero no, the ground vehicle turns towards the boat docks.

One hand still on the wheel, Leron pulls his handheld from his jacket. When Chestla appears in the holofield, he says, "Bring those Jet Skis down to the boat docks now!"

She doesn't ask questions, and he hangs up.

By the time we reach the docks, an overgrown ATV speeds towards us, pulling the Jet Skis. We still haven't caught up to the ransomsnatchers. The purple guys head for a boat that's large enough to drive onto. Once they do, they pull up the ramp. Leron skids our vehicle to a halt. From on board the boat, the ransomsnatchers shoot at us, hitting our car's front end and damaging the engine. Leron backs us behind a building for cover. Pero, we're not going far without repairing this thing.

When I lean back, and I can just see around the building's edge. The boat pulls away from the dock. "Mira! El barco."

Leron squints at me. Right. He doesn't speak Spanish. Pero he figures out what I mean.

Chestla pulls up behind us, and Leron explains what happened as he pulls one of the Jet Skis off the rack. Chestla looks at the two Jet Skis, and says, "Bo rides with me."

She doesn't even consider Jewndel. He's another Guardian. If he dies from injuries received protecting his charge, that would be honorable.

I shake my head. "I'm not leaving an unconscious guy alone en una gran unfamiliar city."

Chestla sucks in a breath, pero before she can protest Leron says, "Good." He smiles and adds, "You're a weak fighter, and more likely to get us hurt protecting you."

He hopes Chestla will let me stay. Pero he's also right. Chestla has to see that.

Chestla points to our appropriated – and now motionless – vehicle. "Do not leave this spot. I left Nellet alone with Ball, and if they decide she's their hidden princess … the Royal Family's already going to fire me, but I'd prefer not to lose anyone I've sworn to protect."

Leron drags his Jet Ski towards the agua. Chestla takes the other one. She doesn't look back.

CHAPTER THIRTY-SEVEN

From the car, I call Kayla on my sublingual to warn her to be careful. When I explain that Stephen's failed quest got someone abducted, her loud wracking sobs echo inside my brain.

Hey, amiga, it'll be okay.

If you rescue Watae, tell him I'm sorry. She hiccups. *I'm – I'm trying to disappear. So that nobody has to worry about me.*

I look out where that boat was docked. *I don't think that'll work anymore, Kay-Kay. People are searching for you. And if they can't find you, they'll look for people who know you. Like me. And Kaliel.*

Kaliel is trying to find me an ally. A protector. Kayla's chatter sounds more under control. *I begged him not to risk himself, but he feels so bad about Stephen, I couldn't talk him out of it.*

He really loves you, I tell her.

He's not being completely altruistic. Kaliel thinks that with the right allies, I could make a diplomatic plea to save Earth.

I suck in a breath. *Would you do that, amiga?*

I can't! I told him I can't. You know what happened to my brother. If I come out into the open – I would have to challenge my uncle, or wait for him to have me killed.

I murmur a sympathetic noise. *Then hide well. And try to get Kaliel to hide with you.*

There's a scrabbling sound on the roof of the building. I hang up on Kayla and sit up straight. Two guys up there are aiming oversized pistols at me. They're both tall, with flat faces and incisors that hang out like fangs. One of them has unnaturally orange hair. The other one's missing an eye.

Leron dumped Jewndel 's gun on the seat. I grab it and point it at the hombre who's come closest to the roof's edge – the one with the orange hair. "Stay where you are."

"Hey. It's okay," he says in heavily-accented Universal. "We just want the dead Evevron."

These muchachos must have seen the Guardian get shot in the square and followed us.

"He's not dead," I protest. "And what for?"

The guy nods towards Jewndel's hand. "There's a small, ridiculously expensive trade in Evevron claws. Are you sure he's not dead? I could make it worth your while."

"He's alive," I gesture with the gun. "So I suggest you leave."

If they rush me, I'm in trouble. I've never shot anyone before, nunca, and I'm not sure I have it in me. Pero they don't know that. According to Tawny's spin, I'm Bo the Spuckslayer. A force to be reckoned with.

"What about the other one?" The guy points towards where the boat went. "You'll be there when he's executed, right? What's the difference if they burn his corpse with a few less fingers? They'd each be worth a fortune and a half, with the fingerprints intact."

"Oi! That's horrible!"

"That's not a no."

"No. En serio."

The guys edge forward. The Evevron Guardian's breathing is shallow. He won't suddenly regain consciousness and help me.

"The nice lady said no." A voice comes from behind my vehicle.

I glance at the figure – then I do a double-take. Ay, no! He's one of Jack's crew – the injured pirate Gavin pulled out of the environment suit. He holds a pistol-sized vapgun in each hand.

Pero I can only deal with one threat at a time. I look back at the guys on the roof, keeping my useless gun pointed at them.

"Why do you care?" the orange haired scavenger asks the pirate.

"That's my business," the pirate says. "But I just escaped from local law enforcement, and a fleet of police drones is looking for me. Do you want to keep us all here long enough for the drones to find us?"

The one-eyed scavenger pulls out a pair of field glasses. He says a single word, then the two guys beat a hasty retreat across the roof.

I turn and half-heartedly point my gun at the pirate. I doubt I could beat him in a gunfight, even if I was willing to shoot him. He was probably heading for the docks, to find a boat to stow away on – until he spotted me and found a way to get leverage. I sigh. "You need me alive, right? I'm not letting those guys come back and cut off Jewndel's hands. Wait until my friends come back into view, and I'll put this gun down and go with you."

He laughs. "I'm not here to kidnap you. This time." He lowers the vapguns. "That Krom friend of yours – the one who spared my life – I want you to thank him for me."

Why isn't he kidnapping me? He's a henchpirate. Doesn't he want what his employer wants? "But what about Jack?"

"Jack's gone off the deep end. And today he got my friends killed, trying to start a war that's already underway. I'm done."

I drop my gun onto the seat and check Jewndel's pulse. It seems strong, and his breathing hasn't worsened. "Why is Jack working for Greftash, anyway?"

The pirate blinks. "Jack isn't working *for* Greftash. He's *from* Greftash. A lot of us are. And Jack's part of the group that's still pushing space exploration as a way to solve the resource shortages the colony's dealt with since we eliminated our prison guards."

I blink. "That makes no sense. Jack's a pirate. He's been one for years."

"On Greftash, that's not an issue. He's more powerful than you think."

"He tells everyone he's from Earth."

The pirate nods. "Wouldn't you?"

Pues, I guess I might. Greftash has a nonexistent reputation. And Jack's DNA would scan as Earthling. He could even be who he claims – the descendant of a crime familia that shadowpopped off Earth a couple of generations ago.

A thrumming noise shakes the air.

"I wasn't bluffing about those drones," the pirate says. "I'm out of time to find a boat."

My stolen vehicle has an open area behind the seats that serves as cargo storage. It holds a bunch of junk, including a tarp. This hombre just saved me and Jewndel. It's like with Frank and Brill – if we keep helping each other, maybe we'll survive. I gesture towards the tarp. "Get under there, mijo."

He does, unfolding the tarp to conceal himself among the junk.

A fleet of thirty drones flying in a grid head this way. They surround the vehicle. Oye! The driver must have reported it stolen. The lead drone holographically projects a cheerful, yet rudimentary face. "Pardon the inconvenience, Galactic Citizen. We are pursuing this criminal." The face fades to a picture of the pirate. "May we search this vehicle?"

Maybe the driver hasn't reported the vehicle stolen yet. Still, if they look under the tarp, the pirate and I will both be in trouble. I gasp and put my acting skills into use. "I saw that guy! He stowed away on that boat!"

I climb out of the vehicle, hurry around the building, and point to the boat that carried off Watae. Several drones follow me, pero the others still surround the vehicle. In the distance, the Jet Skis are returning – with three figures aboard. Yay! It's about time.

The drones all pivot and fly off after the boat. They pass the Jet Skis without even slowing down.

"Stay down," I tell the pirate. "I'll sort this out with my friends."

Watae is driving one of the Jet Skis and Leron rides with Chestla. When they reach the dock, she helps Leron up onto the pavement.

Chestla gives me a dirty look for leaving the spot where she left me. "Get the emergency kit from the ATV, Bo. Leron's shoulder needs seeing to."

"I don't know why," Leron grumbles. "It's not like I'll be alive long enough for it to get infected."

Todavía, he doesn't resist as Chestla pulls off his jacket and shirt and runs a line of healing foam over a deep cut running from the top of his shoulder to halfway down his bicep. He's in excelente condición físico, with built shoulders and well-defined abs. Which makes executing him even more of a waste.

Leron puts his jacket back on and zips it. A gaping slit at the shoulder still shows bare skin and stray foam.

"We need to get back to the ship," Chestla insists. "The longer we're in the open, the more risk that girl calls in backup."

Watae says, "I'm still confused. Who do they think I am?"

"I'll explain once we're inside." Chestla gives him a reassuring smile. He starts to protest. Chestla says, "Consider me your temporary Guardian, on loan from your wife."

That closes Watae's mouth. Tears flood his eyes. "Yes, Guardian."

He moves towards the vehicle. When he gets close enough to see inside, he turns back to me. "You saved Jewndel. I thought he was dead."

I say, "Leron put him on the car. I assumed he was dead too."

Leron shrugs. He takes a small object from his pocket. "As long as this isn't poisoned, he should be okay."

The barb on the object matches the mark on Jewndel's abs.

Watae blinks, then swallows hard. "I'm not in immediate danger now. The priority should be getting Jewndel medical attention."

"The priority is getting you back to the ship, and getting that ship off this planet," Chestla insists. She moves to the front of the vehicle, pops the hood and starts fixing it. "If you die, so does our hope of newfound peace."

"You think I can found that peace without my Guardian?" Watae pulls out his phone, pulls up directions to the hospital. "He taught me honor and how to look beneath the skin to find out who a person really is."

Leron looks to Chestla for a decision. Part of me can't believe how cold she's being. Todavía – is that how she thinks of herself? Easily expendable? It's clear that she would expect the same treatment if her and Jewndel's positions were reversed. She slams the hood and gets in the driver's seat. The vehicle starts properly. I guess we're abandoning the ATV.

I climb into the open-top vehicle's back seat. Jewndel's breathing has grown even shallower. Panic jolts through me. Whether intended as poison or not, injecting a substance into the wrong alien physiology can have disastrous consequences. I put a hand on his chest. His heartbeat's erratic. "Chicos, Jewndel needs a doctor."

"Please." Watae climbs in and clasps Jewndel's hand. "He's been watching out for me since I was six years old."

Chestla looks conflicted. Our ship is so close. We could be safe. Only, we all want to take the risk, to save a life. "Fine. But once he's been admitted, we leave."

Leron gets into the front. He gives Chestla a little smile. I think it is important to him that Jewndel lives.

Watae sniffs the air. He looks at me, then at the tarp. "Bo, are you aware someone else is in this vehicle?"

I nod. "He helped me save Jewndel from some muchachos who wanted to harvest his claws. The least we can do is give him a ride to the spaceport."

Nobody protests.

The doctors think Jewndel will live, that it wasn't poison – just an allergic reaction to a sedative. He needs treatment and observation, so we have to leave him behind on this planet. It looks like vehicles actually the spaceport are being searched, and we are harboring a fugitive in a stolen car, so we park near as we can and walk the rest of the way. The poor pirate is on his own from here.

As we walk back through the bazaar, a wide, silver-toned bracelet catches my eye. Black metal is layered in a geometric pattern that includes two twined hearts – that somehow still look masculine. The bracelet reminds me of Brill. I know. Chestla will be upset that I'm still shopping. She was willing to sacrifice the life of a fellow Guardian to leave this place. Pero that bracelet is the perfect gift for Brill. I won't find anything like it again. This is muy importante por our relationship.

I stop.

"Bo," Chestla says sharply.

"Un momento, por favor." Like Watae said, we aren't in immediate danger. I buy the bracelet, despite the three pairs of Evevron eyes boring into my spine, raising the hairs at the nape of my neck and sending goosebumps down my arms. I don't mention that I still need un handheld nuevo. I won't push it.

We reach the ship before Brill and Gavin, and Chestla is antsy, ready to take off. "We should leave the two Krom. They can catch up."

"No y no y no." I bar her way into the bridge, despite her glare, which makes my bladder want to give way.

Ball comes to meet Chestla in the living area. "Where's Jewndel?"

Chestla and I recount what happened. When Chestla says we all put Watae in danger by refusing to leave Jewndel behind at the docks, Ball scowls at her.

"No one's expendable, Stala."

"He's a Guardian," Chestla says. "If he'd been conscious, he would have agreed with me."

"If he'd been conscious, you wouldn't have tried to leave him."

"Sometimes you're impossible." Chestla stalks into the galley.

I follow her. "You okay, amiga?"

She waves back towards the living area. "You heard Ball. Is he more Evevron or more Krom?"

"He's both." I open the fridge, looking for comfort food to prepare for this broken crew. "That makes him something unique. Ball should be a living contradiction. Instead, he's developed a unique mindset. You have to love both sides of him or let him go so he can find someone who can."

"I don't know if I can do that," Chestla says. "I don't understand Krom."

"You and Brill are sparring partners, right? He's all Krom and you're friends"

"You don't have to agree with a sparring partner."

Que? Does Chestla believe that to be compatible, you have to agree about everything? "I don't always agree with Brill. We've overcome some muy serious issues. Like the time he left me for dead. It made sense to him, porque he saw me bleeding bad and Krom can't survive that kind of blood loss."

"You guys understand each other now."

"That took time. And a lot of work. We're still working on it."

Chestla asks, "What does Brill think about you being shipped with Daschel?"

I shrug. "I've been avoiding the polls. What are people saying?"

She hesitates. "They're horrified. Daschel's hot, but they don't think you should get together with someone who tried to kill your boyfriend. Though a strong minority contingent thinks you would be trading up, mostly the ones who are disappointed Brill isn't dead."

I sigh. "Janvier is a horrible person. He tried to—"

Chestla's not listening to me anymore. She stares off into space. "Maybe I *should* let Ball go. But I don't want to." She pours a tablespoon worth of salt into her palm and tosses it undiluted into her mouth. "Sometimes I love how he challenges me. And sometimes he makes me so unsure of myself. But if he goes Krom vegetarian, I'm out."

"And Eugene?"

"He challenges me in different ways. To be smarter. To be better. With logic puzzles and experiments." She wrinkles her nose. "But morally, he takes me as I am."

From her softened expression, I see her choosing Eugene. She's pushing the Duracell away, so the decision to be with the fun scientist will be easier.

"Still, you should make up with Ball," I say. "Otherwise, this could be a long trip."

We all wind up in the living area. Watae looks like he's about to cry, and Nellet keeps patting or squeezing his hand. Leron finally asks him what's wrong.

"You helped me save Jewndel. But I can do nothing to save you. That's a debt of honor I can't repay, and I really will have to learn how it feels to lose a friend. Jewndel's not here to help me deal with that." Watae really is a teenager. He's made decisions, though, that mean he will have to grow up fast if he wants to lead his people to peace.

"I'll help you," Leron says. "For as long as I can."

Dios mio! It's not right that they're going to execute Leron. Surely Tyson will find him a way to win that appeal. Right?

I feel angry and empty. I can't wait to get off this planet.

Brill and Gavin soon return and we take off, leaving Jack in a cell and his ship in impound. We stripped everything from Gavin's ship and abandoned it. With all its vapgun-induced holes, we can't justify anything besides making an insurance claim.

Brill and I sit on that heart-shaped sofa. He tells me not to give up hope. He's not very convincing. He thinks the cryostasis plan has zero chance. Pero, like he promised, he's supporting me and my decisions, because it's mi planeta.

Frank told Janvier I put all my eggs in one basket, y so far he's right. I need to try other options. Janvier said we need to steal chocolate back from someone we shared it with. Pero what if we just asked? Both the Krom and the Nilka know Earth is in crisis. Maybe they'll help. Either race would tell Janvier, 'No' straight out. But if I ask Jeska directly – maybe he could talk the Civic Gardens into parting with a pair of seedlings. I didn't tell Garfex

that you need two trees for cross-pollination. If I get him one –
exactly what he asked for – he has to keep his word.

"Can I borrow your handheld?" I ask Brill. "I want to talk to
Jeska, and I don't have his number."

"What? You don't have it memorized?" Brill gasps in mock
horror.

Hace poco tiempo, Brill got jealous when Jeska showed
romantic interest in me. Now, he's trying to show he's over being
jealous, that he trusts the strength of our bond.

I scrunch my nose. "I could have stuck it in my sublingual,
pero then I might have been tempted to call him."

I'm teasing. Brill looks serious. He hands me his phone, with
Jeska's number queued up. "I appreciate that. I've talked to Jeska
twice, now that I can tell people I'm alive. We talked about
everything that happened with Ball, how close he came to
bleeding out in my arms. It brought back all the stuff about Darcy.
Jeska and I had never settled our feelings over my role in his
brother's death. We're in a better space now."

I touch Brill's cheek. "Muy feliz that you've found closure."

"What do you want to ask him, anyway?" His eyes tint pink.
He was trying not to ask. Trying to show he trusts me.

"I'm hoping he'll get the Krom to opensource share our
commodity back with us. After all, your entire purpose for
discovering commodities is to prevent the kind of conflict Earth
has with the Zantites."

"Now you're thinking like a Krom." Brill grins. "Actually, I
should have thought of that. The Civic Gardens might say no,
since there isn't an established grove of trees yet. But it's worth a
shot."

I punch send, and Jeska answers in Krom. He's not even
looking at the holofield, probably thinks he's talking to Brill.
"Suavet ten tekta shon. Suaverae ranvet peb pont?" Roughly, *I've
got a crisis. Can I call you back?*

I answer in his language with what translates as, *We have a
crisis here too.*

Jeska focuses on his phone, his eyes tinting a startled pale pink. Jeska is still handsome – his skin warm and brown, his jaw chiseled, his hair dark and thick – pero I don't feel that instant frission of attraction. More a logical admiration of his form. Maybe that's an effect of my heart bond with Brill.

I hope so, porque the last time my feelings about a guy changed so drastically, he'd been infected with a mind parasite.

"Bo!" Jeska smiles, and the attraction returns, just a little. He's outdoors, the holo's background lined with tall, stately trees. "Thank you again for my freedom."

"I got the fruit basket you sent." I crack a smile in return. I got Jeska – and a handful of Zantites – released from lifelong military service aboard Crosskiss's warship. "We're on our way to the *Layla's Pride* right now. Crosskiss agreed to help us try to salvage relations between Zant and my planet. Garfex says if I get him a single cacao tree, he will call off the invasion."

Jeska's eyes go an embranxious rose-tinted gray. "I'm afraid I know what you're about to ask."

Does he think I will blame him if his planet won't share chocolate back with me? Does he feel he owes me, because I kept him from being executed? And does he think it's unfair if he has to say no? We both know what's at stake, pero, I still have to actually ask. "Can I have a cacao seedling to give him?"

"I really, really wish I could give you one. Ita, ita, ita. Only. I've been helping with the official gardens since I got home, and we had a problem last night." One of those purple bat-like creatures Krom keep in their gardens flitters past. The kresp whistles at Jeska. He whistles back. "Every spring, an insect migration passes through this area. They ravage certain plants, but usually leave this garden alone, because we don't plant anything that attracts them. We didn't realize they would have a taste for cacao. I arrived this morning to find everyone dealing with this."

Jeska turns the holofield. The insects attacked the cacao, y many of the support plants the Krom had added to recreate a section of Earth's rainforest. Some of those ecosystem supports are full-grown trees. The insects stripped every leaf, and ate the bark raw on some of the trunks. One cacao sapling has a single leaf. As cold horror zings through my chest, the leaf's edge disappears. Some small bug is eating that last green speck of hope. No y no y no.

Heat builds behind my eyes.

Chocolate can't be gone on Krom too. I cannot accept what I see.

The kresp swoops into the holo and snatches something off the plant. It flies closer to the camera, a teal bug the size of a peanut clutched in its foot. Still in flight, the kresp brings the foot to its mouth and crunches down on the still-squirming bug. I feel a jolt of angerzentment. "Hest! Where was this creature last night? Isn't its job to keep the plants safe by eating insects?"

Brill puts a hand on mine. "They're not nocturnal, my heart."

"What did you call her?" Jeska asks Brill.

Brill grins. "It's reciprocal."

Jeska's eyes go a shocked hunter green. "But you're both so young."

I hand Brill his phone. They'll be talking for a while.

I head into the galley. Gavin had the right idea. I could use something to drink. Brill's talking to Jeska. I don't try to make out what they're saying.

A bug. Un estúpido insecto ruined my only logical chance of saving my world.

Ahora, only the Nilka have chocolate. And they aren't known for sharing. HGB once sent a saboteur to destroy their cacao grove. I saw the gritclip. Almost as soon as the woman broke into their secured plantation, the Nilka captured and interrogated her – and then executed her with her own garden shears.

Still, Admiral Alabaster, a senior military leader, once told me I have the makings of a diplomat. He's likely commanding the Nilka ship that made the demands against my planet. I tremble at the thought of approaching him, then ball mis manos into fists to make it stop. I tried to send Kaliel to talk to him in person. I shouldn't be afraid to call Alabaster on the phone. *Pero* what I'm asking for is more likely to anger the Nilka than what Kaliel wants.

Getting Alabaster's contact information takes a bit of doing — during which I drink a very large glass of J'Lespet. Brill's still using his phone, so I call Alabaster on my sublingual. I imagine the Nilka's gossamer wings and his narrow face, with his *grande* mustache framing both a mouth and a butterfly-like proboscis.

I was expecting your call, Alabaster says.

You were? I can't hide my confusion.

The pilot you sent is in my interrogation room. You are calling to check on him, aren't you?

My breath catches. At least it sounds like Kaliel's vivo. I choose my words carefully. *Many apologies for not checking in sooner. I didn't realize Kaliel already approached you. I believed he had not yet returned from dropping off passengers onto the* Layla's Pride. *We are headed there ourselves to assist the scientists.*

Alabaster bubblechatters, *He was telling the truth about that? Next thing, you'll tell me he's telling the truth about where he got the Nitarri DNA database.*

If he said he was helping the lost Nitarri prince establish his identity, then sí, he's telling the truth. I hesitate. *Please, if his approach to your ship insulted you in any way, blame on me. I told him you might be willing to help a weakened princess, who is grieving her brother, with her people scattered.*

Alabaster bubblechatters, *I hold you responsible, Bo, for whatever happens. But I will hear what he has to say.*

Uf! I blow out a breath of relief. *Many thanks.*

So why did you call me?

I chatter it fast. *Earth complied with your request and burned the cacao trees. Only now, the Zantites demand we give them an undiseased tree or they're going ahead with the invasion.*

Alabaster's growl bubbles through my brain. Despite their appearance, the Nilka are some of the most lethalriffic people en la galaxia. *You bring insult by even suggesting I return what I rightfully purchased. Were you not in a ship heading in the other direction, I would kill you where you stand. As it is, that is too much trouble. Do not compound the slight. I do not have time to come destroy you.*

I wish I could see his body language and facial cues. How indignant is he really? And how much is for show? *Please let me apologize on behalf of my planet.*

When Daschel Janvier apologizes, it will be on behalf of your planet. That man irritates me to the point that I find myself cheering the Zantite invasion fleet to wipe him from existence. He still denies sending that saboteur to destroy the commodity your planet sold to mine.

Which explains why the Nilka were so quick to lobby for Earth being destroyed as the source of a plague that could wipe out that commodity.

I'm not telling Alabaster that the Nilka now hold a choco-monopoly. Assuming their plantation is growing as well as they claim. Maybe they've lost chocolate también, and not a single tree remains en toda la galaxia. Diplomacy can't get me a cacao tree. We have to turn to science. We need to get Chestla and Leron to that ship, so they can work with Eugene and Murry.

Well, I apologize on behalf of myself, I tell Alabaster.

CHAPTER THIRTY-EIGHT

It should take only a few more hours to reach the *Layla's Pride*.

Frank comes into the galley and turns on the coffee maker. "I've called in all the favors I can, but nobody can find the signal for the tracker on your phone – or any signs of HGB property hitting the black market. Which is good, in a way. How's Murry taking the news from the Court?"

I shrug. "Better than expected. He's being very philosophical about it."

Frank takes a mug from the cabinet. "If they line me up for the shave, don't expect me to be the same way. I intend to fight. They'll have to shoot me before they can get me on that stage."

Oye. That's an image I don't need. "Nobody seems to have the microdot. Maybe the pirates destroyed my phone."

Frank stares at me. "Or they're figuring the best way to sell it. If Jack's crew can't prove they destroyed the dot, HGB won't be happy. That element of uncertainty tends to get people killed." Frank slams the mug onto the counter. "The shave in public or a bullet in the dark. Which one properly repays me for killing your father?"

I shake my head, trying to shake away the gory images his words just conjured. "I never wanted to see you shaved. Not even when you were hunting me. Verdaderamente. I just wanted HGB to stop hurting people. That's what I still want."

Frank gives me a hard look. "You opened this box of trouble without thinking it through. You may not be able to close it."

I hesitate. Should I tell Frank that Janvier ordered his death before 1.0 even knew I had the microdot? Pero that seems cruel. I swallow a lump of sympathy. "What do you want me to do?"

"Accept responsibility for your actions. That's all."

"I wish I had done some things differently. Though I still believe things had to change." Tears dance in my eyes. "I can't help but admire Murry. He's losing his life, and he's more concerned with trying to make up for what he did to Earth. When the lawyers said I might still get shaved if I failed on Zant, I only thought how unfair it was, porque I kept trying to do the right thing. And I get now what Mamá said. You were trying to do the right thing too. It would be unfair if–"

The coffee pot in Frank's hand freezes halfway to the mug. "What do you mean, what he did to Earth?"

I flinch back from the ferocity in Frank's eyes. I guess it doesn't matter now. What can Frank do? Kill a couple of spucks before the courts execute the hive mind? "Murry created Pure Rot, back before he became Murry."

"Why, that stupid–" Frank can't even finish his sentence. He sweeps the mug into the sink so hard it shatters. More carefully, he puts the coffee pot back in the maker. "And you brought one of the Murry monsters to Earth?"

"Mira! Murry was already on Earth, inside HGB. At one point, he had a hug on Daschel Janvier. He gave up his foothold on Earth and confined himself to the spucks." I make solid eye contact with Frank. "Eso– This box you say I've opened – the lid was coming off one way or another. All these secrets couldn't stay hidden forever."

"What secrets, exactly."

Either I trust Frank or I don't. Considering he risked everything to save Brill, maybe it's time I trust him.

I stammer out an explanation, of how the Evevrons engineered the Mindhuggers to be susceptible to theobromine poisoning, and how the emerging consciousness was terrangerated that HGB made chocolate addictive, which spread an antidote to the mindworm infection to all choco-addicted planets. It's all intertwined. Serum Green makes HGB chocolate addictive. And the whole invasion coalition consisted of addicts wanting to invade Earth to get the source of chocolate for themselves – addicts HGB and the Evevrons created. Of course, these addicts didn't want to wait for the Krom to inevitably secure chocolate as part of their commodities trading.

Looking more thoughtful now than angry, Frank takes out another mug. "When I executed your father, he had a bar of HGB dark and two vials of liquid on him. I assume you think he was close to figuring all this out."

I set my wine glass next to the sink and get myself a mug. I look Frank in the eye and realize I'm over the heartshattered angerzentment that has made it impossible to talk about this. Sí, Frank killed mi papá. And it doesn't hurt anymore to hear him say it. I hold out my mug for coffee. "I think Papá was still chasing leads and phantoms – like Jane Smith."

"Who?" Frank pours the coffee with a steady hand.

"The leader of a resistance group Papá may have been working with. She posted a holo of the warehouse where she thought HGB kept the chocolate contaminated with Pure275. And after that, it's like she shadowpopped off the planet."

"Mexican, maybe thirty-five, fidgety, with crazy eyes?" Frank blows on his coffee. He takes it black, like I do. When I nod, he nods back and squints like I'm un poco estúpido. "Stop looking. You won't find her."

Porque Frank killed her too. I take a steadying sip of my coffee. "She's been dead longer than I've been looking for her, no?"

Frank looks at me like, *do you really want to know?* Then he nods. "We traced her off of visual clues in that holo. She never answered any of my questions."

Brill comes into the galley and holds out his phone. "Murry wants to talk to you."

"Sí." I hold out my hand.

"Not you, Babe. This viejo."

Frank takes the phone. At least he can't hurt Murry over a virtual connection.

As usual, Murry enters the conversation like it's in the middle. "So when I was a couple of people from HGB, they thought a lot about alien weapons. And some of what they thought makes me think you might recognize this."

Gracias a Dios I just explained about Murry having been inside HGB. Frank looks under control, though muscles cord in his jaw.

Murry's not holding the phone. A more agile hand runs the image over a bloodied uniform shirt with a strangely familiar insignia, to where a green hand holds a strange-looking gun. The slack fingers belong to a dead man.

I suck in a breath. "Mijo, that's the same insignia we saw in the mountain's core in Hawaii."

The phone turns, showing the image of a blinking spuck. "Is it? These eyes have a hard time with that kind of thing."

"It is," Frank says. "Where are you?"

"Outside of Sheweh City on Evevron, trying to finish the irrigation system before the appeal period ends and I am killed. We are with Ekrin and her squad, and we were attacked."

"Did you find the ship?" Frank asks urgently. "The aliens would have burrowed down somewhere out of sight."

Ekrin, the one holding the camera, says something in Evevron.

Murry says, "No, but Ekrin wants to look for it. Which is funny, because she couldn't have understood what you said."

"Great minds think alike." Frank straightens his collar. "Do you have drones? I'd like to help."

My lips purse in as I process this unexpected shift in Frank's demeaner.

Murry translates Frank's request to Ekrin.

She has the tech and she's happy for the help. Not that she needs us – her squad has drone pilots – pero we're freeing up those pilots to keep sweeping the area with the rest of the squad. And Frank's prior experience with these aliens may come in handy.

So we'll use the VR setup on the *Just Married* to pilot the drones through the miles of underground tunnels the spucks have dug, while the spucks look for signs of disturbance from the air. Hopefully one of us will find evidence of the invaders.

After we've hung up, I ask Frank, "You won't hurt the spucks, right? Those drones have weapons."

Genuine sympathy shines in Frank's eyes. "The Court will carry out justice soon enough. And Murry will pay for everything he did, including destroying chocolate on Earth. But the entire planet of Evevron is at stake. These same aliens destroyed the Nitarri home world and attacked Earth. If Murry wants to stop them before he dies, I'll help him. But don't expect me to cry when they fry him. He ruined Earth just as surely as these planetsnatchers would have."

CHAPTER THIRTY-NINE

We head to the VR lab and get plugged into the gear. Frank's holding his goggles, hesitating.

"Are you okay, viejo?"

"I will be." Frank's hands tremble, though. "Everyone thinks Earth's borders closed because of the Krom. But we could have gotten past that, developed normal relationships with the galaxy, so that we'd have friends now. But the Gevexix marauder ship – that solidified our course."

"That's not exactly true," Dash says, examining Frank's setup.

"You weren't even there." Frank smiles bitterly. "You or 1.0."

"But I – he – read enough of the records. The First Contact War was a bit of a free-for-all. HGB Operatives found connections between different factions and half a dozen other different offplanet interests. We just happened to be approached by the most effective group. One way or another, we were bound to be caught up in someone else's problems."

Frank's face reddens like una manzana. Probably because a man who's less than a year old knows more about the secrets Frank's spent half his life protecting than he does.

"Is that true?" Brill asks.

"There were rumors," Frank mutters.

"The Greftash colony was formed thirty years before the Krom made First Contact," I say. "They were prisoners shipped off Earth. So someone made deals well before the war."

"We need to talk more about how you know that. After we save Evevron." Frank jams his goggles on.

Ekrin's group only had three drones handy, so Leron, Dash and Ball watch from the sidelines. None of them are pilots. Y

Chestla's busy flying the *Just Married*. Brill was teaching me to fly his ship, back before he faked his muerte, so I'm actually the third most qualified.

We're sitting in chairs, pero it's supposed to feel like we're inside the drones, which are each about the size of a large dog. The drone cameras project real-time holofeeds, and I'm terrified I'll crash mine into a wall.

Ekrin's squad is aboveground, making a spiral around the area where they ran into the intruders they killed. Part of my view shows them driving slowly in open-sided vehicles in a rectangle at the bottom of my sightline. They use devices complicados to image the ground under them as they go. Ekrin's got the camera on her, keeping in touch with us through Murry's translation.

"Keep these cameras rolling," Frank emphasizes. "Record every detail of what happens. These people have to be stopped, here, now, or they will keep destroying planets."

My sublingual rings. It's Tawny. *Give me access to that VR system, and I'll run live feed. Stop it! This is cashmere. I am not picking you up.*

Her voice is almost laughing, though. Botas may be growing on her. I relay the message to Brill, who patches Tawny in.

The drone's lights are bright enough that it looks like day underground. I see some abandoned tunnel-starts, like maybe the water table had looked promising until the spucks got a look at the rock structure. Verdaderamente, Murry is an amazing being. It's a shame the Court can't see that. My hand tightens into a fist, and my throat goes tight. I try to focus on the current mission.

We each go different directions down here, looking for a disturbance. Nothing feels out of place, and once I get a handle on the controls, remote piloting the drone feels monotonous.

I glance at the other displays ranged at the bottom of my view area. Brill's doing fine, and Frank seems to be zooming in on the wall, looking for something specific. The spuck in flight keeps looking down in a way that makes me dizzy. And Ekrin is driving through thick foliage.

As Ekrin's vehicle enters a clearing, she slams on her brakes. In the clearing's center, there's a starship that likematches the one in the depths of that Hawaiian volcano. Near the ship, a group of green-skinned guys stand in a wide circle, focused on the ground. Their heads jerk up towards Ekrin.

The tunnel bends and I nearly ram my drone head-on into the wall. Ay-ay-ay. My whole body tenses as I navigate the tight turn. I slow down and let the drone settle to the tunnel floor. By the time I focus back on Ekrin's view, a skirmish is already underway. She's crouched behind her vehicle, exchanging fire with the intruders, who are standing their ground behind an energy shield. Behind the barrier, a device burrows into the ground, disappearing at a steady rate.

Frank says, "That's the core-killing weapon. The one we observed on Earth had an extensive disarming procedure, with keys and codes we didn't have. So those jerks are the only ones who know how to just turn it off."

The energy shield sizzles, and then goes down. There's a pause in the fighting, as both sides re-evaluate.

"And they're not likely to talk, even if Ekrin leaves them breathing," Brill says, assuming that without the shield, these invaders are toast. "They'll want leverage in exchange for their lives. Babe, look at the dots in the map at the right of your periphery view. If both our tunnels continue arcing back towards that point, you and I are close to the action."

"And each other. I'll race you there, mi vida." I examine the map then get the drone flying in the right direction.

"Absolutely, my heart."

I'm smiling, despite the situation. "Awww. Te amo."

"Will you two stop being mushy on a group line?" Frank complains.

"Lo siento, viejo." I fly the drone muy rapido, pero I keep glancing down at Ekrin's view, catching snatches of the battle in progress. The green guys have four arms and an equal number of guns. Y todavía, the ferocity of the Evevron warriors freezes them in place. When dozens of spucks fly over the horizon, the guys stop shooting and run for their ship. The spucks reach the ship first.

The Gevexix surrender.

"What do we do now?" Murry asks.

"Get them to turn off the device, if you can," Frank instructs.

Murry says something to Ekrin, who holds out the phone to the least surly-looking captive. Murry speaks rápidamente in a language I've never heard.

The green dude shrugs all four shoulders and spits on the ground. So no, they won't turn off the device.

"Ideas?" Frank asks.

"We're hunters," Murry says. "We have the net we use to capture rogue predators. It's made of a metal stronger than anything you have on Earth."

"Really?" Brill asks.

"Don't get any Krom ideas, Brill Cray," Murray says. "We've had quite enough of being 'discovered' for one lifetime."

Oye! I bring my hands to the sides of my face, though that movement makes the drone slow. Can't we even come together when we have a common goal?

Murry adds, "A huge branch of our tunnel system sprawls deeper and deeper under where the weapon went down, now that we avoid digging where we might damage the city. Maybe we can get below the device and catch it."

"That's dangerous." Frank seems to have found whatever he was looking for. He turns his drone down a side tunnel.

"And letting them destroy my home's not?" While Murry talks to Frank, a spuck gestures at Ekrin with its claw hands, in a rough pantomime of diving into the tunnel system. He must be saying something to her via her phone, because she nods and moves towards her open vehicle. She pulls out a canvas bundle. The spuck takes it in his teeth and starts digging. The spuck wearing the camera watches the others, who are all disappearing into the tunnel the first one made, or making secondary entrances in circle grande enough to avoid destroying the tunnel system's structural integrity.

I can almost feel the vibration of all those spucks tunneling into the ground around us.

Brill and I both reach the spot where the shaft that the device is drilling intersects the tunnel junction.

En un túnel diferente, Frank's drone lights up the faces of two green guys pushing a cart filled with ore. "I take it that's the special metal you were talking about?" Frank asks Murry. "These guys are collecting commodities in case the planet blows. That's their consolation prize if a planet's leaders won't pay up."

The su's draw multiple guns and fire at the drone. Frank fires back, and the green guys jump back behind their cart, still taking pot shots at the drone.

Frank, vengezentment in his movements, growls and maneuvers the drone above the cart. He's about to kill two people. He's not inside the drone, so it isn't justifiable. Nunca y no.

I suspend audio on the actioncast, so we can talk without the audience listing.

"Viejo, don't!"

"Bo–"

"Por favor. You once told me you promised yourself that you would never kill in anger."

Frank shouts a frustrated wordless, "Aarrrgggghhh!" and releases a line of bullets into the wall, just above the green guys' cabezas. As bits of rock shower around them, they duck and shield themselves. Frank flattens each tire of their cart with a single bullet, then backs his drone up the tunnel.

Hopefully, Tawny shifted away from that camera.

"Wow, su," Brill says. "Is that how you think of the Krom?"

"Once I did," Frank says. "Remember, I tried to put a bullet between your eyes."

"I'm not likely to ever forget that." Brill sounds shaky, just thinking about it. "But you said that was the job, as a weapon for HGB."

"Some targets are easier than others. You were going to be easy. So easy. You have no idea how–"

"Wal, su, I get it."

"But Bo forced me to get to know you, and I realized Krom motives are different from these vultures. I still don't agree with you, but I understand."

Where mine and Brill's drones are, a hatch opens on the Gevexix device, revealing a quill of arrows. The launcher angles them towards us and shoots a barrage. I dodge, and my drone manages to keep clear. Pero it takes intense focus.

"Thank you, Bodacious." Frank's voice startles me. "I needed a voice of reason there for a minute."

"Would killing those muchachos have made you feel better?" I ask.

"No." Frank's voice sounds small. "It would have broken me. But flattening those tires was oddly satisfying."

Brill laughs. "I get why. You've needed closure on these keks for a long time."

"Too long," Frank says.

More oversized arrows fly from the device, closer this time. I cringe, though they aren't actualmente flying by my face. An arrow hits Brill's drone, sending his view spinning and skewering the tiny craft to the tunnel wall.

My own drone flies safely past.

"Here, mi vida. Fly this drone. You're the pilot. Not me." I'm terrified I'll mess this up.

"Ga, Babe. You got this. Just keep it moving steady." He reinstates the audio on the live feed.

I'm close enough that I take a shot at the device. I see the weapon hit, pero the laser blast just leaves a scorch mark on the metal.

"You have to get right up on it," Frank says. "Use the heavy-duty laser to burn through the carapace and start pulling out wires."

Right. Because I've totally done something like this before, no?

I glance at the other views. Hundreds of spucks flood the cavern below me, spreading out the net, holding parts of it in their teeth, pinning other parts to the floor with their long, blunted digging claws. Por favor, let it hold. The Evevrons are geniuses with tech, and the net should be strong enough to hold a struggling predator. Even though I'm still piloting the drone above the device, I watch the scene in the cavern playing out at the bottom of my viewfield, from the camera-wearing spuck's point of view. The drill on the device breaks through the cavern's ceiling, then spins in open air. The device turns sideways as it falls, so that the drill doesn't cut through anything inmediatamente.

The device rights itself, starts drilling again, snapping a few of the net's threads. The net holds, glowing with a forcefield, constraining the device. The weight hauls some of the spucks forward as the device struggles to free itself from the net.

My drone plummets into the cavern, and I pull back on the controls, so that instead of crashing into the weapon, the drone's nose just besos the outside hull.

"Murry, let go of the net and get out of there," Frank instructs. "Otherwise, those spucks will die when Bo drills into the weapon. It has a failsafe that will cause an explosion big enough to obliterate all evidence that the device was ever on your planet, even if it hasn't reached the target for triggering core instability."

Frank's drone isn't catching up to me. I check his viewfield at the bottom of mine. He's doing something to the wall, still above the cavern.

Murry says, "But if I let go, the device may reach its destination before Bo disarms it. These me's are due to be executed soon. Losing them here is better, don't you think?"

"How many of you will be left?" Brill asks.

"Fourteen of us are too far away to get there in time to help."

Murry needs at least five or six human-quality minds to hold onto all his memories. Pero with spucks? "Will that be enough, mijo?"

"I think so." Murry hesitates. "It'll have to be."

"Lo siento por this." I start the laser, and it burns a neat hole in the device's hull. The device stops drilling and scuttles sideways across the net, where a spuck tries to grab it. The device is still fighting the net, trying to dig down through the holes in the surface, and the spucks, making unhappy noises, keep pulling and adjusting the net. Another spuck releases the net edge and opens its jaws, bellowing displeasure. It leaps into the air and closes its teeth around one edge of the device's shell. Oye! That won't work for long before the spuck's teeth snap.

I bring the drone in close and finish burning the hole. I make a few stabs at the virtual control menus. I finally get the extender arm working and start pulling out wires. No sé what's connected to what, so I grab everything.

The device stops moving. The spuck sets it down. Blood streams from its mouth.

For un momento, I think that maybe, just maybe I disabled the device in a way that won't trigger the failsafe. Then it explodes.

When hunters killed a small number of Murry's selves, he had freaked out from the pain. Ahora, he's experiencing that pain on a massive scale, taking the blow of death after death as hundreds of spucks take damage from the blast. My drone gets zapblasted and my viewfield goes blank. Frank's drone, the only camera left, takes center screen as the dirt caves in around it.

Murry screams through the electronic device covering my ear, more human than any sound the spucks could make. It's so heart-wrenching I have to mute it.

Frank flies up, out of the tunnel system. He reaches an area where the dirt is falling away from an open chamber. Que es esto? The bare rock has been painted a soft pink, and dozens of large boulders glow with strategic lighting. A waterfall cascades down the back of the cavern. A clutch of eggs lies in the center, and not far from it, one of the smaller female spucks lies still, either stunned by the blast or outright dead. Some of the eggs are cracked.

The cavern is an incubation lab. The still-functioning computers show heartbeats inside the eggs or rows of scrolling data. Near the far wall, una pequeña reptilian head pokes up over the rocks framing a small pool.

The drone hovers, watching.

I turn my sound back on. Murry is whimpering now, raw grief that penetrates deep into mi corazón. After this preview of what muerte for a hive mind looks like, I'll crumble when the Court finishes him.

Frank's voice sounds a lot more sympathetic when he says, "Murry, what is this place?"

"Please." Murry's heartshattered. "Turn off the cameras."

This is FeedCasting straight to the public. Esto es horrible. Murry told me he wouldn't fight his execution as long as no one realized Awn was a separate consciousness. And he just told everyone that all of the spucks in this area under his control died in that cavern.

Frank kills the camera. Pero people are still listening in when Murry says, "All we wanted is a child. A third consciousness, as a legacy after I'm gone, something that's both me and Awn and not. So that she won't be alone, like I was. Awn never hurt anyone. Please don't let them punish her, too."

"Murry," Frank's voice comes out soft and choked up. He said he wouldn't cry for Murry's death. He was wrong.

Y of all the things that have made my life feel like a novela, this one's the hardest to live through. On the shows, there's always a secret pregnancy, or a baby fathered by a now-dead character, or a muchacho claiming paternity for someone else's niño. It keeps the audience guessing, adds another layer of surprise. Ay, though. Living inside this trope could break me. Especially if the Court decides to execute Awn.

"Gideon Tyson wants to get patched into this call," Tawny says.

Tyson says, "Murry, you were condemned because te guy who examined you could tell tat you were hiding something. He believed your motives were untrustworthy and deemed you dangerous. He never imagined you might be protecting someone else. Tis shows you are completely different tan what he tought. Tere are a few time segments left in your appeal. Will you submit to reexamination?"

"Oh, goodness, yes." Murry sounds relieved, despite the pain.

"I will get it set up. Your lawyer will be in touch shortly." Tyson sounds all emotional, too. "Your examiner will also collect your testimony regarding te men Ekrin captured. If you help bring justice to te galaxy, tat will also count in your favor."

"Full disclosure?" Murry says. "I have a single spuck that isn't on Evevron anymore. But the people I'm with can vouch that I'm on board a Zantite warship on a mission of mercy."

Murry needs to be honest answering whatever questions they ask. I just hope they don't ask him anything that will reveal everyone else's secrets.

After we exit VR, Brill goes to talk to Chestla about our plans once we arrive at the warship. I'm tidying up the gear when Frank pulls me aside and hands me his handheld. "Your mother wants to talk to you."

Cold sparks through my chest. "Is everything okay?" I glance at the holofield, and no, everything is most definitely not okay. Mamá is crying again. I hold up the phone. "What happened, Mamá?"

She wipes a handkerchief across her nose and gets herself a bit more under control. "The invasion fleet is ahead of schedule. They've already emerged from our side of the wormhole."

"Ay! No."

Crosskiss hadn't guaranteed a certain amount of time. He just said until his fleet arrived at Earth.

"There is panic at Earth's spaceports. Your abuelita y your sisters y Minerva y Mario's girls made it off of Earth, but transport space is limited, and your Abuelo y Mario volunteered to stay behind to make room for four niñas who were booked on a later flight."

"No, Mamá. Por favor."

In theory, they could survive the invasion – Earth can only sustain so much damage before it surrenders. Pero it feels like two members of mi familia volunteered to stay aboard the Titanic.

CHAPTER FORTY

The Court takes all of twenty minutes to try and condemn the planetsnatchers – including the guys Frank refrained from killing. Given the detailed holographic evidence, they don't bother to appeal.

After another hour, Murry finds himself spared – though the Court plans to monitor him closely, and is still determining the limits they will allow for his existence. The executioners en route to Evevron to kill the spucks get redirected to un objetivo diferente: the planetsnatchers. Unlike on Earth, the executions won't be FeedCast, Gracias a Dios. Still, those green men, glaring surlily into the camera, facing muerte in their cell on Evevron, trouble me.

After the trial recap goes dark, I say, "They look like they don't care that they are about to die."

Brill puts a hand on mine, "Mercy only goes so far, Babe. Eventually, there has to be justice."

"It's still horrible."

Frank looks dazed. "When this happened on Earth, we shouldn't have kept it a secret. We were brand new to a post-Contact galaxy, and we didn't think anyone would understand that we were defending ourselves."

"I think HGB was already wrapped up in so many other secrets at that point, they didn't want anybody digging into their business," Brill says.

"I agree." Dash comes into the room, now that the cameras are off. "I don't know everything that happened before 1.0 took the helm at HGB – he never bothered to read through all the archives – but it's a tangled mess that dates decades before First Contact."

"Que? You've seen the records?" I should have realized. "How did HGB go from an organization trying to rescue the people who shadowpopped to Greftash to a faction in the war? En serio, they went from protecting people to murdering civilians."

Dash shrugs. "I expect it was a complicated web of decisions. Shelly was always more interested in HGB's past than the rest of us. I'm sure he could have given you details."

"Maybe you did kill the wrong one," Brill tells Frank. "Everyone wants apologies and statements from the head guy of HGB, and the Janvier we know won't do it. Shelly would have done it with grace." Brill looks significantly over at Dash.

Dash goes red all the way to his ears. "Don't look at me. I am not going back to Earth."

"I'm sure Janvier's not on Earth anymore," Brill says. "You don't think Tawny was FeedCasting from Earth, either, revwal? They're probably together somewhere safe from the invasion, with a contingent of HGB officials."

Dash nods, very reluctantly. "That's the standard plan."

"Can we track their location through the castsignal Tawny made?" I ask Brill. I doubt anyone has ever used Tawny's tech against her before.

"No," Frank says. "I cannot condone that. Yes, we threatened to replace Janvier with a clone, but we got our concessions. We're not murdering my boss."

"I'm not suggesting we kill Janvier." Brill looks offended as his irises shift towards red. "Shtesh! I though you have started to understand Krom ways."

I say, "Tawny wouldn't condone that either, viejo, and we know she's listening. We wouldn't need to kill him. Just put Dash in his place long enough to make decisions Janvier can't easily take back. Like what Shelly did, making that statement for Murry." And it hits home why Shelly got so passionate when I asked him to defend the mindworms. Verdaderamente. He felt his position likematched theirs, since he too was the product of hidden experimentation. He wanted to make a world in which he would be allowed to live. And I crashbanged it.

"And how do you plan to put Dash in Janvier's place?" Frank looks skeptical.

I shrug, reluctantly pulling myself away from memories of Shelly. "I don't know the specifics. Pero we would need to distract Janvier and cut his communication to the outside for a strategic amount of time."

Brill's eyes go deep purple. "Maybe Tawny'd help. It sounds right for her skill set."

"Wait," Dash says. "I couldn't pull off being 1.0 in front of cameras. I don't have his desire for power, or his craving for the spotlight." Dash straightens his shirt collar. "And it's pointless anyway. All of your plans hinge on having a clean sample of cacao."

"I still have hope we'll get one," I counter.

Dash bites at his cheek. Then he lets out a long breath. "You said you would drop me off on a backwater planet. Back when 1.0 was in college, he was a barista in San Jose. It was the happiest time of his life. I just want to find an interesting town and do coffee art, maybe sideline repairing copy machines."

"We can't force him to do this," Brill says.

I put mi mano on Dash's arm. "I tried running away from the spotlight. I made it almost three years before being pulled straight back to Earth. Maybe you can manage it longer than I did. If Earth still exists in three years."

Dash's face becomes a hard mask. "I. Am. Not. Daschel. Janvier. I shouldn't have to pay for his mistakes."

"Earlier, mijo, you said you were Daschel." I point out. "You bear his memories – and his gifts."

Frank says, "We don't have time to make stops now anyway. We need to get the scientists to the Zantite warship. And we will stay there while they work, right up until the invasion starts."

"At least consider the plan," Brill says. "Avell."

"I'll think about it," Dash says.

And that's the most we can ask. Después de todo, if we coerce him into playing Janvier, we likematch HGB.

It takes forever to reach the warship, and I feel time and hope slipping away. And as we near the *Layla's Pride*, the Evevrons get more nervous, thickening the predator pheromones in the air.

When we finally arrive, Gavin is asleep inside a cabin on our ship. Everyone else has assembled in the ship's living area. I turn to go knock on Gavin's door.

Brill takes my arm. "Mira, Babe. Leave him. He'll be much more himself when he wakes up."

Ball gives a close-fisted salute in the direction of Gavin's cabin. "I'll see about securing him a vitamin drink or some yewstral." He smiles over at me. "Yewstral's the only alcohol I know that's actually good for a hangover."

"Best not go too far on your own," Watae warns. "I've heard that when Zantites decide to eat their enemies, there's no evidence left for anyone to lodge a complaint."

Ball's face goes pinched. He is, después de todo, as much Krom as Evevron, and Krom are all about finding and keeping peace – something Watae is just beginning to learn. "I intend to take Crosskiss at his word. If we don't bring our own grudges on board, we could make massive strides towards truer peace between our peoples." His eyes unexpectedly tint lavender. "Strides. From someone like me." He gestures at his leg. "I don't care if we've had two wars with them. They'd have to be in a dark place to want to fight someone who's already this broken."

Leron glances at his phone. For about the tenth time in the last hour.

"Are you expecting a call?" I ask.

He gives me a sad smile. "I'm counting down the time until the end of my appeal. There's only a few time segment partitions left."

"I truly am sorry," Brill says as we troop out of the ship into the docking bay of the *Layla's Pride*. "I thought that when they showed Murry wasn't dangerous, that that might sway things for you, too."

"Like you told Bo, mercy only goes so far." Leron glances at Chestla. "I'm sorry about before, when you first uncovered the secrets about Murry. I shouldn't have hurt you, trying to keep my guilt a secret."

With a whoosh, an airlock pressurizes on the other side of the docking bay, and then a sleek silver ship glides in.

Leron goes pale. "My executioners, right on time."

"You told them where you were going?" I splutter. Oi! They're really going to kill him the minute his appeal expires?

Leron points to a shaved spot on his cabeza, near the nape of his neck. "I didn't have to tell anyone. They chipped me, remember? If I try to take it out, it will rupture and spill poison into my bloodstream."

Brill whispers, "They probably dispatched these su's the minute the original verdict was passed. They're not often late."

My chest feels tight and dread drops into my stomach. The silver ship parks next to the *Just Married*, and two guys get out.

One is a willowy humanoid with a soft opalescent glow to his skin. He's wearing loose-fitting gray clothing and has a black backpack slung over his shoulder.

The other muchacho is built like a fur-covered linebacker, with a canine-looking snout beneath very human-looking eyes. They walk slowly toward us.

The willowy one says, "I am Fendigsh, certified Galactic Executioner. I am here regarding the case of the Galactic Court verses Leron of Evevron."

Leron steps forward. "I still have two time segment partitions."

"I respect that. May we chat during that time? Or do you wish to do something to further your appeal?"

Leron says, "I have nothing else to offer. I pled guilty and asked that my sentence be commuted to life in prison. I assume that's been denied."

"Sadly, yes. And I sympathize. These last moments of hope are never pleasant. But you still need to make a few decisions." Fendigsh pats his backpack. "We can do this here, where you're among friends, or we can take you back to the official facility. That'll take about two days, so you get to keep breathing longer, but you'll spend your last breaths in a white room with just me and Okveng here as company. Your co-defendants have already been executed. They opted to die together, on Evevron."

Ay-ay-ay! He's talking about the whole line of Evevron researchers, who sat contrite and broken at Murry's trial. Now they're probably lying in another line, fría y silenciosa, being prepared for a ceremony of salt. Leron winces.

Sympathy wrenches my heart. Brill wraps his arms around me from behind. Porque he feels what I'm feeling.

Leron glances at Okveng. The guys fangs protrude out of his mouth, and he doesn't look like much of a talker. Then Leron looks around at the rest of us.

Ball's eyes glisten with tears. Chestla clings to him. It's obvious how much it hurts her to hold back from physically defending Leron, whom she grew up with.

Eugene runs into the bay and scans the scene. Obviamente, he came to comfort Chestla. Eugene sees her with Ball and freezes. Chestla doesn't notice him.

Watae steps forward. "Surely this sentence can be commuted. Leron saved my life, and I am my people's crown prince. And he is needed here, for at least the next six time segments, to assist with vital research."

Which means only a few hours remain until the Zantites arrive at Earth.

Fendigsh gives Watae a sad smile. "There are only a few circumstances where the Galactic Court refuses to defer to local planetary law. This is one of those cases. Sentence has been passed, and appeal denied. I am truly sorry."

Watae growls.

Leron laughs. "You're right. It is better to die here, among people who care what's happening."

"Do you have a will?" Fendigsh asks. "Or do you need assistance making one?"

Leron flexes his hands, stretching his fingers with their claw nails. Chestla does that to calm herself. "It's on file with my attorney."

"Very well." Fendigsh unzips his backpack. "I assume you want your body sent home."

Dios mio! When they said they'd execute Leron here, they meant the docking bay. I thought they'd at least take him to the Doc's office or something. And I still have no idea *how* they plan to kill Leron.

Pero he does. His eyes intent on the backpack, Leron swallows visibly. "Quick and painless, right?"

"Quick and painless," Fendigsh says in a comforting tone. "Do you have any last words, or messages you'd like conveyed?"

Leron looks over at me. "Tell Murry I'm sorry I wasn't brave enough to face him."

Brill's phone rings, and he starts to quiet it. Pero his eyes go apricot in startled shock. He holds out the phone. Murry's voice comes from it, loud and panicked. "Stop! Wait!"

Amid a clattering noise, the spuck races out of the hallway. As he leaps, wings spreading to half-fly across the open space, he digs gouges in the carpet. He snaps those feartastic teeth at the two executioners, bellowing, which given this place's acoustics, practically deafens me.

Okveng pulls a gun, pero Fendigsh stops him from firing. The spuck picks up Leron in two clawed hands, holding him protectively to the side.

Brill's phone says, "I won't let you kill him. I forgave him. That has to count."

Those teeth snap shut on the ominous backpack, and the spuck hurls it against the far wall.

"Put me down, Murry," Leron says, prying at the claws holding him. "This won't change anything. I've accepted that my death is justice. At least let me keep my dignity."

The spuck brings his cabeza very close to Fendigsh. Brill's phone says, "This individual is unique. He tried to reverse the cryostasis. What he is does not deserve to be lost."

Murry threads his teeth through Leron's sweater and, leaving the Evevron dangling from his mouth, turns and races back down the hallway.

Okveng grumbles, "That thing attacked two officers of the Galactic Court. Why didn't you let me shoot it?"

Fendigsh looks at him sadly. "You'll understand when you've been doing this job a bit longer. Life is precious and punishing those who don't want to see it end – that's cruel. Besides, he didn't touch you, did he?"

"Well, no," Okveng admits.

"Then let's go talk to him."

Chestla stares as Okveng and Fendigsh amble into the hallway. I can't read the expression on her face.

Ball says, "Remember when Leron and I took that ship into orbit? I thought your father would blow a gasket."

Chestla manages a weak smile. "You two built it out of a kit. And scavenged his restaurant for parts."

"This isn't your fault," Eugene says, stepping closer to the two Evevrons. He looks ready to pull Chestla away from Ball.

"It's really not," Ball agrees.

Chestla pulls away from Ball and glares at them both. "Oh yeah? Why was I spared, after the Court implicated me?"

"I was implicated too," Ball reminds her. "The Court showed leniency to a lot of us."

Eugene puts a hand on Chestla's arm. "Let's go see what's happening. We need Leron to help with the research."

Chestla nods. "Okay."

Now Ball's face goes tight and pinched. He can't blush, and his eyes don't betray a shift, pero he looks jealous.

Eugene guides Chestla into the hallway. He says something, and she laughs.

Brill and I lag behind. He whispers to me, "Now that's just awkward."

I agree. Chestla has to make a decision before this gets feo.

CHAPTER FORTY-ONE

It isn't hard to figure out where Murry went. Cierto, we just follow the gouges in the carpet and the dents in the walls. A gaping hole in the wall's been ripped below a sign that says "Emergency Medical Kit," in Zantite. Shortly past that, Murry entered the mess hall. We arrive just as a stream of soldiers rushes the other way, and the mess hall door slams shut.

We could enter through windows that open between the galley and the mess, pero I don't feel obligated to share that information. Por qué habría.

Okveng tests the door. It doesn't budge. He slams his sturdy bulk against it. The solid Zantite construction doesn't give.

Fendigsh takes Brill's phone. "It's Murry, isn't it?"

Murry laughs, the sound awkward and stilted. "I was once Gideon Tyson. All Galactic Enforcers are trained in hostage negotiation. So let's skip all that please."

"Okay, Murry. You can't stay there indefinitely. We'll just carry out our orders whenever you come out. Are you asking for time to make peace with Leron? Because we don't mind giving you that."

"Hold on." After a shuffling noise, the spuck huffs into another phone. Ni idea where he got it. "Now Leron can hear us too. I spoke with Tyson, my friend who is familiar with the law. He says that if a sentient Evevron chooses to infect himself with me, it won't violate my prohibition from the Court against expanding outside the borders of Evevron. That's right, isn't it? There would be no repercussions?"

Fendigsh looks at me like *is he serious?* "I would have to look it up to be sure, but I don't think there would be. You'd want it confirmed that the Evevron agreed."

"For this to work, this me will have to be dead, so he'd have to do it all himself – guaranteeing that the Evevron's making a free choice. But this body is just an animal, so truly, nothing will be lost."

"What are you asking me to agree to?" Leron is una buena distancia from the phone, his voice muffled. "Hey! Get out of there! That's a blast freezer."

Murry ignores him. "And a bystander who helps in a voluntary procedure would face no repercussions, right?"

Fendigsh hesitates. "Again, I'd have to look it up to be sure. Who's in there with you?"

Crosskiss's voice is unmistakable. "Only the captain of this ship."

Oye! If it had been anybody else, Murry might have found help. Crosskiss is more likely to shoot the spuck, or open the door and let the executioners in.

"Leron's the closest living person to those who created me. Becoming him, even briefly, will give me answers about my past I can never get otherwise. Even if you kill him once we leave this room, I will have absorbed that which is noble about him into myself. And I can glean the research he's willing to share in those moments, to better try to save Earth. But Tyson says you might not kill him after all if, when we walk out of here, there is no way to untangle Leron and me. I need a voice. I'm tired of talking through electronics, hoping someone will pick up the phone so I can speak. People assume I'm stupid because spucks can't talk."

There's a loud buzzing noise coming over the line, like a machine experiencing an error, then a metal door bangs shut.

Leron picks up the phone. "The spuck locked itself in the blast freezer and turned it on. I'm trying to turn it off, but he pulled out some of the wires. How would he even know how to do that?"

Crosskiss says, "Mertex Makanoc once worked maintenance on this ship."

There's a thrashing noise in the background.

Leron says, "Spucks are warm-blooded. They can't survive being deep-frozen. And I don't have the equipment to transport the parasite in its contracted form. Without another host, this pearl will die. With so few of Murry left, and the verdict uncertain as to whether he will be allowed to create more pearls, each one is precious." Leron sounds like he's trying to talk himself into becoming one of Murry's hosts, justifying finding a way to stay vivo. "And it's comforting to think that Murry wants to hold onto part of me, even after I'm executed. And that he thinks he can use what I know to save an entire planet."

"What did he mean that you couldn't be untangled?" Crosskiss asks. "I've watched this case develop, since Mertex was one of my men. The parasite has suicided part of itself before, with no ill effects to the host."

Leron's talking to Crosskiss now. "The Galactics chipped me as a possible flight risk. If a hug unfolds around that chip, damaging or removing the parasite would almost certainly poison us both. But if my executioners want to contract the Mindhugger into a pearl again, all they have to do is freeze me immediately after my death." He hesitates. "Or before. Like what that spuck is doing. If they complete the process on Evevron, then they can move the parasite to another spuck."

"And you're willing to do that?" Crosskiss sounds skeptical.

"I'd rather live to be Murry's voice. Though I doubt the Court will go for that." Leron sighs. "I have to die for my crimes, but saving one part of this new species grants me a little redemption."

"Isn't becoming infected the same as dying?" Crosskiss asks. "Your body's alive, but your mind belongs to the hive."

"With Murry's documented hugs, the individuals retained relative control of their own minds. Murry only exercised complete control in times of great stress or need. Now that he has developed a self-sacrificing moral code, the hug would almost be what the original researchers intended – a voice in your head encouraging you to be better, do better things."

Crosskiss says, "What can I do to help?"

Que? En serio? Did I hear Crosskiss right? Are we rubbing off on him somehow?

Then Crosskiss adds, "My mother hopes to see the cryostasis issue resolved. She has a soft spot for Earth. Knowing I tried to help will make her feel a bit better, even after you fail and the planet is destroyed."

So maybe not.

Fendigsh pulls out his phone to contact his superiors and find out what *he's* supposed to do.

A ding comes from Brill's phone. I remember that sound. The blast freezer has finished its cycle. The spuck is dead. Leron says, "We don't have much time. We don't have proper tools to work with, so to extract the pearl, we have to cut open the spuck's head. Carefully."

I shudder. They have the tools for that, cierto. There's a room near the blast freezer full of tools for butchering game.

Brill makes a soft, unhappy noise.

"What, su?" Gavin asks.

Brill replies, "I doubt Crosskiss has ever done anything carefully in his life."

After some unpleasant sounds, Crosskiss asks, "What are we looking for?"

"The pearl is small enough to be injected into the bloodstream, so it won't be readily visible. But a pocket in the flesh near the brain will show where the pearl first expanded. If we extract the blue fluid, the pearl should be in it."

The whole procedure takes just a few minutes.

I tell the two executioners. "It will take a bit longer for the hug to unfold."

"You've seen it?" Fendigsh asks.

I nod. "I've seen the effects."

Eugene says, "In that case, we should get to the lab. We're short on time, and the latest test should almost be completed. I can use a biochemist's take on why the beans keep turning that weird green color."

"You sure they're not peas?" Chestla jokes, and Eugene laughs.

"Stala," Ball says, then falls silent, porque she came here to help Eugene, and Ball has no right to stop her from bantering. The tewakelle clears his throat. "I'll ask in the medical bay for yewstral for Gavin."

Leaning on his cane, he walks relatively quickly down the hall. Chestla looks like she wants to go with him, then she glances at Eugene, and a blush spreads across her cheeks.

"Wait up," Watae calls. "Chestla said that if we aren't going to the lab, we should stay with you." The young Evevron seems to be looking for guidance. I think he wants to ask privately if he can do anything for Leron.

That Chestla trusts Ball to look after her charges says something mega grande.

That leaves me, Brill, Frank and the two executioners listening in as Leron and Crosskiss wait to see if they successfully transferred the parasite. Fendigsh gets a text response on his handheld, pero he angles the device so that we can't see it. Pues, bien. He pulls his companion aside and they speak animatedly for several minutes.

While we're waiting for the hug to unfold, Leron and Crosskiss talk about plans they've had for the future – when Leron had one. Leron wanted to travel. Crosskiss has been many places. True to the Zantite belief that a man should not be left waiting for death, Crosskiss tries to distract Leron with stories of far-flung adventure. Maybe Crosskiss does believe in mercy, on his own terms. They've forgotten they left the line open on the handheld.

Eventually, Leron opens the door. He bows his cabeza and holds his manos out, wrists crossed as though expecting to be bound. "You heard everything Murry said. I know it's not one of the choices you gave me, but I'd prefer if you take me home to Evevron alive. If it's not too much trouble. And then, after you transfer the pearl to an untamed spuck, we can pick up where we left off down in the docking bay."

"Ay de mi." Heat bites the back of my nose and my eyes, and my chest feels tight.

Watae never came back. I'd assumed that he had something else to say to Leron. Pero he is just a kid. Maybe he's not up to seeing Leron's muerte.

Leron touches his own chest, obviously thinking about whatever is in that backpack. Then he drops his hand back to the submissive crossed position. "Please."

Fendigsh looks at him with solemn, sad eyes. Then he turns to Okveng, whose fangs are hanging out again. "Are you ready to do what the Court instructed?"

Okveng replies, "Of course."

Leron's shoulders slump. He smiles sadly at me. "Tell Ekrin and the others I'm sorry I couldn't even save this one hug. But I hope Murry can use my knowledge." Then his face becomes more animated. "No. Please. This isn't fair! You should see into his mind. It's fascinating."

Murry has pushed through, and we're talking to him now, not Leron. So the improvised transfer worked.

Brill steps closer, puts a mano on Leron's arm. "Murry, you have to let Leron be himself when he dies. Remember, he asked for his dignity. Give him that."

Leron tells the executioners, "Sorry about that. Murry promises it won't happen again. He just wants to watch and remember. And he's pressuring me to tell you that I've had a crush on Ekrin for forever, and one of you guys should tell her I loved her, even if it is too late." He stops speaking, then looks frustrated – like Murry's voice in his cabeza won't shut up. "Something about Mertex waiting too long, and Murry being tired of individuals making the same mistakes because they won't talk to each other."

Okveng smiles, his fangs even more prominent. He looks like he's trying not to laugh at the guy he's about to execute. Which is feo y cruel, no? "Relax, kid. I'm not supposed to kill you yet. The

Court wants to know how you relate to the hive mind now. If you help guarantee that Murry will not be a threat to others, I'm authorized to commute your sentence."

Leron looks to Fendigsh, who seems to be in charge. And además the one more likely to show compassion. The he looks back at Okveng. "Why you?"

Okveng grins. "My people are telepaths. Not as strong as the Nitarri, but we do okay."

Which explains why he didn't strike me as much of a talker. I suddenly wish we'd been nicer to this muchacho. Offered him some coffee or something. Now that he holds Leron's life in his hands. It's extraño that telepaths don't automatically sense each other. Otherwise Murry would have spoken directly to Okveng earlier, and not nearly gotten the spuck shot when he'd snatched Leron. Okveng will have to "talk" to Murry, through Leron. And Leron will have to prove he can keep Murry from overriding his mind. That'll take mucho tiempo.

I say, "Let me get both of you some coffee from the galley, no? And maybe I can whip up a batch of cookies?"

Crosskiss comes out of the galley. "I have a conference room where you two can sit quietly." Why is he being so nice? He points a massive yellow index finger at me as he walks past. "But I will be back to snag a couple of cookies fresh from the oven." He grins, showing those feartastic teeth. "You'll have me so spoiled. I need to think of a way to keep you on board after six months is over."

"Not likely, su," Brill says coldly. "Bo needs to think about building a real future. You said she could leave after this to graduate school and put a few things in order."

"And she'll come straight back afterwards, because she always keeps her word." Crosskiss grins at me, and for once it's not predatory.

"If you could come up with a treatment chamber for the IH shakes, I'd run back here, no?" I'm only half-kidding.

Crosskiss wrinkles his spongy brow. "What are you talking about?"

"HGB designed a treatment program for Earthlings who have taken the Invincible Heart," Frank tells him. "It involves stabilizing the metallic residue in the blood."

Crosskiss says, "Bo, if you can get me a schematic, my scientists can build something like that on board the ship. If the Court lets Leron live, he might be grateful enough to stick around to improve the technology."

Brill's been doing something with his phone. "Gavin's on that. Despite the hangover, you can expect those schematics soon."

Crosskiss nods. "This could allow for groundbreaking research. A willing subject that won't die after a single test."

Ignoring Crosskiss, I smile at Brill. Mi vida's eyes shift from purple to gold. He's okay with me staying on this ship, as long as it gets me away from dependence on HGB. That's – actually really sweet.

Crosskiss rolls his eyes at us. I turn towards the Zantite. "Why did you do that for Leron? What's in it for you?"

A teal blush breaks out on Crosskiss's face. He pulls a green balloon out of his pocket. It's flat, and worn at the end, like the knot has been re-tied several times. It has to be the balloon that niña gave him in France. He wasn't making it up after all.

"She keeps sending me pictures of Paris. Mother insists I respond." He says it like an accusation. "Pictures of her cat, and the little boy she likes, and of the city's lights. She thinks I'm a good person, doesn't realize I'm going to help end her world. Today, she sent me a picture of her baby brother. Ugly thing, all red and wrinkly. He was born last night." Which has nada to do with Leron. And yet, it explains everything. Crosskiss stuffs the balloon back into his pocket.

Heat burns behind my eyes. "Thank you."

"Whatever." Crosskiss's gruff exterior returns, his scowl as feartastic as ever. He waves to Leron. "This way."

After Crosskiss takes the executioners and Leron down the hall, I ask, "Will they commute his sentence?"

Frank says, "They wouldn't interview him if they weren't looking for an excuse to reward his self-sacrificing choice. Especially because he told them that all he wanted was a quick painless death, and being frozen is the opposite of that. He's lucky that Watae spoke up for him. And that this executioner is sympathetic enough to contact the Court instead of proceeding according to orders. Most wouldn't have done that."

"You would have," Brill says.

My eyes go wide at this shift in the relationship between Frank and Brill. And no sé, maybe I finally understand Frank too.

CHAPTER FORTY-TWO

Being back in the galley of a Zantite warship is a surreal experience. A nuevo set of cooks have replaced the guys I got released from here last time. One wears a MIAG bracelet, so they know who I am, though they just nod at me and let me wander straight into their pantry.

I come out carrying a bag of questionable-origin flour and manage in passable Zantite, "Where did you guys move the coffee maker?"

"Over there," MIAG guy says, then hesitantly adds, "It is a pleasure to make an initial impression of you."

"And I you." I give him my brightest megawatt smile.

He blushes green. "Let me know if you need any help."

I'm not used to having fans anymore. Pero it's nice to have help – and company – while cooking. It's also nice to have someone tall enough to mix things easily at these oversized counters. We get the cookies mixed and baking in record time. And while they are in the oven, I help these hombres prepare lunch.

One of the Zantites catches me looking at the labels on a stack of boxes. "That's for the special dinner tomorrow night. They even sent us a setup for doing fancy stuff with edible nanites, but none of us has ever worked with it before."

He points to a corner counter where a sleek laptop sits closed. The nanites and attendant gear are in the box beside it.

"Any of you have an aptitude for both coding and art?" Porque, if not, they're in trouble. Working with nanites isn't easy. And on this vessel, a mistake that makes your soup tornado fly apart at the guests is more than a failtastic grade – it could merit muerte.

"I code," the one wearing the bracelet says.

Pero none of them are into art. And I don't have time to help them. Not that I'm eager to deal with the nanites again. No y nunca. I know it's illogical. The microbots aren't the reason mal things happen. And still, I shudder just imagining opening those vials.

I – no sé –something's wrong. Like more than just my dread about the nanites. I don't know how to place it. I bring a hand to my chest, where my heart hammers in fear. After a few moments, the feeling passes. I really have to get a grip about these nanites. Only first I have to get out of this room.

I suggest to the one who codes, "You should pull up some holotorials of effects other people have done. Sometimes they post the whole program open-source."

He opens up the laptop. "That's a great idea!"

Chestla calls my sublingual. I hope she wants me to come see some exciting breakthrough in the lab. Pero no y no. She sounds upset. *Bo, your phone just popped up on my tracking software. It's on this ship.*

My chest goes frío. *Que? How?*

I don't know. Just be careful. Someone hostile to you could be aboard this ship.

You mean a stowaway? I stowed away on this very ship, when I'd been fleeing the Galactacops. It's not a good idea. Zantites eat stowaways. I'd wound up with Crosskiss's teeth scraping down my back, a breath away from severing my spine.

Bo, this is serious. Chestla's growl echoes through mi cabeza.

I'll be careful, chica. I'm taking coffee to the conference room, and then I will join you in the lab.

I get the cookies out of the oversized ovens and pile them on a plate. Crosskiss still hasn't showed up to claim his portion, so I put some aside, with instructions to the galley crew to save them for him. Then I put the plate on a tray and add the carafe of coffee and some Zantite-sized mugs.

The ship's hallways are usually busy, pero the conference room is in an area that doesn't get frequent use. I'm just glad it's in the opposite direction from the room with the drain, which is set aside for executions and duels. If they'd taken Leron there, I wouldn't have much hope for him.

Thinking about all the blood that's been washed down that drain, and how close mine had come to joining it, mi corazón hammers again. Then I wonder. My body is overreacting. Could it be the heart bond? Trying not to panic, I call Brill on my sublingual. He doesn't answer.

Then I feel normal again, and I feel silly. Though I can't quite calm my worry por mi vida.

The carpet in this hallway seems even thicker than in the others, and the wall has been painted gold, with silver and black accents. Crosskiss is treating these executioners like dignitaries. I will have to thank him later. Spoiling him with good food for six months isn't so high of a price to pay.

An odd smell, maybe a leak in the wastewater recycling system, wrinkles my nose. Pauf! At the next intersection, the smell seems stronger. Someone grabs at me from around the corner. A strong hand clamps around my upper arm. I push my tray into his face and wrench away. That's going to bruise. "Oi!"

"Hell, Bodacious," Jack splutters, as he bats away the tray, mugs, and crumbling cookies.

I quickstep backward and turn to run.

Jack says, "Stop!" so coldly that I glance back. He's leveling a weapon at me, and not his usual vapgun. He fires, and suddenly I can't move. I fall, unable to even brace myself on the way down. Jack leans over me. Every time I've faced him before, someone was there to protect me. He's a lot more menacing when I'm alone and helpless. I try to scream for help. All that comes out is un minúsculo squeak. Still. I managed to make a noise. My vocal cords aren't entirely paralyzed, and I can blink.

Aunque, I can't access my sublingual.

"Can you stop freaking out?" Jack grabs my shirt collar and drags me into the side hall. "You'll be able to move again in a few minutes. Just in time to commit murder."

Eh? Jack had wanted to take me back to Zant. This ship is heading in the opposite direction. How have I played into his plan?

Jack drags me through a wide golden door into a room with a double-high ceiling and a lavish printed rug. Everything is black, edged with gold – even the furniture. It looks like a formal living room for Zantite royalty. Brill is sitting against the wall. Mi vida! He's vivo, doesn't look in distress, pero he doesn't move. Jack must have shot Brill with the paralyzing gun también.

My tongue is loosening up a little. "What do you want with Brill?"

Jack smirks. "You really want to know?"

I probably don't. How long will it be before Brill can move? I can't fight Jack by myself, and who else will rescue me? "I thought you just needed me, to start your war."

Jack says, "The war is just a catalyst to expose all the secrets, all the crimes, and make Earth pay."

"For sending your grandparents to Greftash?"

He studies me. "For being a total jerk to all the little planets in the galaxy." So no y no, he can't admit that this is a personal vendetta. "Once you kill a Zantite royal, Garfex will be so vengeance blind, the attack on Earth won't just be an invasion. It will be a total massacre. Especially with Frank on board to imply that HGB was behind the assassination."

The only royal Zantite on the *Layla's Pride* is Crosskiss. Whom I couldn't kill, even if I tried. I *did* try, once. In a moment of desperation, I took Crosskiss's vapgun from him and shot him with it. I'd just made the nine-foot-tall Zantite mad.

Jack's need to make Earth pay has him grasping at straws – just like me taking that microdot. I'm seeing too many painful likematches between myself and Jack. I understand what Frank meant, about me needing another goal than justicia, something to move towards instead of just things to fight. If I don't, I could wind up as bitterly vengezentful as Jack is.

"Killing Earth won't make you feel better," I say, frustrated that I still can't move. "Let me talk to Janvier. See if he can bring you and your people home. We can share the planet."

Jack laughs. "You're kidding, right? We're not looking for a kumbaya moment. We want our birthright. If we'd had charge of Earth, we wouldn't have squandered everything in a senseless fight over chocolate. New Greftash can be so much more than Earth ever was."

"Squandered what, mijo?"

"The Sol system." He gives me a look like, *duh*. "Why fight the survivors of the invasion of Earth when we can trade with the Krom for the technology to terraform Mars? We'll put an observation port on Pluto and keep invaders from getting a foothold in the solar system. Lease rights to people who have the tech for mining on Jupiter. Do what the Earthlings would have done if they hadn't been so busy closing themselves off to protect chocolate."

"Why would you inherit the solar system if Earth dies?" I ask.

Jack looks less certain. "Our lawyers have looked into it."

I blink. Jack may be a kek, pero maybe the people who sent him aren't. It could be a valid threat.

I try to move my arm, manage to lift my fingers. Bien. I need to keep Jack talking long enough for me to recover. "How did you even get here? You were still prison bound when we left."

"I stole a faster ship. And a few interesting weapons. And then I snuck in through this ship's un-bionetted waste system." Which explains the smell. "And don't look to loverboy to help you. Krom are a lot more susceptible to paralysis."

Mi corazón se enfría. Jack pulls me into a little side room, shielded from view of the doorway. Away from Brill. Jack reaches into a bag slung over his shoulder and withdraws four syringes filled with murky liquid shot through with swirling gold. He puts one in his pocket.

I gasp with fear and longing. The Invincible Heart.

My fingers twitch, and my arm leaves the rug. I'm still mostly paralyzed, or I'd grab a syringe. Pero I swore to Mertex, as he was dying, and to Brill and to mi mamá that I would never take it again.

"Three should be enough to overdose you, without killing you immediately," Jack says. "The fourth dose is for Brill, in case you need incentive. I took these from the med office, after I killed some kid assistant and broke a few things. Just like a junkie looking for a fix."

I groan. I met the kid Jack is talking about, last time I was on this ship. "Poor Quayex."

"Don't you mean poor Bo? You always complain that I'm being unfair to you. But you got four of my men killed. So now, *this* is justice." Jack kneels next to me. "I just need you to kill one Zantite royal. If you don't do it in the rage haze that comes with the overdose, I'll torture Brill. With that new heart bond of yours, it should drive you over the edge. Of course, if you cooperate, things will go easier for your boyfriend." Though for his plan to work, he still needs to kill Brill.

"How–" I mean, what could Jack know about Krom heart bonds?

"I bugged Gavin, when he was taking me to the Galactacops. I wanted to blackmail him into getting me terraforming equipment. Sadly, Brill and Gavin didn't say anything in the recording solid enough to use." Jack moves out of sight. "I've heard rumors of such bonds. Fascinating. Brill can't move. I could easily inject him with the IH at any point. This vein in his neck would make death pretty much immediate."

I get the impression Jack is bending down, touching Brill's skin.

My heartbeat pounds in my ears, and suddenly sweat beads on my arms. Y sí, I'm sharing mi vida's fear. It's a visceral threat. IH makes a Krom's heart more or less explode.

"Leave him alone, por favor! There's no need to scare him like that."

Why can't Brill speak for himself?

"This is so much more effective than threatening to kill Gavin. You'd actually feel Brill's heart explode." Jack moves back to me. The syringe isn't sticking out of his pocket anymore. He must have left it where Brill can see it. "I'll give you a gun with one bullet to shoot Queen Layla, if you want her to die fast and easy, but if you try to use it on me, I'll push the plunger on your Krom before I hit the ground."

I gasp. "Layla's here?"

If I killed the crown prince, that would angerate Garfex. Pero what he'd do to my planet if I killed his beloved wife … the cinders of Earth wouldn't cool for decades.

CHAPTER FORTY-THREE

"The Queen's visiting her son. There's supposed to be a special dinner and everything. Ironic, isn't it? You ran to the very place I planned to take you." Jack puts something in my mouth that tastes like bitter peppermint, and suddenly I can't talk. He looks relieved. "You sent Layla a message that you wanted to speak with her privately, the minute you got on board. She will be coming to meet you soon." He takes my phone out of his pocket and waves it at me. "I took a closer look at this, after both your boyfriends scoured my ship for it. I found the microdot, and I *will* use this information in Greftash's case against Earth. I assume that makes you happy at least. Too bad you won't be there to watch everyone associated with HGB get shaved."

I jerk away from Jack and roll onto my side. He's been monologuing so long that whatever he shot me with is wearing off. Bien. I try to get up off the floor. I make it to a crawling position. I still don't have the strength to fight Jack when he flips me over and pins my arm. He uncaps the first syringe and slides the needle into my vein. I watch in mute horror as the liquid disappears. I've wanted this, so badly. Even though it will kill me.

"This should take, what, twenty minutes or so to take effect? The full load of it should hit you like a truck." He turns to retrieve the next syringe. Oye! No. This cannot be the pointless, kalltet way I die. Riding the adrenaline that my own body has dumped into my system, I knee him hard in the groin. Groaning, he falls onto his backside, releasing me. I scramble away from him, and get to my shaky, rubbery feet.

He follows, still wincing.

I still can't make a sound. Moving like an awkward duckling, I flail over to the remaining two syringes of IH and scoop them off the floor.

Jack's brown eyes go wide. "You wouldn't."

I'm holding the syringes like I'm going to stab him in the face. Sthesh. I wouldn't curse him with an addiction like mine. I can't say that, though. I can't say anything. I drop the vials to the rug and stomp on them, breaking the glass with my boot.

Jack grabs for me again. I elbow him away, a move I saw Chestla practice a dozen times while sparring with Brill. I'm shocked that it works. It didn't when she made me try it on her.

The door to the main room opens and closes. I don't take my focus off Jack. It must be Layla, coming in for our meeting.

"That door locked behind her," Jack whispers. He smiles, because I can't say a word to warn her. "She'll just have to wait for you to be ready."

No y no! I will not murder anyone. My legacy will not be the destruction of my people in retribution. And mi vida cannot die in this room, as a collateral victim – chosen because of our heart bond.

I rush Jack, feeling stronger, more in control, even though I just took the IH. It must have reawakened what was already in my blood, completing it, making me ready to run, fight and scream without the time it took to build the first time I was injected. Jack goes flying, pero then he's back on his feet, swinging at me. We're fighting and some of what Chestla taught me clicks into place.

Ciertamente, we make enough noise to warn Layla. Ciertamente, she'll save me.

Pero no one tries to stop this fight.

Jack's more experienced with his fists, and he no longer seems to care if he marks me, which could ruin his illusion. He punches me hard in my weak shoulder and I crumple. On my way down, I grab the gun he used to paralyze me. I shoot him and he thuds to the floor, his cabeza hitting the carpet. His mano flops to the hard surface in the anteroom threshold, making a thwapping noise.

General Crosskiss leans at the doorway to the anteroom, arms crossed, just watching.

I make a gesture like *Seriously, you couldn't have helped me?*

Crosskiss pushes away from the wall. He holds the still-capped syringe of IH. "My culture considers it insulting to step into the middle of a friend's duel, especially when said friend has it handily in control."

Wait. Did Crosskiss just give me a compliment? And call me his friend? I might be speechless, even if Jack hadn't rendered me mute.

Crosskiss glares down at Jack, who is still flat on the floor. He asks in gravely Universal, "How long until Bo can speak again?"

Jack tries to talk, manages a few squeaks and half words. Finally he says, "Ten, twelve minutes tops." And then after a few more tries, "There should be no lasting damage."

I get to my feet and step shakily over to Brill, who still hasn't moved. Mi vida is breathing and otherwise looks fine.

"You are a stowaway aboard a Zantite vessel carrying members of the royal family and you have assaulted an adjunct member of my crew. Have you any complaints?" Crosskiss leans down, hands on his knees, to get a closer look at Jack. He scrunches up his nose at the unpleasant smell. "We'll get you washed up first, of course."

I gasp in a breath. Crosskiss just announced his intent to execute Jack.

If the charges are incorrect, Jack is supposed to offer a valid complaint. Otherwise, he'll die.

Jack doesn't get it. He probably has no experience with Zantite formalistic language. "About having a shower? No complaints here. This ship reeks."

He really is a kek. Pero I need him vivo, at least long enough to find out what his planet's plans are. I step in front of Crosskiss waving my arms in a frantic *No* gesture. Crosskiss purses his thick rubbery lips. We stand there, unable to communicate for a couple of minutes.

I gesture for Crosskiss's handheld, and when he gives it to me, I type, *This man is part of a conspiracy to use me to get your father to obliterate my people instead of just invade them. Frank will want to question him first. Please.*

If Jack survives that, Crosskiss might still be required to take a bite out of him. I bet the pirate'd give the Zantite a stomachache.

Crosskiss looks troubled. "It is unusual for outsiders to be involved in our interrogations." Before he can decide whether Frank should be allowed into the room with the drain, the door rattles.

Layla, obviamente. I cross the room to let her in.

Layla wears a sparkling long tunic over flowing pants and has a silver circlet on her bald head. She takes in my torn, disheveled clothing. "Rough flight?"

I laugh, pero no sound comes out. I still have Crosskiss's handheld. I type, *You have no idea. I am pleased to make a new impression of you and am grateful for all the attempts you have made to help my planet.*

"And I likewise," Layla says, looking down at the phone. Her rubbery brow furrows. "What conspiracy?"

I left several spaces after what I typed to Crosskiss, but she must have scrolled up.

I point over to where Crosskiss stands over Jack. I take the handheld back and type, *Jack has escaped from the police several times. Keep a careful eye on him.*

"An eye and a tooth," Layla says, and it feels like part of the Zantite formalistic language. I hope she means it.

I follow Layla to where Jack lays. Crosskiss brightens up. "Mother! As Queen you outrank me. Which means this stowaway is your responsibility."

They've switched to speaking Zantite.

Layla scrunches her flattish nose in distaste. "A responsibility I intend to escape. He looks downright toxic."

"Maybe we can talk Sawyer into shooting him during the interrogation," Crosskiss says thoughtfully as Layla hands him his phone.

I lean down and take my handheld from Jack's his pocket. I open the case, and the microdot is nestled inside, safe and sound. I let out a silent breath of relief. Uf. I show Brill the phone. He gives me a thumbs up, though he still can't lift his hand.

Jack turns his cabeza towards me, finally looking a bit troubled. He asks in English, "What are they talking about?"

My voice is coming back. It's cracked and papery as I say, "Zantites eat stowaways. They're arguing over which one has to execute you. They both think you'd taste awful."

Jack goes pale. "I thought that was a myth."

So did I, once upon a time. "I suggest you offer to trade Frank information for your life. Though no sé if the Zantites will go for that." I step towards Crosskiss.

Crosskiss looks at the syringes I smashed on the rug. "Leron's examination didn't take long. The telepath fitted him with permanent studs through the tops of his ears that give him limited control over what the Mindhuggers can do to his mind. But the Mindhuggers will still know what he's thinking and what he's doing – and he will know the hive mind. So it makes for checks and balances, as long as Murry can't afford to lose a single hug. It was quite fascinating, and only when it was over did I realize you never showed up with the coffee. Imagine my surprise when I found a carafe leaking all over the hallway."

Crosskiss is being so rational, it's hard to believe how often his face has loomed in my nightmares. I ask hesitantly, "Are we friends now?"

"I'm as surprised as you." Crosskiss grins. "But like I said, once a conflict is resolved, there's no reason to hold a grudge." He looks at the syringe in his hand. "Many of my men admire you for taking the Invincible Heart. I've come to admire you for surviving – and becoming stronger from the experience. The girl I nearly executed would have just frozen and let this pirate kill her."

I blink, unsure what to think. Finally, I say, "I'm sorry about that time I shot you."

Crosskiss's smile gets grande. "I've wondered whether you would have done that without the influence of the Invincible Heart. All of your talk about respecting the life of others, versus the instinct to personally survive."

I've wondered the same thing. "I'm sure the IH had something to do with it, no?"

"Are you high on it right now?"

I look at my arm, with the tiny mark from Jack's needle.

Crosskiss follows my gaze. "I will warn my crew to be cautious."

CHAPTER FORTY-FOUR

As soon as my sublingual is working, I call Frank. *Where are you viejo? I need to give you something.*

I don't want to hold onto this microdot any longer than necessary.

Frank's sigh rolls through mi cabeza. *I'm in the medical bay, trying to convince a half dozen Zantite soldiers that Ball, Watae and Nellet had nothing to do with murdering one of their crewmen.*

Tell them to call Crosskiss, I bubblechatter. Brill and I are still in the room where I fought Jack. The two Zantite royals took Jack with them when they left – and for once, Jack had looked frightened. *Crosskiss has Jack in custody. The kek did it to get syringes of IH.*

Why am I not surprised? After a beat, Frank says, *Wait. Is the thing you have to give me what I hope?*

Sí, y I need to get it out of my hands before anything else happens to it.

Frank chatters, *My leaving would not be advisable at the moment. Find someone to escort you down here.*

I know how to get there, viejo. I don't need an escort. I hear an edge of irritation creep into my bubblechatter. It's the IH talking. I take a deep breath. Frank has every reason to be concerned for me. I was just assaulted in the hallway. *Lo siento. I'll bring Brill, right?*

Brill seems fully recovered from the paralysis gun and has been texting feverishly, trying to get more information on Jack, while pacing at near-blur speeds.

As we walk down to the Doc's office, Brill slides his hand into mine. He looks uncertain, like I might reject his touch.

"I felt your fear," I tell him. "When Jack threatened to dose you with the Invincible Heart. Que no when Frank was about to shoot you?"

His eyes go bright pink. "Because I wasn't as scared. I'd made my peace with not walking out of the HGB compound, and I knew Frank would look out for you. But if Jack killed me here, I couldn't have done anything to save you. Not that I did anything anyway." His gaze moves ahead, though his hand still clasps mine. "Plus, after what happened on Zant, the thought of dying from the Invincible Heart terrifies me. You'll only notice the bond when my heart reaction is significantly different than yours – and you're not that scared of the IH. I wish you were."

"Maybe Crosskiss is right." I tell him. "Maybe I'm no longer the girl who needs saving all the time. And more than matching lifespans or biology, that makes our relationship fair."

"I've never thought of you as that girl. You've saved my life multiple times. Gracias por this one." His eyes are solid gold. "But now you know what I meant. A bond is a risk and a responsibility."

"And a privilege, mi vida."

He looks so pleased, I stop him and kiss him.

We finally break the kiss and get to the Doc's office. The door has been busted off its hinges. Inside, Nellet and Watae sit in the waiting area, looking nervous, holding hands. Nellet has her shoulders hunched up against her ears, and Watae's body language is closed in. I feel bad for assuming Watae didn't try to get back to the bay and support Leron.

Frank stands outside, talking to a half dozen Zantites soldiers.

I don't see Ball. If something's happened to him, it will break Chestla. She needs to decide about this love triangle she's landed in. Pero not that way.

I rush to Frank, dragging Brill along. "What happened? Where's Ball?"

Frank glances into the office, towards a closed door behind which the Doc performs surgeries – and, in a smaller antechamber, prepares bodies – or parts of bodies – to be sent home. Doc's late assistant Quayex is probably in there, right now.

"Don't worry, Bodacious. The Duracell's not dead," Frank says. "Dr Tassiks offered to perform a procedure used on Zantite soldiers to help regain muscle function after battle injuries. He says he's studied enough Evevron physiology during the wars that he believes it will work. If Ball's body rejects it, though, he could wind up paralyzed."

"Oi! Ball's only half Evevron," I say. "Why would he take that kind of risk?"

"I think he did it to prove he trusts his former enemies. It diffused the tense situation," Frank says.

Brill says, "Or maybe he thinks he needs to be physically sound to win Chestla."

"Either way, it'll take a while." Frank squares his shoulders. "Now that this is under control, I need to borrow Bo for a minute."

Brill squeezes my hand and lets go. I follow Frank to an oversized supply closet filled with boxes of bright yellow bandages, sterile gloves and other things needed to keep a medical bay running. We easily have enough room to step inside.

I take out my phone and start to open the case.

"Wait," Frank says.

I blink up at him. "Que?"

"I just – Dash told me in detail about what all is on this dot. It has kill lists – everything I and the other operatives have done. You finally have proof HGB ordered your father's execution and that I carried it out. With all these other secrets coming out – you could delete your mother's information off here, so there's no official connection between HGB's involvement in her husband's death and her rise to stardom – I mean, this dot is your last chance to go to the Courts."

I feel my lips purse together. "Why are you offering that? Do you feel you deserve to die for what you've done?"

"What? Of course not." Now Frank's the one blinking at me. "I hope you will give me the dot. And that you will give your blessing for me to marry your mother and have a place in your life. But I don't want you to feel like I've ever used or coerced you."

I raise my chin. "And if I don't give you the dot? Won't there be consequences?"

"I won't hurt you." Then Frank's eyes go cold. "Though I can't say the same for whoever might receive this information from you. Or for the HGB operatives heading for this ship."

I laugh. I can't help it. Frank looks so much like a papá, frustangerated at the thought somebody might threaten his daughter –un papá with the cold eyes of a man who will kill to protect his daughter.

"You love me," I say, emotimazement thick in my voice.

"Of course I do," Frank says gruffly. "I told you a long time ago, I've fallen in love with your family, even though, given how I came into contact with all of you, I shouldn't be part of it. I don't expect you to love me in return."

My heart squeezes, and my hand trembles. I'd thought he meant he loved Mamá y la niñas. The ones who'd let him get close.

Frank loves me, and I hold his life in my hands, as surely as if this microdot was his still-beating heart. Chocolate and blood and life, and cacao pods, like Janvier said. How could I withhold Frank's chance to live?

I hold out the phone case. "I don't want to see everything crumble, with nada in its wake but more war and pain. I want change for my world, pero not like that. Jack showed me that."

"Jack?" Frank cocks an eyebrow. He takes the dot from my phone case and folds it into a proper blue plastic case.

I stuff the phone in my pocket and sweep a box of bandages off the shelf. "He's the descendant of a prisoner who got sent to Greftash. Jack wanted to take the microdot to the Courts to prove that HGB morally forfeited Earth's rights to our own solar system. Had I brought this to the Galactics, he would have swooped in and said I made the case for his claim." My hands crush the bandage box. I throw it onto the floor. Realizing what I've done, I take a breath. The IH has me so mad at Jack, I just want to smash everything. I force myself to sound calm. "He thought I would be fizzbounced to watch HGB collectively face the shave. Earth turned its back on Jack, and he would love to see it destroyed, innocent people and all. Looking at his face, I saw how feo that is." I shudder. "Crosskiss is keeping him alive so you can interrogate him."

Ignoring the box I crushed, Frank turns the case over in his hands. "So that's it? I can't imagine you're giving up on trying to change the status quo. You don't want to see Janvier get shaved. But Shelly asked you to help take HGB in a new direction, and you said no to that too." Frank slips the case into his pocket. "What *do* you want for your world?"

I consider the question. "No sé. I don't really fit on Earth anymore. If I showed my face in the streets, people would kill me. I just want everyone survive this invasion."

"Then you'll hide out on this spacecraft for a while, then run away back to Larksis?"

My shoulders stiffen, making the old gunshot ache. "That's not running away. They've offered me a teaching position, as soon as I graduate."

"So graduate."

I glare at Frank, and he glares right back.

"What are you afraid of?" he demands.

"That the future I thought I wanted might not make me happy." I didn't mean to say it out loud. Pero once I do, I can't stop. "If I'm stuck on Larksis, and Brill's off having adventures, and you and Mamá are back on Earth, then I'll be stuck on the sidelines of my own life. I've spent so much time at school, and I love teaching others about food. And it's selfish to worry about whether I'd be bored with the future I've worked towards, or if

I'll be too embarrassed to admit to the whole galaxy that I wasted my time. Eso es when mi hermano y mi abuelo could be muerto before the day is out."

"Stop worrying about what people think," Frank grumbles. "Worry about whether the life you choose gives you the joy and strength to withstand taking the IH treatments indefinitely."

He's right. I can't deny myself un futuro feliz, just because I'm worried about the polls. All that matters is that I take responsibility for my actions, because no matter what I do, some people will criticize. Frank wraps me in a hug. I am so startled, I stand there, stiff as a wall. Frank rubs my back. "It's okay, kiddo. We'll figure this out."

If I accept this comfort, it's a turning point between us, and I have no right to complain if he proposes to mi mamá.

I return the hug, as fiercely as anything else I've done under the influence of the IH.

After a moment, Frank and I let go. I feel fragile and hopeful, the drug magnifying that emotion too. "Te quiero, viejo." *I love you, old man.*

Sudden, unexpected tears glitter in Frank's eyes. He blinks them back and opens the closet door. "I'll make arrangements to return this dot to Janvier. Be cautious – the other operatives will have figured out where we were headed. If that idiot Jack can sneak aboard this ship, my colleagues will have little trouble."

Brill stands just outside the door. "Don't worry, Mr. Sawyer. If you believe there's a threat, I won't let her out of my sight."

I wrap an arm around mi vida. "Por favor, let's go to the lab. I want to help."

Of course, that means fetching coffee, since I know nada about cryogenics technology. Pero I can't stand around doing nada, not with the IH singing in my blood.

I dread the crash, the fall back into withdrawal.

Brill glances towards the Doc's office. Watae and Nellet stand outside the waiting room, talking with the Zantite soldiers. Watae does a cartwheel, illustrating a story he's telling, and they all laugh. Brill's eyes shift towards blue. "Anything you need, Babe."

In the lab, Eugene, Chestla and Leron huddle around a small glass box holding a single cacao bean. No sé what they expect to happen.

Four Zantites sitting in giant-sized chairs monitor a dozen oversized displays. One stands and flips a switch in the wall. Green light flashes inside the box. At first, nada happens. Then the cacao bean crinkles, wrinkles and turns mushy.

The researchers let out a collective groan of dismay.

As Eugene and Chestla reach to open the box and replace the bean, their hands touch. Chestla seems in no hurry to move it. She takes his mano in hers and squeezes. Eugene blushes crimson.

"How's it going?" Brill asks.

They all jerk upright and look towards the door – except Chestla, who must have been keeping a better eye on her surroundings.

Chestla addresses me instead of Brill. "I'm sorry, cesuda ma. The barrier between death and life remains unbroken. We must think of alternatives to present to the Zantites before the invasion begins."

"But it feels like we're so close," Eugene protests. "If they gave us more time, we could figure it out."

Leron says, "The Zantites won't want the carob Murry brought. Now that the spuck is dead, nobody wants it."

Amid a grumble of assent, one of the Zantites says, "The spuck made us taste that stuff. It was awful."

"Garfex wants a tree," I point out. "I doubt he'll settle for a box of bars anyway."

"What if we come up with a synthetic chocolate that's easy to mass produce? Then you don't need a tree." Leron taps his chin. "Murry spent so much time obsessing over Serum Green that he keeps coming back to that as a possible solution. He's still terrified of it, since it prevents his expansion, but he needed to understand it. It contains some of the same base chemicals as HGB Dark."

I step forward. "I tried creating synthetic chocolate for a homework assignment in culinary school. It never came out right. Pero maybe with your help?"

Leron backs away from me. "Serum Green is hazardous to my health. If the parasite in my head dies, so do I."

"I'll help you, Babe," Brill says. "If we have questions, we can call the lab."

"I'll get you some samples of the serum." Eugene hurries towards the door. "They're still on board the transport."

Leron looks at Eugene reproachfully. "Murry believes you brought that box as a threat to keep the spuck under control."

Eugene's wide eyes look shocked, and holds up a hand. "Tell Murry I'm sorry for giving him the wrong impression. When we raided HGB for the cacao beans, I just picked up everything related to chocolate."

"I'll pass that along." Leron already sounds tired of being Murry's go-between. I doubt, though, that he will regret the decision. No y no. The task might be daunting, pero at least he is alive to do it. "Now, Murry's glad we have the Serum Green, just in case this works."

We follow Eugene into the hall.

His world is about to be invaded, pero Eugene can't stop smiling. "Did you two see the look Chestla gave me as we were leaving? We've really bonded over this project. If we can break this problem, it will be the perfect moment to ask her out."

"Su," Brill says. "Won't it be the perfect moment to rush to save your home planet?"

Eugene looks confused. "Isn't that somebody else's job?"

Brill's eyes tint violet. "Fair enough."

Ay-ay-ay! Here's Eugene trying to prove he's intellectually the man for Chestla, while Ball is in the Doc's office trying to become physically man enough. I don't know which guy to root for. I trust that Chestla will choose the one who will make her happy. Pero Eugene has less history with Chestla, and is also shy and awkward. It wouldn't hurt to give him a little advice.

"Maybe you shouldn't wait for the perfect moment, mijo," I say. Porque if that happens after Ball returns from a successful treatment, it could be too late. "Just be honest. Tell her how you feel and what you want from a relationship. She won't get subtle."

Just like Eugene doesn't get subtlety. Which is why they might be a good match.

Brill's eyes remain violet. I doubt he believes Eugene has a chance. He might be right. Pero Eugene deserves to know he tried.

When we reach the transport, Eugene unlocks it. The ship is stuffed so full of carob – some boxes broken open, their silver interior wrappers tossed everywhere – that it's hard to imagine where they'd put the spuck. I pick up a bar. Even the raw silver-toned paper looks more attractive than the garish pink wrappers. I'm glad Janvier stopped production before this lot got double-wrapped.

Eugene threads through the boxes to an area where he stored what little gear he could gather since the fire. He brings back a small box with a dozen vials of Serum Green.

I've always considered Serum Green as peligroso. This liquid holds so many secrets, including the original reason for the invasion of my planet.

Reluctantly, I take the box. My handheld buzzes in my pocket. I pass the box to Brill and pull out my phone. Jack must have turned the alerts back on for the Spice Road News App. Brill's phone alerts him too, and balancing the box in one hand, he pulls his out.

Blizzard and Feddoink appear in the holofield. The headline reads, *Preliminaries begin for the Invasion of Earth. Planetary weapons systems knocked out of orbit. Deaths and injuries reported.*

I stuff the phone back in my pocket. I don't need to see visuals of the destruction.

My handheld buzzes again. It's mi hermano Mario. Brill's still watching the FeedCast of the destruction when I answer.

"Hola Pequeña," Mario says. "I just got off the phone with Mamá. I wanted to let everybody know we're okay." His smile is strained, though, and behind him, flames and smoke billow from his casa. In the capture field behind Mario, mi abuelo faces away from me. Abuelo, in a bathrobe and slippers and, stares at el fuego. He and Mario must have been playing a game to pass the time while waiting for Earth's inevitable destruction. Mario says, "HGB will surrender. They must know now we can't win, no?"

Mi hermano is braver than I ever gave him credit for. He doesn't believe any more than I that HGB will surrender. I should have trusted him with more information. I should have spent more time with him.

Brill's watching holo of Earth's fleet of starships scrambling in the wake of the energy pulse that attacked Earth, while the Zantite warships were still hours away. The voiceover helpfully notes that these ships have shielding against pulse weapons, so they're still flying to face the Zantites. Some are drones. Pero not all of them. People are going to die out there.

Tears brush my cheeks. "Muchas gracias por helping Abuelo through this."

"De nada." Mario glances at Abuelo. "He's always been the strong one. Remember when we went camping as niños, ? He sang to us and told us stories. Now, he's falling apart. What can I do?"

My heart hurts, and the IH amplifying my frustangeration makes me want to fling my handheld. Why didn't mi familia get offplanet sooner? Why weren't there enough ships to evacuate everyone? That fleet scrambling into the sky could have taken thousands more people away from the danger. I kick the nearest box of HGB New. It doesn't help.

"Now you have to be the strong one," I tell Mario. "We're trying to appease the Zantites. Don't give up hope."

"Then I should let you get back to work." He manages another worried smile.

"Tell abuelo I love him." I blow un beso at the phone.

Mario mimes catching it. "Te quieros también, Pequeña." *We love you too.*

When I hang up, Brill's eyes are shining mahogany. "I didn't realize those two were still on Earth."

"It doesn't matter whose familia we're talking about," I say bitterly. "Innocent people will die. We have to stop the invasion."

I grab the box of Serum Green away from him and stalk off of the transport.

CHAPTER FORTY-FIVE

Brill follows, pero Eugene wants to grab a few more things. As Brill and I walk across the docking bay, shouting erupts from inside the transport. Eugene flies out, cradling a box full of test tubes, and lands on his backside. Miraculously, nothing breaks.

The cargo ship's door slams shut.

"It's that pirate again," Eugene says, setting the box on the floor.

En serio? How did Jack get away from Crosskiss and evade the docking bay guards? Y how did he get around behind us without us noticing?

Eugene adds, "He thinks we're carrying chocolate."

"Did you tell him otherwise?" Brill asks.

"I didn't get a chance."

The transport fires up.

"Get out of the way!" Brill blazebangs over and pulls Eugene to safety.

Jack maneuvers the hijacked ship towards the airlock. He doesn't have clearance to leave. It doesn't look like he cares. If he tries to bust through to open space, we're in serious trouble. He probably wouldn't make it, definitely not without damaging the transport. Pero he's desperate enough to try.

Rather than risk damage to the airlock, the panicked Zantite guard standing between us and the main portion of the ship frantically punches clearance codes to open the lock doors.

We watch the ship leave. Brill's eyes are lavender as he hands Eugene his test tubes.

I ask, "Que, mi vida?"

"If Jack thinks that payload is chocolate, and he's alone with no crew to help defend it, he'll need to turn the cargo into cash and grab a less conspicuous ship. Uan, whoever he sets up a buy with will be ita ita mad when they find out it's carob."

Eugene says, "Surely he will examine the merchandise first."

I laugh. "Not necessarily. This is Jack we're talking about."

Eugene hurries towards the lab, while Brill and I head for the galley.

Before we even reach the ship proper, a sleepy-eyed Gavin calls Brill's handheld. Gavin's hair pokes up on one side. "You su's be careful. Jack Wolfe escaped the police and is in the area. He just listed a massive shipment of chocolate as a one-hour auction. Every alert on my phone went off."

I can't help but laugh.

Gavin blinks. "What's so funny?"

I tell him, "We already fought Jack, captured him, turned him over to the Zantites, and watched him escape again. While you were asleep."

"He took the transport with Murry's carob," Brill says. "He's selling fake chocolate."

Gavin's irises dip to black. "The joke may be on him. One of the bid signatures is from the *Onyx Shadow*. They look pretty determined to win."

That ship's name should terrify me, pero the IH blunts it. Grundt, the captain of the *Onyx Shadow*, shot Brill in the chest because he thought we tried to steal from him. If mi vida hadn't been wearing body armor, he wouldn't have survived. While Brill's been "dead," he's been off Grundt's radar. Pero now that he's vivo again, Grundt might still want to settle the score.

"Shouldn't we warn Jack?" I ask. "Those muchachos will kill him."

Both Krom look at me like I've gone loca. Then Brill sighs. "I'll call him."

When Brill dials, Jack refuses the call.

"We could contact Grundt and warn him to withdraw his bid," I say.

Brill's irises go black, and he looks like he's going to say no. Pero, he makes eye contact with me and hesitates. He knows how much I need him to be the kind of guy who shows mercy. Finally he says, "Haza. Grundt will find out I'm vivo soon anyway. If he doesn't already know. I might as well tell him myself."

It takes a few minutes for Brill to secure Grundt's contact information. Then Grundt's gray, granite-like face appears in the holofield.

Anxiety fills my chest. He es muy, muy peligroso.

"Brill Cray. Give me a reason not to rip your heart out and crush it."

"Because this is a phone connection?" Brill tries for levity. Grundt's not having it. Brill goes somber, lets the color of fear show in his eyes. "Maybe because I'm calling to save you trouble. The lot you're bidding on – Jack stole an HGB transport, uan he thinks what he's selling is chocolate, but it's not. It's HGB's new chocolate substitute. Withdraw your bid and let some other su's deal with it."

Grundt studies mi vida. "Is this a trick, Cray?"

"Why would I want you any madder at me than you already are? Check the other bid signatures. None of them are mine."

Grundt freezes his end of the holo, either checking on Brill's story or consulting with his crew. Dios mio, his paused expression is muy feo. The holo jumps, with Grundt in un place completamente diferente. "I don't think we'll withdraw that bid. Jack has caused a lot of trouble with this pirate coalition he's been building. It's time we pay the Commodore a little visit anyway." He says the word *commodore* muy muy sarcastically.

Brill sighs. "So I put myself back on your radar for no reason."

Grundt laughs. "No, I appreciate the heads up. Let's say I won't go out of my way to hunt you down and kill you, as long as you don't dig into any more of my secrets." Brill shifts and Grundt glances towards me at the capture fields' edge. "Miss Benitez. Many condolences on your planet."

I smile sadly. "We haven't crashbanged it yet, no?"

Leaving Brill talking to Grundt, I head towards the galley. Guilt gnaws at me. The green serum in the box may chemically likematch chocolate, but really, how does what I hope to do differ from HGB's attempt to sell people carob?

Bien. There's one big difference. The Serum Green mocklate is a stopgap, something that tastes like real chocolate, to offer Crosskiss, so he will give Eugene and the others more time to work on the real problem.

Krom-quick, Brill catches up to me. "You were right, Babe. Kindness can be paid forward too."

It's nice for once to help Brill put his life in *less* danger.

When we reach the galley, I say, "We need a vegetable fat that is solid at room temperature. And something to give a bit of nutty oomph. And some coffee and a little wine."

"Wal, mi corazón." Brill heads to the pantry.

I set up a workstation. The galley crew give me a wider berth. I guess Crosskiss told them I took another hit of IH.

Brill carries a half dozen bags from the pantry. "This is everything I could find that resembles nuts. I didn't taste any, obviously."

Krom are universally allergic to peanuts from Earth, which are technically not nuts – pero also tree nuts from several planets. Though tree nuts from Earth don't bother them. I, on the other hand, taste everything. Cocoa nibs always remind me of pecans. There's no pecans on board, pero the bag marked k'vekk has a promising flavor profile.

I get out a baking pan and turn on the oven. Chocolate is made from fermented, roasted beans. Uan, I'd like to get a roasted flavor into my concoction.

Chocolate is then conched for days, crushing the bean particles finer and finer until smooth, but not too small, which would ruin the mouth feel. I have neither the time nor the equipment for that. This concoction will be gritty, no matter what.

I approach the galley chef who's been the friendliest to me. "Do you have a grinder or blender?"

"Sure." The Zantite relaxes visibly. En serio? Despite all the teeth and his massive size, I intimidate him. "Do you need help?"

"Please!" I explain what we hope to do. Which the galley cooks find fascinante. What we produce isn't chocolate. It's a bit green – I think from the k'vekk, not the Serum Green – and a bit grainy. If you close your eyes and make your taste buds squint, the fake chocolate has fruity notes, earthiness, hints of acidity, and waxiness from the fat. The Serum Green fills in some elements your brain's expecting when it thinks chocolate.

The kitchen has no molds, so we pour the mixture into flexible bread pans and hope for the best. Meanwhile, Brill arranges for Queen Layla to meet with me in the galley as soon as she finishes another meeting.

"I just hope it's in time, mi vida." I pick up a tray of the bread pans to take into the freezer.

"If we have to, we'll call Garfex and plead for mercy directly," Brill says.

I say, "He'll be more likely to listen if the plea comes from Layla. She's here, and she'll see how hard we've worked on this."

I enter the walk-in freezer, which is pretty much how I remember, with dressed meats and bags and bags of frozen produce. It's not as scary this time.

Oh. They butchered the frozen spuck. I recognize the claws still on one of the hands. No es sorpresa, realmente. Without the parasite, it's technically just an animal. Waste not, want not, and all that. It hammers home why Brill, a member of the galaxy's most extensively traveled explorer race, is a mostly-vegetarian. I might need to become one, too – at least until I fulfill my promise to Crosskiss. Back home though, if I get a chance to eat some of mi mamá's chicken tinga, all bets are off.

I place my tray in an empty spot on a shelf. The last time I was in this freezer, I was desperate and dying. Y ahora, mi planeta está en the same predicament. Everything is coming full circle.

When I return, the galley is a frenzy of activity. The crew are terrified of Queen Layla coming here and finding so much as a crumb out of place. Layla wears her Mercy is a Gift bracelet all the time and is the least likely Zantite on this ship to order an execution based on a minor infraction. Pero if they insult Crosskiss's mother, he might. Though, even if they did insult Layla, I doubt she would tell her son.

We wait, pero Layla never shows.

Finally, Brill says, "The invasion fleet has almost reached Earth. This is your last chance to talk to Garfex."

I call Chestla. *Any breakthroughs, chica?*

Unfortunately no. I'm afraid it's over. I'm sorry we failed you.

I understand. I hang up and retrieve my tray from the freezer. As it cooled, the mock chocolate turned a sickly purple. I pop the bars out of the bread pans.

Brill calls Garfex, holding the phone so I'm in the center of the capture field. The Zantite king looks shocked that I actually contacted him.

"Bodacious? I'm a bit busy at the moment. Our ships are almost in range of Earth."

I glance at my tray of almost chocolate bars. In the face of everything that's happened, it's a paltry offering. "I just – I had to try one more time to get you to change your mind."

Garfex nods towards the tray. "Are you growing me some cacao trees?"

"If you give us more time, I think we can give you trees. Eugene thinks he's close to breaking the cryostasis barrier."

Garfex wrinkles his rubbery brow. "Then what is on that tray?"

"A peace offering. Of sorts." Ni idea how to present this. I hold up a bar. "I've worked up a product to substitute for chocolate while we work on bringing back the real thing."

"That's not what I asked for. I see that your heart is in the right place, but I'm sorry, I can't – oh, dear."

The bar shatters in my hands, one of the alien ingredients behaving unexpectedly as it returns from frozen to room temperature. Ay! The other bars start to explode, popping wildly off the tray, the particles half-solid and goopy.

Layla picks that moment to enter. She rushes towards me. The last few bars pop all at once, splattering us both in near-chocolate. Brill flashed out of the way, shielding his phone.

"Layla? Honeycake? Are you okay?" Garfex says through the phone.

"I'm fine Garfie!"

Brill pulls off his jacket to prevent it from getting stained with the sticky mess, then he brings the camera in closer.

On Garfex's end, the actioncast rocks, like his ship's been hit. He did say he'd be in the vanguard vessel. "I'm sorry, Bo, but really do have to go. Your guys are firing on me."

The invasion has started.

"Oh honey!" Layla leans down and squeezes my shoulders. "You tried your best. Always remember that."

I wrench away. "No! No y no. It can't end like this."

The phone in my pocket buzzes with another alert. Brill pulls up his app. He mutes it, pero I still see one of Earth's ships exploding. Brill looks like he can't decide whether to keep showing the gritcast, or to drop the phone and crush me to him. He finally hands the phone to Layla and wraps his arms around me.

My handheld buzzes again, and this time it's not an alert. It's Mario. He takes in my disheveled, chocolate-covered appearance. "What happened to you?"

"Long story, mi hermano. Let's just say I failed to impress the Zantites."

And now, there's nothing else to do. Crosskiss can't help us. Neither can Tyson. Layla's already offering condolences. The planet is doomed.

Mario sits on a bench, Abuelo beside him. "I'm calling everyone to say goodbye."

Abuelo tells him, "Te rindes demasiado fácil." *You give up too easily.*

Mario turns to him. "Estoy aceptando que hay cosas que no puedo cambiar." *I am accepting that there are things I cannot change.*

Now that I see him hollow-eyed from lack of sleep, resting his mano on mi abuelo's, I realize how importante it is that Mario and I finally started building a relationship again. I've been the kid sister tagging along throughout his life, and maybe we never got along, but he held everything together in those first years after la muerte de Papá. When we were teenagers, I looked up to mi hermano, and I was devastated when he believed the worst of the lies the vulturazzi had told about me. And now, just when it looked like things between us might be repaired, he's preparing for the very real chance he's about to die.

My heart clenches, and my hands go tense. It isn't fair. None of this is fair. We all tried so hard.

Layla turns Brill's phone towards us. "You two might want to see this. They've already compiled it as a recap."

"Que?" I let mi hermano go and hang up the phone.

In the actioncast, the ships are blowing each other up, and while the Earthling ships are losing, they have disabled a surprising number of Zantite vessels, even scuttlepunched a few. I'm trembling, the IH taking me to a place of rage. So many people are dying needlessly.

Then the firing stops. A small fleet of ships appears below the two combating sides, sliding around from the far side of Earth.

The audio patches us in, and I recognize Kayla's voice. Surprise jolts through me.

Kayla says, "Please stand down. We have filed an injunction with the Galactic Court."

"And who are you?" Garfex demands.

It takes a second, pero the FeedCasters get a splitscreen holo, with Garfex on the left and Kayla on the right. Kayla stands on the bridge of a ship, with Kaliel in the pilot's chair beside her. She wears a glittering tiara and a flowing black gown.

Kayla said she couldn't risk coming out of hiding, not even to try to save Earth. Y todavía … she did just that. Pride por mi amiga fills my heart.

"Shirazende Okkawashilede, princess of the Nitarri royal family," Kayla says. "I am also a citizen of Earth, courtesy of my adopted parents. With the Nitarri scattered and in need of a new home, I have prior claim to this planet. Also, the Nilka feel they must be included in any grievances you have against Earth. I have a communique from Admiral Alabaster himself."

Somebody off screen asks Garfex if they can do that, and he replies, "I have no idea."

If this turns into a firefight, Kayla and her amigos are outgunned *and* outnumbered. Pero if they're Nitarri, they could inflict casualties on the Zantites without weapons – just by spilling feedback into their brains. This could easily turn into a bloodbath. I hold my breath.

Nobody fires. The Zantites probably don't want to offend Alabaster – in case Alabaster, who can be capricious, has chosen to see Kayla as an ally. If so, injuring her could start a war between the Zantites and the Nilka. Garfex and his bridge crew debate if this claim has merit, until someone reminds them that this is being FeedCast. Garfex looks at Kayla and growls, "I'll call you back."

He disappears. After a second, Kayla's side of the holo goes dark también, and the image changes to the outside of the ships, the three fleets forming a triangle.

Kayla calls my handheld. "How are things going with the cryostasis barrier? Murry and Tyson asked me to play for time."

"Gracias, mi amiga. The lab team's still working on it." I smile at her. "I'm surprised you've been in touch with Murry. I thought he was afraid of you, since you have the power to collectively kill him."

Despite Kayla's official garb, she's got her knit green hat balled up in her hands. "We've been talking since I sang to that spuck on Earth. We're friends now. Murry and Tyson helped me figure out how I can help Earth without getting myself killed. I've looked into the legal aspects of this claim Tyson cooked up, and the Court won't uphold the injunction. It won't change things in the long run, but the Court is required to process the request and deliberate and issue a decision. Afterwards, the Zantites may be within their rights to blow us out of the sky." Kayla looks terrified. "It won't be a lot of time, Bo. Maybe a couple of hours. Don't waste it."

I'm confused. "People still want to assassinate you. Why show yourself, when there are so few guarantees?"

"Because Earth is my planet too. It may be my adopted planet, but parts of this world made me who I am. I never wanted to be anything except an Earthling making five-star desserts in one of the galaxy's hottest kitchens. I still don't want to be anybody's princess, but if it gives me the power to stand up to these bullies, I'll take the responsibility." She gestures at me with her hat. "I learned that from you."

Tears bite at my eyes. "Mi amiga!"

"Where'd you get a fleet?" Brill asks. "When I talked to Kaliel he said Stephen couldn't assemble one before he was killed."

Kayla gestures to the bridge crew behind her. "There are a number of Nitarri ready and willing to believe in me." Preng, the Nitarri who had been called to examine Murry, stands at one of the stations. Eh? Did Murry contact him, after the hive mind had been spared? Kayla shrugs. "I am my people's Anastasia."

Kayla has long felt a connection to the myth about the Russian princess. Only, unlike the historical Anastasia, Kayla actually survived her family's slaughter.

After I hang up with Kayla, Queen Layla gestures at her chocolate splattered clothing. "It looks like we do have a little more time. I suggest we change clothes and then meet back here to discuss options."

CHAPTER FORTY-SIX

In the hallway, Brill and I cross paths with Frank, who is on his handheld. He scowls at me, mumbles something and hangs up. He gestured to my ruined clothes. "What happened to you?"

"I tried to make synthetic chocolate." I haven't seen Frank since we left him sorting things at the Doc's office. No sé what he's been up to. "Who was that on your handheld?"

"I've been trying to get your brother off of Earth."

"Gracias, viejo." I rub my face and come away with chocolate on my fingers. "You once said Mario annoyed you so much you wished he could be your assassination target."

Frank blushes. "A lot has changed since then. He's changed. Mario's reaction when I admitted to killing your father was a lot more mature than I expected." He clears his throat. "Besides, Botas likes him. I must be missing something."

Brill's eyes are violet, though his face is somber. Mi hermano could well still die on Earth. And he and Brill didn't have the smoothest relationship either, not since Mario revealed himself still distrustful of Krom when we all were on Zant. Familia es messy and complicated, no?

Frank's handheld rings again. He looks at it, hopeful, then scowls as he recognizes the caller. He puts his finger to his lips, requesting silence, then answers.

Daschel Janvier appears in the field. Brill and I can only see the flattened back of the image. "Are you alone?"

"Yeah," Frank lies. "They're all busy working in the labs."

"Good." Janvier hesitates. "I can trust you, can't I?"

Before a few days ago, Frank's loyalty to HGB had been unquestioning and unshakable. Now … no sé.

"Of course you can, Daschel. Because I'm trusting you to do what's right."

"That's fair. I care about Earth, and all the people left on it. I've dedicated my life to keeping them safe. And now I'm about to make the hard decisions necessary to restore order."

Mi corazón goes cold at his tone.

"Then why call me?" Frank asks.

"Keep Bo working on her pointless task. If you want to keep her alive, keep her off the feeds. The operatives I sent should arrive soon to make sure she doesn't cause trouble. I'd say take her phone, but unless you're prepared to disable her sublingual, that's pointless."

I shudder. Without access to blocking technology, Frank would have to rip the tech out of my head.

Frank's expression fills with distaste. "Really, Daschel. What are you planning to do that makes Bo such a threat?"

Janvier says, "We're about to throw Murry and the Evevrons under the bus. We reveal everything – how they developed Pure275, how they sold it to us to help us win the war, how Murry's the one who took that tainted chocolate to Zant. I'll get Tawny to spin it so that Earth is the victim."

Frank says, "That'll take more spin than a pro leaguer's curveball."

Janvier asks Frank, "Where's my microdot?"

"I have it," Frank says. "I told you I would get everything under control."

"Let me see it."

Frank takes the blue case out of his pocket.

"Up close enough that I can see the dot itself."

Frank opens the case. His soft gasp makes me realize the case is empty.

Obviamente, Janvier's picked up on that too. "I thought you had things under control."

Frank swallows visibly. "The dot has to be somewhere on this ship. I'll find it."

Janvier makes a few vague threats before Frank hangs up.

Frank arches an eyebrow at Brill.

Brill takes a step back. "Don't look at me. Ga. I wouldn't touch that thing for all the money in all the worlds."

Frank looks at me.

"Seriously viejo? I just gave it to you."

Frank curses softly. Then he looks past us, up the hallway. Four guys in dark suits are walking towards us. All four have brown hair and steady, fríos eyes. Frank curses louder.

"Miss Benitez," one HGB goon says, as he draws a gun. "Please stay where you are, and we can do this in a civilized way." From his expression, he means more than just detaining me. Maybe Janvier isn't so trusting of Frank's abilities after all. Or maybe this guy thinks I deserve execution for ruining chocolate.

I want to flitdash, pero there's nowhere to go.

Frank steps between me at the HGB goons. "Come on, Sam. She has a meeting with the Zantite queen. If she disappears, diplomacy here gets even harder."

"Janvier said you may have gone rogue." Sam points his gun at Frank, slowly walking up to him. "And if you showed any signs of it, to eliminate you too. We all know that you're an old man, that you've slowed down, gone soft. It won't be that hard."

"Trying to get you to see reason is going rogue?" Frank asks.

Sam shrugs. "Looks like it. Janvier didn't say what specific behavior to look for."

Without warning, Frank strikes Sam's hand and the gun goes flying. Frank whips out his own gun and grabs Sam, holding the weapon against the younger su's temple. "Come on now. Seth. Cal. Pete. You know that even if you drop me, I can still pull the trigger."

"We know," Cal says. He shoots Sam, who tumbles from Frank's grasp and sprawls on the floor.

Seth and Pete are so startled, they don't even register Brill blazebanging at Krom speed to grab their guns. As the two stand weaponless, Brill shoots Cal in the leg.

Despite the obvious pain, Cal keeps his footing and turns his gun towards mi vida – at the same time Seth tackles Frank and pulls the viejo's arms behind him. Seth is kneeling over Frank.

Brill zips away, drawing fire as Cal hobbles after mi vida, down the hall. Pete just stands there, like he's not sure who's side to take.

"I'll make this painless," Seth says, shifting his weight up to get an arm around Frank's neck. "For that time you saved me in Peru."

Dios mio! He's going to break Frank's neck.

"No!" Fueled with the Invincible Heart, I grab Seth, pull him off balance, kick him hard in the side. He falls, pero doesn't release Frank. Seth hooks his leg around mine and jerks me off balance. Ay! I go sprawling. The three of us are all on the floor. I get to my knees and clamber over Seth, get between him and Frank, making it difficult for him to keep a tight hold on Frank's neck.

Frank's still breathing, though Seth choked him hard enough he has trouble speaking. He may be telling me to run. Not that I would leave Frank like this. Seth grabs my shoulders. He's either going to kill me or shove me away so he can finish killing Frank.

"Everybody stand down!"

We all freeze. Dash stands in the hallway, wearing a suitcoat and tie, just like 1.0. Gracias a Dios por Nellet's obsession with Earth. That's the suit Watae got married in.

"Mr. Janvier." Pete straightens up, and Seth tries to get up off the floor.

Dash's shyness and hesitation is gone. "This doesn't look like the quiet operation I asked for. And I had to retrieve the case myself, so the entire job is a failure. Plus, one of you may face the shave for killing Sam. This is not the time to turn on our own."

Pete goes pale.

Seth asks, "The case." He sounds hesitant. I don't think they know what they came to retrieve. "Where is it?"

"Safely back where it belongs."

"I'm sorry," Seth says. "But seeing you here is unexpected. Can we get verification?"

Oye! That's a problem, no? I hold my breath, though my body tells me to flitdash or try to tackle Seth.

Dash scowls. "Scan me if you need verification." He takes off his suit coat and rolls up his sleeve. There's a minor bruise on his arm, in the same spot where Shelly had the microdot. It's not noticeable unless you're looking for it.

Shelly had said both he and 1.0 have talent for sleight of hand. Dash must have taken the dot off Frank and had Doc insert it in his flesh down in the Zantite medical bay. At this point, it's only his word versus 1.0's on who is the original Daschel Janvier.

And these guys have no idea Janvier has a clone. They scan Dash's arm. They have to accept the results, no?

They take Sam's corpse and a hobbling Cal back to their ship, where Dash told them to wait, so they can escort him to the rendezvous point to meet Tawny and the others. Como si eso pasara – *like that will happen.*

By the time they're gone. Frank is sitting up, pero his neck has visible bruises.

Brill and Dash half-carry Frank to the Doc's office. Doc wants to keep him for observation. I go into the examination room. Frank's lying on the exam table. He doesn't look comfortable being there and starts to sit.

Dash clears his throat.

"Fine." Frank's voice sounds like a frog's. He sighs and lies back on the table. "It took guts to stand up to Seth like that. You have no idea how many people he's killed."

"One less than he wanted to," I quip. En serio. I don't want to think about it.

Frank grins. "You've gotten seriously attached having me around." He stops, swallows, like talking is painful. "Attached enough to give me your blessing if I propose to your mother? I know I said I'd wait until after everything–"

"Sí." Heat and moisture dance in my eyes. I bring a hand to my face. I'm always saying no to things. This time saying yes feels right. "Sí y sí. Siempre. Todo. Mucho."

He looks so happy. I'd like to stay in this moment, pero I have to use the remaining time Kayla bought us effectively. After what Jack did, a half-dozen Zantites guard the medical office. Dash stays too, so I assume Frank will be safe.

As we're leaving, Dash says, "If you pull this off, I'll be Janvier for the cameras, long enough to make the apologies."

CHAPTER FORTY-SEVEN

I get myself mock-chocolate-free and changed, then check in at the lab. They're working desesperadamente on a set of calculations.

"No. That's the wrong coefficient. That should be a three," Chestla says, smacking Eugene's shoulder.

Ni idea what she means, pero Eugene beams at her.

"You are a genius." Eugene draws Chestla to him and kisses her.

Nobody but me seems to notice. I pretend to be absorbed in the data scrolling past in the holos. Really, I'm totally watching mi amiga kiss Eugene – despite what I told Murry about kissing being private.

When they break the beso, she looks flushed. And happy.

Leron comes over to me. He sounds un poco bored when he says, "Murry's about to be recognized as a native species on Evevron, and therefore have the rights of a person before the Galactic Court. He wants me to thank you for helping to save him."

"De nada." I put a hand on Leron's arm. Does he understand Spanish now, since Murry does? "Don't worry. He can use a phone to talk to people directly. The new will wear off soon and he won't keep putting so many demands on you."

"I hope so." Leron blushes. "That sounds ungrateful, doesn't it? I really am beyond happy to be alive."

"It's an adjustment, no?"

"You can say that again. You know the old saying that if someone tells you not to picture a pink-speckled gelk fish, all you can think of is pink-speckled gelk fish? It's like that. Kind of. I keep feeling that Murry's impressed with your ingenuity, and he's sorry that your mock-chocolate didn't work out. And I can't stop thinking about some nanite-effect food carousel you did. I've never seen anything like it. But I can't stop picturing it in my mind."

I blush. "Sí. I made that on Zant, for Minda's show, and my school was going to accept it for my final. Only, I thought nobody got to see it."

"But that thing was amazing. You're one project away from graduation? With such talent, you shouldn't give up."

I roll my eyes. I already had this conversation with Frank, no?

I'm still not ready to work with the edible nanites. They remind me of the most traumatic days in my life. Of darkness, death, and destruction.

And graduation is the last thing I should be worried about right now.

From the corner of my eye, I glimpse a freezer box on the counter, obviamente filled with cacao beans. More death and cold.

Pero then I start thinking. Most of the worlds' most spectacular chefs use edible nanite in ways that make food seem alive. What if the edible nanites could animate the cacao beans, forcing them to germinate and grow, despite having been frozen. Could they then be induced to produce viable pods of beans?

I gasp.

"What?" Leron asks.

I hesitate. It's a stupid idea. And even if it wasn't, I'd have to work with edible nanites. Last time I tried, I wound up as a puddle of tears on the floor. "Nothing."

Leron rolls his eyes. "Bo, if you don't tell me what you're thinking, Murry will literally drive me insane asking."

My chest feels hot with embarrassment. "Es estúpido. I can't propose something loco in front of all you scientists."

"Murry says you're giving up, just when you figured something out. He's been watching you, learning from you, and now he's disappointed in you. When there's one last chance to save your planet, there aren't any stupid ideas. Stop caring what other people think. He wants you to–"

"Haza!" I say. It's like with the heart bond – imagine how muy diferente things would have been if I'd just told Brill how it made me feel instead of feeling too silly to speak up. "Murry's right. I need to get back to the kitchen."

I try to snatch the freezer box off of the counter. It doesn't move. It's the size of a picnic cooler – and it's a lot heavier than it looks. Either there's a thousand cacao beans inside, or the cooling system weighs a ton.

"Hey!" Eugene protests. "We're using those."

"Then come with me. I'll transfer some of these beans to the galley's walk-in freezer. Then you can take the container back."

"I'll go," Chestla says. "You guys keep working with the current sample."

Muy bien! I can use the help of a biochemist.

"I could help too." Ball steps through the doorway, walking without a cane. He picks up the freezer box and balances it easily.

Chestla's mouth slides open, displaying all her teeth. "What happened to you?"

"He underwent surgery the Zantite doctor suggested," Brill tells her. "Risky surgery that apparently paid off."

Amazing what can happen if you work with your enemies instead of fighting them, no?

"I knew you needed," Ball starts. He moistens his lips and starts over. "I knew you found my injuries repulsive. That I would never be worthy of you as long as I was broken. Right before I got hurt, it seemed like we'd reconnected. That maybe you could love me back. And I didn't want to lose you to somebody stronger."

As in Eugene. I never thought I'd hear anyone say a human could be stronger than a Duracell. Especially not a Duracell.

Chestla still looks shocked. "Is that why you thought I pulled away?"

"Isn't it?"

"No." She bites her lip. "Ball, don't you remember how long I was in the hospital after I failed my test in the Canyon?"

"You sent everyone away, because you didn't want them to see you broken."

Chestla steps over to Ball, takes the cooler from him and puts it back on the counter. "I sent everyone away because I was ashamed of my failure. I was never ashamed of my body." She gestures down at her clothes. "You have no idea how many scars I have under here from when they put my back back together. I don't care if you're scarred, or if you're slow. But I am glad that you no longer seem in pain."

"Then why? What did I do that made you feel like you need someone else?"

"You needed me too much." Chestla bares her teeth at him. "I was scared, okay? I'm a Guardian Companion. I'm supposed to be willing to sacrifice my life for my charge. How can I do that, if you could literally die from grief? And now Bo's talking about this Krom heart bond—"

"Duracells don't usually have that problem." Ball looks over at Brill. "Or that gift. I can't even shift towards the colors of love." He looks back at Chestla. "I'm stronger than you think, Stala."

"But I'm not sure I am," Chestla says. "What if I risk my heart, and it doesn't work? I'm not the girl you grew up with. Living off Evevron changed me. What if I don't turn out to be what you want?" Chestla stares at him and gasps.

"What?" Ball touches his face, like something might be wrong after the surgery.

"Your eyes are hazel, so maybe I just never noticed. But at the edges of your irises, where they sometimes shift to lavender – they just shifted towards gold."

Ball eyes go wide. He grabs Chestla and kisses her. Deeply. Aggressively. Like the Duracell he is. And she wraps her arms around his shoulders in response.

Eugene is staring down at his work, correcting a calculation. He'd kissed Chestla not half an hour ago. And now, he acts like he can't see her kissing someone else.

I walk over to him. "You okay, mijo?"

He still stares at his calculations. "I will be. I like Chestla. A lot. But I don't need her. Not the way she needs him." He meets my gaze. "Whatever your experiment is, I hope it works. Because right now, I what I need is to still have a home."

I follow Chestla and Ball into the hallway.

Brill falls into step with us. "Sounds like you have a plan."

"These beans are just plants. We don't need them to be alive like you and I are alive. They have no personality or memories to worry about. We just need to trick them into germinating, and spooling out that perfectly preserved genetic code." It sounds muy estúpido out loud. Still, I get out my phone and enter search terms. "Once, one of my professors forced a flower to bloom in moments. If the base program for that effect is posted, that will save time. Though I'm so afraid this won't work."

Chestla turns to me. "But Bo, if it does, it will save your planet."

"I'm trying not to get my hopes up, chica." Pero somehow this feels like a more solid plan than begging other planets for help or trying to appease Garfex with fake chocolate.

Tawny calls my sublingual. *If you really think this has a chance of working, I will delay Daschel's communications. I just found out what he's planning to say. I don't want to start a third Zant Evevron war any more than you do.*

Where's Botas? I ask.

He's distracting Daschel. That dog has a thing for feathers, and he's threatening to chew up Daschel's five-hundred-dollar pillow. I may have pulled out a feather to give him the idea.

I smile, and Brill raises an eyebrow, like he wants to know who I'm talking to.

I can't make any promises, amiga, pero the theory with the nanites is sound, and Dash is on board to help with the spin.

Amiga? Tawny's bubblechatter sounds happy. *Are we finally real friends?*

I think so. You'd better check on Botas, though. If he eats too many feathers, he might get sick.

When we reach the galley, the cooks are still scrubbing near-chocolate out of the cracks between the countertops. The nanite station has been taken out of the box, though it isn't hooked up. Chestla starts connecting the cables, attaching the machine to the laptop. Several Zantites pause in their cleaning to stare at her. She turns, as though she feels their eyes boring into her neck. "Is there going to be a problem?"

"I've just never seen an Evevron this close before while it was still alive," the one wearing the MIAG bracelet says. "I have to say, those pheromones pack an unexpected punch. I was at Kfeny Hill. And I thought the death musk there was bad enough. I never imagined it'd be stronger when …" He trails off, as though unable to think of a polite ending to that sentence.

Chestla gives him a sad smile. "You don't have to get that close to someone to kill them, do you?"

The Zantite blushes green.

"At least no one took claws as war trophies from Kfeny Hill," Ball says. "I've always admired your culture's respect for our dead."

"Come on, Babe." Brill takes the cooler box from Ball and jerks his chin towards the freezer. "Let's get some beans on ice so I can get this back to the lab. Then I'll grab that brooch with Tawny's good camera. If this works, you'll want it documented."

We store the samples, and Ball goes with Brill. As they walk out, Ball says something to him.

Brill replies, "Actually, it's reciprocal."

After that, they're too far away for me to hear them.

I find the program I'm looking for. By that point, Chestla has the laptop set up. She moves it to a bench that's at a much easier height for me to work with.

I take a deep breath. Sí, this idea may not work. Y sí, I have to face everything I've partitioned off inside my mind about the bombing and all the deaths that have filled my life. I picture Mario's face, y mi abuelo's. They're still vivo —for now. If I don't do this, then I'll have to live my life knowing I didn't try my hardest to save them – after they sacrificed their ticket off the planet to give others a chance to live.

I brush away moisture that keep building in my eyes. It takes me a few minutes to get the program downloaded from my phone to the laptop. I'm muy feliz that this is the same program that we used at school, and that it allows you to work in your preferred language. For Chestla's sake, I leave it in Universal.

She dumps in the specifics of the plant we're working with into the laptop. She has more data than we need, from all the work she's been doing in the lab. We confer on the best overall approach for this program – thinking of the nanites as being alive *for* the cacao bean, because it can't be alive for itself.

Queen Layla walks in, looking shocked to see an Evevron in the galley. She's not royalty por nada, and as a trained diplomat, she recovers her composure inmediatamente. Her voice still sounds strained when she asks, "Bo, who's your friend?"

Chestla stiffens. And I realize mi Evevron amiga still has a weapon at her hip.

"Queen Layla," I say quickly, "Meet Chestla of Evevron, Guardian Companion to Nellet, Princess of Pendosha. And Chestla, meet Queen Layla of the Zantites, protector of the weak, sojourner of planets, wife of Garfex who holds the trident of awe."

Layla asks, "What is an Evevronian bodyguard doing in this meeting?"

Chestla's body language draws in on itself. "Perhaps I should leave."

"Perhaps you should." Queen Layla smiles tensely, revealing far too many teeth.

Chestla's mouth drops open. Before she can speak, I step between them. It should be my worst nightmare, no? A physically

puny human trapped between two alpha predators with a history.
Pero the Invincible Heart runs through my veins. "Crosskiss
promised there would be no trouble. He said soldiers carry no
grudges after the war is over."

Layla grits her teeth, leaning close to me. "My son did not
have to catalogue the records of the dead, which I did as royal
advisor. I had to write down the names of my father and my first
husband. Were I allowed to challenge every Evevron on board to
a duel—"

"Barbaric custom," Chestla says bitterly.

Layla unhinges her jaw, which Zantites only do when they
plan to bite someone in half. Chestla draws her short sword from
her hip.

Frustangeration builds in my chest, tightens my muscles. I
grab Layla's wrist, angling the MIAG bracelet so that she has to
look at it. "Do you believe what this says or not? Chestla wasn't
even born when that war started. She—"

"Tak spevn grawkgraw azks krekk plek akkat." Chestla speaks
awkwardly in Zantite. She's looking at her phone, where she must
be reading phonetically.

"What did you say?" Layla straightens, looking over me at
Chestla.

"I said I am thoroughly sorry for your loss." She switches to
Universal. "My father is a chef and a hunter. He has put himself
in much risk, just to feed the city. I cannot imagine what I would
do if anything happened to him. I wish I could offer some comfort
regarding your family. But today, Bo's family is at stake. Her
brother and her grandfather are still on Earth. Would you have her
record their names on the list of the dead?"

Layla looks like Chestla slapped her.

"Por favor." I take a deep breath, to calm the emotion sparking
in my chest. "Let's start over."

"How do you say that phrase?" Chestla asks me. "The official
greeting."

I say, "Tak spevn ginkkt a flekk stet bikket vokk ne pletk."

She repeats me. Despite her unfamiliarity with the language, it actually translates as, "I am pleased to make an initial impression of you."

Layla replies, "And I likewise." Then *she* switches to Universal. "I am embarrassed for my overreaction. I'm not sure if I should wear this bracelet at all. I'm not like Minda."

Minda's una gran proponent of peace between cultures. I never asked Minda what she thinks of the Evevrons, pero I doubt her initial reaction to anyone starts with hostility.

Layla starts to take the bracelet off. I place both of my hands over one of hers. Layla has made a huge stride toward understanding her own heart. And in making peace with the past. "You've earned this more than you realize."

The galley is un poco emptier. At the threat of a duel in their kitchen, the galley crew fled into the freezer.

"I was unaware of any meeting," Chestla says. "We are conducting a final experiment to give Garfex the cacao tree he asked for. I can work while you two talk."

Mi amiga is trying hard to keep peace.

"What are you working on?" Layla bends down to look at the laptop. Tension still sparks between her and Chestla, pero it's toned down a lot.

"In addition to being a bodyguard, I've trained as a biochemist," Chestla says. When Layla looks confused, Chestla shrugs. "I'm Evevron. We multitask."

CHAPTER FORTY-EIGHT

Chestla and I relate my idea for reviving the cacao beans to Layla, and as I explain, the program comes clearer in mi cabeza. As we talk, I type snatches of code.

I retrieve a handful of cacao beans from the freezer to demonstrate my point. The galley crew are all shivering, pretending they're catalogue the freezer contents. In their heads.

"You guys can't stay in here. Why don't you go clean the mess hall?"

"Great idea," one says. The guys rush through the galley.

I show Layla the cacao beans. She picks one up. Each seed is purple-brown, and wrinkled-looking, about the size of the first joint of my thumb, with a white spot on one end, that should become the tree's tap root.

"This is what chocolate comes from?" Layla looks fascinante, holding it between her spongy thumb and forefinger.

"I know, right? It doesn't look like much to stand between my planet and destruction."

Layla says, "But it is a seed of hope. I want to help."

I look at Chestla. Mi amiga smiles, and a spark of joy lightens my chest.

Chestla says, "Garfex can't back out of supporting a project his wife helped with."

I take my spot back by the bench and review my notes. Jimena Duarte once called chocolate *una semilla de muerte*, a seed of death. Pero right now, with the program outline in front of me, it feels like what Layla called it, la semilla de la esperanza, the seed of hope.

Leron had to talk me into taking a chance on this. He shouldn't have had to. I came close to giving up on mi planeta y mi familia y todos mis amigos. Letting all the deaths overwhelm me, and forgetting about the sacrifices and the love – and the last-minute rescues. All because I'm afraid to work with the nanites.

Leron himself had been seconds away from having his heart stopped. Brill had been one decision away from having a bullet in his. Maybe these nanites aren't death. Maybe they're a way to rebel against giving up.

My fingers fly over the keyboard. Coding is an art, and when I was in school, it was the class that gave me the most trouble. Pero, right now, what I need this program to do makes perfect sense. Pieces of everything I've learned come together. As I work, I think about each bad thing that's happened to me, from the moment the pops started buzzbashing me to now. I let the memories in, finally processing the trauma. Accepting that I was shot. I was bitten. I was used as a pawn by someone I love and left to die. And worse than any of that, I was lied about. I survived each of those things, which would have killed or broken someone else. I am stronger than anyone would have believed. Crosskiss even said so.

I pause. Eh? Why are the lies más importante than the violence? My nightmares always feature Crosskiss's teeth about to close over me, or Tyson's fangs about to sink into my heart. Pero I don't think muerte is what I really fear. My fear is that no one will understand what I've been through. That the sleazarazzi will still hate me, and people will write nasty notes begging for my death. I flitdashed halfway across la galaxia because Mamá's old boyfriend lied and said I kissed him – and people believed him. Crosskiss implied that I was a bad person, deserving of execution as a stowaway – but he was wrong. Murry-Tyson claimed that I wasn't a good friend, that I manipulated people – and it took a long time to convince him that wasn't true. Each of these traumas were followed by malcasts and plummeting horrorstats in the polls.

Mis amigos keep telling me to stop caring about what's mediaceptable, that there will always be haters, that you can't expect everyone to understand. Y ahora – as this program comes together on the screen, proving empirically that everything I learned in school about food and science is valuable, whether people have confidence in me or not – I get it. In my heart and not just my mind, I get it. I am good enough. I don't have to continually prove myself to anyone. Not Brill, not Frank – not even Mario. None of them asked me to. Heck, Frank even said he loves me, despite all the trouble I caused him.

And the public? I don't owe them anything. If I decided mañana to audition for another cheesecast, it wouldn't matter what the polls said afterwards about my hair. Or the meaning of the role I chose to play. People who don't know me have no right to judge me.

It's a blinding moment of insight. And it changes me. I feel like, even after the IH buzz recedes, I'll feel at peace. And I can focus even more clearly now on pulling this program together.

Chestla leans over my shoulder, watching, offering suggestions. When I finish the last line of code, Chestla takes my seat and goes back through the program, closing brackets and fixing minor mistakes. We're short on time, so there's no room for estúpidos errores.

Queen Layla watches Chestla. She says softly, "Evevrons are really quite graceful."

Brill comes back into the room, a blur as he moves over to me. He sets a double-armful of gear from the hydroponics lab on the counter. Ball follows. The Duracell sets a pair of heavier buckets of planting material on the floor.

Brill gestures towards Chestla. "Ven? How's it going?"

"Haza." I answer. "She should be about done proofing my work."

"I am done." Chestla pushes a final key, and the software starts coding the program into the nanites.

That will take a few minutes. I pull Brill aside – not that this space has much room for privacy. I touch his face. It's smooth, where the scar from the first time he'd been aboard this ship was repaired. We've been through muchas muchas cosas together. "I don't know if you found the time to get me anything, mi vida. But I want to give you your heart bond gift."

Brill's eyes tint pink, then dip back to gold. "I bought something for you the day I first felt the bond. I've been carrying it ever since."

He takes a packet of folded white tissue paper from an inside pocket of his jacket. It's a little beat up. When I open it, a silver bracelet slides into my palm. It's thin and elegant, and at one-inch intervals, there's a heart with a jraghite stone set into it. The stones glow from his body heat. Porque he kept it close to his heart.

I laugh as he fastens it around my wrist.

"What's so funny?" His eyes are tinting pink, like he's afraid he messed this gift thing up again.

I grab his hand. "It's perfect. You'll see when you open yours."

I take the narrow box from my pocket.

When he opens it, a slow smile takes over his very kissable lips. "Babe. I just … wow. For once, we're on the same page."

He slides the bracelet onto his wrist, on the opposite hand as his proximity band. I lean in and kiss him, brevemente, because people are watching and I don't want to embarrass him. Pero I can't let this moment pass without marking it.

Across the room, the nanite system chimes, showing that the tube of edible microbots is ready. I hurry over to it, Brill at my side.

I keep glancing at his bracelet. It looks so right on him, like he's telling the worlds he belongs to me. I wonder what his mother will make of it – since Brill said he's not telling her about the heart bond until he can do it in person.

Tawny calls my sublingual. She wants un mejor ángulo for her camera. *Brill brought the brooch with the good camera, but it's still in his pocket.*

We set up the cameras. Then I draw the tube of nanites out of the machine, and Brill hands me a syringe from the hydroponics gear. He moves to use a punch to pierce the hard outer coating of a cacao bean.

"Wait!" I put a hand on Brill's. Then I look over at Layla, who's watching the proceedings curiously. She looks a little left out. I hold out the syringe to the Zantite queen. "You should do this, please. Your husband can't deny the experiment's authenticity if you are part of it."

Layla blushes teal. "I wouldn't know how."

"Chestla will walk you through it, no?" After all, I've already done the hard part. Nerves dance in my stomach. Now, this really had better work. The last thing Earth needs is Layla feeling embarrassed.

Brill hands Chestla the punch and the cacao bean. He gives me a look I can't read. Does he think I should be doing this myself, to show that Earthlings are capable? No. Detener, Bo. I refuse to second-guess my decision.

"That was brilliant, Babe." Brill leans against me, near-hugging me with his shoulder. "Tawny is getting feed of you convincing a Zantite and an Evevron to work together to save your world. If that doesn't convince everyone that Earthlings deserve a place in the galaxy, nothing will."

Despite the stakes riding on this, happiness bubbles through my chest. Mi vida thinks I'm brilliant.

Together, Chestla and Layla make un minúsculo hole in the cacao bean, inject in the nanites, and settle it in the clear planting medium from the hydroponics lab.

"Why does this bucket need to be so deep?" Layla asks. "I thought we were just sprouting a seed."

Chestla flashes Layla a grin, displaying her predator's teeth in a way that's the opposite of hostile. "Bo went a little bit beyond that."

She pushes the bucket to the center of the floor.

Layla looks over at me, her expression impressed. "Now what happens?"

"Hopefully the viability ring at the neck of the bucket turns green." Which it hasn't done yet. I take a deep breath. As seconds tick past, mi corazón beats faster, the IH amping me up for action.

Brill takes my hand. "It's going to be diay, Babe."

He steadies me. I don't know how much is the physical contact and how much is the heart bond, pero my heartbeat slows. Which feels wrong. If this experiment doesn't work, my whole planet falls to the Zantites. So how can my body tell me that everything will be fine? It has to be the heart bond. Which means mi vida has that much confidence in me.

There's a flicker of green, and the viability ring lights up. The cacao bean, suspended in the clear plasma, looks like it's shattering, then splits open.

The light goes out.

"Oi! No. No y no!" I take a shuddery breath. "Por favor."

I stare at that bean. It had definitely started to sprout, despite the bean itself being muerto. I must have done something incorrect with the code. Pero what did I do wrong? I turn back towards the nanite station. Maybe there's time to debug the code. Maybe–

"Look, my heart!"

He'll have to stop calling me that, or someone will tell his mother before he gets the chance. I turn back. Brill points to the bucket.

The ring has gone green again. A slender stem shoots up from the planting medium, taking the two halves of the cacao bean with it. Leaves form at the top of the stem, looking like tiny fuzzy spikes, then widening and forming veins. They're each the size of my thumb, green and beautiful and perfect. The leaves strengthen and lift into an arched shape. Another set of leaves form at the center of the first ones and raise the stem, lifting and gaining strength. And then another set forms, then another, each set of leaves significantly larger than the last. Meanwhile, the trunk thickens, and roots form deeper in the bucket.

"Quickly," I tell Layla, "Start the second one."

Porque you need two cacao trees to cross-pollinate and make actual pods.

Layla and Chestla work together, and by the time flowers form along the first cacao tree's trunk, the second bean has split the dirt.

I draw out the second tube of nanites and open it, and a fleet of tiny bot-clusters flies out, clouding the air, surrounding the flowering tree. We don't have midges here to pollinate the flowers. We have to hope the clusters of nanites can do the job.

By the time flowers start forming on the second tree, they're falling off the first. The nanites move over to the flowers, which fall moments later, replaced by the beginnings of cacao pods. The pods form, the size and shape of Nerf footballs, all red and gold and waxy. Tan hermosa! – *So beautiful*. And then the program finishes, leaving the trees pushing against the galley ceiling. In the wild, these trees can grow thirty feet tall. The pot size constrains these two.

Chestla takes her short sword from her belt and slices a cacao pod from the growing pad on the trunk. She cracks the pod open with the blade, and the scent of pineapple fills the air. She hands the pod to Layla. "Please. Call Garfex. We have what Bo promised."

My sublingual rings. It's Tawny. *I already have live feed of this going directly to Garfex's warship. But he said he needs Janvier to deliver the tree. Layla's call should buy you a little time.*

Sudden tears bite the back of my eyes. *Live feed? You have that much faith in me, amiga?*

I'm starting to, Tawny admits. *But your plan better work. Daschel will kill me when he finds out a solar storm isn't what shut down this planet's communications.*

I laugh, pero then I hesitate. *You don't mean that literally, right?*

No. Tawny chuckles, then goes somber. *At least, I don't think so. But I can't let him condemn Murry. For some reason, that alien reminds me of Frank's corgi. And they're both growing on me.* Tawny adds, *Daschel and I had a long talk. His heart is in the right place, but he always thinks he knows the best way to handle things. He came close to admitting he needs help.*

Pues, we're about to do a few things for him whether he likes it or not.

CHAPTER FORTY-NINE

The *Layla's Pride* is en route to Garfex's flagship, which is still orbiting Earth. Layla talked him into waiting for us, even though the Galactic Court determined the Nitarri can't claim the planet. At least the Zantites let Kayla's little fleet leave in peace.

Now that the scientists have taken over the resuscitations, I stand awkwardly in the lab. I thought we only needed for a dozen cacao beans from the new pod to light up cells in a viability box, showing that what we made could be sprouted to form new trees. Pero Garfex wants chemical proof that this stuff really is chocolate.

We asked Dash to meet us in the lab. So far he hasn't shown up, pero I don't think he'd bail after giving his word. I'm grateful to him for saving Frank. Choosing to have that microdot embedded in his skin must have been muy difícil, because it makes him a target for anyone looking to get that information. Pero only 1.0 could have stopped HGB's assassins, so he had to do it. Dash never wanted to be Janvier, and after this, he may not be able to escape being taken back to where the real Janvier waits.

Eugene keeps leaning towards the live cacao beans in the viability box, repeating, "Astounding! Absolutely astounding!"

Eugene, Chestla and Leron finish the chemical analysis.

Dash finally shows. He and I prepare what to say once we reach Garfex's flagship. I explain my concerns about Garfex's reaction when he finds out the chocolate he's been eating was laced with Serum Green.

Dash laughs. "It's officially called Plenzoxin. I suggest we tell Garfex chocolate bar formulation is a trade secret and sell him the serum as a bonus to enhance the flavor when he makes chocolate. With the warning that some species may find it mildly addictive."

"Dios mio! I never would have thought of that." I gesture at Dash with the tablet computer I'm holding. It displays the analysis of the cacao beans. "That's logic worthy of 1.0 – pero with mejor diplomacy. Since you and Shelly can both exist, there is a lot more to Janvier than I give him credit for."

"Let's hope so," Dash says. "After we finish our plan, he can still act in the fallout. He could undo what we hope to accomplish. And he'll realize that I'm holding his microdot hostage."

"Then you and he will have some muy importante decisions to make, no?"

He looks up at me. "Can I ask you something?" He waits for my nod, then asks, "Why did you hate HGB so much, even before you found out we murdered your father?"

My shoulders stiffen. I look him in the eye. "You abused your power, and took over everything. Not only that, you were so patronizing about using people. Like when Tawny first asked me to come home to be your Princesa de Cacao. She said mi papá's ancestry could be traced back to Montezuma."

Dash blinks. "But your genealogy does trace back to Montezuma. We DNA tested your father after his death. It's standard procedure, with remains that aren't otherwise identifiable. And while there's always a level of uncertainty when so much time had passed, the gene pool is a match. That's why we wanted you for the project. It was supposed to honor you."

I laugh. "Montezuma's tomb has never been found. There's no way you could know that."

Dash's eyes widen in shock. "Surely Tawny told you. HGB funds a number of grants for archeological expeditions throughout the chocolate belt. A Mexican research team uncovered the ruins. As long as the body inside the tomb was correctly identified, Earth's most famous chocolate addict was your ancestor."

I'm starting to believe him. "How did they find it?"

"They cleared away debris from where bombing during the First Contact War had leveled a town near Mexico City.

Construction efforts to rebuild were abandoned, decades ago. In the past, that's what's hindered the search for Aztec history – the buildings built on top of the history were too valuable to knock down to look underneath."

"How come nobody knows the tomb has been recovered?"

"We were supposed to reveal that information in a huge media blitz after you finished the holomercials, when you went to Mexico. But you derailed that plan. A museum is set up near the HGB's Mexico Facility, with the artifacts on display for visitors and the local population. But we kept having to delay the opening, and after things went sideways, Tawny wanted to hold onto the information in case she could use it."

My eyes widen as I take in the implications. "I guess I was too angry to really listen to Tawny, mijo."

I've been so focused on the mal things HGB has done to keep their choco-monopoly that I never thought they might be doing good things too. They funded a lot of art and culture – including mi mamá's cooking show. Pero when you live in the shadow of the shave, it's hard to see it as anything other than propaganda.

My mind is still spinning when the door opens, and Brill enters, wheeling a cacao tree on un cart grande. Queen Layla walks with him. Just the four of us will board Garfex's ship. None of the Evevrons are going, and Frank is still in Doc's office, though he's texted me constantly.

We take a transport to land inside Garfex's ship. The hardest part is getting the tree through the transport doors.

Garfex himself meets us at the docking bay.

Layla steps forward from our group and embraces him, which seems to put the Zantite King in a better mood. He looks over at me. "I never thought I'd have to back up my rash words."

I grin. I offer him the tablet, which looks ridículamente small in his giant hands. "I'd have never believed it either."

Garfex gestures to Dash. "And how did you get him here? He knows he's supposed to apologize, right?"

Dash reaches out a hand for Garfex to shake. Garfex's palm engulfs part of Dash's forearm, yet the clone never loses Janvier's confident swagger. On some foundational level, he really is the same as 1.0. "I've learned a few things from this Krom. You might say I'm a completely different man."

Now that's an understatement.

Brill chokes out a laugh. "From me?"

We follow Garfex to a luxuriously appointed conference room. On the table before one seat, there's a gold-toned paper box. We all look at each other, not sure who's supposed to sit there. Garfex takes the seat at the head of the table. Brill places a bowl of cacao pods on the table in front of him. Garfex grins, and though Brill's standing close to all those shark teeth, he doesn't even flinch. Garfex says, "I understand it is customary for Krom to begin negotiations by exchanging gifts. That box is for you."

"Really? Tanyaliesh mucho. Thank you, so much." Brill sounds fizzbounced as he rushes around the table and sits in the oversized chair with the golden box in front of it.

"Nothing for me?" Dash grumbles.

"Mercy is a gift," Garfex says. "I've heard that often enough. I still don't like you, but I'm not destroying half your planet and enslaving the rest."

"Fair enough." Dash sits next to Brill and looks into the box. "What is that?"

"I have no idea." Brill's eyes are an intensely curious deep lavender. "But it would be rude to ask."

Garfex laughs. "It's a new kind of star drive. Unlike anything on the market."

Brill's eyes shift through several colors, landing on apricot surprise. "That's a very generous gift."

"It was Minda's idea. She said you're young and rash and need something to solidify your reputation. She's quite taken with you. And Bo too. She's working on something for Bo, but wouldn't say what."

Brill's eyes go emerald green. "That sounds intriguing, too."

Dash rolls his eyes. "Can we get on with this?"

"Sorry nobody got you anything, su," Brill says.

"Look, Garfex," Dash says. "I apologize for everything that has happened between my planet and yours. I'm giving you the first of a new strain of cacao trees, and the tablet contains the code required to quick-grow enough trees to maturity for you to start a new industry. But." Dash hesitates and leans forward, both hands on the table. "But we're taking a note from the Krom. That code will be open-source. There will be enough chocolate for everyone, so that everyone will leave Earth alone to lick our wounds and recover."

"I promised to leave several crews to help with your environmental disaster." Garfex glances at me. "Another thing I never imagined would happen in a century of lifetimes."

I tell him, "We have ideas for looking outward, at the rest of our solar system." Some pieces of the plan we've worked up are things Shelly had talked about. Some if it came from what Jack told me Greftash wanted to do. A few bits I added myself. "We have first claim, so we hope you'll back off and let us put an observation post on Pluto and a mining operation on Jupiter."

Después de todo, the Zantites had expressed interest in Pluto, back before the invasion began, so they might be able to file a claim.

"By all means," Garfex says. "We don't want it anymore. But do it soon, while you still have help."

Layla's handheld rings. She walks away from the table to answer it, then comes back, her grin showing about a million gleaming teeth. "Minda came through with your surprise."

She activates a holofield that takes up the far side of the room. In half of it, Mamá and Minda are sitting at a café table on some planet. I don't think it's Larksis. In the other half, several of mis profesores from school sit at a conference table.

"Bo," Minda says, "We contacted the Culinary Academy with holofeed of your graduation project."

"Graduation project?" I repeat stupidly. Que? I haven't outlined a project yet. Though now that I'm over my reluctance to work with nanites, I've got at least a dozen ideas.

"Your effort is quite remarkable." Blegart Pau, a native Larkssian and one of mis profesores favoritos, waves all four of his hands. "No one has ever interpreted the prompt quite this way. Most graduation candidates do something that's showy at best – a cyclone of candy, or drinks that pour from glass to glass. But you've shown that you understand the whole cycle of food, and then circumvented it by turning processed food back into a renewable source. Which is genius. To accept your project, we need to compare your code with what is readily available, to make sure what you did is unique."

My mind reels. When I turned frozen cacao beans into cacao trees, I wasn't working on a graduation project. I was trying to save my planet. Pero what I did with the edible nanites likematches the project guidelines. Only … "I can send you the code, pero when you look at it, you'll see part of it isn't unique. I based that section on an open-source program I found for quick-blooming a flower. I had time constraints."

And I had no idea I would get graded on how well I reversed a biological disaster. The teachers murmur to each other, too low for me to make out clear words across the holographic connection.

Finally, Blegart Pau says, "Send us the code, and we will decide."

Cierto, that decision won't be unanimous.

We break for the time being, and someone brings in snacks.

Brill pulls me to the side. His eyes have gone gold again. "Babe. In about five minutes, you'll be a college graduate. An actual chef. It's what you've always wanted."

"We don't know for sure yet." I put a hand on his. I take a deep breath. I need to be honest with him. "I don't know if I want to be a chef anymore. Life in a commercial kitchen seems a lot smaller than before I crossed half de la galaxia. And being with you – you won't want to give up a life of adventure. And I'll find myself wanting to go along for the ride."

"So, like a trans-galactic food truck?" Brill blinks. "I'm not sure how practical–"

"Dios mio!" He just gave me an idea.

Brill flinches back, startled. Layla looks over at us, concerned.

"Not a food truck. That's loco." I tap my lips with my finger. "But I could talk to Tawny about setting me up with my own holoshow, where I could teach about cuisines from across the worlds."

"And you could film some of your episodes on site. That's what you're getting at, right?" He looks even more fizzbounced than when he opened the star drive. "I could set up transport jobs that would match, and take your equipment and crew wherever you need to go."

"HGB might even pay for the gas, mi vida." Maybe I could combine everything I love, and at the same time, return to the spotlight on my own terms. Some of Mamá's most popular cooking show episodes were filmed off of Earth.

I can see myself on out-of-the-way planets, with culinary traditions nobody's bothered to holo and seeking out the best bottles of wine nobody's heard of, while the cameras roll and I interview the people who grew the grapes or vipzas or jenkts. And of course, I'll show my kitchen – wherever I wind up living – with my own take on galactic fusion food.

And if I need to help Brill out with the trader thing, or keep him out of trouble, I have a legit reason for being in any neighborhood, on any planet. Which helps him too. We could even go looking for the fountain of youth plant, like he wants. Y who knows? Maybe that star drive will solidify Brill's reputation enough that he will propose, despite his familia's objections. If not right away, then sooner than he thought. I'm still not ready to go to Krom, pero it's a huge step in the right direction.

Suddenly, I am very anxious to graduate and move on with my life. My planet has a future now. I deserve one too.

Garfex calls us back to the conference table. The holofield springs back to life. Blegart Pau is smiling, so even before he speaks, I know they've accepted my project. Mamá and Minda leap up from their seats and grab hands, jumping up and down, though Minda has to stoop awkwardly to keep from pulling Mamá off her feet.

"Gracias a Dios!" Mamá shouts. "It's about time."

Brill pulls me into a hug. "My heart and my life. And the most amazing person I've ever met."

EPILOGUE

I can't believe Crosskiss is coming to pick me up personally. Well, he's also coming to Earth for a mediatastic ceremony to be held during the nueva version of the chocolate festival. Pero he's bringing a small ship, and I'm supposed to return with him for my six months aboard the *Layla's Pride*. He's also bringing my camera crew, since Tawny received approval for my show to start filming while I'm aboard the *Layla's Pride*. At this point, I can do pretty much whatever I want with it. Though I'm sure Tawny will have suggestions.

Without Tawny's live feed of me helping Murry save Evevron, and then of me guiding Layla through recreating the cacao trees, my new place in the polls would have been unimaginable. 86% of respondents look forward to mi nuevo show. 68% are back on Team Brill. And 96% think I should receive an award for my work with nanites. Tawny warned me I'll have to work with nanites regularly on my show to keep the ratings. A few vocal holdouts would like to see me muerto. Pero you know what? I don't care.

I'm in a car with Jack Wolfe and Kayla Baker. Kaliel is driving, and I'm up front beside him. If you'd ever told me I would see Jack and Kayla sharing a bench seat – yeah, it's muy muy surreal. Pero they're sharing a planet, so they might as well get used to it. The Krom are donating the tech to terraform Mars, since Janvier offered the planet to the Greftashians and the Nitarri as their shared new home. The Greftashians will get citizenship of Earth and a choice to move back to the home world, if they want. Relatively few are taking us up on it. Almost all of them are willing to trade environmentally poor Greftash for a brand-new blue and green Mars, though.

The Nitarri – well, that's more complicated. Kayla's supporters are flocking to Mars. But her Uncle's not fizzbounced about it.

I ask Kayla, "Does this make you a Princess of Mars?"

Kaliel laughs. "Nice."

Jack scowls. "Greftashians won't bow to any royalty."

"Relax," I tell him. "It's a reference to classic Earth sci-fi. *A Princess of Mars* is a book title."

"Oh." Jack's scowl lessens.

Kayla fidgets with a pendant hanging around her neck. It's a crystalline cube carved with Admiral Alabaster's likeness. It marks Kayla as under his protection. "I have no desire to challenge my uncle. I hope this mark from the Admiral will be enough to keep me safe. I don't know if I'll stay on Mars forever, but I need to be there for a while to encourage people to settle there. I'm opening a bakery."

I can't help but laugh. Kayla always did have a gift for frosting work.

Kaliel says, "You know I'll be there all the time."

Kayla reaches over the seat and puts a hand on his shoulder. "For me or the cupcakes?"

"You, of course." His mano covers hers.

"Chestla's friend Ekrin agreed to take me as cesuda ma," Kayla says. "Now that her people have found peace with their neighbors, Ekrin wants a new challenge. She's learning English and Nitarri, and will meet me here before I go on stage. Having a bodyguard is weird."

I shrug. "You get used to it."

Leron agreed to stay on Crosskiss's ship for as long as I'm there, to work on the research into IH withdrawal.– I don't think Murry would forgive him if he hadn't. So that'll be interesting. The poor guy will worry the whole time that someone will tell Ekrin about his Murry-induced confession of love.

As we near HGB headquarters, crowds line the streets, wandering between booths staffed by chocolatiers and chocolate makers from across la galaxia. These new artisans have been exercising their creativity, stretching the bounds of what is possible with chocolate. And they've all come to the birthplace of chocolate, to celebrate it with us.

Some people still wear alien costumes and antennae on springs, pero nobody seems to mind.

I spot Brill. He sees the car coming and waves. When his jacket cuff shifts, the bracelet I gave him flashes in the sunlight. I'm wearing mine too. I love having a gentle reminder of my heart bond with my Krom. My paladzian pendant, which I have to keep until one of us really does die, is tucked in a corner of my dresser drawer, where I hope it stays for many, many years.

Brill will meet us at the ceremony. Pero first, how could he resist making a few purchases and trades when half the galaxy's producers of the hottest commodity are all in one place?

"I'm not apologizing to him," Jack grumbles.

This is turning into the world's longest car ride.

"And he's not giving you back the jacket," I say. "Sí. You both made yourselves clear. You know as soon as the ceremony is over, you'll be arrested for murdering that Zantite niño."

Jack shrugs. "So they say. I'll take the chance, because being here helps my people."

"The Zantites want to impress you onto one of their ships," Kaliel says. "Your service in exchange for the young warrior they lost."

Wha–? No. Por favor, no. If Crosskiss takes Jack back on board the *Layla's Pride*, I'll spend the next six months with this kek breaking everything.

I hope he escapes this time.

We drive through the gate into the HGB compound. It looks the same. Pero HGB's role has changed. It's still a clearinghouse for commodities trade, with a huge presence here and on Interface Station. And they have a good deal of influence on Earth. They don't hold a monopoly on anything anymore – and Earth is diversifying in ways that don't require HGB's moderation.

Kaliel parks, and we head towards the group gathered on the grass between two of the pools.

"Mija!" Mamá approaches and gives me a giant hug.

"Let me see the ring." She showed it to me over the handheld half a dozen times, pero this is the first time I've seen her in person since Frank proposed.

She holds out her hand. It's the piece of jraghite más grande I've ever seen. One of Brill's friends designed the custom setting. The guy usually works as a forger and counterfeiter. Pero he does have an eye for art.

"Are you sure you want me to be the first guest on your show?" Mamá asks. "This is your project."

"Pero Mamá, I want to honor mi familia too. I was never more unhappy than when I isolated myself from all of you."

"Bodacious." Janvier walks up behind me. A chill goes down my spine. I still don't like him. At least, I'm ninety percent sure it's him and not Dash. Frank keeps assuring me that while Janvier's clones are safe, 1.0's back in charge. I hope Dash is somewhere making coffee foam art. And finding someone to fall in love with.

Chestla and Ball are dating. Murry and Awn created their child. Fizzbounced endings are in the air. So por qué no for the Cloneviers too?

"Mr. Janvier." I offer a hand for him to shake, and angle my cheek for him to kiss, like we are friends. Or at least friendly. "And muchas gracias por the follow-up treatment at your facility."

With the research Crosskiss's doctors will be doing on me, I have hope for a more permanent cure to the IH shakes. In the meantime, I'll take the temporary help before I go aboard a ship where I could score another dose of IH.

"As long as you remember you're grateful when you give your speech." Janvier's smile is cold.

I point to the ground at the edge of the manicured lawn, where a few stray cacao seedlings are bringing the wilderness closer in. "I plan to talk about new growth from the ashes. And about all the friends I've lost, and how, despite that, I've found joy. Don't worry – I won't implicate HGB."

I start to walk away. Janvier says, "Can I ask you something?"

"Sure, mijo."

"How serious is Tawny about Hosei?" For the first time, the real Janvier looks vulnerable.

I give him a smile. "Your guess is as good as mine. But if you have him killed, she won't turn to you for comfort."

"You have to save everyone, don't you?"

I sweep a hand towards where the microdot has been presumably reinserted in Janvier's arm. "Even you, mijo." I look him in the eye, and for a moment, I see Shelly. "Just – thank you for not putting a kill order back on Frank."

Janvier actually blushes. "You knew about that?"

"Dash intercepted the information. Frank doesn't know."

Janvier nods. "Don't tell him, will you? Now that we're not the only game in town, we'll have to change the way we do business. I'm still trying to figure out a new role for him and his colleagues, and some of them will be unhappy. The last thing I need is Frank showing up with a vendetta."

"Cierto." I gesture at the rainforest again. "Like I said, new growth from the ashes. I hope it all does turn into something better. I risked a lot for this world."

"This solar system," Frank says, as he joins us.

Janvier smiles, like we hadn't just been discussing how he ordered Frank's death. "Indeed. A lot happened while I was out of communication with the rest of the worlds."

"All good things I hope." From Frank's expression, he probably knows Janvier wanted to have him killed. "I, for one, am proud of Bodacious. I don't think anyone else could have brought us to this point, without the company, or Earth, or a good chunk of the galaxy imploding."

"If you say so." Janvier glances towards the parking lot. "Oh, goodie. The Zantite is here."

Close to nine feet tall, and lemon yellow, and bald, Crosskiss looks awkward and out of place. I rush to greet him.

"I need your help," he tells me.

"Eh?" I ask.

"While you're aboard my ship, I want you to solve a little mystery."

I smile. "Nothing dangerous, I hope."

Although anything that happens aboard a Zantite ship is bound to be feartastic.

Before he can say anything else, Janvier and Frank approach. And Minda gets out of a transport that just landed in the parking lot.

Tawny zeroes in on us from the other direction – and she's holding hands with Brill, like he's one of her clients. I feel an echo of the uncomfortable feeling I had before – something predatory in the way she's holding on to him – pero it seems more subdued. His eyes are a nervous orange-tinted gray.

Crosskiss straightens and looks properly scowl-y again.

Tawny presses Brill's hand into mine. I can't hide the shock that sparks through me. En serio? Tawny has spent all this time keeping me and Brill apart – and she's finally okay with the face of HGB being together with a Krom. "Mi amiga. You really don't hate Brill."

Tawny laughs. "Brill's got HGB's protection, and we made a deal with Krom for their terraforming technology. He's finally helping you in the polls." She leans towards me and whispers. "You two kiss now for the cameras."

Then she backs out of the way of a passing camera drone.

I tell her, "Krom don't do public displays of affection."

"Diay, Babe." Brill gives me a soft beso on the cheek and drapes an arm around my shoulder. The leather sleeve against my neck is comforting.

Tawny rolls her eyes. "Subdued. But I can work with the shy bad-boy thing."

She's already planning my show. Wait! Does she plan to go with us?

Before I can ask, Tawny turns to the others and starts arranging them for an "impromptu" conversation.

She brings Crosskiss up next to me. He towers over me. He smiles for the cameras, but it displays shining rows of his feartastic teeth. Which are still intimidating – pero no longer the focus of my nightmares.

He says in a formal tone, "It is an honor to make a new impression of you, Bodacious Babe Benitez, the Merciful, Bearer of the Invincible Heart, Spuckslayer, Champion of Kaliel the Mindworm Murderer, Guardian of Murry the Misguided, Uncoverer of Secrets, Healer of Worlds."

It's quite a mouthful, pero I've earned it. Every single piece.

Don't worry. I won't let it go to mi cabeza. I smile at Crosskiss, pero I'm talking to the cameras – to my fans and to the haters and those who were just morbidly curious as to whether I'd survive. "Por favor, amigo. Just call me Bo."

ACKNOWLEDGEMENTS

I want to give a special shout-out to all the people who supported our IndiGoGo! Thank you for believing in this book – and in me – when I had absolutely no idea how to make it happen. You know who you are! Now it's time to tell everyone else.

Andrea Amosson	Travis Mondok
Carl and Linda Armand	Jackie OConnor
Jennifer Crippen	Grace Roeber
Sonja R Godeken	Melissa Shumake
Phil and Nancy Golden	Tex Thompson
Jennie Goloboy	Jay Quietnight
Ross Irvin	Mattias Wadenstein

Jake also deserves a HUGE thank you for his work on this one. This is our first time indie publishing fiction, and the learning curve on the setup and marketing side of things has been super steep. He's put in late nights researching, formatting, proofing and e-mailing. There is no way this book would have made it out without him.

Thank you to my fans, for reaching out and sharing the Chocoverse in reviews and on social media. I decided to become a hybrid author for you guys. Bo's story deserved an ending. You deserved to know how Chestla's love triangle turned out. I couldn't just leave you with that cliffhanger at the end of Book 2. Fake Chocolate has taught me a lot about finishing what you start, and how that can help a writer arc along with the characters. I'm a better, more confident person than I was when I started writing this trilogy, and it wasn't until I was writing the ending to Book 3 that I realized everything I'd been using it to teach myself. I never could have gotten there without your encouragement.

I'd like to thank Heri Irawan for an AMAZING cover. Mira! There's Botas! Heri worked with me to make sure it was exactly what I wanted.

I'd also like to thank X27 Films and Media for the GORGEOUS book trailer, and all my friends who starred in it. You guys. En serio. I don't know what I'd do without you in my life!

Thanks to Monica Benitez, Tessa Gegg and Cassie Koerber, for listening to my complaints and setbacks every step of the way. You all three know you went above and beyond. #ragtagforever #benitezgirlsrock #imnotcryingyourecrying #thatonetime

Thanks to Kathryn McClatchy for rallying support for this book. And my agent, Jennie Goloboy, for encouraging me while I'm becoming a hybrid author. Thanks to Julia Mandala for editing the manuscript, and to Eduardo Olazaran for consulting on my use of Mexican Spanish.

And I have to thank the chocolate makers, farmers and cacao sourcers who were willing to share their time and expertise for my research. Give them some love, you guys! After all, they're the ones dealing in Real Chocolate.

AMBER ROYER writes the CHOCOVERSE comic telenovela-style foodie-inspired space opera series (available from Angry Robot Books and Golden Tip Press). She is also co-author of the cookbook There are Herbs in My Chocolate, which combines culinary herbs and chocolate in over 60 sweet and savory recipes, and had a long-running column for Dave's Garden, where she covered gardening and crafting. She blogs about creative writing technique and all things chocolate related over at www.amberroyer.com. She also teaches creative writing in person in North Texas for both UT Arlington Continuing Education and Writing Workshops Dallas. If you are very nice to her, she might make you cupcakes.

www.amberroyer.com   Instagram: amberroyerauthor